Dark Days

Part I

by

Lorel Clayton

I0639359

DARK DAYS

First edition. November 21, 2024.

ISBN: 978-1763800809

Written by Lorel Clayton.

What is to give light must endure burning. -Viktor Frankl

Chapter One ~ After the End

D inah looked upon the wretches who would feed her army. Whatever had become of gleaming nobles and men with flesh to hold between her teeth? These were skeletons, better meant for the ranks of the God-fed.

Ash rained from the sky, obscuring the twisted silhouettes of buildings and slowly burying the multitude that filled the rubble-strewn square before her. Men with scars and missing limbs still clutched the rusted remains of their rifles. Women and children stared with empty eyes set in faces hollow from hunger. They had fought beyond reason, beyond endurance. Now there was nothing left. Husks. What sort of offering was this for her Lord?

"He comes!"

"He comes!" the black-winged angels cried as they perched on the broken machine that had been the last defense of the newly conquered city.

Heads bowed around her in a rustle of cloth and scrape of metal. Dinah fought as long as she could, until the tendons in her neck were taut enough to thrum and droplets of sweat beaded on her lip. In the end, even she, Bringer of All, looked down at the dirt and the savaged captives she must call a meal.

She fell to her knees as the Presence washed over her, a shadow across the sun and the sun itself. The Last God was with them.

Dinah felt him beside her, a glimpse of creaking leather, or was it ancient skin? She had never set eyes on her Lord, but she felt His power every moment of her life. It ran through her veins, made her beautiful, immortal, and it bent her will to His.

"He has come," she heard herself intone with the masses. "The Last God has come."

A breeze and brush of feather against her cheek as the angels flexed their wings in rejoicing.

"Hear me." The god's words reverberated through her bones. "To all who called this world theirs, know it is mine, as you are all mine."

"Always, Lord," Dinah echoed the rest.

She felt a putrid familiarity with the captives at that moment. She and they were the same. Nothing.

Then she saw a small face, wide-eyed and curious. A jolt disturbed Dinah's holy restraint. Her docile emotions, calmed by the god's presence, were rippled by a stone, a tiny pebble, a child in the crowd.

<u>The boy sees him.</u>

Was she dreaming? She had not slept for millennia. Was she mad, finally, after all these years?

She would never have noticed the child if her neck weren't fixed downward, might have spent all eternity as she was now, trapped. No. Everything changed as she met his innocent gaze and felt a fragment of her mind free to think, free to feel ... hatred.

A face was reflected next to hers in the boy's pupils. Its features were obscured by the glow of captured suns burning within its eye sockets. The face of her god. She was seeing it for the first time—and she was not dead.

RALEN GREW ANGRY AS he looked into the man's golden eyes. The light in them was warm and whispered of home, making him think of sweet scents filling the air and of arms holding him, his mother's arms. His mother never held him like that. All lies. The ache in his chest pushed the untruthful thoughts away.

"The Last God has come," the crowd said reverently. They were on their knees now, all but Ralen, mud and fresh blood soaking into their clothes.

<u>God has come for me</u>. He shivered, still dripping with water from the river. He had tried to run, to take a boat, but its motor had rusted solid in the latest attack. Magic, miracles. Whatever it was, no one stood a chance against the invaders.

An acid taste coated his tongue. His neck stung where the Grey Men's claws had dug in when they pulled him from his hiding place in the shriveled grass beside the poisoned water.

"You are all mine," God said. His face was twisted, the corners of His mouth turned down, and His voice held no joy.

Ralen had nothing, but even he was not so empty. He looked away from the glowing eyes, preferring the glow of the fires chewing at the edges of the city. Ash caught on his eyelashes in thick clumps. He blinked, and the flakes fell away. He was the only one not staring at the ground. The lady and the bird men noticed. The bird men were like no angels he had ever imagined.

"Despair," the bird men said, as their black eyes studied him. "Our Lord God departs. Weep and pray for his return!"

As soon as their high voices quieted, God vanished. Ralen saw it happen, saw the light beneath crystal skin grow bright, blinding. When it faded, the brief, deceitful happiness bestowed by those golden eyes was gone, and he did despair.

"Mommy." Ralen gasped the word. He searched for his mother's yellow hair and saw it everywhere, but none of the women were her. She was dead. He had waited for her to push the fallen bricks aside and come out of the house, but she never did. And now God had come to punish him, just as Mother always said He would.

People stood up around him. He hugged a woman's bare legs, not minding the sharp feel of stubble against palms as his tears soaked into her ragged dress. He was nine: too old to cry, Mother had said, and too old to believe in monsters, but the monsters were real.

The woman's hand shook as she patted his head. "I want my mommy too." He clutched her tighter, but she pried loose his fingers and pulled away.

"The End has come," a wrinkled old man with an overripe strawberry of a nose whispered, as though it were a secret. "The End." The man's clownish cheeks were caked with white ash except for two thin lines where tears had washed away the grime, as he stared at the broken fountain in the middle of the square. Its water boiled, cooked goldfish bobbing on the surface.

The old man was wrong. Nothing ended, especially not suffering. Today was only the start.

Grey Men descended into the crowd, picking people at random and dragging them up the broken steps to where the lady waited. Calm and sure, ash swirling around her, nothing touched her skin or stained her red gown. Not even the cries of people torn away from their families and chained in rows disturbed her. She understood this new world, Ralen knew. She was the way.

The lady stared at him as she had throughout God's speech. Her gaze did not stray as she whispered to one of the Grey Men, and the creature went back into the crowd to fetch more people. Ralen was one of them.

He did not fight this time. He looked at the monster's hand on his arm and saw that it wasn't grey: there were rainbows in the scales. Each thick claw was longer than his longest finger, the tips colored silver. The monster fastened a heavy shackle around his wrist. The loop was too large, and it would be easy to escape, but he didn't try. They ate anyone who ran.

Thunder rumbled through the warm air. He looked to the black sky and saw a thread of lightning fork cloud to cloud. When he looked down, he saw them choose her—one child among hundreds, a girl with hair like his mother's.

She didn't wait to be shackled but hid among the legs of the adults. The monsters let her be.

"Hello," Ralen said.

The girl's lip trembled. "Hello."

He slipped out of the manacle and crouched beside her. It felt safer with tall legs all around, like a forest of trees where the monsters couldn't find them.

"The Bringer of All descends." Only one bird man spoke this time. The other swooped across the massive square and alighted on a pile of charred metal and broken glass. Ralen felt him watching.

The lady glided into the crowd like a mist, bare feet hovering just above the ground. There were thousands of people crushed together between ruined buildings, but they somehow found space for her to pass. When she was in the center of them, a hush fell.

Dark hair and pale skin, eyes unnaturally green and bright, the lady was as perfect and unreal as a picture from a magazine when she smiled. "Join with me."

She held out her arms, and a murmur began, close to her at first and then spreading to the outer edges of the crowd. The murmur turned to hisses and screams. One by one people fell, shriveled and blackened like burnt wood. Waves of death poured from the lady until she was surrounded by a sea of dried skin and polished bone.

When everyone in the city was dead—everyone except for the invaders and their captives, including Ralen and the yellow-haired girl hiding among the legs of the other prisoners—the lady took a deep breath, loud enough for him to hear in the silence.

She turned and smiled at him. "Let us go home."

DINAH WAS NOT THE ONLY one to notice the boy's unbowed head. Ashkal and Amseel saw all, knew all, spoke all. Angels, messengers, trophies, even they had not seen their Lord's face until it was reflected in a child's eyes.

Ashkal stayed behind and watched as the boy was herded into the Lady's wagon with the survivors and then trundled towards the Portal. The child would be taken to another world, one conquered long ago, while the Last God's armies finished destroying this one.

Interesting, Ashkal whispered into his twin's mind.

Should we snatch the boy up and offer him to our Lord? Amseel asked.

It is our duty, Ashkal thought, except...

What?

When has our Lord ever needed our protection? When has anyone ever resisted?

Never.

So, this cannot be. We do not see what we see, thus there is no need—

—to do anything. We do not see?

No. The Watchers are blind.

Amseel stretched a wing, eager to depart. The boy will be eaten anyway.

Perhaps. We do not guide Fate. We only see.

But not the boy?

Never. Except, we must continue not to see him as long as possible. We must learn what becomes of this, Ashkal insisted.

Dinah noticed the child.

I know. This is what we must watch, my brother.

Chapter Two ~ Darkness

The Last God took form again in His private chamber. His citadel was carved from the iron heart of a meteorite, a dead world crashed into the plain of this one to scour it of life. He stroked the twisted white Tree in the center of the craterous room. The thing continued to cling to existence. The meteor had not worked as well as He had hoped.

A multitude of windows surrounded the Tree. Some were set in the metal walls, some rested on the sandy earth, while others floated, unsuspended. Each looked upon a different scene—winter, summer, flood or fire—and His soldiers marched across every land He beheld.

It was not enough.

He studied each scene, feeling the itch of something forgotten, something overlooked.

He did not realize He was alone until the angels emerged from a pane, from the world He had turned to volcano and ash, and He was alone no more. Alone. What an imprecise term. The presence or absence of the angels made no difference to His state of being.

"What did you see?" He commanded them to answer. Every breath, every syllable was a command. His creatures had no choice but to obey.

Ashkal and Amseel shared a glance and then said as one, "Nothing, Our Lord. We saw nothing. No Daemon, Shadow or minor god."

"There are no other gods."

"Forgive us, Lord. We are flawed, foolish. We meant there was nothing but a curious child and a crowd humbled before your glory."

"How disappointing." All the gods were gone, torn apart by His hands, and He missed the feel of greater beings, missed how their power shredded and was so easily subsumed to His. Nothing since had provided so much pleasure.

"What did my Bringer do?"

"Dinah fed greatly. She was severely weakened by the battle," Ashkal said.

"She failed me."

"The weapons of that world were surprising."

"Do not defend her." He wanted so much from her, yet she continued to disappoint.

"Yes, Lord. Your Presence was a gift undeserved."

"It is time to choose another Bringer. Past time. Send Adarmis into the field. Let it be known that I will watch and judge ... and that Dinah is in disgrace."

"That should please him, Lord."

"All that matters is *my* pleasure."

"Yes, Lord."

The angels departed, silent and invisible to all but Him, and He returned to studying the windows. He knew what was wrong. There were more worlds beyond His sight, beyond His Presence. He felt them: tiny sparks of power yet to be claimed. Time to build another Portal.

The Last God closed His eyes and gazed upon the Void.

RALEN WAS IN CRAMPED darkness, the air still and thick and filled with inhuman whispers. Cloth rustled as the others twitched in fear. They were all damned, he knew, so they had best get used to fear. To pain. He went to stir patterns in the dirt as he often did whenever he was waiting for something, but there was no dirt on the cave floor. Instead, his fingers walked across cold stone and found the soft hand of the girl beside him. She laced her fingers through his, and he didn't feel like Ralen anymore. Together, they were something more, something that wasn't afraid of the dark.

The whispers drew closer. Hungry.

"It's touch-ing me," a man said, his words clipped and horror-stricken.

The man screamed, and people tore in different directions, the chains joining them rattling like some uncoiling snake until they were pulled up short. Ralen, long free of the shackles, stayed where he was and held tight to the girl. She shivered and put hands over her ears to block out the sounds of crunching bone and the shrieks of the dying man. Ralen wished he could cover his ears too, but he needed to still her shivers. The girl trembled so violently he thought she might fly apart.

"Back." A husky voice cut through the chaos, and fires burst into life in the small cave. It was the lady in her red dress. At her feet, green-skinned ghouls gnawed on human limbs. She kicked at them, and the monsters scattered.

"These are not for you," she told the creatures. They whimpered into bloody hands, like children scolded for doing what they could not help but do.

Grey Men, rainbow scales flashing in the light from the torches they held, came forward with short rods. One by one, they branded people. Ralen felt the cold metal touch the top of the hand he used to clutch the girl's shoulder. The brand did not burn, but still it left a glowing red symbol behind.

"You are the Bringer's now, and the gobels cannot touch the Marked," the Grey Man said.

"We work for you?" a bearded captive huddled with the others asked.

The lady curled her lip. "No. The Drakein and the gobels and the Conquered work for me. _You_ are food for later."

NO ONE SPOKE DURING the long hours after the gobel ate a man and the lady's monsters branded them. Ralen heard the girl's moans when he woke from a restless sleep full of strange images he could not describe. He shook her, but the nightmare held her tight. It was some time before she escaped it. When she did, her eyes opened wide, and tear-filled whites reflected the reddish light put off by the new Marks on their hands.

"Are you alright?" he asked. He had seen enough during the war to know that some injuries were invisible and that some could never be mended.

The girl shook her head. "Hungry. Just hungry." She lay back down and buried her head in his shoulder, but he knew she didn't sleep. He felt her muffled sobs through his skin.

He thought a day had passed, but there was no sunlight to be sure. The Grey Men, Drakein they were called, returned, leading more people behind them who were already Marked. The newcomers had faraway looks, like those who had seen war too, and worse.

The new people carried woven baskets. Shriveled apples and brown-spotted vegetables lay at the bottom of the basket held under Ralen's nose. He took a carrot, but when he reached for another for the girl, an old woman slapped his hand. The empty look she gave him held no anger, but he had broken some rule. The girl had to stand on tiptoes to reach in and take her share. He'd been starved for so long he ate every bite, even the yellowed leaves at the thick end.

The adults hadn't finished their breakfast before they were herded toward the exit. "Where are you taking us?" the bearded man with all the questions asked.

"Work," a Drakein said. The monster glanced at Ralen but left him and the girl behind.

"My name is Anjee," the girl said when they were alone.

Names are not important, Mother always told him, only our sins. That was what God saw. What He judged. Still, he told her, "I'm Ralen."

"I..." She looked down.

His stomach rumbled, and he thought of the half-full baskets of food the others had taken away.

"Are you still hungry?" he asked.

She nodded. He took her hand and led her out of the cave.

They followed a line of smoking torches down limestone stairs to an underground lake. Water dripped from ancient stalactites, and the peaceful sound echoed through the vast darkness beyond the reach of firelight.

He stopped. There were thousands of people in the cavern. All silent. A few Drakein walked among them, prodding stragglers into the river of people that poured up a dirt slope to a blinding white opening in the stone that must be the surface. So many human faces, except ... they stared at nothing, mouths open in unvoiced screams, scratching at their skin, at the glowing brands on their hands. It was how he'd always pictured this place. No burning fires, no sound of cracking whips, just silent pain. Unending pain.

"We're in Hell," he told the girl. Anjee. He thought her name over and over, letting it fill up his head and push out the fear.

"We can't be. We're not dead."

"Death doesn't make any difference." He looked at the red light streaming from the half circle and lines branded on his hand. A devil's mark to claim his soul. The Bringer's Mark. That's what the Drakein had called it. It was supposed to keep gobels away, but scores of them lurked in the shadows, whispering, waiting for another bite of blood and marrow. Ralen would never forget the slurps they'd made.

He sucked in mouthfuls of water from the still lake. It tasted sour and old, despite its enticing color. The water glowed turquoise, like the lagoon of some far off paradise. More lies.

Away from the torches, he noticed that the stones all around glowed too, putting off a cold blue light. He reached out and touched something soft. He pulled and came away with a broad worm that shone brightly against his palm.

Anjee poked at it. "Eew."

He put the worm back and then held Anjee around the waist so she wouldn't fall in as she drank.

A scream echoed from some dark corner. Anjee lifted her head like a startled yearling. He heard struggles, the scrape of feet on stone, and glimpsed a moon-faced woman just before she was dragged deeper into the caves by Drakein. Food for monsters.

Ralen saw his food in baskets on the other side of a finger of lake. He couldn't swim, so he kept to the edge of the water. Anjee's hand never left his as they hopped from stone to brick, feet wet again, until they reached the pile of stores.

They crept past the vacant-eyed adults tasked to watch the supplies. Stealing was for the weak, but hunger would make him weaker. He held Anjee's ankles as she rooted inside the deep basket and came up with three figs. Sticks cracked, and the basket broke apart, spilling a meager stream of fruit. An apple rolled against the foot of the old woman, and she woke from her daze with a gasp. She cast stones at them but threw poorly and missed.

They hurried back to the small cave—one among a honeycomb of caves along one side of the cavern—where they had spent the night. It had no torches or glowworms and was unoccupied, a good place to hide. They ate quickly, even though the old woman did not come to reclaim what they stole.

"Three blind mice ... three blind mice..." Anjee sang. Her voice was sweet and rose above the constant mutters of the gobels. Ralen made his fingers dance on her arm like a mouse on two legs, and she laughed. It was the most beautiful sound he'd ever heard.

"If we grow up," he said, wondering if anyone grew up in Hell, "we'll get married." People got married when they were older. His mother had told him that when she showed him a picture of his father. Ralen couldn't imagine marrying anyone but Anjee. The moment he saw her, it felt as though he had always known her and always would.

She kissed him quick, missing his lips. "Okay." They held each other for warmth, and he fell asleep to her singing.

When he woke, the room was quiet, the adults not yet returned from the surface. The gobels were quiet too. He sucked in a breath and held it. The monsters were never quiet.

His eyes adjusted to the red light emitted by his Mark. A leathery form hunched over his feet. He tried to stand, but the gobel grabbed his ankles.

"Don't hide the little toes. I love to see little toes." The creature wiped thick mud from Ralen's foot with an emaciated hand and then licked the remaining smears of dirt away.

Ralen shivered and pushed the glowing Mark into the gobel's face. It squinted but kept licking. "These are not for you," Ralen repeated the words the lady had used.

"The Bringer is cruel to bring little toes and not let me taste. What harm a nibble? She won't know."

Ralen scratched at the monster, fingers digging into silver eyes. It hissed and caught his wrists in a long-fingered hand.

"One little toe." It bent forward and sucked Ralen's small toe into its mouth.

"No!" he cried, waking Anjee.

Sharp teeth stung his skin. The pressure grew and grew, and he gaped at the pain, strings of saliva dangling across his open mouth.

Crunch. Suck, suck…

He couldn't move, couldn't draw breath. The pain.

"Bad! Bad! Bad!" Anjee slapped and kicked the gobel with a flurry of arms and legs.

The monster ignored her clumsy fists and drew Ralen's blood into his throat like a babe at the breast. Ralen felt lightheaded, his veins weakening and collapsing, empty tunnels with no use. Darkness closed in, the sucking sounds faint with distance, his heartbeat drumming against his skull.

After a last, longing lick, the gobel pulled away. The stump oozed then sealed as the saliva dried. The monster crawled toward the exit. Anjee gathered gravel from the floor and threw it. "Stay away," she ordered.

It held up an arm to shield itself from the stones and chuckled. "The Bringer will never notice a little toe... now and then." As it disappeared down the tunnel, it whispered a new chant, "Many, many, little toes. No one to know. Tomorrow, tomorrow. Time for more to grow...."

Ralen stared at his mangled foot, the skin clammy. All his skin was pale and shivery. Pain twisted his guts.

"Stupid monster," Anjee said. "Toes don't grow back. Do they?"

"I..." He shivered. "I don't know." Tomorrow. He'd find out then. Unless ... he wasn't here anymore.

He would run away. There was supposed to be no escape from Hell, but it was stupid not to try. After everyone came back from working on the surface, they'd be tired. When they slept, he would climb up the path to the cave mouth and never look back. All he had to do was wait. Even monsters must sleep.

Chapter Three ~ The Other Side

Ralen peered between stalagmites at the Drakein who blocked the path to the surface. He'd been wrong. The monsters never slept.

"Is it still there?" Anjee whispered.

Ralen nodded. His foot ached where his toe had been. He needed to escape. There was scrabble on either side of the rise, the only way not guarded. "Come on," he said.

The glowing Marks on their hands were wrapped in cloth torn from Anjee's dress, and they crept through the deepest shadows to avoid being discovered. He put a foot on the shale, and bits broke apart, clattering together like dried bones.

"I see you." The Drakein turned, and its yellow eyes reflected the light from the torch it held.

Ralen scurried up the slope on all fours but only managed a few feet before sliding back down. Anjee grunted, caught beneath him. She pushed, and he was lifted into the air, surprised to feel dry scales on his neck. The Drakein held him in one clawed hand and took Anjee's arm with the other, nearly singeing her with the torch in the same hand. She scowled.

"Return to your sleep den," it ordered.

"The gobels will eat him! They ate his toe!" Anjee said.

The Drakein hissed. "Impossible. They cannot touch anyone with the Mark. Come this way again, and I will eat you both."

Ralen squeezed the creature's wrist, trying to make it let go. He punched and kicked, but the Drakein didn't budge. It carried them, kicking and wriggling, back to the caves and tossed them onto the ground. Ralen's breath left him, but he climbed to his feet, smiling for the first time since the war came to his city. It felt good to fight.

"You should be cowering," the Drakein said.

"Why? You said you wouldn't eat us unless we tried again." Ralen swiped the torch and took Anjee's hand. They ran until they realized no one was following.

Gasping, he said, "Well, we can't go that way."

"You have to do something. Don't worry about me. You need to go. Find another way outside."

"Let me think. For now, there's fire…" He used the stolen torch to navigate the uneven ledge outside the caves. He stuck his head into every cave mouth they passed, searching for a good one with people that didn't snore too loud or weren't too smelly. "…and we can always steal more fruit."

"Stop smiling. It's scaring me. You said we are in Hell. It's nonsense, of course. My parents taught me there's no such thing as Hell, but you seem certain."

"Why can't I be happy in Hell? For now. I know I won't be happy when the gobel comes back."

"What will you do then? Laugh at it?"

Ralen ignored her and stepped into the cave he'd chosen. A few sleepers littered the floor, grumbling at the light, but once Ralen extinguished the torch they quieted.

"Why did you do that?" she asked. "I hate the dark."

"I know how to start a fire when I need. For now, we rest. Ideas always come to me in dreams."

"I don't like the things I see when I dream."

Anjee eventually stopped grumbling and leaned her head on his shoulder. He stared into the dark for a long time, thinking. On the verge of sleep, he had the answer.

"We kill it," he whispered.

Yes.

THE NEXT DAY, THE CAVE was theirs, the adults gone up to the surface to work, nothing but the drip of water from stalactites and the whispers of gobels for company.

Ralen gathered broken metal and dried reeds, grunting until he had a spark and then a flame to relight the torch. Then, he and Anjee gathered every loose stone they could find, feeling for them in the cracks that ran through the cavern walls. Soon, they had a pile.

They built a cairn, a cave within the cave, and Ralen put the torch inside. He lowered the last, heavy stone into place and peeked through a crack to make sure the fire still burned. There was enough air to keep it alive. He sat so as to hide the slivers of light from view, and they waited in the semi-dark for the whispers to stop.

When quiet settled on the cave, he heard skin scrape against stone. It came from his right, where there was a narrow crevice in the cave wall. The monster crept between the bones of the mountain.

He waited for it to come closer. When something cold touched his foot, Ralen pulled off the cover stone and grabbed the torch. The gobel covered its delicate eyes. The monster was not alone this time. Two more crouched nearby, teeth bared, hungry drool running across their chins.

Anjee threw stones at them. "Get!"

Ralen waved the torch. The monsters hid behind their arms but didn't budge. He pressed the fire against the nearest one's flesh. *Sizzle.* The gobel mewled and backed away.

He pressed forward, listening for the sizzle and feeling lighter every time the creature whimpered. He hated the monster, and wanted it to feel pain, like he'd felt when it bit him.

The other two gobels ignored Anjee's punishing rain of stones, the fragments bouncing harmlessly off their leathery skin, but they feared the fire. They covered their eyes. "Burning! Burning!" They turned and ran. She cast one last rock after them anyway.

The first one stood its ground. "Little toe. One little toe."

Ralen pressed the torch against its leathery flesh, but this time the fire went out, leaving orange embers, ash flaking to the ground, and encroaching darkness.

"Hee hee," the gobel laughed.

Ralen took Anjee's hand and ran for the steps leading down to the great cavern. The gobel leapt onto his back. He crashed onto his stomach and slid until he was looking over the precipice. More torches burned along the edge of the lake far below, like twinkling stars.

Anjee's hand slipped out of his, and she rolled down the staircase with the *thwack, thwack* of soft flesh slapping stone. The monster's weight crushed his lungs. Dust filled his mouth. His hands pushed uselessly at empty air, and foul breath warmed his cheek.

"So cruel," the gobel said. "Now, all toes mine. All mine." Teeth cut into his ear, but Ralen could not cry out, could not even breathe.

"Bad!" he heard Anjee say. She was back. She hadn't tumbled far, and she'd found a bigger rock. Relief filled him.

She swung the slab of stone hard enough for it to crack in two, and the gobel mewled. Ralen wriggled and turned until he was free, and then he pushed. He pushed the gobel to the edge. It teetered. He and Anjee together gave it one more shove, and it went over, falling into the night below.

They heard nothing, not even a splash.

"Is it dead?" Anjee asked.

Ralen went back into the cave and found the largest of the rocks they had used to shield the torch. He carried it two-handed down the long flight of steps to the water, Anjee at his heels.

Gobels scattered as they approached, the ones Anjee had pelted cringing as she tossed the broken fragments she carried at them too.

It took a long time to find the monster where it lay, broken over platters of shale. It writhed and moaned. They studied the yellow blood that spread with each beat of its heart.

"It's not dead," she said.

Ralen lifted the heavy stone and dropped it on the gobel's head. He picked it up again and dropped it, over and over until the writhing stopped. There. It would never hurt him again.

Killing was simple. Had it been this simple for God?

Mother always said Ralen was an evil child, and he knew he deserved this place, but was there a reason the whole world had to die too? He shook the thoughts out of his head. The gobel had its reasons for eating his toe, and God has His unknowable reasons, but others' reasons didn't matter. All that mattered was what mattered to him.

He felt shivery and hot and panted for breath. He took Anjee's hand and led her away. She looked back over her shoulder and wouldn't stop staring at the thing they had killed. He was already trying to forget it.

MALA TORE THE COVERS away and screamed. Her throat was sore from calling out in her dreams, but the fully conscious cry echoed down ancient corridors. Her father hurried in, two guards behind him. When they saw no one else in the room, half-drawn daggers were returned to their sheaths.

Her father spoke soothing words and petted her hair, but his deep voice failed to calm. She couldn't shake the feeling of loss from the nightmare. Every child in the Kingdom knew loss, fathers and brothers, but Mala had lost every member of her family to the Last God's horde—all but Papa.

He was dressed in ring mail and a long, beaded vest in the blue and gold of Wain Varges. Had morning come already?

"Don't leave." She clutched his arm and pressed her cheek into the brocade on his shoulder.

"It is my duty. You know that."

"I'll be alone."

"There are your tutors and maids and dozens of children within these walls. You are not alone."

That's not what she meant, but she didn't know how to make him understand, so she pouted. "They're babies."

Mala was almost ten and the oldest of the children in the castle. More children lived in the town, but they were commoners, and she did not associate with them. Her mother had warned it led to nothing but tragedy. They were meant to live short, pointless lives, while she was meant to rule them and continue the line. That was her duty.

"I want you to stay, Papa."

"We seldom get what we want. I want to see you dance, but I can't."

She lowered her arms. She was supposed to be practicing the steps and sewing bells onto the dress that hung from the wardrobe, unfinished. Father was leaving and learning the dance for her Decade ceremony seemed pointless. There was no one else she cared to dance for.

He lifted her chin. "I want you to sleep well and without worry, my child. Can you grant me that at least?"

She couldn't, but she could act strong, act like the queen she would one day be. "Yes, Papa."

"Good. Farewell." He kissed her forehead and then left the chamber as abruptly as he had entered.

The silver light of pre-dawn brightened the window frame. Mala climbed out of bed and opened the door a crack. She watched her father, flanked by the two guards who bore his sword and helm, disappear down the corridor.

No one was watching now, so the tears came and would not stop. Even when her maids arrived—one to dress her and one to tend the barely slept in bed—tears kept bubbling to the surface. She furiously wiped them away whenever they escaped the corners of her eyes.

"What's wrong, dearie?" Evlene asked with her gentle voice.

Mala had grown up hearing that voice. Evlene had dressed her mother each morning, chatting away about nothing of consequence. Mala replied just as her mother would have: "It's none of your concern. Eyes on your duty."

"Yes, young lady. Right of you to say. I do go on." Evlene hummed to herself as she worked, complete silence impossible for her. Mala regretted the sharp tone she'd used. It was what Mama would have done, she reminded herself, but without her here or even Papa, she wanted Evlene's old arms around her, and she didn't want to fight the tears anymore.

She did not act on the desire. Evlene's granddaughter, Gemma, was watching but pretending not to as she fluffed the bed. Gemma was only a few years older than her, and Mala would not hug the old maid in plain sight for gossip to spread. She was grateful when Evlene and Gemma left, along with the temptation to make a fool of herself.

Madam Kiel arrived soon after for their morning lesson. The lady took in Mala's puffy eyes and said, "Oh there can be none of that, Highness. Crying girls are dismissed as easily as yapping puppies. No one takes them seriously. You'll never get what you want with tears."

"I'll never get what I want without them, either."

"Oh, I daresay you will." Madam Kiel reached into the velvet folds of her thick dress and pulled out the palm-sized crystal ball she carried everywhere. "I have seen it."

Mala wiped the last troublesome tear away. "What else can you see about my future?"

"You know that is never a good question to ask. How often must I tell you that fortunetelling gives power to the teller, not to the one who is read? I teach you these methods so that you can be the one in league with Fate, child, not someone's supplicant." Madam Kiel was the youngest fortune teller Mala had ever seen, and what she lacked in deep-set eyes and wise wrinkles she made up for in asperity. It was difficult to be taken seriously when not a crone.

"All you've ever taught me is silly tricks and flim-flam," Mala said. "How can any of that make me master of my own fate?"

"All fortune telling is flim-flam and illusion, Highness. That is the point. Do not let the alluring words of others fool you. If I say that you will get what you want once the tears stop, the tears stop, because it is what you need to hear. The outcome is my design. You are a puppet where I hold the strings, as long as you believe a word I say about the future."

"But Fate is real, the gods are real, or were. I have seen what the Channelers can do, and Papa tells us the words of The Prophets. The Prophets! How can I not believe such seeing is possible?"

"Oh, it is, but it tells you nothing. I know everyone holds stock in the words of those old men, but The Prophets are just that. Men. The future never changes, or it always changes. Just be sure it's never what you want. However, I am certain about one thing in yours."

"Yes?"

"There will be a strange man in it."

Mala smiled. "You've taught me this one. That's what you're always supposed to say."

"Well, it's almost always true."

Chapter Four ~ Food for Monsters

When the Drakein soldier came for him, Ralen was not surprised. Perhaps the monsters were angry he had killed one of them, or perhaps they were hungry, and it was his turn to be food. Reasons didn't matter. Suffering was inevitable.

Anjee fought the monster, like she'd fought the gobel, slapping and kicking, but the Drakein was five times her size. It slung Ralen over its shoulder and gave her one push that sent her stumbling away.

"Goodbye," Ralen said.

Her face turned red, and she sunk to the ground.

"Goodbye," he repeated.

He listened to her tears for as long as he could, but the sound was soon swallowed up in the great cavern. The Drakein carried him upside down, and he craned his neck to see the opening at the top of the slope, yearning for the sunlight he would not feel on his skin again. The monster took him into dark tunnels.

He wondered if there would be a kitchen and an oven, like the old witch in the woods in the fairy tale. Ralen didn't think so. He had seen the monsters eat their food raw.

It was a long walk, the winding path leading upward, and they passed more Drakein. Eventually, they came to steps made from pink marble and lighted by bronze sconces. They climbed up and up, as though trying to reach the clouds. Ralen would have been exhausted if he were walking, but the Drakein did not slow or alter its breathing. It set him down next to a large pair of doors made from carved bone. A moment later, golden hinges creaked, and the doors opened.

DINAH, HIGH UP IN HER longhouse atop the mountain, gazed through a massive window at valleys of green wheat. Sunset burned orange, bathing the gardens and orchards along the hills and ridges in one last glorious display.

The filthy boy held a hand to his light-starved eyes and squinted through fingers at the idyllic scene.

"I adore life," Dinah told him. "The Conquered must have food to fight, of course, but this is not for them. It is for me. You are Ralen?"

The boy stayed quiet, not a word, but she knew that was his name. She knew all within her domain. She made him stand there until the sky paled to lavender.

"You killed a gobel," she said.

"It was me. Only me."

He was protecting the girl already.

"Not modest, I see. Good. I have a use for you, and that is another good thing."

More silence. Finally, the boy asked, "What do you want?"

She did not know what she wanted. It was a formless wish, a longing, except when the boy was there. In his presence, she could see it all laid out before her, every step to take, every word to say.

"You will work the fields for now, you and that girl. Otherwise, the gobels will nibble you to death and you will be worthless."

"You're not going to eat me?"

"I didn't say that." She bared perfect white fangs.

The boy looked away, his gaze following the long bones that made up the window frames, and she expected his thoughts to be full of fear, as straightforward as any child's, not that she could remember the childish thoughts she had once possessed. She could barely remember the desires that had brought her to this place, this fortress of death in a valley of life. But Ralen surprised her. He was not afraid. He was resigned to dying, now or later, but for now … he was curious. He wondered what creatures had bones so large.

"Beasts who once dwelled in this land. Formidable enemies." She stroked patterns and symbols carved into ivory, vestiges of a time that no longer existed.

Now a tendril of fear slithered through the boy. She knew his thoughts.

"Do not dream of running away," she said. "This world is mine, and I will find you."

"I wasn't—"

"—Stop. Never try to lie to me again. I can see into your head, wherever you are. That is <u>my</u> Mark you bear."

He looked at the glowing symbol on his hand. "Then why didn't you see what the gobel did?"

Her magic made him incapable of deceit, but she was not similarly limited. There was no reason for him to know she made mistakes, or that she was not always watching. "It took only a bite of flesh, and I wanted to know if you would do something about it. You did. That pleases me. Strive always to please me."

The valley was dark, and the stars did not provide enough light for her to see the fields anymore. She was reluctant to spend another night wandering through her mountain, watching those capable of sleep, discussing strategies with her commanders. She wanted to enjoy the boy's presence a while longer, enjoy the freedom of her thoughts.

"Come," she said. She opened the wide doors separating her foyer from the library. The room took up half of her massive home, shelves stacked with books from floor to high ceiling.

The boy followed her inside. He reached out and touched a leather-bound volume that was thicker than the length of his arm.

"You will learn to read these," she commanded, "and you will study. From rummaging in your head, I can tell that you are quick-witted, but your intellect is undeveloped. You will spend every evening here, as long as I desire it, and someday I hope you will cease to bore me."

"When I do, that's when you'll eat me?"

"If I decide to kill you, you won't even realize until the dried flesh falls from your bones. Now sit."

He carefully chose a seat, and she noticed how he tried not to touch the smooth bones of the chair more than he had to. She placed an open book before him and sat opposite. She read aloud, pointing to each line upside down, and told him to repeat. He obeyed.

It was strange having another being in her sanctuary. Ralen was quiet, but she felt his life, the blood coursing through his veins, and it distracted her. With effort, she focused on tutoring him. She was frustrated by the need to start with small words, but he caught on quickly, considering it was not his native language. He would need to learn many languages, for there were many worlds within the Last God's domain.

Eventually the boy drooped, his face wan. She would not be able to keep him with her as she hoped. Not only did he need sleep, but her aura weakened him. No matter how much she suppressed her hunger, she could not exist without destroying the life around her. None could survive long in her presence.

She called a Drakein to take him away and sat, alone, feeling the clarity of her thoughts slowly fade, her will dampen. Soon, she worried more about Adarmis and how she would regain her Lord's favor than grandiose dreams of how she might make use of the boy to set herself free.

Chapter Five ~ Orders

The Last God turned his gaze from infinity, from the endless glowing branches of Fate's Tree and the fibrous roots that cut through overlapping dimensions as though they were mere layers of sediment, and absently looked on the creatures bowed low before him.

He tried to remember why they were here—the large man who was larger inside his skin, Adarmis, and the two angels on either side with black, feathered wings draped over their faces to shield their feeble eyes from the glory of His might—and when He remembered, He tried to care enough to speak. "Do you know what it is to be Bringer?"

"It is to be the Hand of God. Your hand," Adarmis said.

Did He have hands? He looked and they were still there. When the Tree was gone, would they go as well? Would He be forever unchained, without form, at last? Or would His five-fingered limbs become branches?

"I, Adarmis, swear..." the man who was not a man continued, but The Last God was already tired of words.

"Your soul is mine, so swear no oaths upon it. You will go to the one place I cannot and make it mine as well. That is your only purpose."

"Yes, Lord."

Dinah had once had purpose, but He was beyond what she could offer and in need of new tools for what lay ahead. This clever brute, General or not, Bringer or not, was of little importance, but his elevation and Dinah's disgrace would satisfy the Fae who promised so much.

"Do not enter my abode again," the Last God ordered His new Bringer, "not until you have leveled the Old Kingdom's wall."

"Yes, but..."

The Last God stopped listening. He let His skin fade, let His muscles and bones become transparent, become light. He forced His light into the light of the Tree, into the light that extended in infinite branches throughout the universe, the light He needed to make His own.

He followed a branch into the heart of the crater where the physical manifestation of Fate's Tree stood, a spindle at the heart of a vast web of destinies—including His own.

He was the Last God. He would not let Fate take everything from him. He would not simply die as she commanded.

He pushed against the bole of the Tree with the force of the million million lesser gods swallowed up inside him, screaming His fury. He imagined tearing the primeval wood to shreds and swallowing all the souls it yoked and yanked about like puppets, and finally, finally being free to create His own fate.

The Tree dropped one yellow leaf.

He sagged with exhaustion and then screamed loud enough to shake the ether. But this was not the first time the Tree had thwarted Him, twisting His light into a small tendril of its own and letting that one small strand fall away, empty as one of Dinah's husks. Yet infinite leaves and branches remained.

The Last God needed more power to fight her, more souls, more magic, more.

GENERAL ADARMIS SURVEYED the broken wall from the back of his mount. The black stone was featureless but for a single arch through which the light of another world shone.

When the Last God's messengers first promised him favor and a chance at triumph, at being named Bringer, with the attendant increase in his meager lifespan, he had thrilled. Each battle bought him a year, each conquest a decade. As the Hand of God, he would have centuries. But now, as he and his army faced the gate to the Old Kingdom, he remembered that his Lord was cruel—to promise so much and ask the impossible.

Some said the Old Kingdom had a magic greater than all other worlds combined. In secret, far from listening angels, some even whispered they had their own god. Whatever their means of protection, they remained unconquered.

There were enough undiscovered lands to keep Adarmis occupied. He wished the god had tossed him through a newly made Portal and asked him to bring a strange world to its knees with no weapon and no army. That he could have managed. This place, which had held against them for so long, was the one certain path to defeat.

He sighed and dug in his spurs, racing his mount—a skeletal beast with only shreds of hide remaining after serving the God-fed—across the threshold and into the besieged encampment on the other side. Worse than being in the god's favor and asked to do the impossible was being in disfavor, like Dinah. He would do whatever he must to make sure she suffered in that state for all eternity.

KING KERVALEN AND FIFTEEN thousand troops emblazoned with the blue and gold of his Wain saw the flicker of light, the tear in the heavens that heralded the arrival of more enemies.

"Be ready for a sally," he told his captain. The message was passed along the wall.

Kervalen knew his enemy. Those fresh to the field and confident, those familiar with victory, were eager to smash themselves against the rock that was the Old Kingdom. They did not understand defeat. Kervalen, on the other hand, understood it well.

His people held onto this land, but it was no victory. The fields fertilized by the dead, the hordes of children kept barely fed in every household until they were strong enough to carry a pike, and the constant, inevitable ache of grief in every parent's, every sibling's breast was proof that they, not the Last God, were the losers.

"The gate opens!" The scout's message was passed down the line.

"Archers ready," Kervalen ordered. His soldiers raised bows, and the creak of stretched gut was amplified a thousand times.

The Last God's enclave was a citadel built of white stone fifty feet high. It was surrounded by a moat of spikes and protected by ballista in every other crenel. It received inexhaustible supplies of troops and weapons through the Portal, and no king before Kervalen had managed to take it. He sometimes dreamed he would be the first, but it was a fantasy.

The enemy gate opened wide, and a wave of soldiers poured onto the field. The archers waited. Finally, mangonels and armored wagons filled with workmen emerged, and Kervalen let the first volley fly.

Soldiers guarding the fringes were hit, but the main body of the enemy was untouched. He couldn't let them get a siege engine in place.

"Trebuchets!" Their own large weaponry creaked to life and cast balls of burning pitch down on the invaders.

While the Last God's enclave was a fortress, it was merely a foothold on a land that did not belong to them. Beyond the range of their weapons, generations of Kervalen's forbears had built a fortress of their own, a circular wall that enclosed the enemy on all sides. Archers could emerge from cover and shoot, or catapults rain fire down on the enemy, but there were no gates, nothing on which the invaders could focus their attacks.

In order to assault the surrounding countryside, the Last God's troops needed to destroy a section of the Old Kingdom's wall. They brought siege engines within range, hoping for several good strikes before they were destroyed, or hoping to buy time for their workers to expand their own fortress a fraction further.

Kervalen knew the enemy's tactics and hurried to see the intruders driven back, their catapults obliterated, before any advances were made. If only such a happy stalemate could be maintained, but the God's troops did, sometimes, succeed.

Kervalen once saw an army pour through broken walls and ravage his countryside, saw it pushed back only at a heavy price. He had been responsible for that failure. He had not stopped them in time, and his wife and son were killed, along with many other families encamped near the wall. He had been selfish to want her near, complacent. On that day, he learned what it meant to be king and to carry on when Kervalen, the man, had nothing left to live for.

So, this day and every day, he took each enemy sally seriously and stopped them hard. He watched as their burning wagon was hauled back inside and knew the retreat was temporary. They would try again in the night.

The red pennant flying atop the enemy tower was lowered and replaced by green.

Kervalen felt a weight in his gut. The god's forces had a new commander, a new banner flying over their fortress. His entire life, he had known only the red.

Why change now? What did it mean? Had the attack been a test? If so, he had revealed himself. The newcomer now knew something about his tactics, while Kervalen knew nothing.

"Double the watches," he told Captain Talis. "Be ready." He could not rely on his experience or afford to be complacent.

The captain nodded and turned to obey.

Kervalen would not sleep this night, and after that, not well, not until he had a chance to gauge this new enemy in battle.

"Don't forget the offering," Kervalen added. "This was an easy win, but even those have a cost."

Talis hesitated mid-stride. He'd heard, but he did not look back or salute. No one enjoyed the offering.

Kervalen watched to make sure it was done. He spoke the words over the criminals brought up to the parapet—their wide eyes confused as they protested innocence one last time—and he blessed the executioner before the hooded man slit the offerings' throats and let the blood pour down the inner wall so that it joined with the blood of countless centuries of enemies that had seeped into the soil.

Kervalen no longer heard the words he spoke or remembered what they meant. All he could think about was the blood-smeared wall that was the only thing that stood between them and everything on the other side.

GRIN THE KEEPER DRIPPED his way up rose marble stairs. Gobels surrounded him, hefting buckets of oil and water and drizzling ladlefuls over his taut skin. His massive body, fat and muscle and bone, but mostly fat, was sewn together from the corpses of extinct creatures. He was one of a kind, but poorly made.

He normally dwelled in the lake at the center of the cavern, immersed in calcareous waters, his bulk lightened and buoyant. It was agony to walk on land, and he needed a dozen servants to manage it, to hoist his limbs in slings and keep him from falling apart.

Thus, it was a bizarre procession that arrived at the bone doors of the Bringer's chambers. Dinah's chambers, Grin reminded himself. She was the Bringer no more. The Last God had turned His back on her, hidden His holy countenance, plunging them all into the abyss of despair. Now there was a new Bringer, and Grin wondered if it might be better to serve Adarmis. Surely <u>he</u> did not live at the top of a mountain?

He quickly smothered the thought. The red Marks that covered his body, like overlapping tattoos, glowed. Who knew when Dinah's awareness was on him? She might kill him for such treasonous ideas. Though, that would be a mercy.

"I do not feel merciful, today," Dinah said as the doors opened. "Leave your gobels behind and come to me alone, Grin."

She had been listening. He sighed, but it mingled with the flatulence and air escaping half-decomposed organs. Why did she torture him so?

When his gobels had retreated to the stairs, he crawled into Dinah's home. The doors closed behind him. He couldn't stand, but he looked more obedient with his forehead on the floor anyway. "My sources tell me Adarmis has been named Bringer. My sympathies, Lady."

"I do not need your sympathy, and do not believe all the lies you hear. I have <u>always</u> been Bringer."

"Yes, Lady." He cringed and smothered another automatic platitude. The strain of knowing there was no lying to his mistress doubled the sweat streaming from every pore of his mismatched skin.

She groaned. "I wish you would not drip on the wood. Every surface was hand carved by artisans who passed their knowledge on to offspring far less talented, and it is irreplaceable. You, however, could easily be remade—and better."

"I was thinking the same thing a moment ago, my Lady."

"No. You thought you were unique, valuable. You have no purpose if you cannot follow a simple order."

"Which one was that, my Lady?" Grin, despite his handicaps, considered himself a useful lackey. He managed her realm below, negotiated with the Drakein and the Conquered, and kept the workers and food alive—for a time. Overall, he thought things were running smoothly.

"The boy, Ralen. He was nearly eaten by your gobels."

Something was coming back to him, and he felt a moment of panic. Oh yes, the boy. The one she had said was important, special, to be protected at all times. The one he had immediately resented. He had far more important things to do than guard one morsel of food. She might be fattening the child up for a special feast, but he couldn't be expected to watch the human every moment.

"That's exactly what I expect," she said. "Nothing in my realm is more important to me. Call it a whim, but it is not your place to judge my whims. You exist only to satisfy them. It is your only reason for existence. Understood?"

"Yes, my—"

"—No. I will ensure you remember."

A wave of her hand and his bulk slid effortlessly across the polished wood floor. Grin was helpless as the lady forced him into a patch of sunshine next to an enormous window. He closed his eyes to shut out the light, but it did nothing to protect him from the heat. The moisture on his skin evaporated, leaving a burning itch behind. Dinah adored the daylight; to him it was agony. The skin across his shoulders cracked.

"Mercy," he begged. "Mercy."

"I told you. I'm not in a merciful mood." Her footsteps echoed into the other room, and she closed an inner door, blocking out his piteous cries.

He did not know how long he burned, crinkling into parchment, to ash it felt like. When she returned, he was a fraction of his former self. Every breath seared his lungs, and he was blind, the eyeballs shriveled in their sockets.

"Now..." she said. He heard doors open, the whispering of gobels. "Call out to your pets, let those who love you care for you, because I want you out of my sight. You will obey me now?"

"Yes." But no sound came from his parched throat, so he thought the words as clearly as he could, Yes, Bringer. I will obey.

"Good. Now, go."

He silently summoned his children, letting them feel his need, and they swarmed to his rescue. The pain worsened as a wave of gobels hoisted his desiccated limbs and carried him to the stairs. The oil and water they poured over cracked skin made it burn all over again.

In all their centuries together, the Lady had never punished him so. Gobels could not heal him, not from this. He would never recover. Not unless Dinah took pity and replaced the ruined parts. He had had many parts replaced, and who knew if there was anything of the original left? He did not even know which organ housed his consciousness. At that moment, he wanted all of it gone. He wanted a real body or none at all.

The task of watching the boy had been an annoyance. Now, it was the center of his universe. He had no hope of vengeance against his mistress—he did not even dare think it—and he would obey her will to the letter. He would keep the boy from harm.

There were other ways to cause pain, ways to make the boy suffer as Grin had suffered, without permanent damage, at least nothing Dinah would be aware of when she looked at him. Many of the humans were damaged in the mind. Shattered psyches were typical in this place. He would make sure Ralen was the most shattered of all.

Chapter Six ~ The Surface

When the other slaves rose in the morning and merged with the stream of people headed for the surface, Ralen joined them. Excitement built as he took Anjee's hand and walked with her on the torch-lit path. The Lady had spared them. By her order, they would both work the fields, away from gobels who liked to nibble on toes in the dark.

The white opening to the world above grew larger and larger until Ralen was suddenly there, buffeted by wind. He dodged the adults' shadows to feel daylight on his skin. The air smelled green with a hint of honey.

Ralen smiled, and Anjee squeezed his hand, the only sign she was excited too.

A wide valley stretched before them, terraced hillsides choked with orchards. Steep granite peaks encircled everything, except where one end of the valley spilled onto a hazy plain hundreds of feet below. Obelisks stood to either side of the gap. Silver creatures with long tails and wings wide enough to obscure the clouds soared beyond the pillars.

A Drakein stepped in front of Ralen and said, "Do not cross the boundary stones. The wild tribes will eat you." It bared serrated teeth, as though wishing it did not have to curb its own appetite.

Ralen nodded his understanding, and the Drakein used the butt of its spear to nudge him and Anjee into a group of people headed for the center of the valley. The river of slaves branched out across the landscape, some headed for the orchards and some for the distant hills.

When Ralen reached the fields, another guard handed out sacks of pungent manure and tools. He and Anjee dragged a sack and a rake between them. They copied the adults and spread the fertilizer beneath the shafts of green wheat.

A brown mouse darted past their feet and Anjee pointed, saying, "Three blind mice..." She sang as they worked.

His gaze kept returning to her, to sunlight in golden hair. For too long there had been nothing but firelight and glowworms to see by. Here, in the world outside the cave, Anjee outshone everything. Ralen felt warm, the sun burning his cheeks, and the warmth penetrated inside, to his heart.

He looked to the top of the mountain they had emerged from, where the Bringer's longhouse pressed down on the cavern below. He saw the lady's red dress framed in one large window. The Mark on his hand suddenly glowed bright red to match. She could see him, see inside. The warmth in his chest faded away, and he went back to work.

He was grateful for the Bringer's mercy, but, even in the worst of times, he'd always had the freedom of his thoughts. He did not like that Dinah could read them. He tried to keep his mind blank as he focused on the task at hand.

Time passed quickly. It was good to have something to do besides hide in caves. He chewed on strands of wheatgrass until rations were handed out at noon.

The Drakein guards faced the sun and closed their eyes contentedly from time to time. Their scales sparkled and mouths hung open, revealing white fangs. Ralen tried not to think about slipping away into the field when they weren't looking and testing the boundary stones. The Bringer was listening in. Even if he and Anjee did run, they could not hide. The Drakein could smell them, and the monsters were fast. He'd seen them kill during the war. He would never get away.

It was hard <u>not</u> to think about something.

Black feathers rustled stalks of wheat. It looked like a crow, a giant crow, but a moment later it was gone.

The lunch break was short. They returned to work, and Ralen's gaze searched through the tall grass for another sign of the bird. He'd seen something, but it was a flicker, gone in an instant. It niggled at the back of his mind like a splinter, as though there was something right in front of him that he could not focus on.

Anjee emptied the last of the fertilizer at his feet, shaking the bag. "I'll get more."

"I'll go with you."

"It's just there." She pointed at the Drakein who stood next to the manure pile with its nose stuffed full of cloth. "I can do it." She marched off and left him to do the raking.

The handle was too long, and he held the rake in the middle, resting the wood on his shoulder. His arms ached from the morning's work.

"You need muscle," a high voice, like struck crystal, said in his ear.

Ralen jumped and dropped the rake in the mud. There was nothing there. He looked around. Anjee was filling her bag at the Drakein's feet. The monster raised its face to the sun again.

"Who's there?" he whispered.

He saw black feathers in his mind, but there was nothing for his eyes to fasten on.

"Go into the field," the voice told him.

"They'll think I'm trying to escape," he said.

"The Drakein will not see. I will make sure of it. Come, Ralen."

His curiosity was overwhelming. He took a hesitant step. Then, feeling a rush of adrenaline, he ran into the depths of the wheat. He stopped, panting. The grass reached his forehead, and he had to stand on tiptoes to see. Adults worked the field deeper in, and the giant Drakein were easy to spot on the fringes, but Anjee was invisible now, like the creature talking to him.

"You're not going to eat me?" Ralen asked.

A sharp laugh tickled his skull. "You should have thought of that before."

He still couldn't see anyone, but he felt something brush against his cheek, and the breeze rustled something besides grass. "You're a bird man, aren't you?"

There was silence for several heartbeats. "Good guess." The air before him shimmered and thickened into a black fog. When it cleared, a winged man was crouched in the dirt. "It was a guess?"

"I saw black feathers."

"No one sees us if we do not want to be seen." The bird man tilted his head, pointed beak aimed at the ground, studying him. "I am Ashkal, Angel of the Last God."

"I'm Ralen...Slave of the Bringer." It felt good to have a title. It helped him understand his role in things. He did what he was told and tried not to be eaten. Simple.

"Dinah is Bringer no more," Ashkal said.

"What does that mean?"

"She displeased our Lord and was shunned. His Presence no longer feeds her, and she no longer knows the joy of His service. She must stay here and contemplate her mistakes and pray our Lord forgives."

"So ... she's been sent to her room to think about it?" Ralen's mother used to send him to his room, aching and sore from her beatings, whenever he did something wrong. He never understood why she told him to think about what he'd done. It was too late then. If he'd been thinking, he wouldn't have made a mistake in the first place. Everything that you regretted happened when you weren't paying attention.

The angel slapped the ground and cawed with laughter. "Exactly!"

They stared at one another. Ralen reached out a hand to touch one of the feathered wings. It was smooth and stiff, not as soft as he thought it would be. "You don't look like an angel. There's nothing human about you at all."

"Yet an angel I am, for I am a messenger of the Last God."

"You mean 'God'. I was taught 'Thou shalt have no other gods before me'."

"Oh, there were gods before this one. My brother and I are all that remains of an ancient race of near-gods. Near. The Last God showed us how fragile we were. Others put up a better fight."

"So, He is God."

Ashkal moved so fast he blurred, and cold metal pressed against Ralen's throat. "This is a Blessed Blade," the angel said. "It cannot be broken, and it drains the souls of its victims, burns them up, leaving nothing behind. It wants to taste your soul. I hear it whispering to me."

Ralen stayed silent. If the angel wanted to kill him, he could. Muscles tensed. He wished he had his own knife. Then he wouldn't die so easily.

"It is like our Lord," Ashkal continued, "hungry and merciless, but the Last God is even more unstoppable." The angel withdrew the knife and sheathed it again.

Ralen put a hand to his throat, feeling vulnerable. "What do you want?" It was the same question he had asked the lady, the question he wanted to ask all the creatures around him. He needed to understand the 'why' of things, even if there was no changing it. Mother had often punished him for his questions.

"We watch. We do not want. Not anymore," Ashkal said.

"We?"

"My brother keeps Dinah distracted. She must not know that I have spoken to you. I can cloud your memories. It is best to forget me and return to work."

"Why are you talking to me at all?"

"We are practical. A tool unused, a blade unsharpened, has no purpose. We will sharpen you." Black mist obscured Ashkal before he vanished.

"What do you mean?" Ralen asked empty air.

"Hold on to your rake next time," the angel said. Then even the formless voice was gone. Ralen did not see him fly away, but he sensed a lessening of pressure and felt an absence in his mind.

Why was he standing here all alone? He thought of Anjee and hurried back to the edge of the wheat. She was waiting, her gaze searching the thick grass.

When she saw him, she burst into tears and put her arms around him. "I thought you'd left me." She always seemed to be crying for him. He knew he should reject her weakness, but he could not bring himself to think anything bad about her. Never.

"It was...." He remembered a flash of black, but everything else was hazy. "I went looking for the crow."

Her whole body shook, as though wracked by fever. "Don't leave me alone. I thought I'd be okay if you were gone. It would be better for you. But then I couldn't see you, and I imagined never seeing you ... and I can't. I can't be alone here."

"I'm sorry." He kissed her cheek. It hurt to see her sad.

"Next time we'll fill the sack together, and I'll look at birds with you," she said. "Promise you won't leave."

"I promise." Yett, for some reason, he didn't think the bird would want her there. Black feathers. He shouldn't think about it, but he couldn't remember why.

DINAH WATCHED THE ANGEL, Amseel, depart her longhouse through an open window. It beat its wings and headed toward the Portal in the next valley. She suddenly envied the creature. She never went overland or through the air to reach the Portal, only below ground through dank tunnels surrounded by decay. Life was forever out of reach. She was immortal, but she did not live, and nothing could live around her.

Instead of closing the thick panes of glass, Dinah climbed over the sill and planted her feet on wildflowers. They browned and shrunk into mud. She took a step toward an ancient olive that leaned over the edge of the cliff. Leaves and bark fell to the ground and disintegrated. She placed a hand on its now bleached wood and stuck a toe over the precipice. Pebbles broke off and tumbled hundreds of feet to the valley below. She could barely discern workers in the field but felt their thoughts, their gazes on her, red dress blowing in the wind.

She could take another step and follow the pebbles to the ground below. It would not kill her. Or would it, now that the god's favor was withdrawn?

Amseel had carried her Lord's words of disapproval. He rebuked her prayers and offers of contrition. The Last God would not restore her to Bringer.

Yet, He had not taken away the energy that sustained her. She was still young, still powerful enough to toss Grin about the room with only a thought. Only...she was hungrier than usual.

A hawk dropped from the sky; its life drained in an instant. Her aura did not reach the valley below, for which she was grateful. She could not bear to have her view taken away along with everything else. With a sigh, she climbed back inside her longhouse and closed the window.

Her fury was contained. It had eaten at her for days, abated only in the boy's presence. The god's disfavor was unbearable, but she had borne it.

There had been a time when she could not imagine anything greater than her Lord, a time when she would have wept at His anger and thrown herself from the mountain in shame, hoping it would kill her. At one time, there was nothing stronger than His Presence, nothing that did not bow before Him. Things had changed. She was no longer Bringer, but she had something more than she had ever had before—hope.

She called to the Drakein guard outside her door and told him to fetch food, lots of it. When a dozen people stood in her entry hall, she sifted through their thoughts.

"Not that one," she said, pointing to a gaunt man. The Drakein dragged him back down to the cavern. The magic in him was weak, but Dinah would need all the mages she could find. Another idea was forming, one that would keep her occupied while she figured out what to do with the boy.

She held her arms out and enveloped the humans in her aura. Their screams were music. Her veins filled with life, and she smiled as she kicked newly polished bone into the bin.

In addition to mages, she would need more artisans, ones skilled enough to work with the materials at hand. There would soon be enough bone to build her home a new wing. She had a plan.

KERVALEN WAS NOT A religious man. His god was dead after all. Ironic that he was not only King but High Priest. It was a hereditary position, although not an empty one. More a curse, as the offerings were his responsibility. Besides the Prophets, he alone knew the mysteries and had read the sacred texts. If he fell in battle, his successor would be given access to the Sanctum, and the Compact would be passed down. He wished that burden on no one. Worse than steel armor or the responsibility of command, knowledge was the hardest thing to bear.

He surveyed the field of dying men, wanting to ease their suffering rather than be the cause of it. He could not even bring their bodies back to their families. Whatever the crows didn't get was burned by fire or Channeler's flame and the ashes soaked into the battlefield with the next rainfall. The greenest grass grew there, wherever it was not trampled by boots and blasted by siege missiles.

Mala would be his successor. She was not ready for this. She was only ten years old, but Kervalen already sensed it, the frailty of will. Once she knew... She would not be strong enough. Her aunts and uncles would take over and all would be lost. No one in his family was strong enough to do what had to be done to stop the invaders.

He recalled his son's smiling face, his wife holding him in her arms. Gabriel would have been strong.

"The gate opens, but we see nothing, no torches," Talis told him.

It was midnight. The attacks by the enemy with the green pennant had been non-stop for weeks. His foe wanted to win badly. Kervalen wanted to live even more.

"Launch flares," he said.

Orbs of light flew from the hands of Channelers and hovered over the killing ground. An army large enough to overwhelm their walls and raze their entire kingdom poured out of the Portal and through the open gates of the enemy citadel.

"By Hestian," Talis whispered, invoking their lost god. He signaled to the archers, but Kervalen stayed his hand.

"No need."

"We must defend," the captain argued.

"Look at them, look closely," Kervalen said.

The captain's mouth gaped when he saw what Kervalen had noticed: the white eyes, bone protruding through shriveled skin, armor hanging loose on emaciated bodies. The enemy soldiers were already dead.

"God-fed." Kervalen had not seen them since he was a boy, and never in such numbers, but the size of the army did not matter. They were mindless, nothing but arms and legs and weapons wielded by the Last God's power.

This was the Old Kingdom—there was a reason it had stood for a thousand years.

Soldiers shifted uncomfortably along the wall, but they waited, following orders passed down the line. A stray arrow fell into the enemy ranks and clattered inside an empty ribcage. Kervalen frowned, but he could forgive a frightened youth.

The God-fed raised axes and swords, pounded fists against shields and then charged. Their silence was unnerving. Human soldiers shouted or cursed to build their courage, but many of the God-fed had no tongues. Their bodies crashed against the Kingdom wall, and they climbed atop one another, a writhing, growing ladder, like an ocean wave ready to surge over the fortifications.

The wave ebbed. The enemy mass crumpled. Body parts and armor clattered to the ground as the magic that held the dead together dissipated. When there was nothing but heaps of bone and metal, the metal corroded and flaked apart, and the bones sank into the soil. The earth crawled over the enemy and covered them up forever.

There was nothing left, not even corpses to burn.

The Last God's new general did not believe. He had to learn for himself it seemed. Foolish, not to trust the wisdom of those more experienced. Or perhaps he did not know history?

"I've never..." the captain whispered.

"I know. It is a disturbing sight, but a heartening one. The will of Hestian is unbroken. We are his chosen people, and we will endure." When Kervalen said it, he almost believed it. There was nothing more faith-sustaining than watching a miracle. Unfortunately, he knew how the miracle worked. If only he could conjure a means of breaking this siege and shut out the Last God once and for all, he wouldn't mind being High Priest.

MONTHS PASSED. THE harvest came, and the workload doubled, but no new workers arrived. The Bringer's conquests were at an end. Worse, she was eating more people. Ralen had heard the gobels whispering about it, and he'd seen the groups of doomed slaves herded up the stairs to her mountaintop. Soon, there would be more monsters than humans in the cavern. He wondered what became of souls devoured in Hell.

When will my turn come? Ralen climbed the steps to her door almost every evening. It didn't matter that his arms and legs ached from swinging a scythe or toting bundles of golden wheat on his back. He had no choice but to obey or end up as one of her chairs.

Often, when he read a book aloud and she corrected his pronunciation, he felt the smooth ball of a femur dig into his thigh. Without thinking he would rest his hand on the rounded top of a skull cleverly embedded in a carved doorframe. The massive bones that supplied the archways and ceiling beams had also come from her victims. Her longhouse was like an evil cottage in a fairy tale after all—beautiful from a distance but terrifying up close. At least there was no kitchen and no oven. From what he had seen, when she decided to eat him it would be fast. Painful. But fast.

He waited at the tunnel mouth for one of the Drakein guards to notice him. "I'm here for my lesson," he said.

The one with a scraped nose and yellowed scales slung the long weapon he carried over his shoulder and beckoned for Ralen to follow before setting off. The curved blade at the end of the polearm glinted and winked as they walked.

The main tunnel branched into a labyrinth, each passage edged in the same blue worm-light, but the guard knew which way to go. They passed more Drakein, leading slow-moving groups of slaves loaded down with wooden planks and buckets of nails. One group came empty-handed from the opposite direction, away from Dinah's longhouse. Alive. At least for now. Among them was a teenage boy. He looked Ralen in the eyes, and Ralen started. There was still spirit left in him.

Ralen wanted more than anything to look away. He was not here to fetch and carry for Dinah nor serve as her evening meal, and he felt a twinge of guilt at that, but he met the older boy's gaze. He was alive. Anjee was alive. He would not apologize for that or for what little he had.

Thankfully, they saw no one else until they reached the top of the marble staircase. The bone doors were open wide to an ant's nest of activity. A section of the longhouse wall was missing, and the sounds of hammering and sawing came from the other side. Open sky was visible, stars twinkling in the cold night, torchlight framing busy slaves as they worked.

"I'm expanding," Dinah said. She was beside him, her red dress close enough for him to touch, but he kept his arms against his sides. This near to her he felt chilled, and a scent like old death swirled around him. He noticed that among the piles of lumber and other building materials were fresh piles of human bones.

Ralen shivered.

"This racket is maddening, so we will have no lesson tonight. There will be no lesson until I return. I pray the Drakein will have this done by then," she said.

"Where are you going?" Ralen asked.

"Wherever I must. I intend to change everything. That means, as much as I love the home I have spent too many campaigns away from, I must leave it. Nothing is ever accomplished by sitting still."

Ralen did not understand any better than he had, and he worried. What would happen to him?

"Prepare a wagon, Captain," Dinah said to the Drakein with the scraped nose who had escorted Ralen up the mountain. "I will need provisions, travelling colors..." She gave the Drakein a look that meant more than she was saying. "...and a group of newly trained hatchlings. Remember not to touch this boy. Sniff deeply, recall his scent. Make sure your underlings remember as well."

"Yes, Lady. Will I not be going with you?" There was a strange note in the monster's voice. It sounded sad.

Dinah reached out and stroked the captain's cheek. The yellow scales she touched turned dark brown and sloughed away. "No, dear child. You will be long dead by the time I return. Ensure your replacement is well trained in my absence."

The Drakein captain bowed deeply. "Yes, Lady."

Dinah turned back to Ralen. "What will happen to you, you wonder? You will stay alive, but it will not be easy. My realm is not a kind place. The universe is not kind. I charge you to survive it and be ready to serve when I return." With that, she waved him away, and he followed the Drakein captain back down the rose stair.

Survive. That had been the first thing his mother told him as the invaders descended on their world. At least Dinah had made sure the Drakein would not eat him. She'd said nothing to the gobels though.

Chapter Seven ~ Lessons

Ralen waited for Anjee to fall asleep. When she was snoring gently on the straw-covered floor beside him, he carefully rose and tucked her in with the rag blanket they shared. He waited a moment longer to make sure she was not faking. Fieldwork exhausted them both, but she'd managed to follow him before. When he was satisfied, he crept out of the small cave. The other slaves slept deeply and did not notice him leave, if they even cared.

Dinah had been gone less than a week, and he already missed the library. Not the house of horrors that held it, but the books. He wanted to ascend the marble stairs again and pore through the pages. Sometimes it felt like he should be looking for something, something that he might find there.

Her longhouse was off limits now, but the mountaintop was not the only place there was to go at night.

It made Anjee curious, especially when he returned claiming no memory of where he had been. Curiosity killed the cat, his mother had taught. The only way he could protect Anjee was to leave her behind.

"Come," the invisible voice said in his ear.

A pressure built up, a silent call that drew him to the edge of the turquoise lake, past Drakein who seemed dazed and unaware of his presence. He stopped in a dark alcove bordered by stalagmites. He had no torch, but the blue glow from the worms and the red light put off by the Mark were enough to see by.

He was forgetting less and less. In some ways, remembering was worse, because he had to hide his thoughts from Dinah. He didn't doubt that she could still listen in on him wherever she was. She couldn't be allowed to see the black feathers and gleaming steel in his memories, couldn't know about Ashkal and Amseel.

The angels appeared in a blur of rippling black feathers, and the Mark on his hand dimmed. Their magic shielded him from the lady. He exhaled and let loose the memories tied away in his head, memories from the past months: the rake in the field, learning to hold it and strike imaginary foes, even though he was too small to swing with any force. At least he built strength. Then it was slinging stones from a piece of leather, a stick that floated on the surface of the lake turned into a baton, and now daggers.

Ashkal handed him two rusty blades that must have come from the scrap pile at the edge of the lake. The metal flaked apart and stained his skin brown.

Then both angels attacked.

"Faster," Amseel said for the millionth time. The angel didn't seem to know any other instruction. Ralen was moving as fast as he could. He was ten years old—his birthday had come in the summer, if the summer on this world was even equivalent to his own—and he was exhausted from doing as much work as any of the adults. They were lucky he could stand up without falling over.

Amseel twisted Ralen's arms behind his back and held him, Blessed Blade a hairsbreadth from his neck. "There is nothing to keep me from killing you."

Ralen knew that, knew he had no choice but to do whatever the bird men asked. He didn't understand why they wanted him to learn to fight anymore than he understood why Dinah had taught him to read and think, but he liked learning, so it was no hardship to obey.

"Don't get overzealous," Ashkal chided his brother. "A cut from your blade can take his soul."

"He gains nothing from encouragement. Defeat and humiliation are the best teachers."

"Have they taught us, my brother? Taught us anything but hatred?"

Amseel moved the Blessed Blade away from Ralen's neck. "He is unharmed."

Ashkal held out a hand and Ralen took it. The angel's skin was covered in black down. It looked bare, but every inch was feathered.

"I'll be faster," Ralen promised.

The lesson went on until he fell to his knees with weariness. He would get only a few hours sleep before dawn, but he would endure. The angels did not visit every day.

"It is difficult to evade our Lord," Ashkal said. "We are his eyes and ears, and He demands reports. If He ever guesses at these encounters, we have no choice but to answer His direct questions. The trick is to keep Him from asking."

It seemed the angels had their own equivalent of Dinah. The Last God could ransack their thoughts whenever He chose, and it was difficult to keep secrets.

"Why?" he asked.

Ashkal rested a serene, black-eyed gaze on him. "Why do what we are doing?"

"Yes." Ralen heard nothing but fearful mention of the Last God from Dinah, from the angels, from everyone. Yet, they were doing something the god wouldn't like. "Why risk it?"

Amseel looked at his brother. "I want to know as well."

"Sometimes a weed grows between the stones, and you pluck it, because that is what you are supposed to do," Ashkal said. "But, if you let the weed grow, who knows what will happen? The stone may even crack, and you don't have to worry about protecting it from weeds anymore."

Ralen was the weed. He guessed that much, but what was he supposed to do?

AS EVER, HE WAS CONFUSED when he left his session with the angels. His mind spun with maneuvers and movements to learn, but the fog descended before he grasped any of it. He forgot.

"Lost, lost, lost?" a gobel whispered in the dark beside him.

Ralen stiffened. What was he doing in the great cavern away from the others? He clenched his fist, expecting to feel a rusty dagger in his grip, but it was empty. The angels, he remembered again. They were gone now. It was dangerous to be alone.

There was no nearby precipice from which to toss this gobel, so he kept walking.

"Don't go," the gobel whined, hopping in front of him. Three others crept through the shadows and slowly surrounded him.

He snatched a heavy rock from the ground and held it like a club. "Leave me alone."

The monster shook its head. "No, no, no. We can't. We were sent. Our beloved father sent us. He wants you. Now."

The gobels leaped. One landed on his back, another wrapped itself around his legs, and when he couldn't move they lifted him up onto their backs. The rock was twisted from his grip. He wanted to cry out, ask for help, but there was no one who would. Anjee might hear his shouts, but he didn't want her to come, didn't want her to get eaten too.

The gobels yanked at his hair, making him whimper, but he kept fighting and twisting. He saw the lakeshore from upside down, water reflecting blue light like a field of stars. The gobels carried him into the lake. He kicked futilely, unable to break free. All he could do was gulp a breath before water covered his face.

Water pressed from every direction. He thrashed, lungs hungry for air as they held him down. His heart beat frantically, his chest tight, and when he couldn't bear it any longer, he inhaled, inhaled water. His chest hurt, and everything went dark.

Sometime later his eyes were open, although he didn't remember opening them or leaving the water. He was lying on his back, staring at a ceiling covered in blue glow worms.

"Feels good to be alive, does it?" He didn't recognize the voice. It was strange, as though the words passed through tubes and crossed deserts before reaching his ears. "Gobels get overanxious. Fortunately, I saved you."

Ralen rolled onto his side. He was on a stone island in the center of the underground lake, a limestone atoll with a shallow pool of water in its center. Gobels were everywhere. The fattest man Ralen had ever seen was half submerged in the pool, stomach floating around him, arms stretched out to the sides. On second look, it was a monster made to look like a man—it had extra arms, bits of mismatched flesh, most of it blackened and burnt, and a cloth over its eyes.

"You can't see me," Ralen noted.

"No, and neither can our Lady. When Dinah is away, whatever wonderful dark thoughts we can imagine are free to rampage through our heads and entertain us with their delicious imagery," the creature said. The monstrous smile sewn across its face seemed genuine at that moment. "Just you and me now, boy."

"What do you want?" Ralen should stop asking the same question—no one ever answered—but he needed to know.

"I am Grin the Keeper. I oversee this domain, take care of details, feed Dinah's armies ... and I have been appointed to watch over you. I thought it high time I 'saw' the beast Dinah deemed special enough to warrant my personal attention."

Special. What did that mean? He expected a reply, Dinah always answered his thoughts, but the fat man didn't. Gobels poured water over his body as he waited.

Ralen could be quiet too. He preferred silence, except for Anjee's singing. Her voice transported him elsewhere, someplace safe and beautiful.

"Are you frightened?" Grin asked.

He had come to expect death, so he was only frightened when it seemed the moment had arrived. The existence of monsters no longer scared him. "No," he said.

"Then come closer."

He took a step, his wet clothes dripping on the stone with a patter like rain. The crowd of gobels parted, and Ralen moved to the edge of the pool.

"Closer," Grin said. "I want to see you."

Ralen couldn't swim. He hated water, and he couldn't get closer without jumping in. "No," he said.

"You defy me? I am master here when Dinah is away." The Keeper waved mismatched fingers, and gobels closed in. They pushed Ralen into the pool, the water coming up to his chin, and shoved his face against the fat man's rotting chest. Cadaverous hands felt his skull, his cheeks, stroked his neck and back.

"Stop," he said.

"No," the monster answered.

Putrid breath made him shudder, but he wasn't strong enough to break free of the embrace. The rag across the creature's eyes was covered in mould, decomposing like the rest of him, and, through a gap, Ralen saw sockets with black eyeballs that had shrunk to raisins.

He longed for the rusty dagger, for sharp steel, anything with which to cut off the hands squeezing him. When he stopped struggling, frozen with hatred and disgust, Grin let him go.

"You will do," the creature said.

As soon as he was free, Ralen climbed out of the pool. The gobels would not let him retreat far. They turned him to face their master.

Grin's misshapen face was an eternal smile. "I'm very busy, boy, and I have important things that need done. It is impossible to get Drakein to do more than hold a weapon and look stern, and my gobels, like me, spurn sunshine. I have a job for you."

Ralen had too many jobs: working the fields, black feathers ... watching over Anjee, although no one had told him to do that. He wanted her to be safe. Needed it. He didn't want another job, but he was a slave, and he had to obey, at least for now. One thing he'd learned from the lady and the angels was that obedience was not absolute.

"What do you want?"

"I need someone to carry messages to and from the Portal," Grin said. "Can you read the God's Tongue?"

"Yes." It was the first thing Dinah had taught him.

"As I hoped. You will be useful. Take this." The Keeper gestured to one of the gobels.

The gobel cringed before bowing to its master. It stood up again and extended one long finger, slowly gripping the curved claw at the end. It pulled, keening with pain, until it had ripped its own claw off. The creature offered it to Ralen.

He hesitated before taking the thing, which was smeared with yellow blood. The gobel sucked its wound, sealing the skin, just as one had sealed the stump of Ralen's little toe.

"Use it to open the messages," the Keeper said, "and read what's inside. Close them up again as best you can, of course. Heat, a bit of candle flame, that should allow you to reaffix the wax seal. I want to know what's being said."

The fat man waved an arm dramatically and glow worms flared brighter, illuminating the entire cavern. Ralen's eyes widened. The place had been an empty void to him until now, dotted with distant lights like stars, with only portions of the lake visible: the slave caves, Dinah's staircase, and the path to the surface. Grin gestured at the other side of the vast lake to where a city climbed the walls, windows and doors cut into the limestone, rooms hollowed out of the ground. An entire city he had been unaware of.

"Find Gordon," Grin ordered. "He's Conquered, and he will have correspondence for the armies, instructions for withdrawal, and so forth. I'm not concerned with such things, but, if there's anything else, I want to know about it. You will be his messenger. You and you alone." The Keeper spoke carefully, making it clear this was important.

"How do I get there?" The sight of water made Ralen's lungs ache all over again. The light from the glow worms dimmed, until only the portion of the island on which he stood and the distant pinpoints of the city's lights were visible.

"There are boats." Grin chuckled. "But they're moored on the other side. My children will carry you. Go now."

"No—" Gobels dragged Ralen under the surface before his protest was heard.

They put something on his mouth and nose that felt like seaweed, cold and jelly-like. It sealed itself to his skin with sharp hooks. He could barely breathe, chest tight again, limbs flailing, pain in his face ... but he didn't black out. The seaweed creature provided some air and kept water from gushing into his lungs. It was an agonizing trip, but better than the first one.

They tossed him onto the pebbly beach at the base of the city. Oil lamps hung near the docks and beside doorways; they were smoky and provided little light. A gobel tore the jelly thing off his face and disappeared into the lake.

He lay there, shivering, cold and exhaustion holding him down. With effort, he pushed his palms into stony sand and climbed to his feet. He couldn't sleep until he was back in the cave with Anjee, until he'd done what the Keeper asked.

He staggered to the nearest door and knocked. He thought of the city where he grew up, doorbells and peepholes, but this city was its opposite, buried underground and fortified. His fist produced a dull thud when it struck the heavy wood. He pounded on the door until his hand hurt. When it opened, a human looked out at him. Ralen was surprised by the healthy face, the fine clothes. The man was not like any of the slaves he had met. "What is it?"

"I'm looking for Gordon," Ralen said.

"The First Commander?"

"'Gordon' was all the Keeper said."

"The Keeper?" The man's eyes widened. "Two streets in." The door shut.

The Conquered city was massive, almost as large as the place Ralen had been born. The limestone buildings were ten stories high, jammed together like irregular toy blocks. The structures built into the cavern wall were taller, more than twenty stories. It was "night", and the streets were empty, except for a few indiscernible figures strolling down the narrow lanes.

A Drakein and two humans stood together on the nearest corner beneath a lamp, sharing a grumbled conversation. Ralen asked them where the First Commander's house was, and the Drakein pointed one claw in the right direction. Unlike the Drakein guards who watched over the slaves, it didn't question him being there.

He knocked on three doors before he found the right one and marveled at the maid who left him to wait in the entry hall of a narrow house that occupied the lower stories of a building. She was clean, everything was clean.

The man who must be Gordon came down the polished stairs wearing a long shirt, his hair flattened and cheek red from sleep. "What is so terribly urgent?"

"Grin the Keeper sent me. I'm to take messages to the Portal. It's my new job," Ralen said.

Gordon had a large moustache and small eyes. He stared for a few seconds then burst out laughing. "You're a child! I had no idea the Keeper engaged in practical jokes. I already have a messenger, a good runner twice your age, and he suits me fine. Go back to the slave pens."

"The Keeper said I was to be your messenger. Me and no one else."

"I see." The man chewed his lip. "Very well, come back tomorrow. I'll have something for you then."

Ralen thought about the lake between him and Anjee. "It's a long way."

The man seemed to finally notice Ralen's weariness, the drooping lids and dripping clothes. "All right, you can rest here."

A woman in nightclothes appeared at the top of the stairs. "What's wrong?" she asked.

"Nothing," Gordon said. "Go back to bed, love. I'll join you in a moment."

Ralen couldn't sleep here. He couldn't leave Anjee alone in the cave or let her go into the fields the next day without him. He had promised. "Can't I deliver the messages now?" he asked.

Gordon shook his head. "The Portal is accessed through a tunnel in the city. The way is sealed at night unless I order otherwise, and I am not willing to unseal it for you now. Wait until morning, and I will have my usual messenger show you the way. No. I will show you myself. I must go there in any event."

Ralen wanted to argue, but the man's expression indicated the discussion was over. He went back upstairs and rejoined his wife.

"I'll get some blankets," the maid said. She had the hollow voice and faraway look that Ralen was used to seeing among the workers. She walked with a limp and bore red scars on her hands.

Had the maid been a slave? Was it possible to survive, to please Dinah and the Keeper and come to this city to live?

Excitement built as he imagined bringing Anjee to a house like this to rest, far away from whispering gobels, but he was too exhausted to sustain the vision in his mind's eye. He could not endure crossing the lake again tonight. It was best to wait for morning, deliver the First Commander's messages, and then rejoin Anjee. In the meantime, he would learn about the Conquered, about the city, and perhaps he could bring her good news when he returned.

He fell asleep on the bed without bothering to crawl under the covers. He had forgotten what a bed felt like.

A hundred years of slumber would not have been long enough, so when the maid woke him at dawn, he did not feel rested.

"The commander is ready to depart." She shoved a bowl of what looked like oatmeal into his hand.

It was bland, but it was food. So, this was where the grain they harvested went? He ate so fast he choked and needed the glass of water she handed him. He licked the bowl clean then ran to the front door. Gordon was there, laden with armor. Ralen recognized the helmet he carried—it was what the soldiers who destroyed his home had worn.

"You were in a hurry last night, now I'm the one waiting." Gordon held out a leather satchel. "Letters for you to carry."

Ralen took the bag and slung it across his shoulder. The Keeper had told him to read what was inside, but how could he do that with the commander watching?

"Follow me." The man's tone was as peremptory as Dinah's.

It was difficult to keep up with the long-legged soldier, and there was little time for Ralen to digest his surroundings, not that he could see much in the unending dark within the cavern. Now that it was "day", the streets were crowded. Soldiers saluted when Gordon walked past. It was a city of soldiers as far as Ralen could tell. Even the women wore armor, except for those who appeared to be servants.

Many servants bore terrible scars or limped, and some were missing arms or legs. Were they victims of invasion, those too injured to perform field work? Would he and Anjee be accepted here if they were still whole?

He heard children's voices and glimpsed a courtyard through a barred gate. The children marched in lines with wooden weapons balanced against their shoulders. Drakein were among them. He'd never seen young Drakein before. They were similar to the adults, scaled and clawed, and they were already taller and heavier than the human children. Everywhere he looked, the populace seemed evenly divided between humans and monsters.

He tried to pay attention and remember the route Gordon took him. It was five minutes from Gordon's house to the tunnel entrance, which was blocked by a massive iron-banded door. A smaller door set in the larger one was watched over by soldiers.

"Has Caleb come through here yet?" Gordon asked the nearest guard.

"No, First Commander. Should I send for word from the Portal?" she asked.

"No need. I go there myself." As an afterthought, he added, "This boy is my new messenger."

The guard took in Ralen's size and raised an eyebrow, but all she said was, "Yes, sir."

When they were through the smaller door and walking down the wide passageway, Gordon fished a bronze medallion out of the pouch at his waist. It hung from a red cord. "This is my seal," he said. "I will give it to you whenever I send you on an errand. It is the only thing that will get you past that door."

Ralen nodded his understanding.

The tunnel was long and lit by evenly spaced lamps. It widened on one side, and he was surprised to see a corral of horses. One was already saddled and bridled. The groomsman held it while Gordon mounted. The commander offered Ralen his hand. "Come."

He remembered Conquered soldiers on horses, earthquakes, and falling into water poisoned by volcanic ash. The Last God had called those volcanoes into existence. Ralen had learned many things from his studies with Dinah, but the books in the library had not taught him how to ride a horse.

There was no place for hesitation or weakness in this world, so he took Gordon's hand and climbed up behind the commander. He held on tight as they cantered off. The tunnel was eerily deserted, the clatter of hoofs echoing against stone.

Ralen must have come this way before, when he was captured, but he'd been unable to see anything at the time. He had been jammed into a crate with the other captives and loaded on a wagon. He remembered the swaying motion of a boat at one point. They'd been across the lake and in the darkness of the slave caves before he'd had a chance to see anything. That's why he never saw the city.

His head was overflowing with questions. Gordon was a human, just like him, so he felt like he could ask them. He shouted over the clamor of hoof beats: "So the Conquered are Dinah's soldiers? We work the fields, and you fight?"

There was no immediate reply, and he worried the commander preferred he stayed quiet. Finally, Gordon said, "Yes, but I serve willingly."

"You chose this?" Ralen didn't know what to think.

"In a way. It's either willing fighter or unwilling slave. At least the Bringer, I mean, Dinah, gave us that choice. The Last God would not have. Anything to avoid being God-fed."

Ralen had heard of the god's own soldiers. They had no minds of their own, no existence without the god powering them. He had never seen them, but he imagined they were the one thing worse than being a slave.

"How do I become Conquered?" he asked.

Gordon snorted. "You want to be a warrior?"

Ralen remembered the servants with their clean clothes and bowls of gruel and thought that would be better than burning cities for Dinah, but he also had a memory of steel that glowed and hummed with a hunger of its own, of black feathers. "Yes. I want to fight."

Gordon stopped the horse. His voice sounded distant, a leader ordering his troops into battle, as he said, "Show me your right hand."

Ralen held it out. The Bringer's Mark glowed brightly in the dimly lit space. The soldier removed a gauntlet and held up his own hand—it was bare.

"The Keeper is playing cruel games," Gordon said. "Sending you here to see our city, to play messenger. You have been Marked. Body and soul you belong to Dinah. You are food, and you will die. Today, tomorrow, it makes no difference. The brand can never be removed, and you can never be one of us."

The commander dug in his spurs, and the horse bolted forward. Ralen clutched hard armor and held on, even as he felt his insides falling away. For a night and a morning, he had hoped for something better. Having that ripped away was agony.

He would never let it happen again. Never let himself hope. His mother would have been ashamed of his weakness.

Chapter Eight ~ Messenger

Saren took the leather satchel from General Adarmis's advisor. A mismatched army milled around them. There were creatures from every world—Drakein, Conquered, God-fed, Fliers, Akantha, and more Saren didn't know the name of—but none were as striking as the Fae standing in front of him.

The advisor's skin was luminous, with shifting clouds of color moving beneath the translucent surface. Prismatic eyes peered through vertical lids, watching everything. Saren had heard stories of Fae, and he often imagined being one of them, experiencing orgies of pain and pleasure, free to satisfy every dark desire.

The Fae opened the satchel and showed him a small parcel wrapped in plain cloth. "This will buy the Keeper's gratitude, and this," he indicated a letter with a green seal, "will either convince your commander to trust the general or be enough to condemn him to death when Dinah learns of it."

"That won't be necessary. Gordon will join us. It'll be easier with him on our side, you'll see, Varvec."

"Do not say my name. You mangle it with your crude pronunciation."

Saren could not meet the Fae's disdainful gaze. "Caleb and the Locum will convince him."

Varvec sniffed. "They lack my talents. I do not expect this silly scheme to succeed, but our new Bringer feels he cannot ignore any opportunity to hurt Dinah."

"Why is that?"

Varvec frowned and disappeared into the crowd. Saren knew the advisor did not like answering questions, and Fae had no use for niceties, such as "farewell".

He hung the satchel across his shoulder and ran for the Portal, which flashed continuously as Adarmis's troops streamed through. The new Bringer's army was growing, and anticipation was in the air. Saren wanted to be part of it all, to raze a world and smell it burning. He craved the rewards of a conqueror, fine clothes and women who could not deny him. He was sick of carrying messages. It won't always be this way, he swore to himself. The letter he carried this time was the first step toward setting things right.

He darted past the column of soldiers with practiced ease and stepped through the Kingdom Portal, but he paused on the God's Plain. Hundreds of Portals, arching high into lead skies, and a million soldiers encamped beside them was always a sight to make him stumble.

The wars never ended, and the staging area was never empty.

He noticed the banners of countless lesser lords and a small contingent of Fae in golden armor, but the red of Dinah's army was missing. She had been Bringer, the greatest of them, and now she was nothing.

Lords warred and fought for power, fell in and out of favor. While their feuds could last for centuries, the enmity of the Last God could go on forever. Saren did not want to be exiled with the rest of Dinah's army, stuck in that stinking cavern for the rest of his life.

He reveled in the anger that coursed through his veins these days, but that sweetness dulled on the Plain. Saren could see the edge of the black pit, a broad crater in the red dirt with an angry blue sun fixed in the sky above, chained to the god's will just as they were all chained. In the Lord's Presence, he felt nothing but a desire to serve. And fear. The nearness of the Last God made his insides cold. The Lord was always watching and judging, ready to induct those who failed him into the ranks of the God-fed. Saren decided to stop staring and deliver the message he carried.

The Plain was vast, and the Portal he sought lay on the other side of it. He stopped at the nearest stable and commandeered a horse. He was not wearing a tabard, so he showed his medallion. The stable master sneered when he saw Dinah's symbol and gave him a mount from the God-fed's ranks. The ragged hide and exposed skeleton were meant to unnerve him, but the creature responded well enough to his instructions.

When he reached his destination, he dismounted and left the horse with a decaying soldier. The God-fed were everywhere and outnumbered the living a hundred to one.

A lush valley and soldiers in red tabards were framed by a rose marble arch—Dinah's realm. Here, on the threshold, the anger inside flared to life again. It felt good.

He waited an hour for Caleb's company to arrive. The captain was late. Saren eventually spotted red in the distance and watched Caleb and his troops navigate through the unyielding army on the Plain. It was difficult to coordinate troop withdrawals when wearing the colors of their disgraced Lady. The soldiers of other lords got in their way at every turn and cast spit and ridicule after them. Saren was glad he had chosen to carry messages wearing no tabard.

When Caleb finally reached his side, Saren saluted and said, "Captain," remembering to act formal around the others. They didn't know Caleb like he did. He was more a brother than a brother-in-law. Play wrestling and drunken discussions into the wee hours of the morning was more usual for them. It was during one of those late-night discussions he had convinced Caleb to accompany him to see Varvec.

Once the Fae had filled Caleb in on the cold realities of their status and what the new Bringer was willing to offer, it wasn't difficult to convince him to switch to Adarmis's side. Caleb would be useful. He and Commander Gordon had served together all their lives, and Gordon trusted him. Saren handed over the satchel with the sealed letter inside, and together they passed through the arch.

RALEN WAS STUNNED BY his first sight of Dinah's Portal. It was a rip in the world, like the one that had torn its way into his world, bringing God's judgment, but this tear was contained inside a beautiful marble arch, as though the unwholesome thing was worthy of worship. He did not hear anything that Gordon said to the soldier who helped him down from the horse. He just stared at the arch, at blue sky outside and gray sky inside. The base of the Portal was ringed in giant bones like the ones that formed the structure of Dinah's longhouse, a display warning those on the other side to stay away. But what he saw on the other side would not be frightened.

A truly hellish world was visible through the opening: an endless red plain beneath an alien sky, blanketed by God-fed. Millions of them. They were worse than the descriptions in Dinah's books. Dead and rotting, their cloying scent drifted on the hot wind that blew through the opening. There was nothing to keep them from stepping across and reaching out with skeletal fingers....

Stop, he told himself. Fear is useless. He was Marked, destined to die. He had no future, so why fear the present? He willed his shaking hands to steady and stood silent at Gordon's side.

The Portal flashed blinding white every time someone walked through. He'd learned that Dinah's disgrace meant she had to withdraw troops from wars on a dozen worlds, and armies of Conquered were returning. Officious looking underlings gave directions for their billeting in the new camp city that spread throughout the eastern valley.

The First Commander stared at the Portal, waiting for something. When a ginger-haired officer came through, the tension in Gordon's shoulders eased. "Caleb. Glad to see you made it in one piece."

"A retreat is easier than an assault. The locals were happy to see us go. Of course, they don't realize Adarmis will take our place." Caleb took a rag from his pouch and wiped at the spittle oozing down his cheek. "The rest of the god's army has a different opinion of us, I fear."

Ralen had only noticed the God-fed, but now that he looked again, he saw that Conquered armies also dotted the plain, each wearing the colors of different lords. He had studied the colors and symbols in Dinah's books and recognized Lord Kahl, Lord Bay, Lord Marq ... and plenty of the green of Lord Adarmis.

"It is only temporary," Gordon said. "Our Lady will rise again."

"Of course," Caleb said. "Still, I brought something for you." He handed the commander a leather satchel.

Gordon hesitated before taking it. "Yes. Get some rest now, old friend."

"Gladly." Caleb saluted and headed for the valley encampment with the others.

A scrawny teenager in leather armor hovered nearby. Gordon noticed him. "Ah." He turned to Ralen. "This is the message runner."

A twinge of interest made Ralen ask, "Caleb isn't your runner? Why did he have something for you?"

"No, Saren is." Gordon ignored the second question and spoke to the young soldier instead. "This slave boy will carry messages to and from the city. I still need you to run them to their destinations—the slave is Marked and can't cross the Portal—but it should spare your legs a bit."

"Yes, sir." Saren scrunched up his face. "May I ask why?"

"The Keeper's interference. Naught we can do about it. Show Ralen what to do then see to it that he's given your old bunk near the

Command Center. You will be posted here in the valley from now on."

"Yes, sir." Saren's face didn't lose its sour expression.

Ralen jolted out of his fugue. "A bunk? I can't stay in the city."

"I need you close by," Gordon said. "That's how this works."

Ralen might never know the comforts the Conquered enjoyed, or survive Dinah's hunger, or have any reason to hope for the future, but there was still one thing he cared about. He'd promised not to leave Anjee alone. He had to convince the commander to change his mind.

"I'm supposed to be near Dinah. Her orders are more important than the Keeper's." She had never given such an order, but it was true she would be angry if Ralen failed to appear quickly when she summoned him. Whenever she returned.

Gordon placed Caleb's satchel inside a saddle bag and mounted his horse. "Come every few days then. Anything more urgent will attend to itself." To Saren, the commander said, "Keep your bunk."

Ralen guessed Saren would also keep his job as messenger. They were making only a token effort to obey the Keeper's orders. He was grateful but worried what the Keeper would say.

Gordon gave the satchel of messages he carried to Saren, so the older boy could run it through the Portal. Ralen never had a chance to look inside. Would the Keeper punish him now?

The commander pulled Ralen onto the horse, and they returned to the city. When they stood on the docks at the edge of the lake, Gordon fished a parcel out of the satchel Caleb had given him. "This is for the Keeper. I suspect it's the real reason he sent you. See that he gets it."

The object was the size of Ralen's hand and heavy, tied in cloth. "Yes, sir," he said, mimicking the soldiers he'd seen stand at attention every time they were given an order.

One of Gordon's soldiers oared Ralen back across the lake. Gordon could never understand how grateful he was not to have to 'swim'. As soon as he was on familiar ground, he sagged with relief.

It wasn't over though. Nothing would ever be over.

He hurried to the small cave he shared with Anjee, but it was empty. He hid the parcel in the stone cairn they had built to trick the gobel and ran for the surface. He got a kick from the Drakein guard for being late. Anjee's reaction was worse.

She was alone in the apple orchard on the north ridge, gathering fallen fruit in the folds of her dress. He was breathless when he reached her side. "Anjee."

She turned her face away and kept working.

He circled her, but she kept turning away. Finally, he got a glimpse of red cheeks and nose. She'd been crying again.

"I'm sorry," he said.

"You're always going away."

"I had to. It wasn't my fault." Her disappointment made him feel like someone was squeezing his heart in their fist.

"You go every night."

"Dinah makes me."

"You're a liar. She's been gone for days. There's something else. You say you don't remember."

"Sometimes I don't."

"Go away," she said. He tried to take her hand, but she wouldn't let him. "Go away forever if you want!"

He did not want to cry, but the pain in his chest felt like it was clawing its way out and had no place else to go. When the salty tears were pouring out and filling the corners of his mouth, he picked an apple off the ground and threw it so hard it broke against the tree. Anjee jumped as apple chunks flew all around her. He hadn't meant to do that.

The Keeper had said that when Dinah was away, she couldn't hear anyone's thoughts. And he needed Anjee to know.

"I'm not a liar," he said. "Sometimes the angels do make me forget."

He told her everything, how Dinah taught him about wars and strange lands long dead, the job the Keeper had given him, the city on the other side of the lake, the Portal, and how Ashkal and Amseel were showing him how to fight. "You must keep it secret, even in your mind," he added. "I think they would kill us if Dinah found out. They have knives that eat your soul."

"Everything here wants to eat us." She looked him in the eyes, and he was glad he'd told her. It felt right.

"I don't think that's what the angels want," he said. "They're teaching me, like Dinah's teaching me. The Keeper called me 'special.'"

Anjee dug a calloused heel into the dirt and was quiet for a moment while she thought. "Tell Dinah about the angels, and she'll make them go away. You are special. She won't kill you."

"No." He couldn't do that. The thought of never holding a weapon again made his chest tighten almost as badly as when Anjee had been angry with him. Even when Amseel put a dagger to his neck, he felt safe. He felt like it was okay to fight back. It was a kind of freedom, and he couldn't give it up.

"They'll get you in trouble," she said. "They're not your friends. They're monsters."

"They haven't hurt me." The bruises he got from fighting didn't count. "I don't see monsters anymore. All I see is Ashkal and Dinah and Gordon and the Keeper and you and me. Some I hate and some could be friends."

"You can't be friends with something that's not human," she said.

"What about the Conquered?" he asked. "They fight for Dinah. They attacked our world alongside the others. Are they human or are they monsters?"

She frowned and her forehead wrinkled. "You're smart. You get smarter than me every day. I know that. But, sometimes things are simple."

She left it at that and got back to work. Ralen helped her gather as many worm-riddled apples as they could carry in the baskets she'd brought. They didn't speak, but Anjee sang as she worked, and he listened.

GORDON, FIRST COMMANDER of the Stratia, locked the door and opened the satchel Caleb had given him. It was lighter without the package the Keeper had requested. They had never said "bribe", but now that the Keeper had sent the little slave boy to spy on him, he suspected the Keeper would not easily be pacified.

The only thing left inside the satchel was a letter. Gordon took a moment to study the seal; authentic as far as he could tell. Was this really happening? Would he let it?

A wave of hot fear spread across his skin. He crumpled the parchment and tossed it into the fire. He watched until the seal burnt to nothing. He would be a fool to seriously consider betrayal. He had too much to lose.

He should turn Caleb over to Lady Dinah, but he had let things go too far already. It was his fault. He should not have listened when Caleb first whispered suggestions in his ear, should not have been curious. He encouraged the man, and he would not make Caleb suffer for his mistake.

Saren found him later. "Did you want me to carry your reply?"

"No." It was not too late to choose the right course. He would ignore the letter from Adarmis. It was burnt and gone.

"You need longer to consider?" The message runner persisted.

"No."

Saren's face turned red. "Why?"

"I'm Commander here. I don't need to discuss my decisions with you. Go."

Saren stiffened. "Yes, sir." He eyed the empty satchel before leaving.

Gordon would talk to Caleb, tell him to give up this scheme and order him to rein in Saren. The messenger often forgot his rightful place. They all had a role in things—soldiers, commanders, slaves, lords, and gods. It was dangerous to forget it.

THE LOCUM APPROVED of the sketches for the new temple, but all he said was, "Make the columns taller. People must feel insignificant as they pray for our Lord's forgiveness."

The lesser priest nodded, pulled out a new sheet of hand-woven paper, and set a sharpened piece of charcoal to the surface. He began again.

Locum Paeris continued his sedate walk. His rounds of the temple and cavern city took all day, but he was ever dutiful about performing them. He checked on each priest, whether shut away in study or guarding mages in the Command Center, and let his presence be felt among the Conquered.

Once, he had carried the Lord's Presence with him. He had listened to the soldiers' prayers, attended their sick beds, and closed the eyes of corpses returned from battle before they opened again in the God's service. He had been an extension of God. He had felt the power in his marrow, the ebb and flow of energy between the mundane and the divine. Now that flow was cut off.

"The Lady," he cursed. Eyes found him then quickly looked away again. They feared her, but she could not hear him. She was not a god. If she were, their Lord would not abide her existence. She was a servant like Paeris, nothing more. Too many had forgotten that, including the Lady herself. She would soon repent.

The giant copper doors of the temple opened a crack, and a scrawny adolescent slipped through the gap. The message runner was bold, but it was probably wiser to move with open piety than sneak through a side door.

The boy bowed before the altar. A priest moved forward, but Paeris intercepted him and, with a soft touch on the other man's arm, indicated he would hear the boy's prayer instead.

"Who do you serve?" Paeris said the formal words, looking down at the youth's sunburned scalp.

"God and Bringer," Saren whispered.

God and Bringer. That is where Paeris's loyalty lay as well—with Adarmis now, the newly chosen leader of their Lord's divine army.

"What news?" the Locum asked gently. It did not matter if their voices carried in the temple—there were none but the devoted here at this time of day to hear—but he preferred silence, emptiness, so as to leave room for the Presence of their Lord when it once more returned.

"The general wants us to keep going. Varvec gave me a letter for Gordon."

"Did he accept the Bringer's offer?"

Saren clenched his jaw and did not raise his eyes. "No."

"Ahh," Paeris said. "Unfortunate. I know how you admire him."

"I admire strength," Saren hissed.

"As is right. I understand your disappointment, but Gordon is showing strength. And loyalty. It is simply misplaced. His devotion to the Lady will destroy him. We must see to it."

"Yes, Locum." The boy rose and pulled out a sealed scroll. "This was among Varvec's messages. It's from your new master."

Paeris recognized the High Locum's seal. He held the scroll in two fingers like a thing diseased and said, "Ettiad is no one's master. Adarmis is ill-served by my old pupil, but he need not be for much longer."

After Saren left, Paeris waited some time, continuing the last of his rounds in the temple, until returning to his rooms to read the message.

Ettiad's ornate handwriting was unmistakable. _I order you to leave Lady Dinali's domain and serve me beyond the Black Portal._

There was more, but Paeris snorted and tossed the vellum aside. How dare Ettiad command him like a mere priest?

Ettiad clearly needed him there to cover up his incompetence. The Old Kingdom was an unforgiving frontier that stripped all naked in the eyes of their Lord. Paeris knew that must be the true reason The Last God had not already smashed the Kingdom into oblivion. It was a test. Those who said there was a power that kept the God at bay were revealed as blasphemers, and those who failed to fight hard enough in the name of their Holy Lord and failed were revealed as the worthless slabs of flesh they were.

We have all failed, he thought. _And we are all unworthy in Our Lord's eyes. But when we finally succeed ... When I succeed, then he will grant me everlasting glory and power._

Let Ettiad sink beneath the weight of his own foolishness. There was important work to be done here. Only when it was complete would he return to the Old Kingdom, as High Locum, to serve the new Bringer and to wear the mantle of their Lord's everlasting Presence once more.

Paeris would prove his devotion by exposing the witch's hubris and weaken her army by turning her soldiers against each other.

That evening, Paeris gave new instructions to his priests. He visited the homes of devout Conquered officers and avoided the barracks of Drakein, spreading the word of God and making it clear to all what He wished. "Dinah is disgraced," he told them. "Hated by the Lord. We must all turn away from her or risk our very souls. Leave her and her egg-hatched spawn to wither and die outside the Last God's Presence. We must turn once more to His light."

Division would generate chaos in Dinah's ranks, exposing the weak and revealing those worthy of redemption. And he would be the one to draw the line of separation.

Chapter Nine ~ Breaking Down

It was the middle of the night before Ralen remembered the parcel he'd hidden beneath a pile of stones. He dreaded seeing the Keeper again, but it would be worse to make him wait. This time he told Anjee where he was going. They spoke in hushed tones so as not to disturb the others.

"Be careful," she said.

"Don't you want to come?" he asked. He had been prepared to argue.

"I don't want to get you in trouble. I would never do that, unlike some." Now he understood. She was making a point: the angels were not his friends, not if they endangered him, while she would endure being left behind for his sake.

He adjusted the pile of dried wheat stalks and rags that made up their bed, so she was warm and comfortable. "Goodnight, Anjee."

"I won't sleep," she said. "Not until you come back."

When he moved the stones around the package, they clattered loud enough to wake one of the workers. It was the crazy man who shouted at the clouds whenever it rained. Most of the slaves were crazy, but they were usually quieter about it. The man grabbed Ralen's hand and hissed, "Don't steal from me."

Ralen pulled free of the painful grip, maneuvering on instinct. The angels' lessons were sinking in. He took the package and hurried away.

When he was on the torch-lit path that led to the lake, he decided to look inside the parcel. The Keeper had told him to spy on the Conquered's messages, but it was only fair to spy on Grin as well.

He removed the string and unfolded the cloth to reveal a bronze amulet, etched with words in a language he had not yet encountered in Dinah's library. Its purpose was a mystery, so he re-wrapped the amulet and waited on the edge of the lake for a gobel. He did not have to wait long: they were always lurking and watching.

As soon as one of the creatures crawled out of the water, Ralen held out the package and said, "Take this to Grin."

"Take it yourself." The gobel tugged him toward the lake. He fought free, as he had with the crazy man, but the gobel whispered for its siblings and several appeared out of the gloom. He was overwhelmed by a flurry of slimy limbs and sharp talons, each wound no more than a graze but enough to leave him covered in bloody lines. Then they dragged him under the water.

Not again. The slimy creature they remembered to put on his face this time kept him alive, but he hated the taste of stale water that crept into the corners of his mouth, and he ached for more air, for the wind that blew down from the mountains when he worked the fields.

The gobels tossed him onto the shore of the Keeper's island, and he took a deep breath. The foul sweetness of the Keeper's half-rotted body made him gag. He stood, legs trembling, and held out the now soaked parcel. "This is for you." The fat man could not see, of course.

"What is it?" Grin wiggled his fingers with anticipation. "Bring it over."

Ralen steeled himself and stepped into the Keeper's pool. Cold hands felt across his body, missing the package entirely. Grin seemed to enjoy his discomfort, cooing with pleasure, so he chose not to react or reveal how much the monster's touch bothered him.

"Here." Ralen pressed the package into a grotesque palm. "Gordon said you were waiting for it."

"Yes, yes, yes," Grin said, as he felt the parcel's contours. "You have no idea. I never dreamed he would satisfy my demand. What are they up to over there? Did you run across any interesting correspondence?"

"No." Ralen chose not to mention his inability to access a single letter.

"Too bad. You will have more opportunity to find something tomorrow."

"Gordon said I'm only needed every few days."

"That will not do. You must search everything, watch them constantly."

"What if Dinah returns? She wants me with her. I can't live in the city."

"I see." Grin's scarred lips formed a straight line, his best approximation of a frown. "We will do what we can then. The gobels will carry you every morning."

"I could have a boat."

"What makes you believe you deserve such comforts?" Grin grabbed his hand and pressed a greasy thumb into the raised Mark. "You are food."

Ralen winced at the pain. The Mark was supposed to be his shame, but Grin was Marked even more badly. "How am I any less than you?" he said, defiant.

"You are not Keeper. You do not command. That is how you are less." To illustrate his point, Grin waved a hand and gobels swarmed. They pressed Ralen's face into the water of the pool.

He fought them as hard as he'd fought the people who'd dragged him away from the ruins of his mother's house, but there were too many gobels. Too many monsters ... just as Anjee kept reminding him. He would not swallow water again. He held his breath until bright circles appeared behind his eyelids.

He must have blacked out, because he was staring up at glow-worm covered stalactites as green fingers slapped him awake. "Come back, come back," a gobel whispered in a sing song chant.

"You understand now?" Grin said.

"Yes." Ralen coughed, chest sore from the weight that had pressed him down.

Now that the Keeper had established his dominance, he relaxed into his usual jovial manner. "Since you are here, you can help me." Grin felt the raised writings on the amulet and read them aloud, the spoken language no more comprehensible to Ralen than the written one had been.

The amulet flattened into a thin disc before expanding by an arm's length. It then grew tall, transforming into a bronze cage. Inside was a ball of white light.

"A rare creature." Grin reached for the light, trying to touch what he could not see. "Wisps are concentrated magic. Concentrated life."

"Don't you have magic?" Ralen asked, thinking of the glow worms he could turn on and off like a light bulb and Grin's silent command of the gobels.

"Not enough. Now, no more questions." The Keeper had many different types of fingers, some thick and scaled, some taloned and feathered, and he poked a serrated appendage between the bars of the cage. The wisp recoiled and screeched. The sound hurt Ralen's ears and made him cringe in sympathy.

"Pain is the best way to extract power." Grin sounded happy that this was the case. "But first, I need something, boy. Go into the sleep den and fetch one of your kind."

"What for?"

"What did I say about questions? Pick one and bring him to me."

Ralen listened to the wisp's screams as gobels dragged him underwater again. The jelly thing on his face was agonizing, but he needed to get used to it. The Keeper planned to make him travel to the Conquered city every morning. The wisp wasn't the only one the fat man enjoyed tormenting.

When he reached the cave, Anjee was awake, visible in the red glow of her Mark.

"What's wrong?" There was a tremor in her voice as she eyed the gobels that accompanied him. Six of them whispered in the dark at his back and made the hairs on his neck stand on end. They were there to make sure he obeyed their master.

"I don't know," he said. A gobel reached for Anjee. "No!" He would never bring Anjee to the Keeper for any reason. "Not her."

That one.

"That one." He pointed to the crazy man sleeping next to the stone pile.

The gobels grabbed the sleeping man. He woke, confused, and began to scream, "Don't steal! Don't steal!"

Anjee tucked her knees against her chest. Ralen wanted to stay with her, but the gobels dragged him and the chosen captive back down to the lake. The man was pushed under without a jelly creature for his face, his screams soon choked by water, and Ralen was towed side by side with a dead man.

They hauled the man's corpse onto the island. Ralen hung back, shivering, wanting nothing more than to crawl into the cave with Anjee and sleep until the world disappeared.

"The gobels say he is a fine choice." The Keeper bobbed excitedly, making water slosh over the stones. "Now ... bring me the eyes."

Ralen was paralyzed.

"Bring me the eyes," the Keeper repeated. "Or I'll use yours."

A gobel pulled Ralen to the corpse's side. The man's eyes were open, staring at the glow worms on the ceiling but seeing nothing. He was dead because Ralen had chosen.

He couldn't move, couldn't breathe. He sat rigid.

"Like this," the gobel whispered, placing strong fingers on the edge of one eye socket. With a crunch and a pop, the eyeball was hanging loose. "You have my claw," it said, displaying a scarred fingertip. "You cut the cord. Pull then cut. Pull then cut-cut...."

Ralen fumbled for the gobel's claw in his front pocket. He should have used it to open the Conquered's messages, found some way to be alone with the satchel, found something to please Grin. He should have stayed in the city. Maybe then he wouldn't be here now, doing this. But, he had promised Anjee. He would do whatever he must to return to her each day.

He remembered what it felt like to have a rusted knife in his hand, the quick movements Amseel had taught him. He cut the eye loose, then the other one. He carried them in the fold of his shirt like apples harvested from the orchard.

"Good," the Keeper said, feeling each eyeball. "Perfect." He pulled the shriveled raisins from his own sockets and popped the new eyes in. They pointed in strange directions, one looking at the ground the other at the back of Grin's skull. "Hold the cage."

Ralen did as he was commanded and tried to shut his ears against the wisp's screeches. When Grin was done, the wisp's light had faded, and the dead man's eyes focused on him. "Let's see what other parts I can use," the Keeper said.

Hours later, when they were done, gobels returned Ralen to the cave. He didn't speak. No matter how much Anjee begged, or worried over the blood on his clothes, he didn't tell her what had happened. He would never tell her. It was one more thing he would try to forget.

LOCUM PAERIS MOVED through the darkened tent city and cast a glance at the Portal. "She's not here," he chided himself for his paranoia. The Lady would not return from wherever she had vanished these many months simply to interfere with him at this moment. The Last God was with him, Presence or no. He could not fail.

He had made use of the Lady's absence to spread his influence among the returned troops. They were easily swayed with talk of glory and serving a Bringer again, but he was careful not to speak too openly against Dinah. He preferred to avoid the Keeper's notice.

The Keeper was in the tent city this day as well, relaxing on piles of cushions atop his litter, oiled by gobels, as he oversaw the Drakein and Conquered who labored on the new temple. Newly cut white stone glowed in the moonlight. The material had been carried in from Amarsine, beyond the Plain, and would make a proper domicile for their Lord's Presence.

Paeris felt the Keeper's gaze boring into his skull as he consulted with the architect, and when Paeris left the construction site to continue his rounds among the soldiers' tents, The Keeper sent gobels after him. The abomination was Dinah's tool, encrusted with her foul Mark, and it would not do for suspicions to turn to certainties.

In order to protect his secrets, Paeris often towed a mage around by a chain like a pet. He now twisted the man's power into spells of concealment, and gobels whispered in frustration when they lost track of him. While the Keeper's lackeys searched for him in the overcrowded valley, Paeris slipped into Sub-commander Caleb's tent.

"Locum." The man got on hands and knees and put his nose to the ground.

"Why are you still here?" Paeris said. He did not ask Caleb to rise just yet. "I looked for you in the cavern city, but your family says they have not seen you in weeks."

"It is easier to commiserate with soldiers when I languish here with them. They hear me and what I have to offer."

"Such dedication." Paeris felt a questing tendril of magic from the Keeper and yanked on the slave-mage's chain, startling him out of a doze and silently commanding him to strengthen the protective wards. "I am glad to finally find you. The new temple is nearly complete, but it is missing a sanctifying coat of blood."

"The Keeper will pick slaves to sacrifice."

"I do not mean that. I'm envisaging something more. Conquered."

Caleb raised his head. "What?"

Paeris felt a twinge of annoyance. Why wasn't the sub-commander looking at the ground? "Not a sacrifice. I do not wish the soldiers to blame the priesthood for the loss of loved ones—no matter how much I would welcome such an offering by the devout—rather I am thinking of the greater goal. There are officers unaffected by my words or yours and who blasphemes by showing greater respect to the Lady and the First Commander than to their Locum. Yes?"

"There are," Caleb said carefully.

"Then I wish you to change the Keeper's work assignments. Send these heretics to guard slaves extending the fields at the outer markers. Make sure there are no Drakein among them."

"That would invite attacks."

"Yes. Let the wilderness take them. The army will blame the Keeper and lazy Drakein."

"I don't know if I can condemn them to death for not listening to us." Caleb's head was still raised without permission.

Paeris scowled. "Blasphemy. All are condemned by our Lord. All must die in his service and then serve even in death. You question this truth?"

Caleb lowered his head and sank his knees once more into the dirt. "Forgive me, Locum. I forget myself."

"At least they are warriors and will have a fighting chance. Is that not how God judges? The strong survive and the unworthy perish."

"Yes, Locum. I ... I will see to it."

"Good." Paeris wrapped the chain around his fist several times and tugged the mage along as he exited the tent. Only when he was outside did he call back to Caleb, saying, "You can rise now."

THREE DAYS LATER, SAREN delivered orders to the men chosen for guard duty.

There were groans and complaints about lieutenants being treated like common soldiers, but they believed the orders came from the Keeper, who cared nothing for hierarchies other than making sure everyone knew he was at the top, his every word the same as Dinah's in her absence.

Saren shadowed them to observe the outcome of the Locum's task. The officers arrived at the boundary and found milling slaves, newly enchanted obelisks lying on the ground, and no Drakein in sight. They shifted uncomfortably, but none went in search of a Drakein protector. That would be admitting fear of simple animals.

The slaves went first into the forest, hacking away at thick brush to clear room for digging. They went one hundred paces then erected two small stones. When another hundred paces were cleared, the boundary stones were repositioned. It would be simple to become bored with such repetitive work, and the slaves were lethargic and uninterested, but their guards remained alert, weapons drawn. Even so, they were not quick enough when it happened.

Talons reached out of the wild growth and took a slave. The two closest guards were also snatched. They wounded the creature, whatever it was, its shriek echoing through the valley, but the screams of the men taken were almost as loud. Then all was quiet.

When the surviving soldiers' adrenaline ebbed, they shouted orders and the workers scrambled to finish erecting the stones.

Saren smiled and left to report to Caleb. He was certain everyone within earshot guessed what had happened, but along the way, he embellished the tale. In his version, the Drakein refused guard duty, giving their wild cousins a chance to feast on Conquered.

Chapter Ten ~ Return

For once, Dinah did not wear red. She was cloaked in grey, Drakein at her side, their reflective scales smeared with mud and ash to hide them in the semi-darkness. It was imperative no one learn who was behind the raid.

Their quarry slept in a tent in the middle of an army. Jeera was a nothing lord, with worthless soldiers she had once disdained, but she was the pariah now. She could no longer stride in and demand what she wanted, and she could not take it by force, else the Last God would know she was not in exile.

Instead, she slunk about in the night like an animal foraging for food. She would take a few slaves to serve that purpose, but it was the mage she wanted.

She released her aura, draining everything before her. The encampment was trampled and muddy, so no one would notice a few dead weeds. The soldiers who kept watch drooped. She was careful not to kill them. Let Jeera's officers later find them sleeping at their posts.

"Now," she ordered.

Her Drakein took one last sniff of the old garment she'd acquired and then rushed in and used their sensitive noses to find the mage she sought. They returned with the old man and a dozen other captives previously taken by the lordling's forces. It would be better if no one guessed who the target had been and assumed the prisoners had escaped on their own.

Her aura made the captives as listless as the guards, and they were placed like sleeping children in the caged wagon at the end of the column. The cage was covered with drapes to hide its nature. All the wagons in her retinue were decked in the green of Adarmis's followers.

Drakein kept five captives aside for her wagon. When everyone was stowed, the caravan set off.

The chosen few rested, heads against one another in a weary clump on the bench opposite her. Dinah's private transport was large, with room enough to sleep, not that she ever did. Gauze curtains granted privacy while allowing her to see the countryside rolling by.

A bowl of fruit and a decanter of wine rattled on the sideboard. When the first prisoner awoke, Dinah offered him a drink and something to eat. He did not recognize her, but he gauged her fine clothes and his surroundings and said, "My thanks, lady."

As the others stirred, he overcame his hesitation and ate as many grapes as he could swallow, handfuls at a time. Dinah offered the other four her hospitality as well, and they accepted, eyes wide with fright, but hunger made them bold enough to snatch their share from the bowl. When it was empty, she stopped the caravan and had a soldier bring more food from the supply wagon.

As she took the fruit, she nodded to the Drakein, and he went forward to unhitch the horses. The view outside the window was static, a brown river sluggishly wending through brown fields. She studied the dull scene while listening to the crunch of apples and smacking of lips.

Satiated, the captives leaned back on embroidered cushions, but now that their fear of starvation had fled, their fear of Dinah rose. They looked at their feet and were afraid to talk. Dinah heard their thoughts, so she did not care what came from their mouths.

The first one to find his courage asked, "What do you want of us, my lady?"

She ignored the question. "Do you feel better?"

"Yes, lady. I have not known such comforts in a long while."

"You are reminded of joy?"

"Yes."

"Good." Her hunger could not be as easily satisfied as theirs. She could survive by draining small portions of life from the surrounding land and her captives, but months of reconnaissance and raiding had depleted her reserves. A feast was required. These were still wretches, but their spirits had been bolstered enough to provide some nourishment.

Precious mages, the objective of this excursion, were secured in the last wagon, far from her aura, and the Drakein had moved everyone else to safety, so she released her hold on her power. It felt good to extend the boundaries of her soul, to be free, a beast un-caged.

She sensed the living flesh across from her, felt blood slipping through arteries and the cavities of a heart, a heart that jerked in agony as her aura touched it. Screams bounced off the wooden walls, and one girl almost reached the door before crumpling to the floor. Hearts clenched one last time and then blackened. Their life became Dinah's.

When the wave of satisfaction passed, she noted the clean bones and dried folds of skin mingled with cast off clothing piled all around. She felt a shiver of disquiet upon seeing the girl's long hair, rooted in shriveled scalp, draped across her slippers, and she lifted her feet onto the bench.

Empty husks disturbed her. It was better when the bones were used, made lovely with carvings, and the skin turned to parchment or covers for her books. They were merely items then.

While her soldiers re-hitched the horses, she sent a few Drakein to dig a hole for the remains. This was a poorly populated world. Jeera's army would not remain long before returning to the God's Plain, so there was little likelihood of her kills being discovered. Nevertheless, she preferred to hide all evidence of her presence.

When the wagon was moving again, she leaned back, glad to be alone once more. She sniffed, certain she smelled flesh. Everything had been taken away, even the bowl of fruit she could not eat, but still she felt intruded upon.

She stood, hunching beneath the low roof, and paced the few feet available to her. It did not help. She ordered another halt and waved the guards back who tried to follow her. She walked through the fields, the dead grass immune to her passing, and looked up at leaden skies. She longed for her home atop the mountain, thriving valleys and warm air. She came to a decision.

Her journey had occupied more than a year. The wagons were nearly full. There were one or two more places they had learned would be easy to raid for the mages and tools she required, but it could wait. She was weary. It was time to go home.

Another color change was in order, to the yellow of the neutral Fae. The soldiers tore down Adarmis's banners—it had amused her to hide among her enemy—and hoisted the white sun on yellow instead. When the Drakein were done, they locked themselves in the middle wagon, leaving the Marked horses to steer by Dinah's silent commands. She could not pass for Fae, so she wore a hood to hide her features and drew thick curtains across the windows.

A flutter filled the empty places inside her as they crossed the Portal.

She had visited the God's Plain many times in her long life and did not need to see it now—it was etched in her memory. The land was flat and filled with death, God-fed, crowded with Conquered armies and countless Portals in every shape and construction material from stone to wood and even precious gems, each leading to one of the worlds He had conquered. I had conquered, she amended. She had been Bringer for every victory, and this was how He repaid her. Spurning her, turning on her. She did not need Him. He needed her.

The light of this world's small, blue sun could not penetrate into the dark crater where the god dwelled. The crater that was evidence He could pull all the stars down from the heavens if He chose—and still not defeat Fate.

In this place, Dinah fought against His power, against an intense love for Him that He wanted all to feel. He was a God, and His power greater than hers, no matter how much she wished otherwise.

He had given her so much, and she suddenly wanted to make amends. She would do what no one else had managed and prove that, despite her failure, she was still greater than Adarmis. Her Lord would be pleased by her temerity and bestow His grace on her once more.

Warm thoughts of her god sustained her for a time, but they cooled as she neared the Portal to her own world, and she remembered the curse He had laid upon her. Soon enough, she felt the stirrings of resentment once more.

She thanked Ralen for this gift—this freedom of thought, this ability to hate the Last God and revel in her own power again. She did not know what Ralen was, what gave him this ability, but he was precious and her key to a new existence. She only needed to figure out how best to use the boy.

ANOTHER SUMMER HAD come and gone, and Ralen had grown a few inches, although he was still a head shorter than Saren. Ralen handed the lanky messenger a stack of letters he had read in the tunnel on the way over, each unsealed with a sharp knife made from the gobel's claw and resealed using the candle he kept in his frayed pocket alongside it. The candle was magic, another gift from the Keeper, and it lit itself whenever he spoke a certain word, but the candle was unreliable. It had sputtered out this morning, making it difficult to repair all the wax seals. He did not like magic, no matter how much he saw of it. It didn't seem real. It wasn't right.

"What took you so long?" Saren asked, "Those stubby legs not working? Must be the slave rations keeping you stunted."

Ralen could not mention the faulty candle, so he shrugged and said, "Must be." He travelled the tunnel between the cavern city and the Portal in the eastern valley on foot. He was not allowed one of the Conquered's horses, not that he could ride. At least running had built stamina for his lessons with the angels.

They visited more frequently. Amseel still said, "faster", but he had let Ralen hold a Blessed Blade. The thing did not hum for him, did not whisper of eating souls, and he did not understand how it was better than any other weapon, but allowing him to use it had been a gesture of encouragement, of respect.

The angels were no longer able to cloud his mind. Ralen remembered everything he learned, and his thoughts continued the fighting practice with images of gobels and the Keeper, a daydream that kept him sane each time he reported and told Grin he had found nothing out of the ordinary in the Conquered's correspondence.

Everything was changing. He felt the changes inside, the hardness from watching the Keeper at work. Grin had acquired two more wisps, and the monster's burnt body was now entirely healed. There were also two fewer workers for this season's harvest. All that mattered was Ralen had made certain Anjee was safe.

Sometimes, he missed his lessons in Dinah's library. He missed learning languages, understanding things beyond food and survival. His mind had been sharpened from studying the Conquered, from being an unnoticed spy. He observed everyone and everything, as the Keeper commanded. He was twelve, but he felt old. Saren's jibes were the only childish thing in his life.

"I can't help it if I'm not as fast as you," Ralen told Saren. He did not let on how quickly he could make the trip if he chose.

"Then quit trying to act above your station and leave the job to me. I hate standing around." Saren positioned the strap of the message pouch across his shoulders and loped through the Portal to the God's Plain.

Ralen waited a moment to see which direction the runner went. With Dinah's army recalled, messages were only passed between Conquered families who dwelled with lords irrevocably bonded to Dinah and who shared in her disgrace. He had learned the direction of those lords' Portals, but Saren often went a different way.

Where did the runner go? Should he tell the Keeper? Would it get Saren killed? Were Saren's parts any more precious than a slave's? Ralen disliked the skinny older boy and his superior attitude, but he didn't want him dead. He didn't want anyone dead. Choosing the Keeper's victims had taken too much from him already. He picked men far gone in madness, but he worried sometimes. Was this how monsters were born? One choice at a time?

A line of Fae wagons came through the Portal bearing yellow banners. Foreign visitors were unusual. A hooded figure spoke to one of the Drakein guards, and the soldier lowered his head in submission, allowing them to pass.

Curious, Ralen followed the caravan into the tunnel, along city streets, and finally to the docks on the underground lake. Where were they going? When the wagons stopped, a squad of Drakein began unloading crates. Ralen inched closer and saw they were full of prisoners. More slaves to work the fields? More food?

Then Dinah stepped out of the lead wagon. She wasn't wearing red, but he knew it was her even before she lowered the hood and smiled directly at him with gleaming white fangs.

"Ralen," she said, sensing him in the gloom. "I'm home."

He left his hiding spot and bowed before her. "Bringer." He knew he wasn't supposed to call her that, but she didn't seem to mind.

"One day I shall be again. What are you doing in the city?"

"Work for the Keeper."

"Are all your toes intact?" she asked dangerously.

"Yes." Ralen was unsure about the rest of him. Better to lose a toe now and then to a gobel than endure seeing what Grin got up to on his island. Something was stuck inside him, a piece broken and lodged against his heart.

"So, my Keeper is watching over you?"

"He gave me a job running messages." And spying, he added silently, knowing she would hear, but he didn't want any eavesdroppers to know about his activities.

"Interesting. You're filthier than ever. Don't you bathe?"

"Every day." Gobels dragged him across the lake to the city each morning. He had taught himself to swim, but it didn't help. They insisted.

"New clothes are in order then. Come." She got into a boat and Ralen sat beside her as Drakein oared them across the turquoise water. The glow worms brightened along Dinah's path so that she was limned in blue light.

He eyed the crates on the other boats. "More workers?" he asked.

"Yes, special ones. Wait until we are home. I will show you everything. I have a wonderful idea that you won't understand, but I must tell someone."

For the first time in over a year, Ralen made the long climb up marble steps to Dinah's longhouse. The air was stale, closed up for too long. She opened the windows and beamed down at the valley below.

"I missed the harvest. How sad."

"There are still the figs," he said. "It's too cold for them here, and they grow slowly."

"I always helped them along." She waved a hand, and the fireplace came to life, wood and bone chips catching instantly.

Ralen thought there was something different about the place and realized what it was when Dinah opened a set of doors that hadn't been there last time he came for a lesson. The new room was as large as her library. Drakein must have finished it in her absence.

Unlike the rest of the house, the new wing had few windows, and they were barred. Sleeping pallets lined one wall next to a wash basin and hearth. There was a forge at the other end of the room and long tables laden with tools and metal ingots. Shelves were crammed with vials of colored powders.

Dinah held out her arms and turned to him. He recoiled—it was the gesture she used before she fed.

"Don't be silly." She lowered her arms. "I rejoice, for my laboratory is complete, and I now have mages to work in it."

While the Drakein carried in the new captives and fastened their chains to the wall, Dinah led Ralen to the library.

"Let me explain." She sank into a large chair and rested her feet on a pile of books.

He had never seen her behave so casually, and it disturbed him. "You don't have to, my Lady—"

"—I'll do what I please. I am cut off from the Last God and none but He can command me."

Ralen knew when to stay quiet.

"I had no pity for other lords who suffered His wrath. Most died, I think. I expected to die—well, cease to exist, since I do not live in the first place—but I survived.

"I believe I can construct something that will sustain an army as I have been sustained. I can make the God-fed better. The Last God will be grateful, and He will bestow his Presence on me again."

Ralen noticed the adoring look in her eyes slowly fade. After a moment, she added, "Not that I care for gratitude, only that my punishment end and my armies be free to extend my might to the worlds that are rightfully mine. I was Bringer and none stood before me."

"Why..." Ralen hesitated. The Keeper disliked his questions, but Dinah had once encouraged them. "Why is God mad at you?"

"He needs no reason, but I'm sure it was because of your world. It had no magic, no gods, no daemonae, yet its weapons destroyed half my army. The god intervened before I lost more."

"My world?" He had not thought of the place he came from in a long time.

She lowered her legs and leaned forward, looking into his face seriously. "That is something to remember, Ralen. As powerful as you are, there is always something stronger, and usually something unexpected."

Did she mean that his world had been stronger than her or that the god had been stronger than them both?

She didn't answer his unspoken question. Did she not want to, or was she not listening in?

After a moment, she said, "What tasks has the Keeper set you?"

"I'm to carry the First Commander's messages everyday and read them."

"Come across anything interesting?"

"No. But I've learned new words."

"You can learn more from the First Commander directly than you can by spying. When you're not with me, I want you to be at his elbow. Tell him he is to teach you logistics, strategy...."

"Am I going to war?" Cold tendrils of fear scurried across his scalp. He had seen war.

She looked him over, a sardonic smile on her face. "You've grown since last I saw you, but I think my enemies have nothing to fear as yet. Pay attention to the commander. An army is trained to win long before they reach the battlefield."

What about Anjee? He didn't want to stay in the Conquered city all day. He wanted to be with her out in the sun. "The harvest..." he began.

"You prefer grubbing in the dirt? I have other plans for you."

"Is this what the Keeper meant when he said I'm special?"

"You are."

"How?"

"One day you will know. If you survive. We are all born with potential, much of it never realized. My entire race is dead. Their blood and hearts and minds were the same as mine, but I am the only one standing here. I am the only one who seized destiny. One day, you will seize yours, or vanish like them.

"For now, contain your curiosity. I should tell the Keeper to contain his as well.

"I want to be alone," she added. "Go and make yourself presentable before I summon you again."

"Yes, Lady."

Dinah would not explain her plans for him. No one explained. He was a slave, food, and his life was not his own: That's what the Keeper and the gaze of every Drakein told him. Yet, how could he be nothing and special too?

And Dinah spoke as though it would be his choice whether or not to fulfill his potential. Choice meant freedom. He held on to that thought after he was dismissed, leaving the Lady to her world atop the mountain while he returned to his in the cavern below.

Chapter Eleven ~ Changes

Dinah flicked through an ancient book from her library. Too many, like the one she held in her hands, were in languages as dead as their owners, and what knowledge they contained, profound or common, was lost forever. She returned the book to its place on the shelf. As useless as it was to her, she did not feel like throwing it away.

All the time she had spent travelling from world to world through Portals on the God's Plain, searching for the tools she needed, she thought her goal was to regain her Lord's favor. Only with the boy did she remember the full extent of her plans. Ralen was integral to them, and she needed to pay attention to his development. His presence was powerful, leaving her thoughts clearer than they had been for millennia, but he was like nothing she'd encountered before—god, Fae, or daemon—and it would take time to understand his capabilities and how best to use them.

When the Drakein had finished transferring the mages to her new workshop, she sent one of them off with a message. A short time later, the Keeper answered her summons and dragged his sorry form into her entry room. Gobels loitered at the top of the stairs, and she shut the door against their spying. Grin had enough watchful eyes—including two new ones in his own skull—he did not need to recruit Ralen for his games.

"Why do you have the boy reading the First Commander's messages? Your duty is to oversee this realm, not to interfere in military matters."

"I have my suspicions."

"You suspect everyone, while I suspect only you. I hear the constant whirring of your brain, and don't think I haven't noticed your new limbs. What did you rob from me to trade for Fae magic?"

"Nothing, my Lady. The Gobels have scraped a few precious metals from the bottom of the lake and from the tunnels over the years. Commander Gordon was kind enough to broker the deal."

"I know what you're thinking. The commander wanted to please my Keeper. He is not bribing you. Did he ask for anything in exchange?"

"No, but the Fae are so difficult. Why would they ever agree, especially with you...?"

He was wise enough not to say 'disgraced'. She wanted no reminders from her underlings.

"Fae are neutral. Now, stop harassing the commander."

"Yes, my Lady. And the boy?"

"You have protected him, as I asked, and made him stronger. I am pleased. Plus, he can learn much from the Conquered."

"If I knew your plans for the child, Lady, I could better see to his upbringing."

"Even more unwise than concerning yourself with military business is concerning yourself with mine. Understood?"

"Yes, my Lady."

"Now, leave me."

The Keeper heaved himself towards the stair. The laboratory door was shut, but she noted his interest in it. She would not fully reveal her schemes to anyone, least of all Grin and his whispering gobels.

"Lady," her senior Drakein guard said as soon as they were alone. "Offerings await."

She did not need the reminder. There were a thousand details to deal with after such a long absence, but the health of her army was one duty she never shirked. It was second only to Ralen and her other new acquisitions in importance.

"Begin the preparations," she told him.

He hurried away, and she took a moment to calm her thoughts. Imprinting required concentration. The Keeper always vexed her, but he had been a gift from her Lord, and so she tolerated him—barely.

As soon as she was suitably steeled, she descended into the tunnels and wound her way through the oldest passageways to a small cavern where the roof had collapsed. Midday sun would entice the younglings to hatch.

She arrived before her guards had moved all the leathery eggs into the light, but there was no time to waste. Shadows already crept across those on the periphery. There were over a hundred, at least three times the usual number, but she noted many smashed and rotting eggs swept into the corners. Her guards had destroyed those ready to hatch while she was away to prevent wild Drakein from escaping into the caverns. Nothing was wasted: the remains would feed the new crop of young.

Tiny claws scratched at silver membranes, eager to reach the warmth. As soon as the first one's teeth tore through and yellow eyes appeared, she caught its gaze with hers. "Hello, child. Your mother welcomes you." A guard passed her a tendril of meat and she dropped it into the hatchling's mouth. It swallowed and growled for more. She left it to finish fighting its way out and moved on to the next egg.

Before the light had gone, she had a new generation of soldiers to be taken to the city for training. They were thick-witted and aged too quickly, but their obedience did not require a holy Presence or Marks or compulsions. They would fight and die simply because they loved her.

RALEN OBEYED DINAH'S command to tidy up and went to choose new clothes. The Drakein who showed him the pile of cast offs was amazed the strange material had survived so long after the fall of Ralen's homeworld, although the slaves they'd once belonged to had not.

The pants he chose were too long, but Ralen rolled them up and transferred his knife and candle to the pocket. They weren't as well fitted as his old pair, but they were whole and unstained. Saren would have one less thing to tease him about.

He found Anjee in the cavern. She sang as she separated wheat grains from the chaff. Around her were baskets ready to be taken across the lake to the Conquered. Soon, he would be with them. This was his last day with her. He joined in, wondering what to say, but she spoke first.

"Dinah has returned. Does this mean more nights spent in the library?" Anjee asked.

"Yes...and days spent with the Conquered."

Her face went blank. "You're to live with them?"

"I don't know. She only said I'm to learn from the First Commander, and I'm not to work the fields anymore. I'll come back here to sleep." Night-time was when Anjee was most vulnerable. He wanted to be there to watch over her.

She stripped the wheat ferociously. The gobels' overlapping whispers were loud in the absence of her singing. The hollowness inside him grew the longer she stayed quiet.

He was angry with Dinah, with the Keeper, with everything. He took a handful of grain and threw it into the dark where gobels lurked. "Go away!" he shouted.

The whispers stopped. To Anjee, he said, "I hate Grin. Why couldn't Dinah take me away from him instead of away from you?"

She gave him the look she always used when he mentioned the Keeper. She wanted to know. He shared everything with her except that. He knew she sensed the difference in him, that piece that had broken the night he picked the crazy man and took his eyes. Talking about it would do nothing. Simply being with her mended him as best as he could be mended.

"I'll be all right," Anjee said, forcing a smile. "We do what we're told. I can't change that. Nor can you. But... Do you want to?"

"What do you mean?"

"You hate Grin, yet Dinah commands him and all of us. Do you not hate her?"

He paused. "We would be dead without her."

"Or free."

Anjee's words echoed the whispers that kept slipping out of the corners of his carefully controlled thoughts—fight, defy, freedom—but there was no way out of Hell, not without the Lady there to unlock the door. And to wish her ill was both stupid and dangerous.

"No. No one is free, not anymore. Dinah is not so harsh a master. We talk in the longhouse. She is..."

"Don't say 'kind'. She is not kind. I have known other slaves that go up there and never come back again. They are mad and broken, but they are people. She is one of the monsters. Don't forget that."

"It's not so simple."

"What does she say to you in your hours together that makes you love her so?"

"I do not love her. She talks of history and battles and people she knew long ago. And yes, she can be kind. She is a monster, but not all monsters are the same. She feeds, but do we hate a lion for feeding on people when it has to?"

"I've never known anyone eaten by lions."

He laughed. "Or sharks. I thought about saying sharks. You are right. I have grown used to her, but that does not mean she isn't dangerous. I do remember that."

"Good. I wish you didn't have to go to see her, and I wish you didn't have to go among the Conquered, but what I wish doesn't matter. Nothing I do or want will ever matter."

"You matter to me." He wrapped his arms around her and held so tight she gave a sharp exhale.

When he let her go, he said, "At least in the fields you'll be safe from gobels. I'll come back at night. I won't leave you alone. I'll protect you—I promise."

"Don't make promises. Our lives are not our own. And don't do anything to get into trouble." She looked down, focusing on the task at hand, and began a new song about a tortoise in the sunshine.

"Where did you learn that?" he asked, reaching out for a few stalks of wheat.

"One of the women taught me. They speak when you're not here."

"They do?" A broken wheat shaft caught under his fingernail and drew blood. He put the finger in his mouth.

"They won't say, but I think they're afraid of you and all the time you spend with Her. You're the only one taken up to the mountain who comes back again."

"You're not afraid."

"Of course not. I'm afraid <u>for</u> you. Especially since you are such a poor worker." With a playful smile, she piled a bundle of wheat on his lap.

Her smile was a rare thing. It slipped out sometimes, like a ray of sunlight escaping a cloud-filled sky, and disappeared as quickly as it had come, so he was never sure he'd really seen it. Still, even her brief smile was enough to warm the darkness inside, and he smiled back.

He knew he was a fool to think of freedom, even fleetingly. Dinah had never promised any such thing. He knew he was trapped. Still, he reveled in each day spent working the fields with sky instead of stone overhead, reveled in every opportunity to stretch his legs while running messages for Gordon. And each note Anjee sang was as good as an eternity in paradise.

Freedom was in the gaps between shackle and skin, in the slack of chain, in the breath between screams. There could be happiness in Hell.

The day was over by the time they finished the grain. He wanted to keep working, to listen to her new songs over and over. He did not look forward to the morning: Gobels dragging him across the lake, running messages to the Portal and trying not to get caught reading them … reporting to the Keeper. He wanted Dinah to call him to her, to tell him he never had to do terrible things again, but no Drakein came to fetch him.

As he and Anjee curled up together to sleep, he heard a different call, a glimpse of black feathers, and felt the pull to return to the cavern. He stiffened.

"She's back," Anjee reminded him. "It's not safe to go."

"I have to." The truth was he wanted to. He tried not to notice Anjee's anxious expression when he left.

WHEN RALEN REACHED the secluded section of cavern where they usually met, Amseel and Ashkal appeared out of the darkness.

"Dinah has returned," he told them.

"We know all, see all," Ashkal said. "She plays with her new toys and is oblivious."

"Let us begin." Amseel had a length of rope and used it to catch Ralen's hands. "If you were holding a weapon, I could have disarmed you. Bindings can help as well as hinder. Today we fight with bound wrists."

Ashkal tied his brother's wrists together, and Amseel demonstrated how to defeat an opponent without the full use of his hands. It was Ralen's turn after that, and his attention was occupied for the next few hours.

When he had learned the new moves and felt his body responding automatically, he thought about the task the Keeper had given him. Grin wanted him to find evidence that the Conquered were doing something wrong. If he discovered it, would he no longer need to cross the lake? Would Dinah reward him? Could he stay here with Anjee, protect her from the monsters?

He needed advice, so he turned to Ashkal. "You see all. Have you seen where the message runner, Saren, goes after he passes through the Portal?"

"We see," Amseel answered instead. The angel pulled a steel dagger and stepped forward. Ralen disarmed him by catching the tip of the blade with the coils of the rope tied around his wrists.

"You won't tell me?"

Ashkal said, "So many intrigues in this realm: Keeper, Conquered, Dinah, even the gobels whisper, whisper, whisper. Only the Drakein seem not to care for such things. So much happening around you—because of you—even if the whisperers do not know."

"Because of me?" Ralen weaved away from a series of blows executed by both angels at once. They took advantage whenever he was distracted. Their favorite lesson was the importance of concentration. He was too slow, and Amseel gave him a bruise to remind him to pay attention.

When they were finished, Ralen, dripping sweat and panting, while the angels showed no trace of tiredness, repeated the question. "Where does Saren go? Should I tell the Keeper? Or is it nothing?"

"Nothing here is nothing," Ashkal said.

"Do not interfere," Amseel told his brother. "We are not permitted."

"You interfere with me," Ralen argued. "You say all you do is watch, but..." He held out his arms, indicating the training in progress.

Ashkal's wings twitched. "Your presence disturbs the order of things it seems. Even with us. This lesson is over. Go and forget."

Ralen felt a cloud descend on his thoughts, but it cleared quickly. He shook his head and looked into Ashkal's eyes. "It's not working anymore. It hasn't for a while. I thought you wanted me to remember."

Amseel dropped the steel dagger they'd been practicing with and pulled the knife from his belt sheath. Ralen took a step back. The lesson was supposed to be over. He sensed the tension in the air, noted the way Amseel held the Blessed Blade—this was real.

"Stop," Ashkal ordered his brother. More was said silently; Ralen could tell from the twitch of feathers that the angels were speaking in each other's minds.

Amseel only grew angrier. "This has gone too far. We are in danger now." He struck, faster than Ralen had ever seen him move. Ralen reacted as he'd been trained, and the blade missed. Almost.

His elbow stung. He touched the spot and came away with a smear of blood. It was only a graze, nothing serious, but then he remembered that Amseel was using a Blessed Blade.

"No," Ashkal cried. "You..."

Ralen continued to look at the blood on his hand, rubbing it between his thumb and forefinger. "When I lose my soul, will it kill me?"

Ashkal's high voice trembled as he said, "You should already be dead."

Amseel tightened his grip on the handle of the blade in his hand. "What is he, my brother?" To Ralen: "What are you? What!?"

Ashkal pointed to the caves and told Ralen, "Go! Run!"

Ralen obeyed, confused, wondering what he had said to make them angry—and wondering how he was still alive.

AS SOON AS THE BOY was gone, Amseel sheathed his blade and said, We must kill him.

To what purpose? Ashkal always sounded calm. He'd sounded just as calm when the skies of their world were burning.

I don't understand the purpose of any of this! He endangers us.

I do not fear Dinah.

And Our Lord? What if He discovers?

The risk is worth it.

Worth our lives?

To soar again? To be as we were? To interfere in all things? Yes. But do not fear. Dinah has not learned of this. As our ability to cloud his mind lessens, her ability to read it must also diminish.

That worries me all the more. Amseel could share thoughts with his brother, but as hard as he willed it, he could not change his mind. And the Blessed Blade—it was as though nothing more than steel touched him! Where will this lead?

Not knowing is what I enjoy. Ashkal had a touch of his old, mischievous smile just before he took to the air in a black cloud of obscuring magic.

Amseel thought about following the boy into the dark cavern and slitting his throat. With a sigh, he vanished and followed his brother instead. In all their long centuries, he had never failed to follow Ashkal, wherever he led, but it was growing more and more difficult.

Chapter Twelve ~ City of Soldiers

In the morning, Ralen walked beside Anjee to the edge of the lake. He was reluctant to let go of her hand. It seemed he had been holding it since the Bringer and the Last God came to their world and tore them both away from the lives they should have had.

"At least with me gone all day, the others will talk to you. You can learn more songs," he told her.

"When they talk, you realize how crazy they are. I don't want to end up like them."

"You won't."

She looked at the distant lights of the city. "I used to think they were stars, the lake was the edge of the world, and we would fall into space if we went to the other side. I wish I could see the city you describe. I wish I was going there too. Will you be one of the Conquered now?"

He released his grip and held up his hand, proudly showing her the glowing Mark. "I'm the same as you. I'll never be one of them."

She must have seen the wound on his elbow, because she frowned. "Everyone will want to mark you as their property, Ralen. Don't let them."

He covered the scratch with his palm. It was red and sore and hurt worse than any cut so shallow should, but he was alive, and he still had a soul. Or he thought he did. It had been Marked by Dinah and confined in Hell so perhaps it had not been his for a long time.

He didn't know what to make of any of this, but it seemed the angels hated him now. He wouldn't be sneaking off in the night to spar with them, and that thought made the wound ache all the more. At least Anjee would be happy about that.

"It doesn't matter who claims me. I will never be Conquered. They won't let you be." He had told her what Gordon had said that first day in the tunnel. The Marked were food, slaves, nothing.

"Sorry," she said.

"I'm not." He could tell from the look of sympathy on her face that she didn't believe him.

The water stirred as three gobels rose from the phosphorescent depths.

He pushed Anjee away. "Go."

She scowled at the monsters and gathered a handful of stones from the lake's edge. The creatures reached for Ralen.

"Go," he repeated.

She reluctantly dropped the pebbles. "Goodbye." Her footfalls echoed off the walls as she ran up the slope toward the valley.

He would see her again. Tonight. He had promised.

The gobels clamped the jelly thing, called a scor, on his face and dragged him under the water as roughly as ever, but after they reached the opposite shore and removed the scor, he smiled as he told them, "I'm staying with the Conquered. I won't be done until late." He might avoid the Keeper's island today. The gobels always carried him straight across in the mornings, then to the Keeper to report around midday.

Silver eyes narrowed. One said, "You hiding from us?"

"No. I'm not afraid of you." It was true. He had much worse things to fear. "I'm obeying Dinah's orders."

The gobels cringed. Mention of her name always upset them. "She is cruel to our master. We don't like her," another one hissed.

"I'll tell her that." He chuckled when the creature's wide eyes went even wider.

"No!" It shook its head. "Me stupid. No meant to say. No." The band of gobels quickly vanished into the blue-green depths, as though hoping the water could hide them from Dinah's wrath.

Left alone on the docks, Ralen listened to the creak of wooden boats as his smile faded. He did not belong here. He moved deeper into the city where the clash of training blades and stomp of boots overwhelmed the quiet. A city of soldiers. He had no place among them, but he trudged to the First Commander's door and knocked.

Gordon's wife answered, wearing only a plain nightgown. She and the children usually rose before Gordon and were training by this time. Her face flushed as she coughed. "You're not the physician."

"What are you doing, Kiera?" Gordon said behind her. "You must rest, my love."

"I don't want to rest. I want to be better. Where is that blasted serving girl?"

Gordon took her arm. "You will not be better instantly, even when they do return."

Ralen unobtrusively followed them into the house and shut the door behind. Gordon often ignored his presence until he was needed.

While the commander led his wife back up the stairs, Ralen waited in the foyer. He spotted a gas candle-lighter lying next to a lamp and quickly transferred it to a pocket in his new trousers. The Keeper's magic candle was defective; it was best to have a backup.

The maid and physician arrived and went upstairs. When the maid hobbled back down with washing, she noted the missing lighter and raised her eyebrows. "Children shouldn't play with fire."

"I've never been a child."

"I suspect not. Be careful anyway."

Ralen noticed the scarred hands she clasped around the handles of the basket. "Is that what happened to you," he asked. "Fire?"

She nodded. "I was four. Fire oil took my leg, and I tried to smother the flames with my hands. It would have kept on burning if someone hadn't rolled me through the dirt."

"I'm sorry. Did it happen when you were taken prisoner?"

Her usually distant look turned focused and angry. "I was born Conquered. I would have been a warrior in a long line of warriors if not for this. I'm no slave or convert." She glanced at the stairs, as though afraid Gordon had heard, and continued in a whisper, "I don't need your pity."

She turned her back on him and went on with her duties. He should have kept quiet. Slaves were food, and he needed to remember his place. He was less than Conquered, apparently even lower than their servants.

An hour later, Gordon came down dressed and ready to go. "Here," he said, handing Ralen a parcel of letters and the amulet that gave him access to the Portal tunnel.

"Commander," he began, taking the messages, "there's something else."

"Yes?"

"I spoke to Dinah." The commander blanched every time Ralen casually spoke her name. "She says I am to follow you all day, learn logistics and strategy."

"What?"

"I think she said logistics, but I don't know what that means."

"She wants you following me?"

"Yes, sir."

"...You are not even Conquered. Why, by the Last God, should you learn about command?"

"I don't know." Ralen decided not to mention her talk of specialness or seizing destiny. He knew to keep his conversations with the Lady a secret. Anjee was the only one he confided in.

Gordon's moustache went up and down as he chewed his lip. "Very well." He was too tense to be as accepting as he sounded, and he cast Ralen a suspicious look before grasping the door handle. "Deliver the messages then meet me in the Command Center."

Ralen knew where that was because sometimes he picked up messages there rather than from Gordon's home. The First Commander strode up the street in one direction and Ralen took off running in the other.

He read the letters once he was deep in the tunnel, past the stables and beyond the sight of the soldiers stationed there. Nothing but enquiries about supplies. Stores were running low, and Gordon wanted their allies to contribute to the Stratia's upkeep. The Stratia was the army, he'd learned. Ralen had no idea what information the Keeper was looking for, but he didn't think he had found it.

He slowed to a walk when he reached the eastern valley. It was narrower and steeper than the terraced valley on the western side of the mountain where the slaves grew food, where Anjee was now.

The Portal was unmistakable, tall enough for him to see over the shoulders of the adults who got in his way. He maneuvered along the track past thousands of tents and clusters of soldiers drilling as best they could in the confined space. Taller structures, made of wood and stone, were being erected in the center of the valley around the new temple. The military camp was becoming a second city, and no one but the commander spoke of the situation being temporary anymore.

Saren tossed a rock in the air while he waited. "What's the excuse this time? Too stupid to remember the way?"

"The First Commander's wife is ill."

"How's that concern you?"

"I had to wait." Something occurred to him. "Should I worry about sickness?" The Conquered had physicians, but the Marked didn't. Still, he couldn't remember any slave being sick. Hungry and insane, but never sick.

"They like their food fresh," Saren said, pointing to Ralen's Mark. "That keeps you well. Too bad it can't keep you from being an idiot."

Ralen had no desire to speak to Saren any more than he had to, so he handed over the messages and turned to leave.

"Wait." Saren gave him a small bundle of letters and a cloth-wrapped parcel.

Ralen recognized the feel of the package. "For the Keeper?"

"Tell him it's the last."

Ralen nodded and took off running. He didn't want to deliver it, didn't want to choose anyone else or hear any more screams. He wanted to throw it in the bushes and forget about it, but there was no telling what Grin would do if he did.

He scanned the messages Saren had given him but saw nothing peculiar. The candle-lighter worked well. He warmed the back of the wax seals and re-affixed them before continuing to the Command Center. It took brandishing Gordon's amulet for him to gain entry and find the First Commander.

The space was filled with scurrying aides, officers engaged in hushed conversations, and scribes scratching on parchment. He saw maps and battalion lists covering the walls, but he was distracted by what he knew was coming later, when he reported to the Keeper. He had barely registered the First Commander's words on his arrival but tried to pay attention now.

"We are out of the wars," Gordon said in an instructional tone. "Yet, we stay apprised of the situation on key battlefields, places we will return when the Last God once more casts His light on Our Lady."

A table covered in sand took up the center of the large circular room. Gordon gestured and spoke a word. The sand shifted and formed shapes: rivers, valleys, trenches, horses, and soldiers.

"This is Ektas," the commander said, "and what we know of the positions of the troops Adarmis sent to replace us. The place is nearly won, but he is not taking chances. The new Bringer has surrounded the Ektas capital and will strike in one overwhelming wave, with this group on the hill watching in case of new arrivals from the rear. At least, that is what I would do with such positioning."

Ralen was fascinated by the detail, each figure carved of sand. "How do you know all this? Can you see this world with magic?"

"No. We rely on reports passed from Adarmis' allies to ours and on spies. When we were the ones stationed on the battlefield, we made use of scouts and far-seeing. No matter the source of the information, the pieces must be brought together to form a greater picture. This picture."

"You have spies in the new Bringer's army?" Ralen asked.

"A few."

Ralen thought of Saren's excursions through the Portal. Was the runner gathering reports from spies? How come he had never encountered these reports?

"This is what's in all the letters you have me carry?" he asked, hoping to learn more, without letting on he had read them.

"Mostly. Here in the Command Center, officers break the codes and mages update the map."

Codes. That's why Ralen saw nothing of interest in the messages he carried. The task the Keeper had set him was pointless. The Conquered could hide anything they wanted in plain sight.

When Gordon mentioned mages, he indicated two men in tunics. They did not wear armor like the other Conquered and sat cross-legged in a white circle chalked on the flagstones. Drakein guards flanked them. At first, Ralen thought it was an honor guard, but then he noticed the red Marks on the mages' hands. They were slaves. He was not the only one allowed among the Conquered, but, like him, the mages were set apart.

There was another guard besides the Drakein, an old man in a white robe. Ralen had seen him once before in the city, saw Conquered and Drakein touch fingers to lips when he passed—a priest of the Last God.

"The key to strategy is having the best map possible," Gordon continued. "What is the lay of the land, the distribution of forces? What defensive structures are in place? Where will reinforcements come from?"

Ralen noted the river between Adarmis' troops and the defender's capital city. "It's difficult to cross water," he said, thinking of the lake between him and Anjee.

"Yes. We must know where to fjord, where boats can be used, or bridges constructed."

There was so much to learn. Ralen fingered one of the sand soldiers and it fell apart. He snatched his hand back and cast Gordon a contrite look, but the figure reformed itself.

"This is logistics?" he asked.

Gordon shook his head. Ralen noted the older man's gaze wandering to other parts of the room, his body poised to move as soon as he finished answering a slave's questions: The commander was bored.

"Logistics is finding a way to feed everyone when there are no enemy lands to pillage and not enough slaves in the field."

It sounded like that's where Gordon thought Ralen should be.

Chapter Thirteen ~ New Arrivals

Gordon shifted the sand map through several more worlds once occupied by Dinah's forces. He pointed out strategic positions and what he would do with the current situation. It seemed he was thinking aloud, and Ralen was merely privy to his musings. Ralen tried not to interrupt with too many questions. Whenever he said anything that reminded the First Commander there was a twelve-year-old slave boy examining his decisions, Gordon chewed his lip with annoyance. Ralen wasn't welcome here.

At the end of the day, Gordon went home to his ill wife and his family, and Ralen went to the docks. No one offered him a place to sleep in the city, and he didn't ask for one. He would stay in the caves with the other Marked. That's what he truly was. Gordon and all the Conquered knew it. Why couldn't Dinah see? Why couldn't she and the Keeper leave him alone?

He did not wait long for the gobels. Bubbles carrying their whispers preceded them out of the water. The dim cavern light disappeared as his face was covered by the scor. Slimy hands took his arms and pulled him under. He now knew how the gelatinous scor on his face worked, how it filtered air from the water and concentrated it in sacks from which he could breathe for a short time, and he knew how to retract the scor's hooks from the sides of his face.

He could peel it off, swallow water and be done. Sink to the bottom where nothing could reach him. He would never again soil his clothes with blood from the Keeper's victims, nor listen to the cries and clatter of bones from Dinah's feeding, nor endure the superior looks of Saren and the other Conquered. He would be free.

Except ... Anjee. He wanted to hear her voice, wanted to keep his promise this time.

He pulled the scor off his face and breathed in the scent of decay that lingered around the Keeper's island. Grin was waiting. "You have something for me, boy?"

Ralen tugged the parcel from his pocket and dropped it in Grin's twitching mass of fingers. "Saren said it's the last."

"The last? I must draw this one out then."

Ralen hoped that meant a reprieve. "The Conquered's messages are all sent in code," he told the Keeper. "I can't discover what they're hiding."

"Find out the code," Grin said.

"I'll be caught."

Grin's happy finger fluttering calmed. "No, I can't have that. Don't want anyone to know. No one. You will find a way. Now, let me look at my new friend."

The Keeper read the words etched on the artifact, and it expanded into a cage. Ralen was surprised to see not a luminous wisp this time but a large-eyed miniature man with fangs and gossamer wings.

"A Hasvel," Grin exclaimed. "Magnificent."

"What is a Hasvel?" Ralen asked.

"A Fae delicacy and a potent morsel of power." Grin stuck a finger through the bars. The Hasvel hissed and bit him. Grin did not even wince, despite the ichors flowing from his punctured skin. He flicked the creature with another oddly attached finger, and the Hasvel grunted as he was flung against the bars on the opposite side of the small cage.

"I will kill you," the fairy said carefully in God's Tongue.

"You have it wrong, my little friend. I will do the killing ... and the biting." Grin licked his lips and Ralen shuddered. Anjee had said it: everything here wanted to eat us. Apparently, Hasvels had the same problem.

"What do you think?" Grin asked. "Do I need a new foot?"

Ralen eyed the blubbery mass of parts. He knew everything burnt and rotted on the Keeper had already been replaced. "You're perfect."

"You haven't even looked!" Grin had his servants lift his right leg out of the water. They rested the heel on the lip of the stone pool. "Get closer," he told Ralen.

Ralen inched toward the extended leg. It was pure white except for a network of blue and purple veins. Tiny spines ran along the sides. It was like a bird's foot, with rubbery skin and four yellow talons instead of toes. "You're perfect," he repeated.

Gobels pressed Ralen's nose against the rippled skin edging one talon. It smelled sour and rotten. "I disagree," Grin said. "Find me a replacement."

"Dinah is back," Ralen reminded him. "She and the Conquered need workers. You don't want a human foot anyway, not when you already have something more interesting."

"Your attempt at guile is laughable. No wonder your spying yields nothing." The Keeper sighed. "You are right, though."

Ralen felt the tension coiled in his gut loosen. "Can I go?"

"Not until you find me an 'interesting' foot."

There would be no respite. Ralen's mind raced, thinking of alternatives, of how he might lure a Drakein to the lake. Then he gripped the wrist of the gobel that had held his nose against the Keeper. "How about this one?"

The gobel's eyes widened. "No, Master. Me good to Master."

"You serve me well," Grin agreed. "This will be a more useful service."

"No!" It tried to pull away, but Ralen was stronger than he used to be. The monster was caught.

"Do not defy me," Grin warned. The gobel whispered curses and shook its head, but it stopped fighting to escape.

"Go on," the Keeper told Ralen. "Cut it off."

Ralen withdrew the claw knife from his pocket and held the gobel's leg down. He hesitated a moment, but he had done worse than this already. He sawed until yellow blood flowed into the Keeper's pool and the foot came off. It floated on the water, tethered by a piece of skin until Ralen made the last cut. The gobel mewled in agony throughout. Several of its brothers licked the stump until it sealed.

"Good," Grin said. "Now, make the Hasvel release its energy to me."

Ralen had performed this part of the operation before as well, but it had been a faceless wisp the previous times. This tiny, winged man was too human.

The Hasvel hissed. "Get away."

When Ralen stabbed its forearm with the claw, he said, "I'm sorry."

Fortunately, the Keeper wished to preserve this last prize, so he stopped at one foot. The Hasvel was wounded in two places. It panted, exhausted from screaming and fighting futilely against Ralen.

Ralen carried the Hasvel's cage to the chest where Grin kept his possessions and set it on top. As he draped a piece of embroidered cloth over the bars, he said again, "I'm sorry."

"If you were sorry, you would let me go," the Hasvel argued in broken God's Tongue.

"There's nowhere to go," Ralen said. "We're all trapped here, and we will all die here. If not today, then tomorrow." He remembered

Gordon's words. He never forgot them. They reminded him not to hope.

His work done, the gobels dragged him to the opposite shore, and he climbed up to the sleep caves. Anjee was curled next to their stone cairn. He lay beside her as silent tears dampened his cheeks.

"You came back," Anjee whispered.

"Always," he told her.

THE NEXT MORNING, RALEN returned to the First Commander's home. The maid answered. "The commander says you should not be following him around today."

"I don't have a choice."

"Then you'll be watching a sickbed or three." She waved him in. "You can help me."

She went to the kitchen and returned carrying a tray laden with mugs of broth. He followed her up the stairs, hesitant, as he had never been allowed to go deeper into the house before. The maid gave a frustrated grunt, indicating her rattling tray and then pointed with her chin to the first door on their right. "Don't be all day about it. Are you helping or not?" He opened the door for her and discovered it was the children's room.

Gordon had two boys, whom he had glimpsed in passing some mornings. One was older than Ralen, but he always considered them boys. They had young eyes. Today, they both lay shivering on down mattresses soaked with sweat.

"An awful fever," the maid said. She placed the tray on a side table and took up a bowl of water that sat on the floor. She fished out a cloth and used it to mop the brow of the nearest boy. "Now, prop him up whilst I spoon a few drops of nourishment down his throat."

Ralen did as instructed and was shocked to feel the heat that emanated from the child's skin.

"There you are," Gordon said coming into the room. Dark circles made his eyes look larger, and his clothes were wrinkled and unkempt. "I need more water." He held out a bowl, and the maid hurried off to refill it.

To Ralen he said, "There's nothing for you to learn here."

"They are so hot. The physician did not cure them?"

"No. Nor my beloved." Gordon placed the back of his hand on his younger son's flushed cheek and a wave of agony crossed his features. Ralen had seen similar pain on the faces of dying men.

Gordon closed his eyes and spoke a fervent prayer: "God, Last and Greatest, be merciful. Spare my family as you have spared me. They too are your faithful soldiers. Let them live to fight for your glory." Then, quietly, he added, "Help us, Lady Dinah."

"Can Dinah cure them?" Ralen asked.

Gordon blinked, as though he'd forgotten Ralen was there. The commander schooled his features into impassivity and said, "She sees no one since her return, and the priests say this is all part of the Last God's punishment. We must suffer."

The maid was back with more water. Gordon tended his children then moved to his wife's room. Ralen felt like an intruder, so he quietly made his way outside and onto the busy street. He noticed more flushed faces in the crowds of soldiers and heard distant coughs. The sickness was spreading.

When he reached the dock, he realized he was hours earlier than the gobels expected. He had grown used to their torturous mode of transport, but there were other ways. He eyed one of the boats moored to a pylon. There were no Conquered nearby, so he hurried over to it and dropped inside. The boat rocked and threatened to topple him out, but he placed a hand against the slimy wooden pylon to steady it. The knot holding it to the dock was impossible for him to untie, so he cut the rope with his gobel claw knife. He found the oars and latched them in the rings.

The cavern lake was miles wide. He stuck to the most direct route, and it took an hour to reach the other side. Muscles ached from the unfamiliar effort. The gobels were ten times as fast, but their cold fingers on his body and the drowning sensation from the scor was worse than the new blisters on his hands. Arms and stomach sore, he pulled the boat onto the rocky shore.

The dim light of glow worms and distant torches revealed the greater darkness of the tunnel entrance he was looking for. The Drakein soldiers guarding it watched him approach.

"I need to see Dinah," he told them.

"The Lady is not to be disturbed."

"Can you give her a message then?"

"Perhaps."

"She'll want to know this. Tell her sickness is spreading among the Conquered and the physicians cannot cure it. The priests will not. If she wants me to learn logistics, she'd best make sure the First Commander's family does not die." Ralen turned away. They would tell her or not. There was nothing more he could do.

He noted the scarcity of Drakein in the area—only the two guards. They were usually thick around the tunnels leading to Dinah's mountaintop. He spotted a clump of lights further along the lake shore and went to investigate.

A new tunnel mouth had been excavated. Lamps lined the freshly cut walls. Drakein led chained slaves away from the site. Ralen recognized them: mages from Dinah's workshop.

He hugged the shadows, unnoticed. Once the mages were gone, the remaining Drakein formed a gauntlet between the tunnel opening and several large crates tied to barges moored at the edge of the lake. Gobels surrounded the barges on the water side in a frenzy of whispers. The Drakein held their poleaxes tightly, claws cutting into their own scales. Everyone was afraid.

The crates on the barges shook, whatever was inside causing them to dance about. If they hadn't been chained in place, they would have fallen into the water. Wagons mounted with wooden hoists were wheeled up to the water's edge.

"Get them ashore, now," Grin ordered. Ralen shrank further into the shadows. He was surprised to see the Keeper floating in the lake near the mass of gobels, personally overseeing the transfer of cargo.

Hooks were fastened to the chains, and the first crate was winched up by muscular Drakein, the hoists creaking under the strain. The box swayed. Something inside growled. The sound was low and powerful, sending an instinctual shiver along Ralen's spine. The new slaves, or whatever they were, weren't human.

Once the first wagon was loaded, it was trundled into the depths of the tunnel, pulled by Drakein rather than horses. He suspected the animals would have spooked at the sounds coming from inside. Ralen twitched with curiosity, but he also realized something: The Keeper and his gobels were here, and he had a boat.

Chapter Fourteen ~ Mistakes

The island in the center of the lake seemed benign without the monsters, nothing but a desolate piece of rock. No trace of blood or echo of screams to reveal what had happened here.

Ralen removed the cloth cover from the Hasvel's cage, and the tiny creature lunged at him, its face wedged between the bars, teeth reaching as its jaws clacked together. Unable to reach, it hissed with fury and frustration.

"I won't hurt you," Ralen said.

"You hurt already. Now you feel pain."

"The Keeper needed you hurt, to steal your magic. I didn't want to do it. I'm a slave."

"I never be slave. I die first!"

"That's what Grin plans—for you to die. It was wisps before. First, he will ... he will make me draw out your suffering. What is a Hasvel?"

"Me," it said, growling, as though that would scare Ralen away.

"Why are you special?"

"Me cook. Know nothing. Fitting that cook be eaten."

"Where are you from?"

"Cehlec Var."

"I don't know what that means."

"Home forest. Safe. But me village raided by Fae. Not safe after all. Where me now?"

Ralen didn't know the name of this place. It was just the cavern or Dinah's realm. He'd always called it Hell. "You are in the domain of the old Bringer."

The Hasvel's large eyes widened even further, and it shrank into its cage. "You be right. No hope."

Ralen thought about why he was here. It wasn't mere curiosity. He admired the Hasvel's spirit, and he did not like its sudden despondency, the slackness of its body. There was too much of that among the slaves. It was all he saw. There was no hope—but there should be.

Ralen unlocked the cage.

"What doing?"

"Setting you free." It was impossible for him or for Anjee; they were Marked, but the Hasvel wasn't. Ralen could do this one thing to fill the hollow inside.

As soon as the door was open, the Hasvel jumped out, its wings beating like a hummingbird's. Ralen caught glimpses of red, yellow, and orange, a blur of color. The creature slowly rose then plummeted, crashing onto the slimy rock with a squelch of water and wheeze of pain from its small lungs.

"Ooog."

"Are you all right?"

The Hasvel stretched out its small arms, like it was doing a push up, and shakily lifted its face out of the muck. "No, me not all right. Me broken. Broken Hasvels die. Broken Hasvels get eaten! You broke me, you..." The creature's rough God's Tongue faded into foreign epithets.

"Will you heal?"

The Hasvel shook off green algae and brown mud and looked over its shoulder to inspect gossamer wings. They were mud splattered too, but he gave them a shake and the muck slid off as easily as water running off a gobel's hide. "Nothing missing." The wings stretched wide, ready to take off again, but the Hasvel suddenly winced and quickly folded them against his back as if protecting something precious. "No, not right. Need rest."

"You can't rest here." Ralen thought that was obvious. The Keeper could return at any moment.

"Which way be home?"

"I don't know where Cehlec Var is, but the Portal is in the eastern valley. You can't fly, so there's no way you can make it without being seen."

"Me walk. Me small. Me hide good." The fairy limped away, hesitating at the edge of the lake hemming them in on all sides. "You pluck me from Fate's web and put me on new path. Maybe bad path but is new. I forgive you." It minced its way into the water and began to paddle with chin up and eyes wide with panic.

Ralen sighed. "Wait. Stop."

He used a rock to smash a hole in the cage from the inside and make it look as though the Hasvel had broken out himself. He left the cage lying on the ground and climbed into his borrowed boat. "Get in. You'll never make it to the Portal without my help."

Even a short swim had done the creature in, and it crawled onto the rock as exhausted as if it had crossed the lake twice. Ralen carefully lifted it into the boat.

He found an empty sack stuck to the bottom of his stolen boat. At one time, it must have held grain harvested by slaves or pale fish caught from the depths of the lake. "Climb inside. No one can see you, or we're both in trouble."

"Trouble here mean dead, right?"

"Yes."

The Hasvel gave a long-suffering sigh and climbed into the sack. Ralen pressed his bare toes into the bilge as he grabbed the oars and pulled with all his remaining strength. If the Keeper caught them here, it would be trouble. Much trouble.

He hid the stolen boat among castoff baskets and other debris from the harvest on the western shore of the lake. The Portal was the opposite direction, through the Conquered city, but he could not go that way without Gordon's sigil.

He found Anjee in the walnut orchard. The other slaves working beside her wandered away when he appeared. They were afraid.

Anjee smiled and ran up to him, leaving a half-full basket of black walnuts on the leaf strewn ground behind her. "I thought you would be in the city all day."

"There's sickness," he said. He told her about Gordon's family, his message to Dinah, and the delivery of the strange crates overseen by the Keeper.

When he described freeing the Hasvel, she frowned. "No. You shouldn't have. The Keeper will guess it was you. What has made you so careless?"

She did not know how he had tortured it, and what was to come. If she did, she would understand why he risked it, but Ralen was afraid to tell her everything. He was afraid to see her shy from him as the other slaves did. All he said was, "I had to." He opened the sack wide enough for her to see the Hasvel inside.

She jumped back with a yelp but then her expression softened. "It's so pretty, like a little person with butterfly wings. A fairy, a real fairy."

"Me no Fae! Me Hasvel," the creature corrected.

"I need to hide him until he heals and can escape through the Portal," Ralen said.

One of those brief smiles crossed her face. "I'll help."

There were no Drakein on the nearby terraces, so they were unobserved as Anjee sought out a particular tree. "Here." She climbed quickly and straddled a branch with her legs.

He handed the sack up to her, and she opened it like a gift, with child-like wonder on her face. She is a child, Ralen reminded himself.

"What is your name?"

Why did Ralen always forget to ask such things?

"Gar."

"I'm Anjee. See up there? The bird's nest? Can you climb inside?"

He leaped up and scrambled into the thick mass of twigs. He looked over the side and smiled. "Like home."

"Stay there, and I will bring you food from the fields later."

Gar cooed. "Me feel better soon. Me heal then fly fast and free!" He plucked a walnut from the tree—which Anjee must have missed when she harvested this one before—and leaned back, taking a huge bite from the rough flesh surrounding the shell. A loud crack filled the air.

"I have to get back to work now." She gave the Hasvel a last wistful smile before climbing down.

Ralen joined her. He had missed working the fields together. He spent the rest of the day warmed by the sun and by the new warmth inside his chest generated by his small rebellion against the Keeper. Defiance felt right. It felt...powerful.

THE NEW TUNNEL, WHERE the strange crates had been taken the day before, was off limits. Ralen passed by on his way to the lake in the morning and saw a line of Drakein guards in front of a new, iron gate that blocked the tunnel mouth. From the growls he'd heard coming from the boxes, he guessed the defenses were meant not only to keep the new arrivals from escaping but to keep everyone else from dying.

He wanted to ask Dinah about the crates, but she had not summoned him since the day of her return. He didn't even know if she had gotten his message about the plague spreading through the Conquered.

So many things were beyond his control. Part of him wanted that to change. Part of him wanted to know the layout and structure of Dinah's realm as well as Gordon knew his sand maps. He wanted to distribute food to the slaves, healers to the Conquered, and exile the Keeper and his gobels to the depths of the lake. He had freed one Hasvel, and that small act had awakened a need in him.

Not freed yet, he reminded himself. He still needed to get the Hasvel past the Portal.

Ralen craved a blade in his hand, the flex of muscle and rush of movement, the training of the angels. They made him feel powerful and free too, but they had vanished. They weren't able to cloud his memories, or kill him with their Blessed Blades, and that disturbed them. He was disappointed. In a way, the angels reminded him of the slaves all around, frightened of anything different.

He waited with bare toes in the lake water. Dinah had given him new clothes, but not shoes. He hadn't had any for years. His feet were calloused, able to run across stone or fields thick with brambles and feel no pain. It would be strange to have shoes again, but he remembered laces. They were always untied, and he still looked at his feet to make sure he wouldn't trip.

A green hand emerged from the water and grasped his ankle. The gobels had come. A moment later, he was knocked off balance and pulled into the depths. He held his breath, waiting for a scor to be jammed onto his face, but it didn't happen.

His head was only a few inches below the surface, so he kicked free and swam up to gulp air. The gobel pulled him down again, but he managed to break free long enough to steal a few more breaths along the way. When his feet found stone and he could stand well enough, he exhaled loudly, steeling himself for the confrontation ahead. This was the Keeper's island, and the monster was angry.

"Where is it?" Grin asked coldly.

Ralen knew he meant the Hasvel. "I don't know what you're talking about."

"The cage is empty."

He stayed quiet.

"You helped it. I know it."

"You are the Keeper. You need no reason to punish me. Do what you will." Ralen steeled himself. He had realized there would be repercussions when he made his choice. He was counting on Dinah's talk of specialness to save his life.

Grin was silent for a long time. The gobels' whispers quieted as they shrank from his anger. Soon there were no sounds but the slosh of water against the sides of the pool.

"You will unravel the Conquered's secret code," Grin said finally. "You will find proof of treason within their ranks, and you will report to me every day. Since you've learned how to use a boat, you can oar here each evening."

The Keeper knew how he had reached the island, and he must know how sore his arms were from the task. Being dragged by gobels was uncomfortable but much less work. Yet, if this was the only torment the Keeper could devise, Ralen would accept it happily.

"I will do as you ask, Master."

"Oh, there's more. I want another creature of power, since you robbed me of the last. My gobels will dredge the lake for more precious stones to pay for it, and you will help them. Now."

The gobel, whose stump-leg Ralen was responsible for, smiled before jumping on his back and shoving an angered scor on his face. This scor had been injured and its hooks dug defensively into his skin, as though trying to bore its way to safety. Ralen hissed with pain but endured the punishment. "Stumpy" and a swarm of gobels pulled him into the depths of the lake.

He had never gone down so far before, and his ears ached from the pressure. The phosphorescent water did not illuminate the depths. He fumbled blindly in the black silt, feeling rocks and what could only be the jagged fragments of half-eaten bones. Human-sized bones.

He searched for what seemed like hours before finding a pocket of cut stones. He took off his pants, tied the legs, and filled them with his find.

He couldn't speak, so he grabbed hold of the nearest gobel and showed him the makeshift sack. It pulled him up to the surface so quickly his ears hurt all over again. He climbed onto the shore of the Keeper's island and emptied the gems onto the ground. There were multi-faceted blue stones, large ovals in deep red and amber, and crystal-clear diamonds in rough-cut chunks. He didn't know what they were worth, but he knew they were not naturally to be found at the bottom of a lake. A strange place to store treasure.

Gobels whispered to their master and the Keeper nodded. "Good, but I will need more. Go back."

Ralen put the scor on his own face, gently this time, and waded back into the water.

Chapter Fifteen ~ Power

When his errand for the Keeper was done, Ralen was exhausted. But he was alive. The Keeper somehow knew of his disobedience, and still... he let Ralen live.

The gobels took the scor and left him in deep water on the slave's side of the lake. The rowboat he had concealed beneath a rock overhang was not too far away. He swam towards it, but three-quarters of the way there, his limbs tired and his head went under. Since freeing the Hasvel from the Keeper's cage, he no longer wanted to drown. He could change things.

He fought his way to the surface and saw gobels lurking, silver eyes peeking above the water. If he'd sunk to the bottom, would they have saved him?

When he reached the boat, he looked at the distant lamplights of the city. He could barely move let alone row. Gordon would not want him there anyway, not while his family was ill.

Dinah was what they needed.

He dozed in the boat, thinking about all he had learned about his place in things, listening to the drip of water from his drenched hair falling back into the lake and pattering onto the wooden seat.

He wanted to sleep the rest of the day away, but shivering, he climbed onto the shore. He checked the frayed rope and made sure the boat was secure before trudging over pock-marked limestone toward the labyrinth of tunnels that led to her.

He thought hard on what to say before delivering his message to a Drakein guard. The Drakein bared its teeth at him and marched off. Going up and down the stairs to Dinah's longhouse was never an easy task.

Ralen slumped wearily against a stalactite, its uneven surface pressing into the sore muscles on his back. Sometime later, the grey-scaled guard returned, mouth open as it cooled itself. "You may ascend. Alone."

Ralen had never climbed the mountain unescorted. He nodded and set out, trying to recall the turns that led to the staircase. This was another test. If he had not been paying attention before, it would have been easy to become lost in Dinah's labyrinth.

He made a wrong turn, the stone walls darker and damper than he remembered, but he quickly backtracked and returned to the worn path. Both paths had been worn by the passing of many feet over the centuries, which had confused him. He wondered where the other tunnel led.

Eventually, he clambered up the rose marble stairs and added aches in his legs to the catalogue of pains in his arms and back.

He hesitated at the bone doors. There was no need to knock; Dinah knew he was there. The doors swung wide of their own accord. Dinah stood in the entry hall, dressed in red again, a massive window behind her. The doors to the workshop and the library were closed. They were alone.

"Your message intrigued me," she said. "Is it a riddle? 'Obedience is fear. Among the fearless, the powerful are powerless.'"

"No, something that occurred to me when the Keeper spared my life. I don't fear him anymore, so why must I obey him?"

"Because I say so." Her anger flashed like lightning—he had never seen it before, and he was almost blinded by it. One moment she stood calmly beside her window, the next she snatched him up by one arm and pressed her fangs against his throat. The touch of her fingers on his skin was like the touch of Amseel's Blessed Blade, icy and sharp. Unlike the Blade, she made his soul feel thin and vulnerable, as though it might fade into hers and be forgotten. He had never imagined such a peaceful death.

"There are ten thousand ways I could kill you..." she sucked in a breath and stepped back. Two bright red drops glistened on the tips of her fangs. He felt his neck, but the bleeding had already stopped. The anger slid off her features, and she smiled. Her smile lacked the warmth of Anjee's, but it was genuine and made him regret displeasing her.

"You truly do not fear," she said. "I see it in your mind, the acceptance. There is the initial screaming mass of hopes unfulfilled and regret for things left undone, but you choke them into silence and await whatever death descends."

"Death is the only surety." His mother's words, which he fnally understood now.

Dinah smiled even more broadly. "What a beautiful creature you are." She calmly clasped her hands and gazed on him a moment, the way she often gazed upon her fields and orchards. "But your premise is flawed. Obedience is fed by fear, yes, but also by love. Think of those slaves you and the Keeper stole from me to mend his gruesome body."

"I think of them more than I like."

"And think of what he will do without you there to guide his choices."

Ralen's throat tightened. Of course, the lady knew what he really wanted, why he had come here.

"You do not fear for yourself, but you fear for that girl," she said. "It is from love that such powerful fear is born."

He could not hide it. "Yes."

"My point is made. Love forges the strongest chains and breeds true fear. Thus, obedience is inevitable. Unless one neither loves nor fears. And well, you'd have to be a monster like.... Well, you'd have to be such as our Lord to owe obedience to no one.

"It seems we have already resumed your lessons," she added. "I had not planned to see you again until my work was done."

There was more he needed to say, and many more questions he needed answered before she sent him away, so he spoke quickly. "When I came before, I was told you're not to be disturbed, but you have to know about the Conquered. They are all sick."

"I know. My mages were busy with sensitive cargo and unable to intercede before the plague took hold."

"I saw the crates arrive. What was inside?"

"Weapons. Imperfect weapons, which I hope to improve upon. Now they are secured, I will set mages on the task of curing this illness."

"Gordon will be grateful."

"The First Commander is valuable. I would not risk him anymore than I would risk you or my other prized possessions."

"Something else before I go..." he began.

"There is no need for you to go now that you are here. Come. We will pry open the books and resume your tedious education. It will be like old times."

"I'm twelve now. I am not as dull as I used to be."

She revealed those needle-sharp teeth once more. "That comment alone makes me hope."

"There's something else," he repeated, still searching for the words and hoping Dinah would simply pluck it from his mind. She finally obliged.

"You and the girl. I have not forgotten. You worry for her. You want to be with her in the Conquered city, among soldiers and swords and food, as long as the sickness is healed first. Your thoughts are swarming with wants these days. Do not think they sway me."

"But..."

"Do not presume to know what I know or dare what I dare. I have my reasons for everything. You must trust in me without question."

"I do."

She smiled. "I know, and that pleases me. Have faith that, as long as you serve me well, you will be rewarded with food for your body and for your mind, and I will care for what needs caring and watch over all that is mine, as is right. I have high hopes for you. One day you may yet understand."

He stood straighter, silently wondering if he might be made Conquered.

"Oh, I have much greater designs than that for you."

He beamed at her praise but did not doubt that she was aware his real happiness came from knowing that her favor would spare Anjee another day.

"It is more than that," she said. "You love me—as a hatchling loves the first creature to free it from the confines of its shell—and that pleases me very much."

Dinah did as she said she would and sent mages through the Conquered city to quell the rising disease. Ralen saw them the next day, moving house to house, escorted by more white-robed priests.

The Lady watched over her mages like treasure. Those that worked in the Command Center were encircled by guards, and the ones Dinah brought home when she returned from her travels through the Portal were confined in the new wing, within her reach.

Ralen didn't know anything about magic, but he knew mages were powerful, and he wondered what kept them from escaping back through the Portal. They were Marked, just as he was, so perhaps that prevented them from leaving? Or was it the priests who shadowed them?

When Ralen reached Gordon's house the next day, the maid greeted him warmly. "Glad to see you've returned. I thought the illness would have frightened you off for good."

"You weren't frightened," he said, "and, you weren't protected by the Mark."

"I'd rather risk disease than be branded." She hesitantly put a hand on his shoulder. From the look in her eye, he guessed she pitied him. He didn't understand why.

The maid, the soldiers, none were safe. They only fooled themselves into thinking they were, that they were different. He had told Anjee he was proud to be Marked, and it had become the truth. The brand reminded him of reality. He preferred to face his existence unwaveringly, without delusions.

He heard laughter in the rooms above.

"The children and the mistress are recovered," the maid said. "There is a festival air today."

Did the Conquered have festivals? Ralen remembered his old world, holiday decorations hanging from city poles, and so much laughter in the streets. His mother never laughed. He remembered a sense of wanting... The memories were fading. He did not struggle to remember. Let them fade.

He lingered at the bottom of the stairs as the maid went up and announced his arrival. Ralen was content to wait, to make Saren wait as had become the norm, but Gordon hurried down to see him.

The First Commander had a thick bundle of messages. He stood a foot away, not handing the letters over, even though Ralen reached for them. There was a strange expression on Gordon's face. "Thank you," the commander said. "I know what you did."

"I did nothing. It was Dinah's will to aid you when she could."

"As you say, it was our Lady's will, but I believe she was reminded of us when she might easily have forgotten those so low. The Drakein tell me you demanded to see her, and she acquiesced. She would not hear even my pleas. Thank you," Gordon repeated.

Ralen was uncomfortable with Gordon's thanks. He could not say why he faced Dinah for them, other than he was the only one who could.

He tugged the messages from the First Commander's grip and said, "I'll deliver these and return to the Command Center."

"Yes. I still have much to teach you."

Ralen bowed his head as the Conquered soldiers did to their commander. The maid pressed a bread roll into his hand. He gave her a startled look then took off out the door. The smell was wondrous and warm. He ate as he ran.

He'd forgotten the last time he had fresh baked bread, and he was grateful. If only the maid hadn't looked at him that way, as though she expected him to do something more.

He did not bother opening the messages on his way to the Portal. The Keeper had ordered him to discover the code, and he would gain nothing from the letters until he learned it. He disliked spying on Gordon, but he had already risked the Keeper's wrath by freeing the Hasvel, so he would obey, for now.

Saren paced in front of the Portal, more agitated than usual. He snatched the letters from Ralen's grip and threw a satchel full of reports meant for Gordon at his feet. "You didn't even show up yesterday. Hiding under the Lady's skirts I heard."

Ralen resisted being pulled into another one of Saren's childish arguments. "I have to go."

The older boy grabbed his arm before he could leave. Ralen could pull lose but chose not to. Saren hissed, "I know what everyone's saying, how you saved the First Commander's family and everyone else, but I know what you're doing. You're a spy. You'll never be one of us, never know our secrets."

"No one can keep secrets from Dinah," Ralen said.

"She can only invade the thoughts of the Marked. Our thoughts are our own. That's a freedom you'll never know, slave."

Saren was as deluded as the maid. Ralen knew Dinah's power, knew how easily she took life. It was no different than breathing for her. If she believed the Conquered had secrets worth knowing, she would discover them, killing as many as it took in the process.

Ralen spied for the Keeper, but he sensed it was no more than a game to Grin, a way to occupy the monster's time. If Ralen told the Keeper or Dinah that the Conquered were traitors, whether they were or not, there would be pain. He might be a slave, but he had the power to alter the lives of these people. He could ask Dinah to bring health, as she had done ... or death.

Saren must have sensed some of the thoughts stirring behind Ralen's eyes, because he released his grip and stepped back.

"I have to go," Ralen repeated. He swung the satchel over his shoulder and set off.

On his way to meet Gordon, he pondered yet another realization. Dinah thought he was special, and that had made him so.

Chapter Sixteen ~ Incursions

"The Fliers have arrived," Varvec informed the new Bringer, folding the message away after reading it.

"At last. Prepare them for the attack," Adarmis ordered.

Varvec bowed low to show his acquiescence and set off for the camp. He was supposed to advise, but he knew General Adarmis considered him a conquest, another oddity for his collection, who must obey any command. The general was wrong, but now was not the time to correct him.

"Looks like I am in charge of the Fliers, like some sort of military leader," Varvec told his companion as soon as he was out of range of Adarmis's hearing.

Tharaspi clacked her mandibles, and all eight legs trembled in an Akantha display of mirth.

"Glad I could amuse you." Varvec brushed a pale hand along the wiry black hairs of her forelimb and continued up the bare chitin of her midriff to the pyramid-like protuberances on her thorax. They were like Fae breasts, hard and angular, and she chittered flirtatiously. She was getting him excited.

"If you are bored with war games, I can think of other exertions to be had in my tent." Her voice was melodic, an enchantment instilled in her race long ago by Varvec's kind. An Akantha's mandibles and square mouth were fine for the primitive clacking of their own language, but those structures were incapable of the nuances of Fae or God's Tongue.

"Alas, no," Varvac said with dissapointment. Tharaspi was his inferior in every way, but with no other Fae in Adarmis's service, she was the best company available. "There is work to be done. I am flexible, as you know, and I embrace this new calling as Military Leader of Fliers, or whatever I am. It will not last forever."

Varvec was not foolish enough to believe Adarmis would remain Bringer. He had already wasted an army of God-fed in a futile assault against the enemy walls, and his strategy with the Fliers would not succeed either. Their Lord had set an impossible task. The Old Kingdom withstood all assaults. Perhaps, with a thousand worlds on their knees before Him, the Last God believed He could finally achieve victory here. Most likely, Adarmis was meant to fail.

"Lady Dinah never allowed us to do anything," Tharaspi pointed out. "She would not even let me nibble on the slaves. It was all for her and her Keeper. I'm enjoying it here, and I'm glad we are rid of her."

"Careful what you say. That woman has more spies than I and an unforgiving temperament that rivals Our Lord's. We have not seen the last of her."

Dinah had been Bringer for as long as anyone, including the long-lived Fae, could remember. She was the god's favorite, and He had always forgiven her inability to conquer the Old Kingdom. But, she had failed again with her most recent target, and apparently twice was too much.

Varvec had been there, seen her armies blasted into dust by impenetrable machines and her mages slaughtered from afar by an unending torrent of explosive weaponry. Dinah might have rallied and won—she was clever and adaptable when the need arose—but there had been no need for so long, and her response was sluggish. The loss of more than half her army in less than a year could not go unobserved.

The angels whispered in the Last God's ear, and His awful Presence fell across the enemy world. The ground split with earthquakes, and volcanoes rose to smother everything in fire and ash. There was nothing usable left. The survivors were turned into slaves, not even offered Conquered status for their defiance, then fed upon by Dinah or left to slowly choke in the poisoned atmosphere—broken toys to amuse the god's favorites with their dying.

It had been a monumental failure, and Varvec suspected that their Lord had no choice but to punish her. Yet, He did not kill her, and He set Adarmis this chore. When the new Bringer failed, as he must, Dinah would be restored ... or given the same impossible task to regain her position. Varvec smiled, considering how long this little game could go on and all the pleasure he would derive from watching it.

"Now I have amused you. What was it I said?" Tharaspi spoke his language, had been raised in his society, but as a servant, and she could never comprehend the subtleties of his mind.

"Nothing," he told her.

The Fae people understood better than anyone how their Lord thought. Some called the Last God cruel—when they believed themselves unobserved—but only the Fae saw the truth their Lord revealed: the cold, mercilessness of existence and the beauty in pain. Only those who embraced the void, who awakened the passions and who loved death, only they would know life.

Dinah never understood this. Varvec had visited her mountain retreat, where she gazed longingly upon fields and thriving things she could never touch, and he knew she believed herself cursed. The bones piled around her, the death that emanated from her, her very existence on the edge of life and death, these were the greatest gifts the god could bestow. He loved her to teach her this lesson. Varvec wished he were so loved by his Lord.

He recalled his assignment. "Already I forget my duty. You must not distract me so, my darling Tharaspi."

"I have never known a Fae to work so much as you. Pleasure is all they crave."

"Work is my pleasure."

The Fliers were gathered in the courtyard at the center of the citadel. The creatures held javelins in tiny, three-fingered hands attached to muscular arms and membranes of purple skin. They could not throw accurately while flying, but the javelins were not designed for battle. They were for demolition. If enough Fliers speared the enemy wall, the javelins would release a wave of energy and open a hole in the Kingdom's defenses, a hole through which Adarmis could send his army. Or such was the plan.

Varvec smiled to himself again, looking forward to the coming entertainment. "Are you ready?" he asked the Flier captain. He was the only one present who spoke their language, a series of finger signs. They were deaf, so verbal commands, even if they could understand the God's Tongue, were useless.

With a dip of his right, central finger, the Flier captain conveyed his assent.

"Then go," Varvec signed.

The lead Flier launched himself skyward and the others followed. The Fliers could stay above bow range, and hopefully, the Kingdom soldiers would not have time to aim their catapults at the sky.

"Masterful," Tharaspi teased. "You are a born leader. Now can we play? I have found a way to secure those silk bindings so I can't struggle free this time. I'll be ever so good, I promise." Her high cheekbones and heart-shaped head were nearly Fae, boring and ordinary, but the multitude of eyes that stretched across her forehead were alluring in their awfulness. He saw his scowl reflected in each one.

"I told you, I'm working." Varvec twisted the sensitive hair beside one of her antennae until she screeched and skittered a few feet away.

Her delicious pain nearly distracted him again, but he turned his awareness toward the sky.

He watched the beasts ascend into the clouds then dive down just enough to see the Old Kingdom's wall. They had sharp eyes and let the javelins fall from on high, allowing the weapons time to gain momentum, confident they would not miss, even from such a distance.

It took a Fae's far-seeing ability to appreciate the entire display. He watched the Fliers in the air with one part of his mind, the enemy soldiers on the wall with another, and Adarmis' anticipation with a third. A hundred Fliers let their weapons fall, a silver rain that skewered soldiers and split stones on impact. Every one hit, and Adarmis looked triumphant.

Wait, Varvec thought.

Electricity danced along each javelin, arcing from one to the next, killing Kingdom soldiers who got in the way. The air hummed as static built. The anticipation was unbearable, the energy needing release... Then it vanished. The threads of lighting dissipated, and the javelins disintegrated into metal shards.

The Fliers had glided across the enemy line. A wall of wind pounded them back and smashed most into the ground of the killing field. Only a few managed to stay aloft and return to the enclave.

It was a beautiful defeat. Dinah had tried something similar centuries ago.

The Old Kingdom's magic, whatever it was, negated everything used against them. The only tactic that had ever won even the smallest victory was overwhelming force of arms, soldiers dying by the tens of thousands to breach the wall in one place. Of course, once the army was on hostile ground, beyond the range of the Portal, this world fought them even more ferociously.

Dinah had done it, captured the king's encampment. No one remembered that victory or gave her due credit. It would have been more spectacular if the king's wife and child had survived the attack to be taken prisoner.

Dinah, as brilliant as she was, had been unable to hold what she took. Land and sky turned against her. Adarmis was wasting his time here, but he had no choice. Once again, the Fae thrilled at his god's design. Such wonderful torments.

"Now, you may speak, Tharaspi." He smiled as though the battle had been a triumph.

"What do you want me to say?" The Akantha's head was bowed, tears glistening across all those eyes like a child. If only she had lips for a pout. By the Last God, she knew how to inflame him.

He grasped one of her mandibles and twisted, thrilling at her squeal of pain, and then he kissed the smooth surface of her mouth flaps. "Tell me how you want me, how you would die without me."

"I would rather die at your hands."

"Yes." He pulled her towards the overflow tents that had been erected in the courtyard outside the main barracks. They were attracting strange stares from the Conquered, and he preferred to have his play in private anyway.

The Portal flashed: An unexpected arrival. Varvec sent out his far-sight and spotted the messenger. Curse his timing.

"Go ahead, Tharaspi. I will meet you there." He liked to keep the identities of his spies a secret, even from her.

"Don't be too long. I miss you." He sensed the falsehood in her words but said nothing. He enjoyed it all the more that her fear of him was real and not feigned.

He waited for the messenger in an alcove of the temple. The human was an annoyance, reporting on every little occurrence, as if the Keeper passing wind was of importance, but, sadly, Saren was one of the best spies he had in Dinah's ranks. The Drakein were incorruptible, the gobels useless, and the Keeper watched so closely it was as though Dinah assumed he would try to betray her at any moment. The Conquered were not close to Dinah, and they did not have her confidence, but they were Varvec's only source of information. Varvec liked information, whatever advantage he could get to serve his god and His Bringer, whoever filled that role now.

"Yes?" Varvec was in a hurry to get this over with.

"She's got werelings," Saren said.

"What are you talking about?"

"Dinah. I saw the new crates brought through the Portal in a wagon with yellow pennants, like the one she arrived in."

"More Fae yellow." Varvec said, annoyed by her using the neutrality of his race as camouflage for her disobedience. The Last God had shunned her. She should be in exile. It had not been a direct command, but it was customary. She was not wallowing in anguish as was expected.

"What does Locum Paeris say about this?"

"He doesn't know any more than the rest of us. She's forbidden the priests entry to the wereling enclosure."

That would not make Paeris happy. Dinah was plotting something. Varvec felt a twinge of regret that he wasn't by her side to watch her plan unfold, but he had different priorities now. He had a new Bringer.

"Then what are you doing here?" he said, curling his lip at Saren. "You said you could get information no one else can. It has been weeks since her return and you still have nothing of use."

Saren looked at the ground. "Don't worry," he said quickly. "There's a slave she lets into her inner chambers. He carries messages to me every morning. I'll learn what he knows."

"Dinah keeps a slave with her—and he still lives?" Varvec was incredulous. He knew Dinah. None survived her for long.

Saren scrunched up his face. "Ralen is a nothing piece of food."

The messenger was jealous. This slave was growing more fascinating with each passing moment. "If he is food, then why hasn't he been eaten? How long has he served her?" Varvec asked.

"Two years, I think. He was brought in with the last batch of captives."

"Perhaps Dinah is attempting to ration her food supply?"

Saren shook his head. "Before she left last year, she was hungrier than ever. There are barely enough workers left for the harvest and rumors she'll be taking Conquered next."

"Is she raiding for new slaves? What use are werelings?"

Saren squinted as he thought. Varvec had tasked his small brain, and he would get nothing useful from it in any event.

"If you wish to earn the respect of the Bringer, discover Dinah's purpose," Varvec said. "And I want to know everything about this Ralen."

"Why?"

He gave the boy a look that sent him scurrying away.

Varvec was no longer in the mood for Tharaspi. Besides, he should 'advise' the Bringer of the Flier's defeat, as if it were not obvious. With a long-suffering sigh, he returned to Adarmis' side.

High Locum Ettiad cringed in a corner of the command pavilion erected atop the central keep. He was hiding behind his mages, among the pillows and goblet-strewn tables, obviously preferring to be back in the comfort of his temple, but Adarmis would not allow him to delegate his duty to a lesser priest when a large assault was underway.

The general was not happy with the Fliers' defeat. Varvec could tell by the way he stood, silent, staring at the enemy wall as though he could will it to crumble. Once, he might have been able to, but Adarmis was confined by his humanity now, another gift from their Lord.

Varvec decided to delay mentioning Dinah's activities until later. It would be better if he knew more. If only his far-sight could cross Portals and reach past locked doors, he wouldn't have to rely on imbecilic humans.

KING KERVALEN WAS ON his arse, having barely avoided a bolt of electricity from the enemy javelin. It was destroyed now, but he panted for breath, stunned by how close he had come to death. The mages scattered among the troops had acted quickly and saved him, saved the wall. His captain was not so fortunate.

"Talis," he said, touching the dead man's shoulder. "Be with Hestian." He did not believe the captain's soul had anywhere to go but into the soil of the Old Kingdom. Still, he was high priest and Talis had been a believer. The soldier deserved the proper rites.

"Papa!"

Kervalen's mind boggled to see Mala there, dressed in armor and flanked by palace guards wielding polished weapons that had never seen battle.

"What are you doing?" He took her arm and dragged her towards the steps on the Kingdom side of the wall. He saw her wagon below, her favorite pale horse hitched in front, and more palace guards arrayed around it, apparently tasked to guard the animal.

"I received your message. You said I still have much to learn, so I'm touring the land as you suggested," she said.

"You were to parade through villages and get the commoners excited, not come here. You are never to come here!"

"What about when I'm queen? I'll be up here like you, leading the battle. I must learn this too."

In another world, he might have lauded her dedication and courage, but he had lost her mother and brother yards from this spot, and he had nearly died a moment ago.

"You are not queen, and you are not to be here."

There were tears in the corners of her eyes, but a pout would not work, not this time. Her ornamental armor made a tinny sound as he dragged her down to the wagon, her guards a safe distance behind. He wanted to kill them for letting her go upon the wall, but he took a breath and calmed himself. They were not to blame. They had no choice but to obey the heir.

"Where is the steward?" he asked his daughter as calmly as he could. "You were to listen to his directions."

"He took sick in the last village. He was weary, and it was too far back to the castle. We left him there to recover with my Channeler to tend him."

She had left her Channeler behind, the one person able to direct magic in her defense. Kervalen sometimes doubted Mala was of his line. If not for his own features reflected in her face and made feminine.... She was like her uncle, Jhared, he decided: impulsive, with no concept of the world outside palace walls.

It was his fault. His fear had closeted her away. He had protected her for so long he wasn't sure he could stop now, but she needed to see the reality.

He unclenched his jaw muscles and said, "Captain Talis is dead. There is room atop your wagon for his body."

"Papa?"

"You will take him home to his family and help them perform the old rituals."

"I don't know how."

"Then learn this as well. The priests have books. Then see to it that the steward recovers. Don't leave his side until he has, or until you must perform the rituals for him as well."

She nodded, her cheeks flushed with exertion or fear.

"This is what it means to rule the Old Kingdom, to see death and make sense of it. We are nothing without our beliefs," he said.

He turned away to fetch Talis but stopped after a few steps. He strode back and put his arms around her. She clutched him, and, as always, he regretted every harsh word. She had nearly seen him die. "I'm all right, child. I'm all right."

MALA HAD BEEN EXCITED, jubilant to see how their defenses defeated the invaders and destroyed the flying creatures that had attacked them. Then Papa's anger almost made her cry, while his hug sent her over the edge, and so she wiped tears away as she oversaw the transfer of Captain Talis's body. She had disappointed her father yet again, but she wouldn't shirk this duty.

He thought her foolish, she knew. He was foolish. Papa was king! What was he doing on the wall? He was the only one who knew Hestian's secrets, the one who was supposed to be teaching her. How dare he risk his life and not let her risk hers? Especially if it was so worthless? She knew he and others did not want her to rule, but how could she prove them wrong if they didn't let her learn?

She didn't say goodbye but set out with her wagons before they lost the sun. By dinnertime, they had returned to the hamlet where the steward was recovering.

"He's dead, milady," Seago said, coming up to her as soon as she removed her dusty riding gloves. She hated rattling around inside the wagons with her maids and preferred a horse.

"What? How?"

"I believe he was poisoned." Unlike most Channelers, who preferred facts and certainties, Seago was always willing to share his opinions. Mala considered him one of her few true allies and advisors. He didn't hide things from her or think her too young to understand.

"He was not my food taster, so the attack was not meant for me. Who is the next most obvious choice to replace him as steward?"

"It would be someone from Wain Varges, but the culprit knows that and probably hopes you will suspect those most likely to gain, even if they are of your own house. They seek to breed fear and distrust, especially as they know you are on your own. They seek to test you or push you into poor decisions."

"Like visiting the wall without the steward to stop me?" Mala had been stupid, playing into her enemy's hands. She was heir and that meant she had just as many enemies as Papa, if not more. Everyone who wanted his favor hated her for standing in their way.

"Father commanded me to oversee Talis's funeral. Now it will be Gella's too. Looks like we are returning home far sooner than I had hoped." Her first instinct had been to send the bodies back, let the priests in the capital manage without her, but her father's command aside, she was learning she needed to resist her instincts. Her rivals were counting on them and her lack of experience.

"A wise decision, milady," Seago said. It was good he approved. She could have asked him directly for his counsel, but he had taught her long ago to use and rely on her own mind first, then weigh others' opinions second.

Chapter Seventeen ~ Questions

Ralen stood in the entry hall, waiting for Dinah to finish in the workshop and begin the day's lessons in the library. There had been "just one more detail" she needed to attend to. The door was open a crack, and he peeked through the opening.

The new slaves were chained to the wall. Unlike the workers in the cavern below, the mages wore fine clothes, and bowls of fruit and plates of bread were left on the tables for them to snack on while they worked. They were well cared for and would have been pink with health if not for Dinah's presence. She made each of them wan, and their hands shook as they worked at mixing chemicals and etching runes.

She circled the room, watching a smith sprinkle blue powder on sheets of heated iron and pound it over, folding the magical elements into the metal. His hammer strokes missed whenever she stepped too near, and the sweat from his brow flowed in rivulets along the sides of his nose. Ralen thought her project would go more smoothly if she stopped draining them.

He knew she had to eat, and he knew what she ate. At least no one had died recently. The mages she had brought with her seemed to be enough to satisfy her appetite. He suspected that was their primary purpose. They worked hard, but Dinah's knowledge far exceeded theirs. It was clear from the orders she gave and the way they looked to her for direction when a task was finished; she didn't need them for their skill but for their energy.

He grew tired and leaned against the door. It creaked open. Dinah saw him. "Stay away."

He obeyed, taking a weary step backwards. He felt better the farther he got from her. He'd been too close. She had drained him along with everyone else. Was that why there were no Drakein guards or white-robed priests to watch the mages? So they wouldn't be fed on as well? She certainly did not need their protection. No one in this world was as powerful as Dinah.

When she finished, she led him to the library. "Stay out of the workshop. It is too dangerous."

"You're feeding," he said.

"Yes and no. I'm teaching the metal to do what I do and to attune itself with me."

"Teaching it?"

"It is not so easily accomplished. Unlike your education," she said, changing the subject. "Where were we?"

"The Twelve Hundredth Conquest," he reminded her. "But ... I'd like to learn something else."

"A request," she said, amused. "Continue."

Lately, he had been wondering about the Keeper's cages, the wisps and the Hasvel. He and Anjee made sure Gar stayed hidden in the orchard and brought him food whenever they could. The Hasvel seemed to be recovering, but Ralen had promised to return him home, and he had no idea where that was. "When I was with the Keeper, I encountered some writing like nothing I've seen in the library." He took ink and parchment and drew the symbols that had been on the amulet before it transformed into the Hasvel's cage.

"Fae magic," Dinah said. "I have books written in their language, and it would be wise to learn it. The Fae interfere throughout the empire, always believing they know best how to satisfy our Lord."

"This writing isn't in any of the books," he said. "I've looked at every one." It had been a test she had set him—to examine the first page of every book on a set of shelves and recite the first line of each. Only half were written in God's Tongue, and of those he could understand, he remembered fifteen. She gave him the memory task often, sometimes making him read the sixth line or something else at random, and he had improved. Now he remembered fifty at a time.

"And you recall the scripts you couldn't decipher? Good. You have not seen the Fae tomes because they are locked away." She went to a chest and opened it with a touch. She retrieved the books from inside and piled them on the table before him.

"Who would steal from you?" he asked.

"Secrets are contained in these books, long lost magic. I took them when I led the god's army against the Fae capital. I was practically a child. Varvec, my old advisor, was always curious about their contents. He may have dared to steal them, or at least read them without my permission."

"You'll let me read them?"

"They are useless to you—you are not a mage."

"How do you know?"

"Magic has an aura. When it touches me, I feel the coiled up power inside of someone ready to explode. That energy is channeled into many talents, but if you're sensitive to it, you can feel it in all its forms, no matter how subtly controlled."

"I don't have anything like that inside?"

"No. You have something I can't define. There is an aura about you, but it is ... calm. A mage's power is a volcano ready to unleash chaos, while you are like the clear air. They are a supernova, and you are the void. I have a void inside me that hungers for life and power, always hungry, an echo of the Last God's hunger for power, but I can turn the energy it swallows to purpose, to sustain me, or give that power over to our Lord. The void inside you contains nothing, a universe unto itself, without form or purpose. If I fed power into you, I know I would never see it again."

"What does that mean?"

"Someday I will know, and then I may tell you." She shook her head as though trying to wake from a daze. "For now, let us read the dirty little secrets of the Fae."

RALEN HAD VERY LITTLE free time, but throughout his evening lesson with Dinah he was aware of the duty he still owed the Hasvel. So, before dawn, he woke Anjee and went with her into the fields to find Gar. The Drakein guards eyed Anjee on the way out, but when Ralen put a hand on her arm and led her past them, they did not interfere.

Gar was still in the nest atop the walnut tree. It was long past the harvest, the tree near nude as winter approached. The nest looked to be nothing more than a bundle of sticks caught in the boughs.

"Empty hands? I no see food, so why I see you?" Gar asked, head peeking out of the small hole in the ball of nesting material.

"I'll bring food from the larder later," Anjee promised. "I have firewood duty, so it will be a good excuse to come back to the orchard. The problem is, I'm running out of excuses. When winter sets in, mild as it is, I'll be sealed inside the cave with the other slaves until spring. We have to move you."

Gar shrank into his hole. "Me like this spot. No one try eat me. Where go instead?"

"Home," Ralen answered.

Gar climbed out again and looked to the east, toward the Portal in the opposite valley, impossible to see with Dinah's mountain between. "Home..." But the excitement in his expression slowly faded. "It long way. Wing still a bit sore." Gar made a point of wincing when he flexed it, but it looked fine to Ralen. He understood if Gar was frightened, but as safe as he felt now, it was an illusion.

"We don't have a choice," Ralen said. "You can't be left alone out here all winter. You'll starve. You need to come with us. I've thought about it, and the only way to get you through the Portal is in a messenger's pouch. I helped the Keeper gather more treasure, and Saren will need to take those stones to the Imperial City to trade for another captive wisp or Hasvel. I looked it up in Dinah's books: Chelec Var is a jungle province just outside the Imperial City that houses the Fae Portal. Once through the Portal, all you need to do is to slip out of the message pouch and fly home."

Gar's eyes widened as Ralen spoke, and as soon as he finished, the Hasvel darted inside the nest so quickly it was clear there was nothing wrong with his wings. Garbled epithets escaped from the dark hole. Finally, he peeked out again to shake his fist at Ralen. "Crazies! Imperial City? Where you think Fae live? They catch poor Hasvels! How me just fly away home? Huh?"

Ralen looked Gar in his small red eyes. There was something about the half bared fangs and angular face that reminded him of Dinah. "You are stronger than you think. I cannot carry you like a baby every step of the way. All I can do is give you a chance. That's more than Anjee or I have."

Gar's wide, frightened eyes softened, and his taut body slowly deflated. "You right. Me want go home. Me rather die than never see me trees again." He reached out and tore a chunk from his carefully built up nest. The dry twigs crackled in his small fist. "This no home and never be. Not with her up there."

Ralen looked and saw Dinah's red dress on the cliff high above.

Anjee gasped. "Has she seen?"

"She knows," Ralen said. "She must have seen it in my mind as we studied Fae history. I could think about nothing else. She doesn't care. Not about a Hasvel. I'm not sure what she cares about."

"Still, I don't want to wait any longer," Anjee said. "I won't be able to hide Gar in the slave caves. Take him with you now."

Gar tore into his nest and came away with the frayed sack Ralen had carried him in from the Keeper's island. "Yes, me go now. Home is calling. But me feel wrong. You trade another Hasvel for me life? Not right."

"No," Ralen said. "But I don't know what else to do. The Keeper will be sending his payment soon, and you need to stay in my boat until then, so we'll be ready when the time comes."

Gar dropped the burlap sack from the nest and Ralen caught it. He held it open for the Hasvel, who flew inside.

"Let's go," he told Anjee, taking her hand for the walk back past the Drakein guards.

He left Anjee to join the other slaves in their morning duties and took the sack to the edge of the lake.

"Don't move so much," Ralen whispered. "Someone may wonder why my lunch is wriggling. Though most here like it that way, they know I do not."

Gar gave one last kick and then said, "There. Me more comfortable now."

"Quiet. We are not alone." Ralen climbed into his rowboat—his because no one had tried to take it from him—and quickly stashed the sack with the Hasvel inside beneath the wooden seat. He clamped oars to rings and pushed off into the water.

The Keeper no longer sent minions to ferry him across the lake, punishment for freeing the Hasvel, but silver gobel eyes still lurked beyond reach of the oars, always watching.

When he reached the city, he leaned down to drink a ladle of fresh water from a covered container he kept at his feet. He pushed it beneath the seat and left the lid askew. He spoke into his hands, hoping the Hasvel could hear clearly enough, "Do not venture far. There is water and a small sack of grain close at hand. And do not leave the boat. I will return."

"When?" Gar asked a little too loudly.

"When my duties are done." He hopped onto the dock and secured the mooring rope, trying not to glance back as he took off down the city's main street.

SAREN KICKED AT STONES in the trampled ground beside the Portal. The valley was filled with tents, the armies that had once occupied a hundred worlds stationed there, ostensibly to defend the Portal, but in effect exiled along with their mistress. There wasn't enough food, and Conquered, <u>soldiers</u> were to join the slaves in clearing more fields and to help them plant in the spring. Caleb and Locum Paeris had warned this would happen. Perhaps now the First Commander would listen and change his mind.

At least Saren's duties kept him from such embarrassing tasks. Nothing would be more humiliating than scratching in the mud next to Ralen's ilk. Varvec wanted to know about the slave, but why? Ralen was nothing. When he appeared—late yet again—with the morning's messages, Saren said, "I want to speak with you."

"What about?"

He had imagined various ways to get the information Varvec wanted, befriending the cur, putting him at ease, but he lacked the inclination. In the end, he decided there was no need to be devious. Ralen was a child and would answer if Saren told him to. He had better. "Have you seen Dinah's new slaves? The ones locked away in her longhouse?"

"Yes." Ralen didn't elaborate.

"Soldiers shouldn't work the fields. Can't the new slaves do it?"

"No."

Was the food being smart? "What are they doing? Where'd she get them from? Where's she been? And why did she bring werelings here?"

"I don't know. I have work to do. If there's nothing else, I'll see you tomorrow, Saren."

The boy left without a by your leave. Saren clenched his fists. He was asking a slave about the Lady. A slave was carrying messages while Conquered were growing food. No wonder Dinah was spurned; she was insane!

He wouldn't let this happen, wouldn't let that snot, Ralen, talk to him this way. He followed behind until they were in the mountain tunnel. Because the Keeper worked only at night, few travelled between the city and the valley encampment during the day, and the path was empty except for the two of them.

Ralen noticed him and turned back. "What do you want?"

"Answers." Saren shoved him against the wall and punched him in the face. The slave was wide eyed with shock, but when Saren's fist came at him again, the boy wasn't there. His knuckles cracked against hard stone, and he cradled his broken fingers. "I'll kill you," he said through the blinding pain.

The boy took off running toward the city. Saren didn't need to go after him. Ralen would find him with tomorrow's messages, and then he would suffer.

RALEN WAS ANGRY, HIS lip bleeding. He always fought to leash his feelings. What would being furious at the Keeper or Dinah or the Drakein get him except death? But the Conquered were human. Saren was human. They were free of the Bringer's Mark, but they weren't better than him.

Saren had hit him! He wasn't expecting that. He had almost struck back, as the angels had taught him, but they had also warned him not to reveal their teachings.

He hurried through the city and to the docks, wanting some distance between him and the source of his anger. Why so many questions? And why the punch? Could the possibility of working the fields really upset Saren so much?

Saren wanted to know about the mages. Dinah had told Ralen to speak of them to no one. She had enemies, she said. Old enemies and new enemies ... and Saren was always taking messages the wrong direction.

Saren was up to something. He should tell the Keeper, but he hesitated at the thought. The older boy might lose his eyes or worse, and other Conquered would be questioned, like Gordon. The Keeper hated all of them.

He felt his stinging lip. He would tell Grin nothing. While he wouldn't mind if Saren felt a little pain, he didn't want any of the others to get into trouble. He would tell Gordon his suspicions instead—when he no longer needed Saren.

He stood at the edge of the dock, listening to water lapping at the pylons. The rowboat, containing his hidden cargo, was barely visible in the oily lamplight. He needed to be done with the Hasvel, and his plan depended on Saren and his long messenger's legs.

He waited for the gobels. They expected him to be in the city with Gordon, so when they finally showed, they were obviously curious to find him staring at the water. One asked, "Why you not working? All slaves must be working, working..." Ralen recognized the gobel that had given up its claw for the knife he still carried in his belt pouch. It and the others began to whisper "working ... working..." over and over.

"Take me to the Keeper. I know there's something he wants done, and I'm volunteering."

Claw cocked his head, as though listening, and Ralen knew the gobels had already told their master.

Most of the gobels slipped beneath the water, leaving only Claw behind, large silver eyes watching. He was quiet, and Ralen felt uneasy.

"What are you waiting for? Bring me a scor... or am I to row? Am I still being punished?" Ralen did not want to bring the Hasvel too near the Keeper again. The goal was to get the fairy far away, but he needed the Keeper's gems and a genuine message for Saren to carry to the Fae lands in order to do that.

Claw listened again for Grin's thoughts. "Not yet. Not yet. Soon I will bring you, but Master is busy now. Busy, busy..." The gobel sniffed at the air and slowly swam toward the rowboat. "Me smell..."

"Where are you going?" The whole plan would be ruined if the Hasvel were discovered now. "If Grin doesn't want to see me, fine. You can leave then." He raced to the boat and found a small campfire inside, built on flat stones, wheatcakes roasting beside it and a sheepish Gar darting back inside the burlap sack.

Ralen stamped out the flames and picked up a cake. It was hot, and he juggled it hand to hand, blowing on it. He tossed it in his mouth and swallowed. It was no bigger than a bite. "My lunch," he told the gobel in words the creature would understand. "Not for you."

The gobel kept staring and licking its lips. Finally, Ralen tossed the remaining cakes toward the center of the lake. "Go get them." Claw took off, as though determined to catch them before they hit the water.

Gar made a disappointed groan beneath the seat. He must be peeking.

Ralen hissed, "A fire? No wonder the Fae caught you!"

"Me is cook. Can't expect to eat mealy old grain raw."

"Shhh." The gobel was back already.

"Yum, yums. But..." Claw looked confused. "Why you give me your lunch? You want trade?"

"No." Ralen hadn't thought about it. The gobel had looked hungry, and he knew what hunger felt like. "I didn't do it to get anything from you. You're a slave like me, and I know what it feels like. Kindness is when you do something for someone just because they are in need. I didn't do it to get anything in return."

The gobel looked even more confused, and then it said the word slowly, testing it out: "K-i-n-d-n-e-s-s."

Ralen had almost forgotten the meaning of the word himself.

The gobel looked about to ask something else, but then it cocked its head again, receiving a silent command. "Master wants to see you now." Claw dived and then quickly resurfaced with a scor. "Here, me help."

"I can do it." Ralen placed the scor on his face and jumped in to draw attention away from the boat and smoky residue of Gar's cooking.

When the gobel took hold of his arm, he thought he saw something in its expression. Not hunger for once. Worry? Then the gobel was off, the water of the lake itself seeming to move aside and push them along, so they went faster than any boat Ralen had ever seen.

THE GOBEL HE'D DECIDED to call Claw dragged him to the island, and he pulled the scor off his face rather than waiting for the gobel to do it. He knew the best places to press to get it to painlessly release its needle hooks. He tossed the jelly creature into the water, and it swam away.

Grin's bulk was visible in the semi darkness. When Ralen drew closer, he realized there was another figure sitting in the pool with him—a yellow haired girl.

The ground seemed to fall away. "Anjee?"

She did not make a sound. He didn't even know if she was alive. He was frozen, unable to move closer, unable to look.

"Anjee?" he repeated.

Grin wiggled his fingers in silent laughter. Dozens of gobels whispered, "Anjee, Anjee..."

"Yes," she said, barely breathing the word. She was too terrified to say more, her body nestled against the monster's chest.

Ralen pulled her out of the water and held her. She shivered and dug her fingers into his skin so hard it hurt.

"You spoil my fun," Grin said.

Ralen looked into the Keeper's stolen eyes and willed him to die. Saren had made him angry, but this was beyond anger. He had endured the Keeper's torturous tasks, helped with the 'parts', and he had not drowned himself, even though sometimes he thought about it, because he had Anjee to return to. Now, the Keeper had her.

"Let her go," Ralen said.

"I was told you wanted to volunteer for a job. I never trust volunteers, not unless I hold a loved one hostage. The gobels tell me you guard her as jealously as the old dragon gods guarded their lairs. What is she, your sister?"

"No."

"A bit young to claim a woman, boy. This one doesn't even smell ripe. Well, it matters not. What matters is that I cannot trust you to do good work for me. You accomplish nothing. Nothing incriminating on The First Commander, no code..."

"I will give you all you want and more. But you cannot have her." He glared at the nearest gobel in such a way that it stepped back, and Ralen took a step toward the lake, Anjee in his arms.

"I am not done talking to her," Grin said.

"She doesn't know anything except wheat and apples and these dark caves."

"She knows you."

"Then talk to me. Not to her."

"You never have anything to say."

"And I'll never tell you anything again unless you let her go."

"I am Keeper. You must obey me."

Dinah had said as much, but there were things beyond obedience and fear.

Yes.

"You can do anything you want to me," Ralen said, "but not to her. Not to her."

He freed Anjee's fingernails from his skin and gently carried her through the green mass of gobels. They bared needle teeth and hissed. Ralen kicked at those that did not move out of his way quick enough.

Nothing followed them into the water except the Keeper's deep, rumbling laughter. Anjee shivered in his arms but trusted him, even as the water inched its way up to her chin. She couldn't swim.

Ralen had learned with a scor on his face, half-drowned by gobels as he was dragged across the lake each day. They had often left him a little way from shore, so he'd had no choice but to flail his arms and legs until he made it back to land. Another thing he'd learned the hard way. Now Anjee would have to learn too.

"Relax and lay flat. Float like a board on the river. I've got you." He made soothing sounds, filled with fear for her and a growing certainty that he could not bear any more such fear.

They floated on their backs and kicked with their legs. When the phosphorescent glow from the worms on the ceiling went out, at the Keeper's command no doubt, there was nothing to guide them but the distant lights of the city. Anjee tired after twenty minutes. He heard her panicked coughs, so he held her, but he was tired too.

"I've got you," he repeated, wanting it to be true, but she slipped down again and choked. He lifted her higher and went under himself, holding his breath. When he came up, she went down again. He sobbed, feeling her slipping out of his grasp, his arms weak and shaking. She fought and thrashed for air, her terror drowning them both.

"Anjee..."

You can't save her.

Who'd said that? He had believed the thoughts his own but now wondered if Dinah were speaking to his mind. She never had before, and it didn't feel like her. Perhaps it was his own fear.

"Here, here, here," a new voice whispered in the dark. Claw rose out of the phosphorescent water, a scor in each hand. He clamped one on Ralen's face, but Anjee was moving too much for him to reach her. Ralen took the second scor and wrapped his legs around her, summoning the strength he needed to hold her still long enough to slap the scor on her face.

She fought the creature, biting at it to keep it away. The gobels must have brought her to the Keeper with one, and she did not want another. He knew the horrible feeling of suffocation, needle hooks in the soft skin beneath cheeks and jaw, and too little air, but some air was better than none. He forced the scor onto her face, shushing her as she flailed and splashed. She eventually calmed, going almost slack, so that he checked to make sure her heart still beat.

Claw pulled them to the rocky shore. The gobel returned to deeper water and waited, watching them with wide eyes. Anjee lay exhausted at the edge of the water and did not stir when Ralen gently removed her scor. He tossed both creatures back towards the gobel. "The Keeper took long enough to send you."

"Master did not send," Claw whispered. "Do not tell, do not tell..." He vanished into the lake.

Anjee's eyes were open, but she was silent, no energy to spare for talk, still in shock from the crossing and her first meeting with the Keeper. He too should have been too tired to move, but anger surged through him, and he rose to his feet.

He paced, his fury growing. "I'm going to kill him."

Anjee did not ask who, but his words made her stir. She said, "He's not a pathetic gobel. He's master of the gobels." She held her side and struggled for breath. "He didn't hurt me. He was scary. That's all. I'm all right." She was trying to calm him, but her trembling limbs and shaky voice belied her words.

"You don't know everything he's done," Ralen said.

The cold certainty of what he must do wouldn't leave him. The angels had taught him to fight, not only to defend, but to strike. They never explained why they wanted him to know those things, but he did know them. He could kill Grin ... if no one interfered, if he didn't fear Dinah's anger. Or want her praise.

He sagged. He had to do something. "Come with me."

Anjee made a surprised sound when he slung her over his shoulder and carried her past hundreds of Marked slaves. They stared at the ground on their way out to the fields, like animals, powerless and unaware. None ever spoke to him, and he had come to expect their fear and silence. He understood why the Conquered scorned him, if this was all they knew of the Marked.

"Where are we going?" she asked. "I told you, I'm all right. Don't ... don't do anything." She knew him, knew what he felt without a word spoken, so she must know she couldn't stop him.

He led her to the tunnel guarded by Drakein. "I want to see Dinah," he told them.

Chapter Eighteen ~ Prayers

Dinah watched Ralen get on his hands and knees before her. The girl copied him. She was as drenched as he was, the water from their tattered clothes forming a puddle on the wooden floor. Dinah raised an eyebrow. "What is this?"

"You give us only what you want, when you want, Lady, and I dare not ask for anything more, but I have heard of prayers. Dinah, hear my prayer," he said.

"...I'm not a god." Dinah heard the tremor in her own voice. She looked around, hoping no one saw the boy's prostrate form. She allowed no priests in her sanctuary, and even her devoted Drakein were out of sight, beyond the doors, but there was no telling where angels lurked.

"If you are not a god then who is?" Ralen asked.

"I am immortal, yes, and powerful, but the Last God is greater. He would destroy me for even thinking myself equal."

"You are greater than me and could destroy me any time you choose," Ralen argued. "Some of the Conquered pray to the Last God. They ask for glory or strong families or promotion, for an end to this exile, but they never get what they ask for. You can grant my prayer. Will you watch over Anjee?"

That was why he'd brought the wretch here. "What has happened?" Dinah asked.

"Protect her from the Keeper."

"I'm all right," Anjee insisted. "Forget me, my Lady."

Dinah had forgotten her. How strange. She would not make that mistake again. She weighed her words before saying, "The Keeper is harsh, and he makes you strong, Ralen ... but there is no need for the girl to be strong. I will answer your prayer."

She was not struck down. The god had not heard her heresy.

"Thank you," Ralen said.

Anjee did not speak. She looked at Dinah warily, nose pointed at the ground but eyes straining to see. Dinah had read the mind of the girl once, long ago, when she chose her from among all the others and deemed her a worthy tool. She had sensed a thread of energy connecting her to the boy who could look upon a god, but that was all she'd been able to do. Now the girl was Marked, her slave, body and soul, and she sifted through her thoughts. There was a vast darkness. Dinah felt her insides dropping away, falling, a glimpse of Anjee's nightmares.

Dinah took a deep breath and withdrew from the girl's mind. She would never allow the Keeper to harm the child. "You will remain here in my home. All will know I protect you."

"Yes, my Lady," Anjee said. She did not sound happy. "Wha..." Speaking to Dinah seemed to frighten the air from her lungs. "...What about Ralen? Will he stay with me?"

"He is not excused from his duties among the Conquered," she said. "Not all prayers are answered. He is allowed to visit my home whenever he chooses. I'm sure we will both see him often." Especially with you here.

"Thank you," Ralen repeated.

The girl looked as though she had been kicked, but she firmed her lips and lowered her gaze in acceptance.

ANJEE FAREWELLED RALEN at the top of the staircase. She didn't want to be here, in this house of bones with the Dark Lady. The Keeper had merely frightened her. What Ralen had done was far worse. They would be separated. She could no longer hold him in the night and make sure he was alright. Her greatest fear would come true.

"I want to stay with you in the cave like before," she said.

"I'm to live in the city and learn from the Conquered, and you're to stay with Dinah. It's better this way. You'll be safe."

"No."

"You have to, or the Keeper..."

"What about the Keeper? What won't you tell me?"

"You'll fear me. Hate me."

"I won't."

He seemed to struggle against something inside. Then, in a rush, he told her. He told her about choosing victims for the Keeper, removing 'parts' and torturing wisps and the Hasvel for their magic.

Anjee had known. She had seen the slaves taken away by Ralen and the gobels, slaves that never returned. She'd seen the way Gar looked at him.

"I don't fear you. I don't hate you." She stroked the back of his head and hummed a soothing lullaby.

Ralen curled into a ball at her feet and wept. He kept no secrets from her now. She wished she could share her fears with him, what she knew, but that would change things. Make it worse for certain.

"Girl," Dinah called from the other side of the door.

Ralen wiped away his tears. For once, Anjee wasn't the one crying. It would do no good. It was too late. "You should go," she said.

He nodded and slowly let go of her hand as he backed down the steps. When he had sunk from view, she turned to the doors of the longhouse. They opened, and she felt Dinah's magic stronger than ever, tugging at the doors, at her body, slipping into her mind. She slunk into the room and got down on her knees before her mistress. "What do you want of me?" she asked.

Dinah circled her, assessing. Anjee heard slippered feet brushing against the polished floor and felt the red dress on her bare arms like the touch of spider webs.

"Stand. Come with me."

Anjee obeyed. She joined Dinah beside a tall window at one end of the gigantic library. Dinah passed her hand across the glass and frost grew over the surface. Soon, the window was covered in thick crystals of ice. Magic. Anjee thrilled to see something from stories come to life, but she knew there was a price. She felt weaker, her energy stolen by the Dark Lady.

"Tell me what you see."

"Cold," Anjee said.

"No. What you <u>See</u>. You can't lie to me, child."

There was no hiding it now. She had hoped to be forgotten by the lady, but that happy future was not to be. She stared at the facets of ice, long streaks and sharp angles, rainbows torn from the sunlight. She unfocused her thoughts, released the barrier she had erected between her and the images and let them come. All her life, she had seen things in her mind, even before she met Ralen—but the visions were always about him.

She heard herself answering without wanting to. "I see Ralen, a few years older than he is now, surrounded by an army of shackled dead. He leads them."

"...I knew you would be useful," Dinah said as she ran a finger down the side of Anjee's face. "Welcome to my home."

RALEN STOOD ON THE edge of the turquoise lake not knowing where to go. Anjee would no longer be waiting in the cave to hold him while he slept. He had lost his home all over again.

It was better this way, better for Anjee. The Keeper was dangerous.

And Dinah is not?

"Who's there?"

There was no answer. He wondered if this place was doing to him what it had done to the other slaves, making him crazy, arguing with himself.

The lady had never lied to him. She had brought him into her confidence, had let him read the Fae books. There was knowledge in them he'd rather be without, magic based on blood sacrifice and torture, of which the Keeper's torment of the wisps and Hasvel were but a pale shadow. The books explained how to raise the dead and send plagues to ravage lands. The Fae no longer possessed this magic, and Dinah said no one but the Last God should. She had trusted Ralen with it, though, and he would trust her with Anjee.

The Keeper's island was visible in the distance. The light from glow worms surged, spreading from the island toward him, turning the stalactites pale blue. The Keeper was watching.

"Are you finished?" he shouted. "I'm tired of threats. I serve, as the Lady commands, so let me serve and be done with it!"

He waited. The glow worms slowly dimmed, and he clenched his fists, frustrated with these games. The Keeper had heard him.

He glared at the wide lake and the distant lights of the Conquered city. His boat and the Hasvel were on the other side. He needed the gobels. He needed the Keeper. He was stranded otherwise. The scors lived deep beneath the lake and only a gobel could fetch one for him.

"I will do whatever you ask," he shouted one more time into the dark. She was safe, and that was all that mattered. "A gobel is all I need."

Be careful what you wish for.

The still lake water rippled and surged. A green gobel head rose above the turquoise water, then another and another. The water boiled with them, more than he had ever seen before. Thousands.

Their emaciated arms and sharp claws reached out for him as a hundred whispers became something like the sound of the sea calling, "Come to Master ... come to Master ... come..."

Revulsion coiled like a brown snake in his stomach, and he took a step back, but a thousand hands reached for him, each covered in claws and each of those a killing blade.

Death is the only surety.

He let go of the fear and walked into the lake. The horde of gobels embraced him, their clammy skin pressed against his, arms that had ripped the limbs from corpses grasping his. A dozen scors were offered, extending their long fingers, and soon one smothered his nose and mouth, stealing his breath and offering a beggar's portion of air in return.

Instead of the water pushing him along, it felt as though the gobels passed him from one to another across the lake, so that each had a touch and a chance to wet him with their hungry, slavering mouths.

He stumbled onto the rocky shore of the Keeper's island, knowing he had crossed a sea of flesh instead of a lake. The Keeper had made his point.

"You have finally met all my children," the Keeper said, grinning as always. "What do you think?"

"You are Master of the Gobels, Keeper of the Lake, and I am only a slave." Let the beast hear whatever would please it.

"Yes, I am Master." Grin gestured to a covered cage on a pedestal of stone beside his murky pool. Ralen tensed, for the burlap sack covering it looked like the one he'd hidden the Hasvel inside, but when a gobel removed the covering, he was surprised to see another gobel inside. It was almost comical, the creature hunched in the broken and too-small cage meant for a fairy. Then he saw the mutilated finger on its right hand—Claw.

"Master ... Please... Master," the gobel begged.

"Silence."

Claw went silent, as did the whispers from the army of gobels all around. Ralen had grown used to the whispers, and their sudden absence was disturbing, making his skin prickle. He was hyper-aware of the vast, dark cave that had long ago swallowed them all.

Yes, Hell should be quiet as the grave, quiet as the small house he'd once lived in, where his mother had stared at herself in the mirror each night, lost in the void of her dark eyes.

"I am Master," Grin continued, "yet this one thinks he serves you."

"I would have died without the scor he brought," Ralen said. Anjee would have died—and that meant more to him. "Aren't you supposed to keep me alive?"

"I may not have chosen this form, this existence, but I choose who within my domain lives and dies and when. I command my gobels, not Dinah. And I command you. I need power, and this gobel has it. You know what to do."

Ralen knew. He had tortured enough poor creatures for the Keeper. It was for that transgression, the pain he had caused, that he owed the Hasvel safe passage back to its home. He pulled the claw knife from his belt pouch and brandished it before the creature that had sacrificed a limb to create the weapon. He saw the fear in the gobel's eyes, the certainty of coming death.

Ralen opened his hand and let the claw knife rest across his upraised palm. "This is yours," he told the caged gobel. "I have no right to it." He needed the Keeper's gems and an errand for Saren to free the Hasvel, but he would not inflict the same torture he sought amends for on another, not even a gobel, especially not this gobel.

"Gaw!" the Keeper spat, furious. "Take him!"

Ralen spun, putting his back to the cage and took hold of the knife the way the angels had taught him—fingers closed tight around the join between hilt and blade, pommel resting lightly against the base of his palm—and it was clear the Keeper, whose dead, stolen eyes he stared directly into, understood he was still willing to fight.

The Keeper raised a blubbery hand, and the gobel horde halted in mid-lunge. Grin laughed like a canyon of dark mirth. "You call my bluff, boy. I would like to kill you and watch my gobels pick your sinews from between their teeth, but Dinah is still master of the Master. I cannot hold fear of death over you, but I can hold your weakness.... 'Claw' use your remaining talons to slit your own throat."

"Yes, Master."

"No." Ralen turned to the cage in time to see Claw obey, yellow blood beginning to pour.

"Stop," the Keeper said casually, and Claw stopped tearing. "Heal him." Gobels encroached on the cage, ignoring Ralen, and long tongues reached through the bars to lick away blood and seal the gash in their brother's throat.

"You see," Grin said, "I am Master. Now, I will spare this disobedient piece of flesh, but only if you serve me well."

"I said I would serve."

"I know, but I feel much happier when I know you have a good reason. I see you do not have the stomach for poking meat in cages—and for that reason I really do not understand what use Dinah has for you—so I do not expect you to do a very good job. I will set tasks simple enough for you to accomplish. You will acquire another Hasvel to replace the one you let escape."

"I will—"

"—I'm not finished. Only when I have that Hasvel in a cage will I release Claw from this one. Understood?"

"Yes. I will need the gems I gathered." Ralen held out his hand.

Grin reached into the pool, shifted aside a layer of fat across his stomach, and lifted out a small bag the exact color and texture of human skin.

Ralen tried not to think about the tiny hairs covering the bag as he reached for it.

Grin hesitated a moment, still not trusting Ralen's agreeableness, but with a sigh of escaping gases, he let the macabre purse go. "Tell the Locum of my needs, not the First Commander."

"Not Saren?"

"I have noticed the messenger has developed an increased sense of piety. I would judge whose lead he and the others truly follow. Now go."

Ralen obeyed, but furiously wondered how Grin's endless paranoia would affect his plan to free the Hasvel—and now Claw.

Ralen swam up to the boat moored beside the city. He placed the bag of gems inside, whispering to Gar to stay hidden. After removing the scor the gobels had given him, he held on to the jelly creature and wrapped a fragment of netting around it. He secured the caged scor to the boat's rope so that it was submerged but unable to escape. Now he would not need to wait for a gobel to bring him one.

He would find the Locum in the morning. Conquered and priests preferred the daylight, and so did he.

Without Anjee, there was no reason to sleep in the slave caves among the cowed and insane Marked, and his boat had been taken over by Gar—it was surprising how much space one small Hasvel could take up—so only one place remained.

A short time later, he knocked on Gordon's door. The corners of the maid's mouth turned up when she saw him. "I thought you were done for the day?"

He stepped inside and saw the family seated for evening meal. The scent of roast meat was wondrous. "I need a place to sleep," he said, trying not to stare at the table. He sucked back saliva that threatened to spill down his chin.

"Here," Gordon's wife pulled out an extra stool. "Sit with us. We were about to begin the Lord's prayer."

Chapter Nineteen ~ Secrets

Anjee felt as though a cold hand was sifting through her insides. She was in the presence of Death.

"I was never blessed with second sight," Dinah said. "I have other attributes in recompense. Strange that I should find you, girl, on a world without any trace of magic, yet bearing one of the rarest gifts of all. And so close to him. It is as though Fate already had plans for you both."

Anjee watched the ice on the window slowly melt and pool on the sill. It seemed Dinah could do anything, steal thoughts and feed on life. Could she taste her regret?

"Fate is beyond gods," Dinah continued. "It is said she dreamed the universe into existence and dreams the paths of our lives each day. I have always trusted in her and let her guide me where she will. Now, here I am and here you are."

"I don't want to be here."

"Fate does not care for wants."

Anjee tried to stay as silent as Ralen often was, tried to calm her mind, make it like a lake, like a mirror, revealing nothing of herself.

The Mark burned.

"You can't win, girl. Your soul is mine."

Anjee shivered as heat poured from the Mark, sending burning tendrils through her veins, along her spine and sinews, into her skull. It hurt so bad she wanted to rip the tatoo from her skin. She scratched at it, but her hand pulled away of its own accord. She wanted to open her mouth and scream, but she couldn't even do that.

"It's called compulsion," Dinah said. "You can fight it, just as I have often fought against the Last God's hold, but you will fail, as I did. We are both animals chained to greater masters, but in your case, I am the one holding the leash. Now, See for me."

Scattered visions of Ralen swirled within Anjee's mind. She didn't need the ice to see them; they greeted her every night when she went to sleep. Whenever she wasn't busy hauling apples from the orchard or focused on the words of a song, the images would come, uncontrolled. Terrible.

Ralen's arms were plastered with blood up to his elbows. Blood was caked into his clothes and armor, so when he finally peeled off his undershirt it came away with a sucking sound, as though the residue of death was reluctant to leave him. Pink lips, painted and perfect, kissed his shoulder.

The image changed before Anjee could focus on what the last one meant, and with the shift came the sound of metal striking metal, of screams filling a gray sky. The sickly sweet smell of gore was everywhere, and the earth was red. Not with blood—the blood looked like black pools around the fallen scattered at Ralen's feet—the soil itself was rust red and lifeless.

The image shifted again, faster this time. A black wall, his fingers searching for a crack, a handhold. A claw cuts the stone...

Again. There is a burst of white light. A giant man steps through an archway...

Again. Translucent membranes flecked with veins and pulsing vessels. The wing stretches...

Again, the image shifts, and this time it comes with a familiar roar, as if all sound in creation was rolled into one and the black night were reaching out for her....

Anjee screamed. The Mark released its hold, and she pushed the images away.

Dinah took a step closer. The Lady calmly watched her tremble and sweat, just as she might watch a thrashing fish thrown onto the riverbank. "I saw," she said. "So many wondrous sights in your mind, child. He seems to be doing all I hoped."

"You have not seen him screaming, his blood spattered on the outstretched wing, his blood pooled around his bloated corpse. You have not seen everything there is to see. I watch him die a hundred different ways every night, hear his dying words every time I let the images come."

"But not this time. This time you saw him a conqueror, saw others' blood spilled at his feet. Fate is on my side, child, and I will lead Ralen to this path."

Anjee shivered. "I've seen you in the visions too. I've seen what you've done. What you will do. You are a monster. But the worst thing you ever did was make Ralen love you, trust you, no matter how much I warned him not to."

"Why did you not tell him about your visions then? Surely, he would have listened?" Dinah bared her fangs in a cruel smile.

Anjee didn't want to answer any more questions. She wanted to curl up in a corner of the caves and hide from everything and everyone, but the Mark broke down her defenses and long pent up words poured from her mouth: "The first night I met him, after I knew Ralen was real, I had a different dream. The worst one yet. One vision after another after another that I couldn't wake from.

"In the dream I told him, and we tried to change his path, to escape you, but everything turned out wrong. Each thing we did made it worse, and soon I saw life after life without him, where he was dead. A voice spoke to me, a mother's voice, but not the mother I'd been born to. She said my dreams were her dreams, dark dreams, and Ralen was not to know about them, for he needed to dream anew.

"When I woke, Ralen said I'd been whimpering. I told him I was hungry, that's all. To keep it secret was the only safe course I saw. I don't remember everything, but, in the dream, when I vowed not to tell him, that was when I finally woke up."

Dinah nodded, as if she could know, as if she had any idea what it felt like to be so helpless. "Fate spoke to you. You are fortunate, but you do not comprehend. She is all powerful, inescapable. You see variations, other paths, but in the end, they are only vapors. We are here now. Ralen's destiny is with me, and that cannot be altered. Fate will not let you take him from me."

Anjee sagged and let the tears come. "I saw this too. It was better when you didn't know. Now there will be only pain. I don't understand. What are my visions for, if not to save him?"

"They are for me." Dinah dug through an ornate chest and brought out a finely made black bowl. She blew the dust from its surface and set it on the table. "There are forces in the universe that want me to succeed. I felt it before I met the god, before I made Him what He is. You were sent to me, child. You will help me see the way ahead and prepare. That is your destiny."

Dinah held a palm over the bowl, and the melted ice from the window crawled across the floor, up the table leg and into the bowl, filling it with clear water to form a perfect mirror. "Look here," she ordered. "I've read this is how seers of old practiced their craft."

Anjee's tears rippled the surface. "I don't see anything."

"You lie. There are always flashes in your mind, too quick for me to discern."

"Most make no sense."

"Figure them out. That is what the tools of scrying are for. You will be a useful seer, or you will be dead. Understood?"

Anjee nodded. Was this her destiny? To be a slave? Nothing but a tool?

She looked carefully into the bowl and saw dark hair, a flowered skirt swirling, and laughter. Ralen laughing. "She will make him happy."

"No, you are the one," Dinah said.

"I can only bring him pain."

"You possess the ability to shatter his soul, and that is more powerful than mortal love. Forget her. Show me something else."

Darkness. Anjee gasped at the aching void in her chest.

"This is what you fear?"

"The darkness ... no air ... I can't breathe. It's here." She slapped the bowl away, and it cracked against the wooden floor, spilling water on the ancient wood.

The drops held a fractured image of black feathers.

A fresh tendril of fear went down her spine. She hadn't meant to reveal Ralen's secret, but Dinah noticed the feathers. The Mark burned.

"Ashkal and Amseel have been here? They've been with Ralen?"

"Yes," Anjee answered, unable to do anything else. "They've been teaching him."

Dinah paced. "What do they want?"

"I don't know, but they tell Ralen to keep them secret."

"He has." Dinah's voice shook, and she looked more disturbed by Ralen's ability to keep secrets than any of Anjee's visions. The Lady recovered her composure and kicked the shards of the bowl. "Clean this up."

RALEN RAN HIS FINGERS across the colored stones he'd dredged from the bottom of the lake. Emeralds, sapphires... he knew the names, and he knew they were considered valuable, but why? Because they were pretty? Did that make them as valuable as a life?

Stones like these had bought Gar's life for the Keeper, and now to save both him and Claw, he would use these to buy another life to take Gar's place.

It was wrong, but nothing had been right for a very long time.

He tucked the frayed sack full of gems into his leather messenger's satchel and showed Gordon's sigil to the guards at the tunnel gate.

"Back again?" the woman asked.

There was usually only a morning run of messages. He'd told the First Commander he needed to do something for the Keeper, which was truth, but he now told the guards a different part of the truth: "Special run. A message for the Locum."

"Locum Paeris is a great man," she said. "It's a shame he's being punished along with us."

"Hopefully not for much longer," the guard on the other side of the gate added.

"Here, here." She inserted her key in the lock and swung the gate open. Ralen ran through without adding to the conversation.

He didn't know anything about the Locum, only that the man was Master of the priests, just as Grin was Master of the gobels.

He clutched the satchel tighter as he entered the Portal valley. The Conquered were looking as hungry as the slaves, and with these they might buy a feast—if they could get it across the Portal. Saren could help with that, but the Keeper had told Ralen to see the Locum instead. It was best to obey.

Someone as important as Master of the priests would not listen to a slave's request without the gems to show, so he carried his satchel up the steep temple steps and knocked. When no one answered, he pushed open the door—solid copper three times his height—and stepped inside.

High, narrow windows set in the quartz walls let in daylight. Giant pillars of bleached wood supported a square beamed ceiling.

He saw Conquered scattered across the massive room, all on hands and knees, foreheads pressed against the floor. Light shone from a dais at one end of the room, not flame but a bright glow that reminded him of the lights from his homeworld. He knew it must be fueled by magic, because there was no glass to contain it, nothing except a circle of priests and chained mages at the base of the dais.

A man robed in white and gold stepped out of the light and stood for a moment before the crowd, as though savoring the moment, even though none of the cowed people had seen his magic. He noticed Ralen staring, and his brow furrowed. Ralen glanced once more at the bowed forms all around and sank onto his knees. He lowered his head to the stone floor, which was carved in symbols and phrases in God's Tongue. He recognized several lines from Dinah's books: *Forsake your gods as He will be the Last.... All shall perish at His hand or in His name...*

Ralen did not bother trying to read more. He raised his head just enough to peek at the rest of the ceremony. The Locum must be the one who had stepped out of the light. The man moved to a marble altar in the center of the chamber and began to read from a book displayed there.

"Any who think they speak for God or who would go against the will of His Bringer—or His chosen Locum—should be burned without pity." He looked up and continued in the same tone, reading the words from memory, "When faith itself is in question, the Last God Himself will sear the unbeliever's soul in torment for all eternity. None are above this order, no matter how high their station. Extreme severity should be shown to those who attempt to shield themselves with the protection of any potentate—be he First Commander or Keeper—and no one, especially one who would call himself holy, should lower himself by showing toleration for heretics of any kind...."

The Locum let his gaze travel across the room. Ralen looked down at the stone once more and waited for the sermon to finish. It was a long time before the final ceremonies were complete and the crowd of worshippers drifted away, many arguing with each other in whispers.

Priests and the mages tethered to them began to drift away as well, returning to the depths of the temple. The Locum turned to leave, pretending not to see Ralen waiting, so Ralen was forced to call out, "I have a request from the Keeper."

The Locum and his retinue stopped and stared as though a mongrel dog had come into the temple and begun to bark. "I sensed the Mark on you. What sort of chattel delivers messages for that cursed construct and yet speaks in the holy language?" the Locum asked.

"One who carries an offering." He lifted the satchel and let the stones inside rattle alluringly.

The Locum stretched out his hand, a mage behind him grunted in pain, and the satchel flew from Ralen's grip to scatter its contents across the floor. Ruby and diamond droplets glistened next to the stone inscriptions and made them look like poor scratches in the sand.

"Gems and gold—riches for those chained to earth. I am sustained by the light of Our Lord, and they hold no luster for me. What use have I for such offerings?"

Ralen wondered if the sermon had ended, for it seemed the Locum was putting on a show for the remaining priests. He needed to get the Locum alone. "The Keeper believes you have friends who would value this offering and who would give something he values far more in exchange."

"Exchange, value ... these are not words that matter to the light. Have you thought much on your soul? Do you have one?"

"If I do, it must be a dark and evil one to deserve the punishment of this life."

"Ah, an agile tongue too. I must say, I have never before appreciated the possibilities of discourse with a slave."

"Then let us speak more." Ralen bent down to gather the scattered gems.

The Locum moved closer and put his sandal over the ruby Ralen was reaching for. "You speak obliquely, but I know your Keeper hungers for the power of the Fae. We are in exile. It is blasphemy to trade for baubles and pleasure when we are meant to be suffering. It is the Keeper's impiety—and the Lady's most of all—that has placed us in these straits. Not to mention the incompetence of the Stratia."

"And what was your role, Locum?"

"Careful with that sly tongue; I have an inkling to cut it out. I am the only one with divine right behind me."

"I thought the Last God was the only one with divine right," Ralen retorted.

"I am here and so He might as well be. You have learned the holy language but not its laws. I would brand you heretic, except you are cattle. I need not invoke the laws meant for men with beasts as low as you—I need no justification to see you burnt."

The Locum gestured and two priests stepped forward. Ralen did not think of shielding himself behind Gordon or Keeper or Dinah, no 'potentates'. He thought of fighting, but nothing would forfeit his life quicker. He might kill a priest, more than one even, but he could not kill everyone on this world and the next and the next, so he relaxed and let them take his arms. He let them lead him to an iron cage lowered from the rafters.

Dozens of cages hung from the ceiling beams. The temple was new but already half the hanging cages were filled with bodies, some barely moving, some stiff and decaying, and some burnt to ashes and charred bone. Magic must be what kept all the smells at bay.

The iron door clanked shut and Ralen grabbed the bars for balance as the cage wobbled its way back toward the roof. The clinking of chain stopped when he was high enough. He looked down, expecting to see the Locum gloat, but the Master of priests walked sedately from the room without even glancing up. Whatever he put in a cage was simply forgotten.

Hopefully, that meant the Locum would also forget to have him burnt. Ralen had seen enough of his neighbors die from either fire or starvation that he knew which he'd choose.

KERVALEN HAD MIXED feelings about returning to Kingsholm. He had endured two seasons of constant war on this last tour, and he and all his soldiers needed a respite. It was customary to rotate tours of duty, but, as he unstrapped his armor and tossed the pieces to a waiting servant, he worried over General Bherim. There were a dozen instructions he'd forgotten to pass on to his replacement. He scribbled them on parchment and told his servant to drop the armor and get the message sent.

When he was alone, he lay on his bed and breathed deeply. There would be fresh soldiers and mages protecting the wall, but were they as experienced? He fretted himself into fitful sleep and woke in the dead of night.

His manservant dozed on a couch in the foyer. Kervalen shook him awake and requested water for bathing and fresh robes. When the sweat of his tormented dreams was washed away, he left his servant and guards behind and carried his own lantern into the Sanctum at the center of the keep.

This was the most ancient part of the Kingdom. Before it was called "Old", this mound had been exposed to stars and sun, a sacred place for consulting the heavens. It was a site of power, where Hestian himself appeared to pass instructions to his followers. A city had grown around it, and a castle was built on top of it, shutting out the sky but not the words of Hestian.

Kervalen opened the secret way and descended past fitted stone to reach the wood and earth that marked the entrance to the original mound. The inside was dark, his lantern barely pushing back the shadows, and it felt as though he were in the womb of the land, an unbeliever defiling its most private place.

"When will it end?" he asked the walls. The sound of his voice was swallowed by soil. Hestian did not answer, never answered. This was now the god's tomb.

"Your efforts are pointless."

Kervalen started. He should have been alone here. An old man, face covered in white stubble and dressed as plainly as a peasant, stepped out of the gloom. Milky eyes reflected the lamplight. One of the Prophets.

"I wasn't asking you," Kervalen said.

"You called out, and I was here. Who else were you asking?"

Everyone knew Hestian was dead. "I want privacy."

"The castle is yours, and the Kingdom," the old man said. "I'd think you'd have all the privacy you need."

"Apparently not." Kervalen turned to leave, there was no reasoning with the Prophets, but the old man took his wrist in a strong grip.

"The darkness comes. All your efforts are in vain."

"I won't believe that."

"Hestian preserved us for a time, but all things must end." The doomsayer slowly released his arm and sank back into the gloom.

Kervalen would not listen to them anymore. They once guided him and his father, had guided all the kings before, had once loved the Kingdom with all their hearts and fought for it with their visions. Yet, for the past ten years, they spoke of nothing but the coming darkness and the end of their visions.

More sacrifices were needed, that was all. He would find a way. He was not about to let anything end.

LOCUM PAERIS WAITED while Drakein announced his arrival. He disliked being made to wait, and it was some time before he was admitted to the Lady's presence, even though she was the one who had summoned him.

"Locum," Dinah said, not taking her eyes off the view from her window. "You've stolen one of my slaves."

Abrupt as always. He would be equally clear. "You have acquired more mages, but they have not been given handlers. I have priests to spare. What is your reason for keeping them from The Last God?"

"You have not answered my question."

"One is a reflection of the other. You take what by rights belongs to God, and so I take your livestock. I daresay it is still I who has suffered in the trade."

"How dare you speak to me thus? You have no rights, priest, but what I choose to allow." She turned from the window, and he felt a chill creep along his spine.

He'd been foolish to speak so freely, and he could not serve his true masters if he were dead. He bowed deeply and said, "Forgive me, Lady."

She turned to one of her lizard pets. "Captain, fetch the boy back for me."

The temple was his domain. Paeris glared at the creature, but the Drakein captain bowed to his mistress and left, ignoring Paeris entirely.

"And..." Dinah said, circling Paeris with a hungry look that made him cower inside his skin, "...you shall not have my new mages either. I know you fear being weak, failing in your duty, but do not worry. What I am planning shall please our Lord, and we will have His favor once more. You can soon go back to groveling in His Presence. But wait. You have never been in His Presence, have you? You are a servant who has never felt His unobstructed light, while I have stood by His side longer than your ilk have existed.

"Even in disgrace I am greater than you have ever been or ever shall be," she added. "I see little use for your kind; especially when you fail to heal the plague that afflicted my Conquered. I keep you alive merely because you have been a useful instrument for our Lord, but even the finest instruments break and are easily replaced. Remember that and do not test me further."

"Yes, Lady. I shall remember. My only wish is to give the Lord His rightful tribute," Paeris said. Though it was true he had never seen the Lord's light, he had known the Lord's Presence before it was taken away, and even with it gone, he still felt the hunger. When not in use, all magic was channeled through handler priests to the Locum, who directed the energy to feed their Lord's Presence on the Plain. The hunger was never satisfied.

"He shall have what He deserves ... when I am done," Dinah said.

Paeris grew red with suppressed fury. Her audacity was outrageous. She was using the mages to feed herself—gluttony—when the God demanded she be punished.

"Now, go," she ordered. Her fearsome gaze made the breath catch in his throat, so he could not reply even if he dared. He merely nodded.

The bone doors opened and Drakein with poleaxes menaced. He scowled at them and paused beside a closed set of double doors. He sensed mages inside and ... something else. It was like a mage, but its energy felt so much sharper, stronger. He drew a tendril into himself and tasted a young girl, felt her skin as his own for a moment, saw the workshop and the fire from the forge. Between ear-splitting hammer blows, metal chains clanked. There were no chains on her wrists or ankles, though. No protections. Her name was Anjee. A girl....

"Go," Dinah repeated. He scurried down the rose marble steps, his thoughts as fast as his heartbeat. He had seen something the lady did not wish him to. Something far more important than a score of mages.

Chapter Twenty ~ Trapped

Anjee was anxious for Ralen. He'd been foolish and gotten himself caught in a priest's cage. Images of him—past, present, future—pounded through her skull in time to the ring of the hammer on the anvil. The smith, oblivious to her discomfort, held a glowing strip of metal in long pincers and smiled kindly, but it would be kinder if he stopped.

She sat cross-legged on a narrow pallet wedged between others in a long row, all empty, as it was impossible for anyone to sleep with the noise. A toothless old man at a nearby table measured green powder onto a scale then transferred the excess back into a glass vial. She winced at the next ring of metal on metal, and the old man chuckled. "The Lady will let us rest for a few hours at dawn," he said.

It wasn't yet sunset. She was so tired. Dinah had forced her to scry all the previous night and day. While it was quiet in the library, she hadn't been allowed to close her eyes or let her weary head fall into the water bowl. The Lady had kept jerking her awake. The rest of the time, Dinah ranted about the angels' interference, until the Locum arrived, and she finally banished Anjee to the workshop.

Anjee now gathered every cushion she could find and piled them over her head. Peaceful darkness enveloped her, but it did not last long. The hammering stopped. The cushions flew away, and red filled her field of vision.

"He is here," Dinah said.

Anjee almost sobbed with relief. She'd seen him hung above the temple-goers to slowly die as they prayed below. She'd seen many worse punishments for heretics—the wheel that turned in the temple basement, crushing bones and flesh instead of grain, the coffin filled with spikes meant for the living—but none of it had come to pass. She'd seen the small army of Drakein march in with poleaxes glinting and lower Ralen's cage while grumbling priests stood by. She'd seen it, but it could easily have been one more mirage, one more vision that did not come to pass. He was here. The weariness made everything seem like a dream.

The Lady yanked her by the arm and dragged her into the foyer, straightening her clothes on the way. The golden clip in Anjee's hair pinched, but the Lady's touch made her too weak to lift her arms to fix it. When the Lady stepped back, it took all her strength to stand normally, hands folded across the silk ties that hung from her new dress.

Ralen knocked, and new worries filled her. What would Dinah do about the angels? What would Ralen say when he learned she'd told? He had to understand ... Dinah put a finger to her lips. She'd heard Anjee's turbulent thoughts and commanded silence.

When Ralen stepped inside, Dinah swept him into a hug. He froze, eyes widening, but when he did not disintegrate, his features relaxed. He quirked an eyebrow at Anjee over the Lady's shoulder. She didn't say anything. He must have noted her stiff pose, because his features tightened once more with fear.

Dinah pulled away. "I see I have confused you both. We have entered a new era, we three. Ralen, you and Anjee are Marked, and that can never be undone, but you are both my pupils. You are special to me. I have elevated you to a position unique among my servants. I have protected you and allowed you to come freely to my home. Now, I embrace you as I would my own children."

She swept up her skirts and glided—feet never touching the ground—to the other end of the large table in the center of the library. Three books plummeted from the shelves behind her and smacked onto the table in a plume of dust. "And I must not neglect your educations." She gestured for them to sit.

Anjee took a seat next to Ralen on Dinah's right. The thicker tome scooted across the creaking wood to him, while Anjee got the thinnest. How was she to read this?

"Ralen will teach you, as I taught him," Dinah said, answering her thought. She felt naked whenever her mind was invaded. Nothing remained that was hers. The Lady owned everything.

Dinah gave her a satisfied smile and called the remaining book into her own hand. She leaned back, settling into a comfortable position to read. After a moment, she looked to Ralen. "Proceed. When you have Anjee scribing her symbols, you can continue your history lessons."

"Yes, Lady." Ralen opened Anjee's book for her and gave her another enquiring look, as if she could explain Dinah's behavior. Anjee could not speak, feeling the compulsion burning into her skin from the Mark, not that she knew what to say.

She looked at the pages inked with unfamiliar symbols and shivered, feeling a chasm opening before her. She felt small, as though standing on the edge of the ocean for the first time. It was a mixture of lightness and vastness, stretching out from her middle to the page and to the library around her. A cold fear lurked beneath everything, certainty of her insignificance. She was so tired. "I don't know about this," she said, glad that her voice worked, although each word came out slowly, censored by the Lady.

"It's not hard," Ralen said. "I managed, didn't I?"

He never understood how special he was. She examined his face and noted the peace in it as he looked at her. She had too much power over his happiness. She knew it was a bad thing—she had Seen it.

Ralen gently turned her chin so that she was looking at the page. His other hand squeezed hers under the table. "It will be fun," he said. "You can leave this place. Books can show you places and times far away from here. You'll see whole new worlds." She saw enough already, but the Lady took control of her muscles and made her nod acceptance.

Ralen talked and talked, explaining how there were fifty-two core symbols in God's Tongue. Each could be modified to carry hundreds of additional meanings.... She couldn't focus. She saw his words swallowed in ash, and a black ocean swallowing everything. She jumped to her feet and skittered toward the door, surprised her body had obeyed.

"Sit," Dinah ordered.

She turned mid stride and resumed her seat. "Yes, Mistress." She had not slipped the puppet strings after all.

"Are you alright?" Ralen asked.

"Feeling cooped up is all. I miss the fields." The words came from her mind, but they were not the ones she would have chosen. The Lady thought them adequate though.

"I do too." He smiled, and she floated. The feeling was hers, a moment of freedom. Her happiness was tied to him just as his was to her. It wasn't right, but it was all she had. She clutched his hand under the table and held on.

WHEN THE LESSON WAS over, Anjee asked him to walk with her. She cast a fearful glance at the Lady, but Dinah nodded her permission.

Ralen led the way through labyrinthine tunnels to the great cavern. He headed for the edge of the lake, but she took his hand and led him up the path to the farming valley. Would distance free her from Dinah?

The Drakein let them pass without a word. How different from their first days in this place. It was dark, but she had no trouble finding the apple orchard on the lowest terrace. Ancient trees closed protectively around them. She loved this place, but she wanted to keep going, take Ralen and flee this valley, this world. Her legs did not obey.

Rows of giant trees, white blossoms perfuming the night air, a glimpse of stars between branches—this was the most freedom she could hope for, and she let it soak into her skin.

"I have the stones needed to buy a new Hasvel," he said without preamble, as though their plans for Gar were still important. As though the world had not shifted forever. "The Drakein took them from the priests and then gave them back to the Keeper. He must have heard what happened. Grin was waiting by the lake on my way here. You know what Grin said about everything?"

Anjee shook her head.

"He said, 'Oh, well. I guess this means the Locum isn't a smuggler. He's still trouble, and you still owe me a debt.' And he handed the gems back to me. I can go to Gordan now and arrange for a new Hasvel, but how do I smuggle Gar back to the Fae lands? Only Saren is allowed to go there, and I can't trust him to take Gar. And even if he didn't look inside the bag and Gar managed to get home, what happens when Saren returns with a new Hasvel for the Keeper? None of it is as easy as I hoped. What do I do now?"

"What do you want to do?"

"It's what I have to do. It's the only way to get Gar out of here—out of my boat where's he's built himself a home—and save Claw."

She would have chided him for his compassion towards a gobel that would have gladly eaten them both given the chance. She would have ... but her tongue was no longer hers.

"I don't want to imprison one for another," he said with finality. "There has to be a better way."

Anjee had a thought, and Dinah must have approved because the words came: "You need to give the Keeper what he really wants. Not what he thinks he wants. He wants power, the secrets of the Conquered and the Locum—not Hasvels."

"You're right. You're right." He smiled that wild, half mad smile of his, and she wanted to smile back, wanted Dinah to command her to, because she couldn't.

Dinah's compulsions kept everything trapped inside, all her shame at betraying Ralen's secrets, all her fears. This was worse than the self-imposed prohibition that had kept her from talking about her visions. The lady's compulsion was like poison building up inside. Only the beauty of the orchard diluted it, kept her breathing and alive.

She was surprised when Ralen said, "I think I'm happy."

"You can't mean that."

"Why not? You're safe from Grin, fed and cared for, given new dresses..." He indicated the rust-colored satin Dinah made her wear. No one noticed the old rag she kept on underneath it. "The Lady saved me from the priests, and now we're together. I don't want to be anywhere else."

She railed inside, banged fists at her internal prison, wanting to shout at him, to scream, *"You're the Lady's now. Can't you see we'll never be free, never be happy? I can never make you happy! Run now! Before it's too late!"*

She didn't say any of those things. Instead, she sank into the deep grass and leaned against the gnarled trunk of a tree. Ralen sat carefully beside her, trying to avoid crumpling her new dress. She slapped it into the ground to show him what she thought of it.

He leaned against her shoulder. She nudged him until his head lay on her lap, and she petted his hair, remembering the time a gobel had bitten him. A lullaby came to mind, and she sang. The notes were far too sweet and soothing—they did not match the fury inside her. He relaxed, his breathing grew regular, and he fell into a peaceful sleep.

Eventually, the frustrated energy inside her quieted. She did not know how to break Dinah's hold on either of them, and she was tired of fighting for the moment. She let out a resigned sigh between notes and lost herself in the song.

She must have fallen asleep too, because Ralen shook her. "You stopped," he said. "It was like the world ended."

"Sorry," Anjee said.

"I should go, anyway. Gordon's maid is expecting me. I don't want to wake her too late."

Why must he return to the city? Why couldn't they live here among the trees, like dryads? If there were such things as magic and monsters, why couldn't the good stories be true too? But all she said was, "I should go too. The Lady awaits."

WHEN SHE RETURNED TO the longhouse, the big doors closed behind her, and Dinah swept into the room. Anjee obeyed the irresistible urge to sink to her knees and put her forehead on the wooden floor. She didn't know if it was a compulsion or if simple fear made her do it.

"I felt you trying to warn him," Dinah said. "You would tell him to leave me. I can't allow that. You must not deny the visions."

"I know, Lady. I'm weak."

"A hammer is not weak because it cannot direct itself; it is merely a tool. Remember and you will not struggle so much. Now, let us commence your most important lessons."

Anjee sobbed. She wanted to sleep, but the Lady never did. She would rather listen to more fretting and curses about Ashkal and Amseel than endure more scrying lessons, so she said, "Why didn't you ask Ralen about the angels?"

"He hides things from me but not from you. It is best he not know I have gleaned your secrets. That way you can continue to pass them on to me. As for those two ... I have not been struck down. They have not turned the Last God against me. I suspect Ralen has had the same effect on them as he's had on me. Perhaps their goals and mine are now the same. Nevertheless, I cannot abide them interfering in my affairs." Dinah brought out the bowl again. "Look."

Anjee was relieved when she saw nothing. She must be too tired. Her glimpses into the future were unbearable. She did not want more, not if Dinah would keep her from changing things. And she had decided she had to try. She could not tell Ralen about the visions, that much she had seen, but she could use them to steer him away from danger, just as Dinah steered him toward it. If only she could fight the Lady's compulsion....

"I know when you're not trying," Dinah said. "Look again. Look hard. I want to know what he will do with the destiny I forge for him—and I want to know what he can endure."

Chapter Twenty-One ~ Illusions

Ralen rowed across the lake to the Conquered city, a small smile on his face. What he'd told Anjee was true: he was happy. It was a strange feeling, one he had rarely experienced, but now he had learned his place within Dinah's realm, and it was a good one. He could protect Anjee and be of use to the Lady, learn and become stronger. And Anjee had made him see he needed a new way to deal with the Keeper—giving him what he wanted.

The maid let him in, and he found his pallet. He had a section of floor in the pantry, between the kitchen and the door to the rear courtyard. Shelves of preserved food surrounded him. It was a comforting place to rest, although he missed Anjee's arms and lullabies. The memory of her voice carried him into sleep, helping to guide him through the unfathomable worlds in his dreams.

At sunrise, the household rose for morning exercises. Gordon asked Ralen to join them in the courtyard, but he shook his head. "It is for Conquered."

"I want you to feel like one of us," Gordon said.

Ralen knew the man was grateful for what he saw as Ralen's aid in curing his family's illness, but he had done nothing and would take no credit for it. "It was Dinah," he said again, "but thank you for making me welcome here."

"I want to do more. Is there anything you need?"

He remembered Saren's strange anger and felt his scabbed lip with his tongue. "I could use your advice."

"Yes?"

"Your message runner, Saren, is acting strange. He asked a lot of questions about Dinah, and the Keeper suspects there are spies among the Conquered."

"No," Gordon said quickly. "I mean, it is possible. We have our own spies in the armies of other lords, but I doubt Saren ... I will look into it."

"Thank you."

The First Commander herded his sleepy-eyed boys out to the courtyard. They would have more training at school later in the day. It was hard work. Slave or soldier, everyone contributed.

The Conquered were the keystone of Dinah's army, necessary for maintaining her power and protecting them all from lords who sought to absorb their rival's territories. With Dinah in disgrace, the Conquered could not exert her will across the worlds as they had once done, but they continued to protect her realm, and they had to be respected for everything they had accomplished in her name. Gordon often told him Dinah's disgrace could not last forever, and when Conquered returned to war, they would show the rest of the Last God's armies how it was done, give them a glimpse of real glory.

With Gordon's family occupied—the hollow clatter of practice weapons echoing from the courtyard and the maid humming as she washed linens in the tub—Ralen used the open space in the main room to do his own practice: the moves the angels had taught him. They had warned him to keep their lessons secret. He could not explain to Gordon where he had learned to fight, so he needed this solitary time to remind his muscles and reflexes of what they could do.

After half an hour, he paused to check on the others. He peeked through a rear window at the lamp-lit courtyard and saw them still engaged in slow warming movements. He wanted to return to his own practice, but the maid was moving about, and he could not let her catch him.

He went upstairs, hoping to find space in the boys' room, but he noticed the door open to a small office. Curiosity made him peer inside. It was Gordon's study. He felt a burst of adrenaline when he saw the books and sheets of parchment piled on the writing desk.

He heard grunts from the courtyard and the maid opening cupboards in the kitchen and knew he had time. He carefully flipped through a notebook then placed it back in the same position. He found what he was looking for atop the pile on the left—the codebook Gordon used when composing messages to their allies.

He scanned the cipher. Words like grain also meant foot soldier, with positions on the page giving numbers. It was fascinating, exactly what the Keeper wanted.

He frowned. The Keeper could go to the Last God. He closed the book and left the room.

He stopped in the hall.

Learning to read the coded messages did not mean he was betraying Gordon. It would be learning, as he was supposed to, and he could choose what information he passed on to the Keeper. He would protect those he cared about, just as Dinah protected him and Anjee, no matter what.

He returned to Gordon's desk and began to study the cipher in detail.

OVER THE NEXT FEW DAYS, Ralen developed a new routine. He practiced the angels' techniques during morning exercises, and then learned each new cipher. Afterwards, he accompanied Gordon to the Command Center and on his rounds through the city, visiting battalion commanders and chatting with the troops, or discussing and debating strategies. He still delivered messages to and from the Portal, and read them whenever he could, but Gordon often gave him a ride on his horse. That way they could survey the valley encampment together.

The First Commander no longer deferred to him as he had after the plague, which was a relief, yet there was clearly a change in Ralen's station. Instead of ignoring him, the Drakein and Conquered nodded to him when he passed. Did everyone know how Dinah had embraced him? Or did they believe he'd been adopted into the ranks of Conquered?

After seeing to Gar in the rowboat, making sure he was fed and hidden, he spent evenings in the library—where Dinah watched him in an unnerving way—and then time in the orchard alone with Anjee. He wished he never had to sleep. When he dragged himself into the pantry at midnight, he passed out and woke well rested the next day to begin again.

One morning, he went up to the boys' room to begin his exercises—the room had the best view of the courtyard, and he could always claim to be examining their toy soldiers if caught—but the maid was already there. She was gathering the washing and entangled herself in the bedclothes and tripped. She sat on the floor, examining her leg. When she noticed him, she quickly covered the exposed skin, embarrassed, but he had already seen the twisted pink flesh.

"Sorry," he said. "I shouldn't have looked. Does it hurt?"

She shook her head. "Not as much as it once did. An old enemy."

"Let me help you." He took her arm, but she pulled away.

"I can do it. This might have kept me from battle, but it won't keep me from my dignity. Go. I'd rather not have a healthy young man watch me struggle." He understood her reluctance to show weakness. There was no place for it here.

It registered that she had called him a young man, and he stood taller as he headed for the stairs. When he was at the bottom, she peeked over the railing. "Wait." He climbed back up to her. She whispered, "There is one way you can help me."

"How?"

"You got Dinah to send mages before. Can... can you get her to heal me? They say my leg can't be fixed, but the Lady is powerful. If anyone..." There was such delicate hope in her eyes.

"I'll do what I can."

She lowered her head and wiped at tears. "Thank you." She clearly didn't want him to see her emotion, so he went in search of a new place to hide his weapons' practice. He also wondered how to fulfill the maid's wish. The Lady did not listen to him as much as everyone assumed.

Chapter Twenty-Two ~ Maneuvers

Saren was surprised when the Locum led him from the nave of the temple to a large office with walls of shelves stacked with scrolls. He usually delivered messages from Varvec like hushed prayers before the altar.

"Is the Keeper watching the temple? Does he know something?" Saren asked, worried.

Paeris shook his head. "His magic cannot penetrate these walls. This place is the god's. I brought you here not to hand you a letter but to offer you a task."

"Name it." Saren straightened, hoping the mission involved swordplay and a chance to kill someone.

"Remember the slave you told me about, Ralen?"

"Him again. Yes."

"He is to be watched, but more importantly Dinah has taken an interest in another, a girl. Do you know her?"

"Everything's upside down, Locum..." the priest looked impatient, so Saren said, "No, I don't know her."

"That must change. I cannot gain access to the longhouse or any of the mages there. I cannot discover Dinah's plans, but I may not have to. The girl will interest Adarmis far more than any of our schemes."

"I can't get Ralen alone to finish extracting the information I need from his hide. He's always under Gordon's arm, discussing strategy like an honored war veteran and not the pack mule he should be. He's even a guest in the commander's house!"

"You are approaching this from the wrong direction," Paeris said. "The girl is the key. I have learned she sometimes walks in the western valley. Her you can get alone."

"Then what?"

"Discover what Dinah keeps from us. Discover the purpose of her new slaves and whether we should capture them or put them to death. And most important—win the girl's trust. Do it quickly. My plans have nearly reached fruition."

Our plans, Saren thought. I started all this. "What does she look like?"

"She's not like any other slave: She wears a satin dress."

ANJEE SNATCHED WHAT sleep she could. The hammering always stopped at dawn, and the air was soon filled with the snores of old men. She wondered why there were no women among the mages. She asked the toothless mage with all the vials of powder about it. His name was Waverly. "They're taken by the god, or they kill themselves first," he said.

"Why?"

"The Last God consumes their power and their souls, unless they escape to the land of death."

"Why didn't you kill yourself?" she asked.

He looked down, shamed, and she realized how it had sounded. "I'm sorry. I didn't..."

"I am a coward, but it doesn't matter. Women have more magic. I have little for The Last God to steal."

"Dinah steals our power too," Anjee said.

"The Lady takes our lifeforce and power to live forever—the god to conquer."

Was that true? Had her life been stolen? Whenever Dinah came into the workshop to feed, Anjee ended up on the floor with the mages, her veins aching and head ready to burst from the pain.

Later, when she was in the library with Dinah, Anjee searched her reflection in the scrying bowl for wrinkles or streaks of grey hair.

"Don't be foolish," Dinah said, reading her thoughts. "I feed from you but not enough to cause lasting harm. You have a mage's power. It fuels your visions, and it protects you. Now, go. I have other work."

Anjee bowed and hurried from the library. She went down the rose stairs as fast as she could—two steps at a time then three—until she thought she would tumble out of control. If she broke her neck, the Lady couldn't have her power or her visions. The moment she thought it, the deep-rooted compulsion that kept her from taking her own life took over and she slowed. It took forever to reach the bottom.

The Lady did not often excuse her during the day, but when she did, Anjee got as far from the cavern as she could. Dinah would want her back in time for Ralen's lessons, but she might be able to climb the highest terrace before it was time to return. As she passed the turquoise lake, she gazed at the distant lights of the city. He was somewhere among the Conquered, where she could not go.

She ascended into the valley and strolled beside golden wheat, reaching out her hand to grab a few stalks. The sun was hidden by clouds, but she turned her face toward it, like one of the lizards, glad for whatever warmth it offered.

"Anjee?"

She turned at the sound of her name. Ralen was the only one who called her by it, the Lady preferring "girl" or "you". It was a soldier. He wore leather instead of metal armor. Because of his height, she thought he was an adult, but his smooth cheeks made her realize he was still a boy, a few years older than her. "Did Dinah send you?" she asked.

"I'm a friend of Ralen's."

Now she knew who he was. Those long legs would be perfect for running messages. "I don't think he considers you a friend, Saren."

"Why? What has he said about me?"

Ralen never said much, but she was good at understanding his silences. "You tease him like a schoolyard bully, and you punched him in the nose."

"It was a bad day. I was frustrated. I didn't mean anything by it."

"I know he didn't send you, and if the Lady didn't, why are you here?"

"I like to walk."

"After running messages?"

"Yeah." He moved ahead of her into the field, trampling stalks as he went. He turned back and said, "They say there's dragon treasure buried out here somewhere. Want to look for it?"

"Wouldn't it be under the ground?"

"I have an advantage. Come on." He walked deeper into the field and drifted to the left where she couldn't see him anymore.

Wind rustled the grass. She heard the distant sound of slaves hacking at the wheat. Soon this would be a muddy field. Once, she would have been with them. Now she was one of the tools, Dinah's blade for carving her way to Ralen. She felt alone.

"Wait!" She hurried after the messenger. It had been a long time since she hunted for buried treasure.

Saren held a tiny brass triangle with a glowing ball of orange light in its center. Magic. "What's that?" she asked.

"The map." He looked at the mountains to get his bearings then walked west. The ball of light grew darker and darker until it was blood red. He dropped the triangle and it buried itself into the ground like an arrow. "Start digging," he said.

"Me?"

"You are a slave."

She frowned as she hiked up her satin dress and dug out a clump of broken wheat stalks and roots. The rich brown mud stuck under her fingernails.

Saren's hands joined hers in scooping out the dirt. "Can't let you have all the fun."

The triangle moved deeper as they dug. Her dress was coated in mud by the time it hit what it was looking for. There was the dull clank of metal on stone. Saren felt around. His eyes brightened, and he pulled out a statue of some creature that was all jagged teeth and protruding claws. He wiped it on his shirt, revealing dark green stone. "Jade," he said.

"Treasure. You were telling the truth. What are you going to do with it?"

"Buy Fae pleasures—if it were up to me. Unfortunately, this belongs to someone else, and I have to deliver it. A messenger's duty never ends."

He held out his hand. She didn't take it, not sure how to interpret his smile. Was it mocking or playful? "Suit yourself." He stepped back, leaving her to stand up on her own.

He put the jade statue in his leather satchel, the sides bulging.

"If it's for Dinah, I can take it," she said.

"There are other powers besides Dinah."

"The god?" she asked.

He tried to look mysterious. "I'd tell you, but..." he pointed to her Mark. "I'll see you around."

After he'd gone a few steps, he looked back. "Can I find you here tomorrow? I might need more digging done."

She looked at her ruined dress and smiled. "I'll be here if I can."

THE NEXT DAY, SHE WAS fortunate Dinah remained occupied with her experiments, so she went to the field again and found Saren waiting. There was no magic triangle this time.

"I thought we could, you know, take a walk." He held out his hand. She hesitated, as she had before. "I won't bite," he said.

She let him entwine his fingers with hers.

He swung her arm as they moved and took large, exaggerated steps. "So, this is a 'walk'. I usually run."

She laughed. He was an idiot, but she didn't mind the entertainment. He reminded her of her big brother. Sometimes she couldn't remember his face.

"Where to?"

She thought of the apple orchard, but that place was special. "Follow me." She broke out of his grip and ran for a low terrace on the northern side of the valley. He kept pace with her easily, and even ran a circle around her to show off. She reached a thick hedge of blackberries and dived into an opening, losing him in the brambles. Speed was not as useful as agility among the thorns.

It reminded her of the rosebushes she had played in before... back home. She found a dark hollow and sat, trying to stifle her giggles. She felt like a child for once.

She heard Saren crashing about and cursing whenever thorns got him. She breathed as quietly as she could and stayed still, but he must have noticed her footprints in the leaf litter. "There you are." He grabbed her before she could take off again and tickled her until she turned red.

"Stop," she begged.

"You'll have to use your magic if you want to stop me."

"I—don't—have...." she slapped him away so she could catch a breath. "I don't have any magic."

He sat back and scrunched up his face. "What? I heard you were a mage."

"Who said that? Ralen?"

"I hear things."

"You heard wrong. If that's the only reason you're here, you can go now. I'm just a slave with nothing to offer."

"Dinah doesn't think so."

"I don't know what Dinah thinks."

"You do know what she does all day long up on her mountain." It was a question, and one she knew she wasn't supposed to answer, even without all the compulsions layered over her soul. It wasn't as bad with Saren, though. Her Mark didn't glow. Dinah didn't seem to be watching her as closely, and she decided to test her bonds.

"Could you carry a message to Ralen?" she asked.

His face scrunched up again. Despite his protestations of friendship, he and Ralen obviously shared a mutual dislike.

"What?"

"Tell him not to trust the Lady and not to trust me."

"What kind of message is that? It doesn't make any sense. If he's not to trust you, why would he trust your message, especially if it came from me?"

"Please. Make him believe it. Tell him to listen to the Keeper. Ralen must choose happiness. He mustn't..." She felt her Mark burn. Dinah's attention was on her, and she nearly bit her tongue when her jaws clacked shut.

"I don't know. I might need payment." Saren lifted a strand of her hair. "An unusual color."

He moved in closer, his lips a few inches away, and she retreated, feeling thorns cut into her back and elbows. He smirked and said, "Not that kind." In a flash of silver, he drew a small dagger and sliced off a lock of her hair.

She clutched the unnaturally smooth edge of the strand in surprise. "Why'd you do that?"

"Like I said. Payment."

"I have to go." She fought her way through a narrow path in the brambles. Saren tried to follow, but he couldn't get through. She left him cursing softly.

Dinah had caught her, and the Lady would not let her pass on any more warnings. She hoped Saren was satisfied with his stolen keepsake. As long as he warned Ralen, she was happy to part with it. Ralen was all that mattered.

Chapter Twenty-Three ~ Progress

Adarmis took off his helmet and hurled it out into the killing field. He half expected the ground to swallow it as it had the God-fed and the bodies of the fallen, but it sat there, taunting him. A cheeky archer on the other side pierced it with an arrow.

This interminable war had tasked his patience to the breaking point. What use being Bringer if he was trapped here? It was a tighter cage than the one that enclosed him in human flesh and bone.

"What would please you, General?" Varvec asked.

"To be crushing Dinah's throat!"

"She is not here, and I think that is little help for our current problem. Of course, we could always leave this to an underling for the time being and take the bulk of your army against her."

"Do not tempt me."

"You are Bringer. Why not invade your rival?"

Adarmis caught a glimpse of his reflection in the Fae's strange eyes and ran fingers through his mussed hair to straighten it. He knew Varvec taunted him, but he would not let the beast feed off his fury. Fae were a hungry lot.

"I never know if the god hates her or loves her." Adarmis suspected the latter, which made it all the more difficult to smother his anger. "I dare not risk it. Not yet. Not until the Kingdom is mine."

"Then you will be waiting forever. It sounds to me like an excuse..." the Fae stopped. He must have realized he'd nearly gone too far. Adarmis would kill him if he called him a coward, if he even hinted it.

"Do what I tell you to do and leave it at that," Adarmis said. "She will suffer for every moment she has occupied the Sacred Cavern. She will know no rest. And soon she will fall before me. I will reclaim my home."

Varvec smiled, disbelieving, but Adarmis planned to keep this vow. He had promised himself long ago, before he was shrouded in humanity, before he bowed to the Last God ... and it was the only reason he craved more life. If there was a way to kill that vile woman, he would find it. Dinah and all she held dear would die.

"So, there is no pleasing you?" Varvec said. "Unfortunate. I'd hoped this token might improve your outlook." The Fae signaled to a soldier who brought forward a small bronze box. Inside was a jade statuette.

"Sethera," Adarmis said with a hiss. He stroked the smooth stone and lifted it in one hand. He remembered this, a delicate bead carved by Drakein servants. It seemed so much larger now. After centuries of serving the Last God, would he recognize anything from his old life? Would nothing be the same as it was? "Where did you get it?"

"I had a spy in Dinah's ranks fetch it from the old battlefield. She has turned the place into a farm, you know."

Adarmis squeezed the likeness of Sethera so hard the jade cut into his palm and blood trickled between his fisted fingers. "Stop goading me, Varvec. I am your Bringer now."

"I know, Lord. I wished only to please you."

That could not be the Fae's true motive. "You know my reasons for wanting Dinah crushed. What do you have to gain by seeing your old mistress defeated?"

"She has a few keepsakes from my homeland as well, which I would like returned."

Adarmis grunted, tired of the Fae's games. He had a war to win before his vendetta could be satisfied. "Don't bother retrieving any more gifts for me, Varvec. I lack the sentiment."

DINAH WAS OVERJOYED with the mages' progress. Half a dozen shackles were ready to try on the werelings. If this worked, she would have the weapons she had always dreamed of and the beginnings of a new army.

"What are they?" Anjee asked.

Dinah saw her staring into the gloomy tunnel where deep rumbles echoed like the mountain shifting in its sleep. The portcullis clanged shut behind them. The girl whirled. Her fright was tangible and sent a delicious shiver through Dinah. "Come and see."

"I-I don't want to," Anjee stammered.

"Come." Dinah put the slightest compulsion behind the command and Anjee jerked, following her into the dark.

Ever since the girl tried sending a warning through that Conquered message runner, Dinah kept her tightly leashed. She had thought to sway Fate and turn Ralen against her, so now there were Marks on both her hands and the soles of her feet, each laced with more vigilant spells to keep her silent.

Lamps lit as Dinah passed, and the chains her Drakein carried reflected the light. The ground trembled as more werelings woke. Their voices could crack stone, but Dinah had warded these walls against their ability.

They were perfect soldiers, strong and fast, able to destroy fortifications with their cries, and immune to all injury except that inflicted by tooth and claw. Since steel was useless and no opponent could get close enough to bite the beasts, werelings were effectively invulnerable. They were also uncontrollable. If unleashed in battle, they were as likely to destroy their masters as the enemy. They bowed to compulsion, but it smothered their spirit, and they would not fight. Dinah hoped her invention would change that.

"Set them down and go," Dinah told the guards. Drakein laid shackles on the dirt and retreated to the portcullis.

"This isn't safe," Anjee said.

"Of course not. We gain nothing of importance in life if all we seek is safety. I will borrow a bit of your power now, child." Dinah did not have to warn her, but there was something about the girl that reminded her of her long ago self. She felt sympathy as well as the urge to shake the timidity out of the child. Such wasted potential.

The girl gasped when Dinah's aura touched her. The mage's core that fuelled her visions provided enough energy to feed Dinah's magic without her having to reach into the earth for it and risk disturbing the wards that protected the tunnel from collapse.

Claws scratched at the sides of the deep pit below her feet, but the transparent barrier over the top trapped the werelings. Dealing with them required layers of both mundane and magical protections.

She drew power from the girl and sent the beasts a compulsion: sleep. They took more effort to compel than Marked, and a few moments later Anjee collapsed. By the time Dinah had lulled the creatures into slumber, the girl was unconscious. She left her lying on the ground. The child needed to regain her strength, in case Dinah must borrow more.

She gathered a set of shackles then descended through the barrier, the magical field parting for her, and into the pit. She had no difficulty seeing in the dark and drifted down beside a fallen wereling. The beast's mouth was open, tongue lolling. Its side rose and fell.

Dinah stroked it like a dog, enjoying the luxurious feel of soft black fur beneath her hand. The wereling was larger than a Drakein. Its strong life force called to her, but she fought the urge to feed. The creatures were too precious to waste.

She locked the shackles around its ankles. The metal joint sealed itself, leaving a smooth surface that no key could open. Even if the beast chewed its own foot off, the shackle would tighten over the stump. There was no escape.

She called the other sets of shackles to her, and they clattered down the sides of the pit and into her hand. She secured the other five werelings as she had the first.

Now for the test. There was no life without risk, and she would risk anything for power enough to match the god's, to make Him bow to her will, to truly live again. "Wake."

They opened their eyes, instantly alert. Massive figures rose to their feet around her, and the first growl vibrated through her bones.

Claws reached for her. She grabbed the wereling's wrist and held it, feeling the muscles and sinews twist beneath her hand. Such strength. She desired more than anything to feed from them, but she was here to test her new magic. Another creature struck, and she held its arm in her stony grip as well. She had the reflexes of a dead race, one she barely belonged to anymore, but it was enough to subdue the wereling. Six was a more uncertain matter. They were angry, the others circling her. A huff of breath moved the hairs on the back of her neck. She sensed muscles tense and heard claws scrape the ground as they all jumped.

Stop. There was no time to speak the command; she thought it instead.

A saber-length claw hovered a hairsbreadth from her eye but came no closer.

"Good," she said, reaching out to stroke the alpha's fur. "You are mine. Now and forever. You and your offspring generations from now and to the end of time."

The shackles were a success. Her scheme would work, and now it was time for the next step. But first, she needed to make sure no one else interfered with her plans for the boy.

She had Drakein guards carry Anjee's limp form back to the house, while she sought out the Keeper. She needed Ralen to be stronger, and Grin would help to hone her greatest weapon.

EVERY DAY, ASHKAL AND Amseel visited the Last God in his chamber with the white tree. Arches of warped sky metal converged at a single point in the high-vaulted ceiling, all carved from the heart of the meteorite. The walls beneath were covered by thousands of oblong 'windows' with hardly a space between them. Each looked upon a different world. The Last God floated in the center of the room, his Presence a blinding light the angels could not set eyes on even if they dared.

Ashkal sensed his master's scrutiny, a thickening of the air, a touch of thought. The god knew all that occurred within reach of His Presence and could probe the deepest reaches of their minds if He chose. Yet, He tasked them to watch certain people who Ashkal knew were, somehow, beyond their Lord's sight. Dinah and Adarmis were of particular interest.

"Adarmis has failed to take the Kingdom." Their Lord seemed to expect another outcome.

"Should we covey your disappointment to the general, or will you name a new Bringer?" Ashkal said.

"I choose to be patient. Dinah has only offered supplication once. Any news?" The god's voice caressed their feathers, slipped into their souls, and they longed to answer Him, to please Him.

"She is locked away with the mages she stole, feeding on their magic," Amseel said.

"She is weakening. Soon she will repent. When she does, I may give her one more chance at the Kingdom." The god's voice drifted away as His attention wandered.

Ashkal nodded, eyes on the floor. He did not know if the god saw his gesture, but he felt the dismissal, a slackening of the tension that told him the god had already forgotten them.

His Presence surrounded them, conveying disinterest or anger or pleasure, His moods became their own, and it weighed them down, uncontrollable, inescapable ... except for one place.

Their audience over, the angels flew through the chamber's only true 'window'—a jagged crack through the thick metal shell of the meteorite core that ran all the way to the surface. They rose out of the crater to soar across the Plain, high above the ocean of soldiers, and to their usual perch on the marble Portal to Dinah's realm. They were invisible to any who passed through the arch below, although few but messengers did these days.

Here, Ashkal felt unburdened. Was it because the god had withdrawn His Presence from the Lady, he wondered, or was it because of Ralen? Ashkal knew the answer and shivered, long black feathers rising along his wings and the back of his head.

I am disturbed, Amseel told his brother. Such emotions were possible nowhere else.

I know, Ashkal said. See the soldiers who pass by here, how they pause, how sadness or anger clouds their faces before they move on?

Is it the child? Amseel asked.

Yes, Ashkal admitted. His influence is growing. Our Lord must soon notice this.

If we kill the boy, no one need know we aided him. He will vanish, and this emptiness will too.

Did his brother feel empty here? I remember our home, Ashkal said. I had forgotten that it was lovelier than Dinah's valley, with no Presence to cage us, room to stretch our wings, to swoop and soar. The red skies swarmed with our kind.

I only remember the ground red with their blood. We are the last. If we do not stop this now, the god will end us, and there will be none to remember.

I also remember, Ashkal continued as though he had not heard his brother, how Our Lord betrayed us. I—

—Do not think it!

I hate him.

He will know! He will know! Amseel drew his dagger, which hummed in response to his fear. I must kill the boy. He toppled backwards from his perch and extended his wings, circling through the Portal and into Dinah's realm.

Ashkal launched himself after his brother and intercepted him mid air. They crashed to the ground in a twisted heap. No one in Dinah's encampment could see them, but they made indents in the grass and turned up soil.

The deadly blade had missed Ashkal by a hairsbreadth.

Amseel saw the dagger against his brother's side and pulled back. Look what comes of this! You are all I have. We cannot be at odds. I would die too.

Then let us be of one mind in this. Something has awakened inside that I will not put back to rest. I will stretch wings and soar again. Will you follow me? Ashkal held out his hand.

Amseel sheathed the Blessed Blade and clasped his brother's hand. The grip was firm, but he said, I fear.

I fear existing forever as we have. I would rather die than remain chained. Our kind is gone, what we once were is stolen. There is nothing else for the god to take from us.

Our souls.

You nearly took mine with that blade. What need have I of it anyway, when it is weighed down by a coward's flesh?

Amseel turned his gaze toward the mountain where the boy lived. <u>Very well. We will see this through. But we will die quickly—our Lord will feel your hatred. He will know.</u>

Ashkal shook his head. <u>He does not care what we feel</u>.

Chapter Twenty-Four ~ Testing

Ralen had been avoiding the Keeper, sending his daily reports through the gobel with the missing foot, Stumpy, but today Stumpy did not wait beside the lake. The gobel stumbled into the Command Center, peeking through fingers to protect its eyes from the lamplight. Officers moved out of its way. It slid its back against the wall, wedged itself into a shadowed corner, and whispered Ralen's name and over and over, as if he were its sole purpose for being.

He felt a moment of pity for the creature and went over. "What does Grin want?" Ralen asked.

Stumpy let out its breath. "Master wants to see you."

"I'm busy." He noted Gordon listlessly flipping through messages. The First Commander would clearly prefer to be organizing a war, but that was impossible while they were exiled. His current concerns were convincing his troops to clear and plant new fields and work like common laborers under the Keeper's directions. Instead of training them to fight, he was training them not to be soldiers anymore. This regimen consisted of barked orders and the occasional, public whipping but did not require much of his time. There was even less for Ralen to do, except watch Gordon's re-enactments of past battles on the sand map. He learned much from them, but it was hardly pressing.

"The Master says..." the creature paused, struggling to form the correct words with its long tongue, "...he is Keeper and Dinah ap-appreci-ates the education he gives you."

"What does he want?" Ralen asked again. He'd made sure Anjee was safe, but there was still a gobel on the Keeper's island crammed into a Hasvel cage.

"This way." The gobel tugged at him, and Ralen reluctantly followed.

When they reached the street, Ralen jerked to a halt. The Keeper was there, lounging on his litter, with an awning to shade him from lamplight, surrounded by ministering gobels who rubbed oils into his flesh and fed food directly into his open mouth. He'd seen Grin several times in the distance, overseeing construction in the Portal valley, but whenever Gordon dealt with him, Ralen managed to hang back. This was the closest he'd been in a week.

He bowed his head slightly. "You have need of me, Keeper?"

"Your cooperation of late pleases me, but I am not here to praise you or remind you of the full extent of our bargain. I'm here because... Our Lady commands..." it seemed difficult for Grin to speak the words "...you to study with me and learn the administration of her realm."

"What does that mean?" Ralen steeled himself, sensing something terrible coming.

"The Lady believes you have learned enough about Conquered. There are many other facets to her strength: gobels, Drakein, and me."

"So, I'm to follow you around too?"

"There is nothing more for Gordon to teach until we return to war. We all pray that happens soon, but until then you will give up your place among the Conquered and never leave my side, night or day."

This wasn't possible. He'd done what Dinah and Grin and everyone wanted. What about his time with Anjee in the orchard under the stars? He lived for those moments. And what about dinners with Gordon's family, morning training...? "No," he said. "No."

Ralen ran to the Command Center and found Gordon. "Tell the Keeper he's wrong. Tell him."

Gordon followed Ralen back outside. When he saw Grin, he said, "Explain."

"The boy is mine now. That is all you need to know."

Gordon's moustache twitched as he searched for words. Ralen could tell he was angry. He waited to hear him order Grin away, but the First Commander bowed deeply. "Yes, Keeper."

Grin gestured for Ralen to follow.

"No," he said again. He looked pleadingly at Gordon. "You can't...."

"The Keeper speaks for our Lady and is second only to her," Gordon said. "We must obey."

There was resignation in Gordon's expression, sympathy, but he didn't need sympathy. He needed to find a way to get Gar home. The fairy couldn't stay hidden in the boat forever. He needed to free Claw. But most of all, he needed to stay as far away from the Keeper as possible. He didn't want to learn to be a monster.

He looked from the bowed commander to the crowd of gobels under the litter to Grin's straight crease of mouth and backed away. He turned and ran. He ran to his boat and rowed across the lake, shushing Gar's whispered questions. He dragged the boat ashore and ran past Dinah's Drakein guards and up the rose stair to the carved bone doors of her longhouse. He couldn't wait for her to notice, so he knocked.

The doors opened, and Dinah stood in the entry hall with a worn-looking Anjee behind her, like a golden shadow to her dark figure.

"Dear Ralen. Why have you come?" she asked.

"I..." Now that he was here, it didn't make any sense. He had run to the Lady looking for arms to hold him and a voice to soothe away his worries. Dinah was forbidding and without warmth. Anjee drooped, bruised circles beneath her eyes, as though she had not slept since last he saw her. "I want to stay with Gordon. I don't want to serve the Keeper."

"Do you want to serve me?"

"Of course, Lady, but..."

"Silence." Her tone sent a chill through him, and he felt he had made a terrible mistake. He looked at the ground.

"Go." Dinah told Anjee, and she scurried into the workshop. Ralen felt her pass so close her scent encircled him.

"I have good reason for my Keeper to watch over you, and I have high hopes, but a whining child is useless to me. You will be strong. You will serve. Or you will die," she said.

He wanted to look into her pale eyes, to beg, but he only stared at his clenched fist. "I'm sorry, Lady."

"Now, return to the Keeper."

"Yes, Lady."

The doors were still open. Once he crossed the threshold they began to close. The sunlight from Dinah's massive window was squeezed into a thin line. Before it disappeared completely, she said, "The girl will still be here. Serve me well, Ralen, and all will be well."

All will be well. He didn't like who he was when he was with the Keeper, but it seemed the Lady did.

When he got to the lake, the boat was gone. He saw the grooves in the mud where it had been—and the small footprints of the gobels who had taken it.

Gar.

It had all been for nothing. There was no chance of rebellion. No chance for the fairy or for him.

RALEN LOOKED FOR ANY trace of the Hasvel, shredded flesh or blood from gobel bites, but there was nothing. He spotted movement farther along the bank and went toward it. Conquered were loading a barge with the last grain from the harvest.

"I need to reach the Keeper's island," he told them. Maybe if he offered his suspicions about Saren, the Keeper would release Gar and Claw. But then Saren would be the one in a cage. He didn't want to be made to choose again. He couldn't...

He would go to the Keeper's island, and when Grin commanded him to torture Gar for his power, he would kill the Hasvel quickly and painlessly. That was all he could do for him now.

The soldier stacking bags said, "I don't think so."

Ralen still had Gordon's seal, and he held it out for them to see. "Now."

The soldier grunted. "Fine." He tossed one last bag onto the barge and then ordered the others to man the oars.

"What about the rest?" another soldier asked, indicating the remaining food on the shore.

"We come back for it, and if Drakein have stolen it, we'll take it out of their hides."

Ralen climbed aboard. He wondered why Drakein would steal grain when they only ate meat, but he didn't ask. His stomach was in knots.

The Conquered soldiers were reluctant to approach the Keeper's island and rowed slowly as soon as the blue-lit rocks came into view. The lead oarsman was old and battle worn, but even he sucked in a breath when silver gobel eyes rose out of the water and surrounded them.

"Keep going," Ralen said. Gordon's emblem hung from a red cord around his neck. The soldier eyed it and obeyed, plunging his oar into the water. Gobels grabbed the oar and the boat, so it was stuck fast.

"Master says only you." The whispery voice was barely discernible above the drip of water from the stalactites.

Ralen took a breath and dived into the cool lake. When he surfaced, he looked for the barge and saw the Conquered had moved on without him.

He pulled himself onto the limestone atoll, and swarms of gobels followed him. The Keeper was in the central pool where the phosphorescence was brightest, waiting.

"You ran," Grin said. He shook as he laughed. "You ran, and she sent you back to me."

"Yes." His voice trembled.

"Dinah dislikes anyone who questions her authority. She commands here, and so do I. That is your first lesson."

"What do you command of me?" Ralen said the words, but he hated them. His gaze darted from green gobels all around to the cage with Claw still wedged inside, but there was no sign of Gar.

The Keeper's fingers wriggled so much Ralen thought they might fly off his hands in his excitement. He said, "Anything I can imagine, boy."

A deep ache filled Ralen's chest and made him want to cry out. He was a slave. He must remember he was a slave. The greatest he could hope for was life. There was no place for defiance. He tried to bury it inside, but it did not fit anymore.

"Your first task will be to feed Dinah's other favorite pets," Grin said. "I believe that to oversee, you must know every aspect of what is overseen, understand every task within the realm, from lowest to highest."

"I know the meanest tasks well." Ralen's tone was bitter.

"I like this situation no more than you do, boy."

Ralen didn't believe him. "Why?"

"She wants you to learn my job." The Keeper spread his arms, indicating his own abhorrent form, the gobels on the barren island, the entire damp cave, and said, "Perhaps, someday, she means for this to be you." He fluttered his stolen fingers and his ever-present grin seemed wider than ever.

RALEN MARVELED AT THE massive portcullis that led to the newly constructed tunnels. The wereling lair. The Keeper's first task had sounded simple.

He looked at the wagon filled with bony meat and entrails: the day's refuse from the slaughterhouse. He'd learned from his studies with Gordon that herd animals roamed beyond the two valleys and provided meat to the army. At least he hadn't been given a job in the slaughterhouse. The stench from the wagon made him gag. The meat was rotten. He closed his nose, but the cloying scent lingered on the back of his throat.

"Feed them," the gobel, Stumpy, instructed before it slipped back into the shadows and slithered off to the lake. He heard a plop as it dived beneath the surface.

A Drakein guard raised the gate for him while two others dragged the wagon into the tunnel. Once he was inside with the wagon, they left and closed the portcullis behind, sealing him in. He had a shovel and no idea what to do.

Light from oil lamps made the limestone walls glisten. There was a precipice to the right of the wagon, and he inched closer to look over the side. A hot, damp wind that smelled of death rose from the darkness. There was no telling how deep it went.

The ground trembled, sending pebbles into the chasm, and a loud rumble filled the air. He threw himself against the wall, remembering the earthquakes that had preceded the volcanoes on his world. Several more rumbles overlapped the first, and he realized it was not the sound of stone shifting but the growls of werelings. This must be the place.

He climbed atop the cart and used the shovel to scoop up piles of slimy, maggot ridden flesh and toss them into the pit. There was a magical barrier over the chasm that flashed blue every time a shovelful passed it. He saw a hand covered in black fur and wielding claws as long as his forearm catch some of the meat. He worked faster.

When the wagon was empty except for putrid stains, he jumped out. At the sound of his feet touching the ground, growls of hunger turned to snarls and sounds of fighting and frustration. Seemed they wanted fresher meat.

"Not so close. Theys gets excited," a familiar voice said from somewhere high above.

Ralen looked up and saw rainbow wings. "Gar. You're alive. How did you get in here?"

"I sneaks. Gobels come for boat and me fly fast and high. None see me come here."

"Then you need to stay here. There's no other safe place."

Another rumble of wereling growls shook the ground.

"Me like orchard better," Gar said.

"I know, but I can't move as freely as before. The Keeper is always watching. I've just thought of another plan. I have the Keeper's gems, and I can bribe Saren, threaten him if need be, to carry you to the Fae lands. There will be no trading for another Hasvel. I just need a chance to get him alone."

"Smells here. Me fly away me think."

"No. You were lucky to make it this far, but you won't make it through the Portal. There are priests and Conquered everywhere in the eastern valley. Be patient. Do you need food? Water?"

"Water okay. Stream runs down wall over there, down to growlies and out crack at bottom to someplace I don't know. Lost the cook pan me made from your old cup down there. Argh. Now me drink high up so theys no sees me. But food?" Gar pointed at the slimy wagon Ralen had just unloaded and made a disgusted face. "Even with cook pan would be yuck yucks."

"I'll bring you something when I come to feed the 'growlies' tomorrow. And I'll find Saren as soon as I can. Now hide."

When Gar was out of sight, Ralen banged the shovel against the metal bars of the portcullis. "I'm done. Let me out."

The Drakein removed the wagon as quickly as they could, disturbed by the werelings. Ralen did not understand why they were so bothered—he was the one who had to feed them. The Keeper had not run out of interesting punishments after all.

Chapter Twenty-Five ~ Stirrings

That evening, Ralen toured the tent city with the Keeper. It was becoming a real city with a temple, granary, and kitchens manned by amputees, warriors turned servants like the maid, and a barracks for the officers built of stones from the fields.

He should have been in the library with Anjee.

"You rule here at night and Gordon during the day. Is that how it works?" Ralen asked.

Grin looked down from the litter, swaying as the gobels carried it, and said, "I rule everything. The sun keeps me away, but what my gobels cannot tell me, the Drakein do. They obey the First Commander in war and me in all other things."

"And where does the Lady fit in?"

"As the Last God is to her, she is to us."

Ralen remembered Dinah's hesitance at accepting prayers. She was their god in all ways, but it seemed to be a dangerous position to hold.

"I always study in the library at night," Ralen said. "I'm sure the Lady wants me with her."

"She has not sent for you. Your education is now in my hands. Now, enough questions. Watch and learn."

He had learned far too much from the Keeper already.

They stopped at the base of the white temple, the gobels shifting under their burden, and Grin's litter swayed. "Locum!" Grin called. "Locum Paeris!" Was Grin the Locum's master too? Was this the lesson for the evening?

Several minutes later, when the Keeper's expression had soured to match his odor, the tall doors opened, and Ralen recognized the dour man in white and gold: self-proclaimed representative of The Last God. Paeris stood with back straight, chin high, and lips set in a condescending expression. "Why have you called for me like a goat in the field?"

"Why weary a messenger when you are in shouting range?" Grin said.

The Locum noticed Ralen but focused his gaze on the Keeper. "Well, you have me."

"How do you find the new temple? Is it constructed to your satisfaction?" An amiable tone often disguised the Keeper at his most dangerous. It seemed only the Conquered thought well of the Master of Priests.

"That's why you called me here?" The Locum huffed and turned to leave.

"Stop." Grin's tone was final.

The Locum stayed where he was. That answered Ralen's question. Grin ruled the priest as well.

"The Drakein say you have a special congregation, one that meets outside the ringing of the prayer bell, one that excludes everyone but humans."

"Nonsense," the Locum said. "Supplicants have always been free to come and go as they please."

"So, you would not prevent me from attending one of these meetings?"

"There are no special services, and you have always been welcome in the temple, Keeper. Not that I have ever seen you answer the bell."

"Our Lord touched me enough when he shaped my flesh," Grin said bitterly.

The Locum's posture stiffened. Apparently, he disapproved of the Keeper's irreverence. "If there's nothing else?"

"I know what you're doing," Grin said.

"You mean the Lord's work?"

"You've something against the Drakein. I don't know what it is, and I don't care. Whether hatched from an egg or born from some bitch, we all serve the god."

"Even if sewn from refuse and not born at all?" the Locum asked.

"Especially. Stop this prejudicial drivel. I'll not stand for it. These walls can be torn down more easily than they were built, and you can preach in the mud ... with the goats."

Locum Paeris did not deign to answer. He sniffed and raised his nose even higher before retreating into the temple. There might have been the slightest nod before his head disappeared from view, but it wasn't enough to satisfy Grin.

"I'd like to dress you in priestly garb, boy, and see what you learn inside those walls, but you were lodged in the First Commander's house and brought me nothing of use. Why did Dinah have to saddle me with such a worthless human?"

Ralen agreed with him on that. He wished the Lady hadn't thrown him to Grin, but he'd far rather shovel rotten meat to the werelings than enter the white temple again.

THE NEXT DAY, LOCUM Paeris took the strand of golden hair Saren gave him and studied it in the ray of morning sunlight streaming through the open door. "Perfect."

He laid it on an intricately etched platter and set about gathering the vials he would need.

"You're sure this will work?" Saren asked.

The Locum did not bother to reply. He had more important concerns than the message runner. He worked carefully, as he did with all things, and whispered prayers at every step. The alchemy did not call for it, but he did nothing without the blessing of his god.

When the potion was complete, he carefully capped the ampoule of clear liquid.

By the time he finished, Saren was asleep on a bench with a bit of gold-trimmed decorative cloth wrapped around his torso. Paeris lifted a sandaled foot and gave him a shove. The messenger rolled out like a ribbon onto the stone floor and landed with a slap of flesh. Once he'd regained his feet and shaken the blurriness from his vision, Paeris handed the vial over. "Give this to her, but make sure none of it touches you. It is absorbed through the skin."

"What's it do?"

"With this, she will tell you all she knows."

"Won't the Lady find out?"

"The girl will forget, and whatever she does not know, the Lady cannot steal from her thoughts. Hurry. The concoction is labile and will not last past sunset."

Saren squeezed the ampoule in his fist and set out at a run.

ANJEE DRIFTED THROUGH dim passageways like a ghost, waiting. Since trying to pass a message to Ralen, she wasn't allowed to enter the great cavern anymore—Drakein barred her way—but there was a labyrinth of corridors between there and Dinah's longhouse, some illuminated by smoking lamps, others by phosphorescent algae or worms, and some dark as the Lady's heart.

She knew the path Ralen usually took to reach the longhouse for his studies, but he did not come. Dinah had forbidden it. Still, she waited.

Each day, Anjee shared her visions with the Lady—there was no choice—and Dinah always said the same thing: "He must be stronger."

She longed for a vision that would keep her and Ralen together always. It never came.

Dinah's feedings were agony. She was not spared them, even though she was exhausted from scrying and working with the mages. When it became too much, she went into the labyrinth to hide and to wait.

The tunnels could keep her occupied for centuries if she lived that long. She didn't understand their purpose. Some were huge, wider than three wagons, but they twisted abruptly and were too steep in some places for anyone to climb. Perhaps they were meant to confuse attackers in case the Portal was breached, the city taken, the lake crossed...? If, after all that, invaders made it here, Dinah could confuse them with the tunnels? As if Dinah would let them get that far. Still, that was the purpose of defenses: one small thing on top of another to wear down the enemy.

Ralen was being trained by the First Commander and the Keeper, while Dinah kept Anjee awake all night and day to share her visions and be drained of energy. They were both being worn down, shaped by the Lady's will.

At least the tunnels were quiet. She curled up in a corner and tried to sleep. It was easier on stone, reminding her of the cave and Ralen. When she thought of him, she sang, her voice echoing into the dark. She missed learning songs from the other slaves, but she had found a book of music in Dinah's library and sung a part of it now, not entirely understanding what it meant, but loving the feel of the notes in her throat.

A scuff of boot on gravel caught her attention, and she cut the song short. Torchlight reflected off the wall.

"Ralen?" she called.

"No." A tall, slim figure appeared around the corner. Saren.

"What are you doing here?"

"I told the Drakein that I carry a message from the Locum."

"Were you lying?"

"No, but the message isn't for Dinah—it's for you."

She shook her head, bewildered. "You're not making any sense."

"This will clear things up." He pulled out a phial of clear liquid and removed the stopper.

"What—?"

He threw it in her face. She was stunned, feeling the droplets trickle down her nose, seep between her lips.

Darkness...

SAREN LOOKED DOWN AT the girl in the satin dress. Pity to waste such fine clothes on a worthless slave.

As soon as the Locum's potion touched her, she collapsed, and now she lay crumpled like a doll with her eyes wide and staring. She didn't even blink.

He slapped her cheek. "Hey, there. Listen. Can you hear me?"

"Yes," she said in a completely calm and even voice.

He was relieved she wasn't dead. Not that she wasn't Marked and likely to die any day, but he'd have looked stupid if he came back empty handed again. If Paeris was right, this slave had all the answers Varvec wanted, and he'd have no need to deal with that close-mouthed imbecile, Ralen, ever again.

"Okay, good." He thought about what he should ask first. Werelings. They were what he was most curious about. "Do you know what Lady Dinah wants with the werelings? Why are they here?"

"Experiments. The shackles. The mages and the Dark Lady have made special shackles, like the ones they themselves wear, but these can control the wereling beasts."

Dark Lady, huh? She was creepy enough without a title like that. "Good. But why does Dinah want to control the werelings?"

"The Lady will breed a new army, but not the one she thinks. Fate has other plans...." Anjee's voice faded.

"Stay focused." He slapped her cheeks again, and they grew red, rosy like a doll he'd found in the ruins of a village their army had destroyed years ago. He'd slammed its porcelain head against a stone wall and laughed at the pieces that flew everywhere. He'd been a child then and easily amused. A lot more than a doll's head needed to be smashed to entertain him now.

"We have forged dozens of shackles," she said. "The Dark Lady plans to breed many werelings. But there is another type of chain we've created in even greater quantities." She smiled as she stared creepily over his shoulder.

"What are they for?" he prompted.

"For the God-fed. The Lady wants to make them better, stronger, able to survive outside the god's Presence as she has. The chains are like the Mark, and whatever wears them will be bound to Dinah just as I am bound. Trapped. You must help me. Kill me."

Saren felt a flash of pity for the girl. Better dead than a slave, but he couldn't slit her throat now, no matter how much she begged. Paeris wanted her and so would Adarmis. That made her too valuable to waste.

He took a moment to look at her. She was pretty, with yellow-gold hair and bright blue eyes. "I can't kill you, but I'll get you free of Dinah. I can't guarantee Adarmis will be a better master. Still, I hope you're grateful." He kissed her on the lips.

"Ralen," she said, eyes unblinking.

He slapped her hard enough for the whole left side of her face to turn rosy, and she fell over onto her side.

"I've heard just about enough from everyone about him," Saren said. "Why don't you tell me what makes him so special? Tell me...."

ANJEE WOKE UP ON THE floor of the tunnel, the oil lamp guttering. She shook her head and the world spun. Her face hurt from resting on stone. Why had she fallen asleep here?

She couldn't remember what she'd been doing before. Exhaustion was to blame. There was never any chance to sleep with the constant hammering of metal in the workroom and the constant torture of Seeing that Dinah put her through.

Her Mark burned. The Lady was looking for her, and she would not be happy Anjee had slipped away. She bounded up the steps and fell through the wide doors, panting.

"Ralen is not coming, so stop haunting the labyrinth looking for him," Dinah said.

Anjee would not let her voice shake, even though the Lady's glare made her want to beg for forgiveness. "I'm glad. He's better off away from me—and from you."

"Oh, not forever. He'll be welcome here again, once Grin breaks him."

"I haven't broken, and you'll never break him."

"You are broken, child." The Mark burned to emphasize the point, and Anjee fell to her knees.

The Lady knew her thoughts, controlled her limbs and tongue when she chose, but she could not have <u>her</u>. Never.

"Return to work," Dinah commanded. "Don't make me bind you more. I prefer to keep your mind intact, but I can control your every breath if you force me to."

Anjee stood like a puppet yanked up by its strings and went into the workshop. The door closed, and the Lady's grip on her eased. She sat next to Waverly and set to work, but willingly. He had been teaching her what the powders did.

Anjee looked at the door and back again. Still no Ralen.

This was her fault. She could blame the visions, but it was her attempt to warn him that had prompted Dinah to cage her so tightly. Had the sacrifice been worth it? Had Saren delivered the message?

She had seen him, she remembered. In the tunnels. Or was it a dream?

"Keep an eye on that," the old mage said.

She stirred a small brass bowl filled with a crystalline concoction that was colored purple and deep rust. The rhythm was important, she'd learned, but it did not require much concentration. "None of this seems like magic," Anjee said.

"It is. But you want the unnatural kind, don't you?"

"Unnatural?"

He spread his fingers and sparks danced between them. "I could cast lightning if the Lady didn't keep me so weak. Call it from a clear sky, from a cavern roof! It's not natural. It takes from the universe."

"I thought it came from inside us. Our core, Dinah calls it."

"And what's inside us comes from the universe. We are but conduits to the well. I'll tell you a secret."

"What?"

Waverly leaned in, crooked teeth and bad breath close to her face. "It's running dry."

"The universe?"

"The unnatural, the magic. All tamed now. Just like us. All tamed."

"Then what happens? When it's gone?"

He shrugged. "Nothing. Or maybe the universe dies. We've stolen its heart after all."

"The universe can't die." Then she remembered the dark ocean swallowing her, separating her from Ralen. That had felt like the universe dying. Her death she could accept, but the death of everything? She would like the orchards and the sky and the songs to remain after she was gone.

She looked at the old wizard's strange grin and shook her head. He was mad, like the other slaves. Still...

"Can you teach me some 'unnatural' stuff? Even the sparks would be more interesting than this." She set down the mortar and pestle.

The old man paused. He eyed the busy workshop. No one was looking at them, and the Lady was in the library. "I can't. You're a woman."

She frowned and felt an angry heat rise into her words: "Dinah is a woman, and I'm a seer. I have power."

"Too much. Women are too powerful, too good a conduit. The god should not be allowed to possess it."

She remembered their first conversation about what had happened to the female mages. "I'm already caught, and Dinah won't let me die." Besides the stairs, she'd tried the window, other ways... "It's already too late. I might as well learn something useful."

He lifted the mortar and sniffed, assessing her work. "Very well. As you say, it's already too late."

ASHKAL AND AMSEEL STOLE into the cavern city from the western entrance. The Drakein guard's head twitched at the passing breeze, but he did not see them. Nothing noticed them, not even Dinah's magical senses. But would Ralen see them?

The boy was growing stronger. He was immune to their manipulation of his memory, and he no longer heard their call, so they split up to search for him.

He is not in any of the caves, Amseel said when they met up back at the entrance.

Nor is he in the Conquered cities, Ashkal said. He was faster than his brother and managed to search a wider area in the same amount of time.

Where then?

I can think of two places, neither good.

Dinah's longhouse and...?

Ashkal led the way over the turquoise lake and to the small island in its center. They remained high above the throng of gobels that covered the surface. The creatures were asleep in the mid morning hour, but they stirred, sensitive to the swirls of wind in the otherwise still cavern air as the angels beat their wings. Ralen's pale form was like a beacon in the green sea of bodies—curled up in their midst.

The Keeper has him, Ashkal said.

What do we do?

Follow and wait until we can get him alone.

Our duties to the god...?

We will take turns. You survey the army and observe Adarmis. I will join you when it is time to report. Then you will return here to watch the boy.

Yes, brother. Amseel was much more accepting after having nearly killed him, but Ashkal would not mind his doubts right now, for he shared them. Why was Ralen guarded by the Keeper? What was Dinah doing?

Chapter Twenty-Six ~ A Message

Ralen woke to the feel of leathery, inhuman skin and mucus. He was coated with it. Gobels. He remembered where he was, and the sick feeling deepened, the emptiness in his gut, the scream building just below his ribcage. The Keeper had ordered him to sleep on the island. He was part of the nest now.

Hungry whispers grew as the monsters woke. Deadly claws stretched and retracted like cats', scratching at him just enough to raise the hairs along his body. The gobel whose head rested on his left shoulder sniffed, enjoying the aroma.

Ralen threw off clutching arms and legs and stood. There was no space to walk, so he climbed over sleeping bodies and sank into the chill lake, trying to wash their scent away.

He floated, luminous water lapping at his lower lip, eyes closed, trying to remember the cold stone of the cave, the mat in Gordon's pantry, Anjee's arms in the orchard.... This could not be his home now.

"Boy!" Grin called, his voice like thunder, causing the water to shake. No, Ralen was the one shaking.

"I'm here." He dragged himself onto the isle, clothes dripping but clean, and made his way to the Keeper's side, the gobels letting him pass.

"While my litter is prepared, go to the First Commander and tell him I require his presence in the North Valley. The Drakein say the humans will no longer supply guards at the Boundary, so tell him to bring some. Tell him I order it."

"Yes, sir." The Conquered city. Alone. He'd see Gordon and the others again. And he'd have a chance to find Saren.

Grin must have noted his sudden happiness. "No dawdling. Deliver the message and meet me in the valley."

"Yes." Ralen tapped a gobel on the shoulder, indicating it should propel him across the lake, and dove into the water. He felt around until he found the scor he had secured in a net with stones—and the pouch he'd hidden with it. He affixed the scor to his face and tied the bag of gems to his belt. He was ready to go by the time the gobel grabbed him.

If he delivered the message fast enough, he'd be done long before the Keeper caught up. He'd have time for his errand. Time alone in the open air, under the stars, and away from the creature who ruled his every breath.

Once on the docks, the gobel squinted its eyes closed against the oil lamps and Ralen got ahead of him. He ran to the Commander's house.

The maid answered when he knocked. "You," she said, taking in his soggy appearance. "You're starved again. Come in and let me fix you something."

He missed her cooking. Gobels ate raw fish and leeches from the lake, and now he did too. He noted her awkward stance, the scars, and remembered his promise to ask Dinah to heal her. He hadn't done it, and now the Lady wouldn't even see him. He did not deserve the maid's kindness, not when he'd failed her. "I can't stay. I have a message for Gordon. Fetch him, please."

"There's leftovers from dinner. It won't take but a minute."

"I can't," he said again.

She looked affronted, and he remembered how easily she slipped into a bad mood, but it was right she be angry at him. "Fine." She left him in the foyer as she had so many times before and went upstairs. But he was not Gordon's message runner anymore. He had fallen a long way: from almost-Conquered to a faceless part of the gobel horde.

As soon as Gordon appeared, Ralen said, "The Keeper commands you to meet him in the North Valley with a contingent of Conquered. He says the Drakein do their duty guarding workers at the Boundary but humans do not."

"Is that what he says? There've been accidents..."

"That's the message. I can't change it." It hurt to see the kindness in Gordon's expression, so he turned his back and climbed the steps down to the street.

He didn't know why Dinah was angry with him, but he knew he had to obey. For Anjee.

He passed through the tunnel without showing Gordon's sigil. They knew him. He saw the Portal, monolithic and impossible, and thought of setting Gar free. There was a sea of God-fed on the other side, but the fairy could soar above them.

A hand snaked out of the shadows and caught his arm. "What are you doing here?" Saren said, frowning. "I heard you'd finally been put where you belong, with the rats. I mean rat-eaters."

Ralen ignored the childish taunt and shrugged out of the message runner's grip. He wouldn't have to search for Saren after all. "I'm glad I found you."

"That's a first. Actually, I found you. You couldn't find the ass end of a donkey."

"But I did find these beneath the lake." Ralen untied the pouch from his waist and offered Saren a peek at the stones. They seemed to absorb the light and send it back stronger than they received it.

Saren whistled. "You know. Holy law decrees slaves can't own anything, so why don't you let me take those off you?" He grabbed the bag, but Ralen held on.

"I'm not stupid. I'm not giving them up without something in return."

"I don't have to give you anything."

"And I don't have to tell the Keeper about your wereling questions, your mage questions... all those detours you take on the other side of the Portal. You called me the spy, but you're the one who will hang for betraying Dinah and the Stratia."

"If you tell."

"If."

Saren snorted. "A month ago, even a week ago, I might have been afraid of your threat, vermin. Not today. Things are changing."

"What kinds of things?"

"For one thing, I'm not going to bow and scrape to the Keeper or Gordon—and especially not you—anymore. Now give me that." He tried to snatch the sack again, but Ralen easily dodged and gave him a shove that sent him flying.

Saren sat up, spitting out dirt and glared.

This was not going the way Ralen needed it to go. "Please. I don't care how much you hate me for existing, but I need you to carry something across the Portal. I can give you far more than what's in this bag. I know where to find more stones. As many as you want." He lowered his voice to a whisper, as they had drawn the attention of the surrounding Conquered.

"You know what I want even more than wealth and comfort?" Saren said as he climbed to his feet. "To be feared." He stepped closer, face red with fury. Ralen expected a fight, but Saren whispered, "I have a message for you from Anjee."

"What did you say?"

"She says—beautiful, golden-haired Anjee in her satin dress—says not to trust the Lady and not to trust her. I'm not surprised. Women aren't to be trusted. Better just to use them and be done with it. I've been visiting her, keeping her company, and I don't think she misses you at all. We take walks in the fields, hold hands..."

"You're lying."

"She gave me a lock of hair." From his tunic, he pulled out a few yellow strands tied with a strip of leather. "I even stole a kiss when she was sleeping in the tunnels one day. Honey lips."

Ralen didn't think. He hit him. It was fast, and blood gushed from Saren's nose. He hit Saren three more times before an answering punch came his way—feeble and hobbled by pain. He dodged it easily and kicked the taller boy's knee, knocking him to the ground. Saren tried to crawl away, but Ralen stood on his legs and then his chest. Bestial sounds of rage came from his throat. He couldn't control it, couldn't make it stop. He didn't believe a word Saren said, but he was so tired of his stupid comments, so tired of everything. He bent down and started punching faster than before.

They had a crowd of onlookers now.

Black talons and rainbow scales dug into his arms and shoulders. He remembered them taking him from beside the river, dragging him back to the burning city where his mother had died, and putting him in chains. He fought them as he'd been unable to fight back then. He heard bones snap and Drakein hisses of pain.

He tried, but he couldn't fight the whole army. They dragged him away from Saren and threw him into a shiny new stockade near the barracks. He shook the bars and screamed. Conquered and Drakein backed away. He saw bruises on many of them, and there was blood beneath his fingernails.

The pounding in his head and heart slowly quieted. The fire coursing through his veins cooled, and he sagged to the ground, emptied of everything.

GORDON FOUND HIM LATER. The pitying look in the First Commander's gaze had grown stronger. Ralen told him, "Go away."

"You need me." The Commander put a skeleton key in the lock and began to turn it.

"No." The word was slurred, nearly unrecognizable. The same went for Saren's face. It was puffy and bruised purple, dried blood in the red fuzz of his beard.

"I told you to go to a healer," Gordon said.

The cell door clanged open, and the sound vibrated through Ralen's skull.

"No," Saren repeated, "You can't blet im out. He's gust a slave. He attacked me. Has eber-thing been 'urned upside down?"

"I'm shocked you let a slave get in so many good hits." Gordon gave Ralen a wink.

Saren looked as though he could spit poison. "The god might favor us if we beren't so squeamish. We'd rather lib with slaves than punish them." Gordon's moustache twitched at that comment, but Saren didn't stop. "He should die for bis, and you know it."

"Don't be extreme." The voice carried, deep and full of accustomed authority. It was the Locum in his white and gold.

Gordon and the surrounding soldiers bowed low. Saren and the Master of priests shared a look before the wounded boy sagged and bowed his head with a wince, clutching a rib.

Ralen stood up straighter.

"It was a tussle between young men. No one was seriously hurt." A few bruised Drakein behind Saren growled, but the Locum ignored them. "Let the child go, First Commander."

That had been what Gordon meant to do, but now he hesitated. He looked to Saren's frown and the growling Drakein all around. To Ralen, he whispered, "I'm sorry." To the Locum and the watching crowd, he said, "Soldiers were hurt, and there must be punishment. This is my call, Locum."

Gordon took hold of Ralen's arm, and Ralen let the commander usher him through the crowd and into the tunnel that led beneath the mountain. A few Drakein and Conquered followed. Gordon looked like he might order them back to their posts, but he stayed quiet. He took Ralen to a heavily fortified building in the center of the cavern city and deposited him in a bigger, older, and damper cell. Only then did he send the guards away.

"I'm sorry, Ralen. I can't show weakness, but I won't kill you. I don't care what law dictates," Gordon said.

"What are you going to do?"

"Imprison you here."

"For how long?" Ralen asked

"For life."

Ralen stiffened.

Gordon's moustache twitched again then stretched over a wide grin. "Don't worry. I've no doubt the Keeper or Dinah will order your release as soon as they hear of it, but for now..." He pointed to the bunk. "...enjoy a proper bed. And I'll make sure you get a full ration. Come here."

Ralen moved closer to the bars. Gordon reached through and squeezed his shoulder. "I can't imagine what it must be like on that island. No fire to warm you. The Keeper..."

Ralen couldn't stand the kindness. It made everything worse in contrast. "I'm alright."

"If you need anything, you can come to me. You're always invited to dinner and morning practice."

"I can't. The Keeper wants me to suffer. I'm not free. My wants don't matter."

Gordon withdrew his hand, and Ralen immediately missed the warmth. Gobels were cold.

The First Commander seemed to weigh his words before saying, "Can I ask you something? You don't have to answer."

"What do you want to know?" Ralen remembered Saren's endless stream of questions, and the Keeper's, but if Gordon asked him something directly, he wasn't sure he could lie. If he even wanted to anymore.

"What has Lady Dinah done to you?" Gordon asked. "When we took you and the other prisoners from the Metal World, you were just a boy. I remember you and that girl. The only children brought back alive. Today you took down grown Conquered soldiers and Drakein. <u>Drakein</u>. You're not a boy anymore. I'm not even sure you're human."

Ralen froze. He'd been foolish to unleash his fury on Saren for everyone to see. He'd just revealed the angels' training to Dinah's entire army. That would not make Ashkal and Amseel happy. But what disturbed him more was Gordon's last statement. Was he human? Had he ever been? Did it mean he was supposed to be one of the monsters?

"I don't know," Ralen finally said. "I honestly don't know what I am or what the Lady wants of me. I don't know anything."

"Maybe you are just a boy after all. A fiendishly fast and unnaturally strong one ... but still a boy." Gordon's moustache stretched again with a smile before he ducked out of the room.

A plate of meat and cheese and fresh bread arrived soon after, but Ralen did not have time to finish all of it before the Keeper came for him.

THE KEEPER WAS FURIOUS, bobbing up and down in the pool at the center of his island. Ralen stood, waiting, gobels on every side. Grin hadn't spoken the entire time since retrieving him from the Conquered city. Now, the fat man unleashed an angry torrent.

"You weren't in the North Valley, and I waited, dawn creeping closer, an hour lost with no Conquered coming to work the border. I finally track you down, and you're in the stockade. The First Commander was so set on keeping you there, I had to threaten him with lashes before he acceded to my command. No one obeys anymore."

Ralen worried for Gordon. Why had he done that? It wasn't smart for the commander to try and protect him. He gained nothing from it. Ralen no longer had Dinah's ear.

"I was in a fight," Ralen said, as though the bruises weren't obvious.

"Oh, I know all about that, fool boy. I thought you were finally going to use my gems to purchase a Hasvel directly from that little smuggler, Saren, but you couldn't even do that right. Now my money has vanished—swallowed up by the crowd of onlookers during your little tussle. A small battle more like it. I hear you took down six soldiers before they caged you. ...You've been keeping secrets from me."

"I serve you, Keeper."

"Not well, and now I realize it was your brawn instead of your brains, or lack thereof, I should have been taking advantage of. Where did you learn to fight like that? There's naught but books in Dinah's longhouse, and don't tell me you learned from the Conquered. No twelve-year-old, muscles or no, can take down six of Lady Dinah's soldiers. You're no mage. I can sniff that much. But there's something about you—something that makes you ever so important."

"I don't know what."

"Or you won't say."

"I don't know. Forgive me, Keeper." Ralen bowed his head and waited, silent.

"I learned forgiveness from Our Lady." Grin's usual jovialness was erased in an instant. "I only threatened the First Commander with the lash, but you will get it."

Gobels moved at a silent command from the Keeper and climbed Ralen, knocking him to the ground. Hard stone scraped his knees, chest, and chin as the creatures splayed his limbs. He thought they would rip his arms from their sockets, and he screamed.

"Save it," Grin said. "We've barely begun. This one has spent many hours crafting the perfect tool for your punishment. I think he's angry with you too."

Ralen craned his neck to see Stumpy, the one-footed gobel, limp over to the chest containing Grin's implements and bring out a bone-handled flail. The creature positioned it in its master's hand with a satisfied air.

"Like Dinah, I hate waste, boy. You see this?" The flail dangled in Ralen's face, so he saw it clearly. The tendrils were made of woven hair, each tipped with ivory molars like beads. "All that's left of the slaves you brought me."

Grin flicked his wrist and the tendrils cut into Ralen's back and shoulders, jagged bits of human teeth embedding themselves in his skin. The pain was sharp and acid, continuing to burn even after the lash retreated. His mouth hung open in a breathless scream. He sucked in a lungful of air, but the lash descended again and stole the breath from him.

"Ten more, I think," Grin said. "One for every pointless question you've ever asked me. Unless you're ready to tell me your secrets?"

"There's nothing ... to tell."

"Too bad."

The gobels whispered joyously each time he shrieked in agony. Tears poured from his eyes as he stared at Stumpy's mangled limb, at the teeth stained with his blood, reminders of his victims. It seemed right he was punished this way. He deserved it for all he'd done.

He wasn't conscious for the last few blows. He awoke to the feel of gobel tongues on his wounds. It burned, but the pain was tiny and comprehensible compared to the lash. They purred at the taste of his blood.

"Yumzie, yumzie." Silver eyes looked at him lovingly.

"As soon as their saliva seals your injuries, I want you on your feet," Grin said. "You don't get out of serving me. And, if for an instant, I believe you do know more than the nothing you've revealed during this interrogation—we will have this conversation again."

"Yes, Master," Ralen whispered, his throat dry, lips cracked. Blackness encroached on his vision again, and he gladly let it take him.

Chapter Twenty-Seven ~ Disintegration

Saren sulked as the Locum tended him. It was the chained mage in the corner who supplied the magic, but the Locum directed it to his battered eye and split cheek. He heard his nose crunch back into position. There was no pain. It was a powerful healing, but it couldn't fix his pride.

He played the fight over and over again in his mind, but he couldn't see what Ralen had done. He'd been so fast. All he could remember was a blur of limbs, pain, reaching out to stop it, and ending up on the ground huddled around his broken ribs. Everyone saw. The humiliation was unbearable.

After he'd given Anjee the potion, she told him everything that Dinah was working on—shackles and wereling armies, history lessons and magic—but all she would say about Ralen was, "I see him. That's all I see. He's all that matters." What did that mean? What had Dinah done to make him so fast? He'd even put Drakein down—what the hell was he?

"It was foolish to try to goad the First Commander into killing the boy," the Locum said. "Very foolish."

"Why? It's what he deserves. Look what he did to me!"

"I am looking, but you need to forget about yourself and remember who you serve. The Lady covets the boy, and whatever she is interested in, so is the Bringer. Adarmis will want him and the girl. The general will be able to learn more from them than we can glean."

"What do we need to know? Kill them, and that will put a crimp in whatever plan Dinah has. That's all there is to it."

"You are not here to do the thinking," Paeris said. To emphasize his point, he stopped the healing and Saren acutely felt the pain in one of his ribs.

"Sorry, sorry. Keep going."

The pain lingered a few moments longer, as did the priest's satisfied expression, then blissful numbness returned, and Saren relaxed again.

"It is nearly time," the Locum said, thinking aloud. "I will make a strong sedative for you to give the girl, and our loyal soldiers can carry her across the lake along with the food supplies. It will be more difficult to sneak her through the tunnel and to the Portal. Perhaps in my personal wagon…"

"You plan to steal Dinah's pet now?"

"The Lady wil be occupied with other matters. Everything is in place. The one difficulty is the boy. We must find a way to capture him as well. You must get him away from the Keeper."

"Me?" <u>I'd rather kill him</u>, he added silently.

"Yes, and quickly. Once I set events in motion, they will be impossible to stop."

GORDON SLAMMED HIS fist against the table. His pens and papers fell to the floor. "Listen!"

Caleb firmed his lips, shutting his mouth as ordered but clearly wanting to argue.

"You cannot take your family and leave. Dinah will stop you," Gordon spoke slowly and clearly as though explaining to a child.

"Not if you help me," Caleb argued. "Not if you come too. You and everyone else who wants to be free of this confinement, who wants to avoid being turned into a slave. We are more than farmers. Dinah insults us, is mad, and shunned for it. Adarmis wants us. He will take our vows, and we will be Conquered again, fighting as we should."

"If you go ... you are a traitor." Gordon heard the weariness in his own voice. This was out of control. He must either kill his friend or join him. The choice was looming, unavoidable. "Vows are not transferred from one lord to the next. No one would trust Conquered who once served their enemy. I know what Adarmis said, but he lies. This is merely a tactic to weaken Dinah, to steal her army. When she has the god's forgiveness, she will fight Adarmis for her title. He wants to get rid of us, to make sure she is never Bringer again."

"Perhaps she shouldn't be."

"Enough." He had to kill him, kill his friend. The moment he decided, images of their smiling boyhood sprang to mind. Neither was born here. They knew love and family and saw it all taken away along with their childhood toys, their tree house in the woods burning along with the real houses of their neighbors.

They were taken to the cavern city and tossed into the training yard with Drakein and Conquered who had dwelled there for generations. The Conquered children were raised in the dark, not seeing daylight until they were old enough to learn to ride in the valley. When he and Caleb next saw the sun again, they had bested all the other children. Those trained from childhood had knowledge, but they lacked the heart of boys who knew friendship, who cared for each other and who remembered what it was to be free.

Gordon fought hard to be the best, to gain command, to be trusted by the Lady, to feel secure enough to marry and build a new family. He had been rewarded for his devotion, and now he knew a life as good as the one he had lost. He could not betray the Lady ... but he could not kill his oldest friend either. "Go," he said. "Get out."

Caleb smiled and reached for his shoulder, but Gordon sat back in his chair and looked at his hands. When Caleb was gone, he breathed deeply. He would have to carefully reassign Drakein guards, make sure none were watching the Portal. He would clear the path, but he would not walk it with Caleb. He could not.

SAREN, EXHAUSTED FROM a long day of running messages and scouting out a way to fulfill the Locum's command, pushed the tent flap aside and crashed onto his cot.

"Forgetting field duty?" his bunkmate said. The soldier wore his plainest underclothes, his armor piled neatly beside his trunk.

"I've done my duty," Saren said. He'd reported everything to Varvec and got General Adarmis's approval to go forward. The Kingdom Portal was a long and exhausting detour from his normal delivery rounds.

"Everyone needs food, everyone works. That's the order. You too," his roommate said. He slapped Saren's feet off the cot.

Saren felt like punching a fist through his face, but the soldier was bigger and glared back dangerously. Saren *mumphed* and put his boots back on. He trudged out to the field, kicking stones along the way.

It was the evening shift—the Keeper on his palanquin visible in the distance—and the area to be worked illuminated by mage light. The mages weren't digging, he noticed, and they ate. So unfair.

When a shovel was placed in his hand, he thought again about hitting his bunkmate with it. The man must have sensed Saren's murderous hostility, because he chose to work at the far end of field, taking the place of an exhausted soldier manning a horse-drawn plough.

New boundary stones, marble obelisks, had been placed at the distant edge of the field. Too bad. A few intruding lizards or primitive Drakein would distract everyone so he could head back to his tent.

He lackadaisically stirred the soil, making a point of not getting any real work done, and wondered why they hadn't tried smuggling in more slaves or used some of the machines captured in the last invasion. He said as much to those around him.

"Even if the machines were reliable," a sergeant answered, "there's no one left alive who knows how to work them. Besides, there are plenty of slaves right here." He indicated the Conquered standing about, and Saren frowned. He wasn't a slave. He was better than Ralen. The Locum's plan was to capture him, but Saren was formulating his own plan, one Paeris wouldn't approve of.

At the end of the shift, Caleb intercepted him coming in from the field. Even his brother-in-law was covered in dirt. Was no one spared this indignity?

"Gordon will let us go," Caleb whispered. "I'll talk more later."

At last. Gordon was on their side. Saren felt a thrill of triumph. Now he could take his rightful place in Adarmis's ranks, an officer, with all its rewards. He imagined even more: piles of jade and gold to make Ralen's sack of stones look pathetic. He deserved all of it and more for finally delivering Dinah's army into Adarmis's grasp.

WHEN CALEB SOUGHT HIM out again the next morning, Saren didn't wait for him to speak before launching a barrage of questions. "How did you convince Gordon? When does the army march? How do we deal with the Drakein?"

The sun rose over the horizon, and the bell for devotionals rang. Caleb silently walked him to the temple, and Saren fought to keep his impatience in check. The white stone turned the red of blood in water in the early light. The temple was full, and the spillover of devotees knelt at the base of the steps. The Locum and his attendant priests stood at the threshold where everyone could see them.

Caleb shook his head and finally said, "The army isn't going. Just our family. Gordon will position the guards so we can pass through the Portal undetected. We have three days to prepare."

"No!" Saren hissed. Heads turned his way, so he got on his knees beside Caleb. "This is not what Varvec wanted. This will not make Adarmis happy."

"It's all I could get," Caleb said. He smiled at Saren. "I planned to bring you along, but if you're this opposed, you're welcome to stay."

"Shut up."

Caleb rustled his hair. "Idiot."

Saren shoved him away. "I'm not a boy anymore. I worked to get protection from Adarmis. I risked my neck carrying messages between him and the Locum. I don't care what Paeris thinks. This was my plan. *Mine.*" Saren got up and headed for the tunnel to the city. The Locum glared from his place high on the temple steps, and the people Saren nearly stepped on grumbled as he wriggled past them.

Caleb thought they had three days, but he did not know the full scale of everything that had been set in motion. He was in for a surprise, and so was Gordon. There wasn't much time. Saren needed to carry out his other plan now. His plan for Ralen, not the Locum's.

Chapter Twenty-Eight ~ Awry

Locum Paeris had given one of his usual sermons at the temple in the Portal Valley that morning, but now, at midday, he stood on the highest step of the Last God's temple in the center of the cavern city, in darkness rather than sunlight, and with a new sermon on his lips.

The old temple. A fitting place to do away with the old. It was larger than the new temple in the Portal camp, but its once white stone was dirtied by centuries of smoke from lamps and cookfires. Paeris did not need their warmth—righteousness burned within him. It was time to bring Dinah low for her hubris, time to serve the god's new, chosen Bringer.

"I must tell you what I know, and you must tell me who you follow." Paeris addressed the entire city, all those who had answered his summons and the summons of his supporters among the Conquered. Their murmurs sounded like wind shaking a forest of trees. Drakein drifted through the mob, carried there by curiosity, but they did not matter. He would say what he would say, regardless.

He clasped his pet mage's chain and felt icy power spill through his body and into his voice. "Dinah has betrayed us. Our Lord has turned away from her, and so must we!"

The crowd hushed.

"What has the Lady done?" someone asked.

"Besides dishonor us in battle and send us to the fields to work like slaves instead of soldiers?" Paeris retorted.

"It was we who dishonored her," an old man further back said. He was on crutches but wore his armor nonetheless. "We first failed to defeat the Old Kingdom, and then we failed again. Her glory is ours, her dishonor is ours."

"She is not so loyal to you," Paeris told him. "To any of you. She will replace you with Drakein and with the army of werelings she plans to breed."

"She needs us," the old soldier said.

"She needs slaves more."

The murmurs returned, louder than before. The Drakein watched, less emotional than the humans, hands shifting to their swords.

Paeris kept going. "Your armor will be exchanged for a cattle brand! We will all be Marked. We will work, and then we will be devoured, by her and by Drakein."

"Enough," a Drakein officer ordered. "This is treason." He drew his sword.

Paeris stood firm and pointed. "See. It begins. There are werelings across the lake," he added quickly, as though afraid the Drakein would strike him down, "breeding stock, meant to produce an army. They were brought here in secret, just as the Lady moved secretly in false colors. She disobeyed Our Lord. And she has acquired mages that she will not give up to the priesthood, to her god. Why would she keep them from us? Why breed an army when she has an army of Conquered already that she cannot feed?"

"I told you to be quiet," the Drakein repeated, shaking his head to clear it of the flurry of words from the priest. "Obedience is our only purpose. We do not talk. We do not ask questions."

"Easy for you to say." Paeris stepped forward, noting the way Conquered grasped the handles of their swords and looked at the Drakein around them with suspicion. "You won't be the ones eaten."

More Drakein drew swords and Conquered followed suit. Metal clashed. Screams of rage echoed through the great cavern as Paeris retreated into the sanctuary of the temple and shut the door. He allowed himself a broad smile.

Now, time to gather their gifts for the Bringer and flee before the Lady put an end to this turmoil. No matter how swiftly she quelled the uprising, oceans of blood would be spilled, and his work would be accomplished. Her loss was Adarmis' gain.

GOBELS DRAGGED RALEN across the lake for his midday chore. He disliked the wereling tunnels, but he preferred them to the Keeper's island. Gobels had healed his wounds, still the thick scars on his back caught at his shirt, and he remembered the pain of the lash with blinding clarity.

Dinah had not come for him, had not saved him.

The stench of rotten meat filled his nostrils as the guards—Conquered this time—pushed the heavy wagon past the raised portcullis. There were twice as many soldiers, but they had a harder time of it than the Drakein had.

He was shut in, all alone but for growls that shook the ground and the shovel that shook in his hands. He set to work, tossing the slimy meat into the pit as fast as he could. The growls slowly quieted as the animals ate. Sweat poured off him.

He took a moment to search the roof for butterfly wings, but there was no sign of Gar. Where was he hiding? He hoped the Hasvel hadn't tried to return to the orchard.

He leaned the shovel against the inside of the wagon and hopped out. A leather flask hung from a rope on the outside. He hadn't noticed it before. Curious, he pulled the cork and sniffed. Nothing. He poured a bit onto his palm. Water. Silently thanking the guards or whoever had stocked the wagon, he took a swig. It was fresh from a spring and not the stale stuff from the lake he was used to.

A cramp bent him over. The muscles along his neck shot tendrils of pain into his skull and his vision blurred. The ground hit him. He lay in the dirt, unable to move, drool pooling around his chin.

The squeak of metal as the portcullis raised woke him—along with a boot to his ribs. A bruise blossomed where the kick impacted, and breath left him.

"I didn't really think you'd fall for that, but I'm glad I didn't need the others' help. This way it's just you and me." The voice was familiar. Saren.

He looked up and saw the message runner wearing full Conquered armor and holding a halberd. The pointed end was aimed at his face. On instinct, he reached out to steal the weapon, but his body wouldn't move correctly. The tip of the curved blade cut through his shirtsleeve and drew blood.

"Careful," Saren said. "I was ordered not to kill you."

Ralen staggered to his feet and found himself trapped between the wagon and the wereling pit. "What do you want?"

"To disobey my orders." Saren jabbed the halberd at him.

Ralen sidestepped, trying to move as fast as the angels had taught him, but the dizziness and pain in his head threw him off balance. One foot slipped over the edge of the chasm. He grabbed the waterskin, and the leather strap tore. He shifted his grip to the rope that ran along the side of the wagon and steadied himself.

"I plan to tell Paeris that there was a 'misstep' when I tried to capture you." Saren jabbed at him again with the halberd.

Ralen dangled from the rope, both feet hanging over the pit now, and swung away from the weapon. The cave shook with wereling growls.

"Let ... go," Saren said, frustrated as Ralen stayed out of reach. The message runner sliced at him again but missed.

Ralen held tight. He focused on the creak of the rope, the burning across his palms from the rough material, even as the world spun and made his guts twist. He thought that whatever he'd been drugged with was wearing off, but he still felt awful.

"Die already!" Saren aimed well for once. Ralen felt the sharp pain of a new cut along his rib.

One of the rings fastening the rope to the wagon broke and the rope lengthened. Ralen kept his grip, but there was no tension, nothing to stop his descent as he fell through the barrier. He hung there, chin just above the stinging blue line of magic and the rest of him dangling in the chasm. Growls rose from the lair of the werelings.

Saren laughed. "This is perfect. Anjee told me all about this cage. There's no climbing back up."

Ralen gritted his teeth, fighting off the last dizziness from the potion, and caught the rope between his feet. He tried to climb but his head would not move higher. In the struggle, he slipped slightly and the magical barrier bit into his lower lip. It stung like an insect's bite.

Saren thrust with the long halberd, aiming for his right eye, and Ralen had no way to defend himself except to slip lower on the rope, so the blue barrier was above his head. The halberd blade glanced off its surface, and Saren shook his fingers from the force of the impact.

"Looks like you're taken care of," Saren said. "I'd love to stay and watch the werelings eat your feet, but I have other work to do. I'll have to tell the soldiers outside that we failed in the Locum's mission—tragic accident you getting dizzy and falling in like this—but there's still Anjee."

"What do you want with her?"

"Sorry. Can't tell."

Ralen braced his feet against the stone wall and climbed as fast as he could, ignoring rope burns and the growls that shook the air around him. The top of his skull hit the magical barrier like a hammer striking stone, and his ears rung.

"Not very smart, are you?" Saren said.

"What did I do to make you hate me so much?"

"Before you broke my nose, you mean?"

"Yes."

"Nothing. You're nothing. And I don't need a reason to want you dead anymore than I need a reason to squash an ant beneath my boot. Enjoy what little time you have left—you've been squashed and are just squirming a bit now before you die." Saren waved cheerily before he vanished from view.

Ralen listened to the smacks and gulps of werelings as they ate rotten meat somewhere in the darkness below him. He clutched the rough rope and breathed in the fetid air, clearing his head of the last of the drug Saren had given him.

Fear helped. It was the type of fear that made others shake and sob, but he'd been raised on fear. Fear had filled his dreams and bloomed stronger each morning when Mother woke him and asked him to recite his sins. There was the fear of uncertainty, not knowing what the day would hold, what penitence would be required for failing to tie his shoes or for not paying attention, for looking out the window at other children going off to school while Mother locked him in his room with only one book to study.

That was why he loved Dinah's library. So many books. So many stories. So many gods. He'd been taught there was only one, and when he finally met him—met the Last God, although he was not what Mother had imagined—Ralen had been angry.

Fear easily turned to fury.

There was fear of dying, fear of pain, fear of certain pain ... so many types of fear. But all could be transformed. He let that happen now. Let his fear of the monsters in the dark below and his fear for Anjee transform into the anger that warmed his muscles and focused his thoughts—that made him ready to fight.

SAREN CURSED AS HE tried to keep up with the squad of Conquered Paeris had given him to command. He liked the idea of ordering blooded soldiers around, but he'd wanted to look the part and now the damnable armor he wore slowed him down.

Ralen was as good as dead. He'd left two soldiers behind to guard the wereling tunnel, not that he was afraid of Ralen getting out—although there was something unnatural about that slave—but just in case the rebellion went better than expected and they could present the werelings as a gift to Adarmis. With them plus the slave girl, Paeris and Adarmis would forgive him losing Ralen—he hoped.

When they reached the labyrinth, the Conquered in front saluted the two Drakein guards and then stepped aside to let the soldiers behind step forward with bared weapons and run the Drakein through. Even gutted, the Drakein managed to slice down with their halberds and kill their murderers. It was like some comedy from a Fae stage play, with bodies locked together in death, blood everywhere.

"Clean this up now," Saren ordered. He'd been here before, so he helped to hide the corpses in the tunnels, while others mopped up the blood.

Saren led them deeper into the labyrinth. He'd found Anjee before because of her singing, but today the walls were silent. That meant she was probably in the longhouse, and he didn't know the way. He took a moment to gain his bearings.

The clatter of heavy armor and running feet was loud behind them.

"Hide," Saren ordered. They stepped into a smaller side tunnel, and Saren peeked around the corner to watch a group of Drakein run past. It looked like Locum Paeris had been busy and everyone not a part of the plan was running around madly, just as they wanted.

He signaled the Conquered, and together they followed the Drakein into the depths of the labyrinth. The Drakein made so much noise that Saren's squad went unnoticed behind them.

Saren shadowed them to the famous rose marble staircase and then hid his people in a side tunnel again. He'd never been up to the longhouse, and he didn't really want to go now. Not even with a squad of Conquered.

He'd handled Ralen and he could handle one little slave girl, but it was the army guarding Anjee—Including Lady Dinah—he had to be careful of.

The Drakein hurried up the steps, and so Saren and his squad waited patiently. Things were going his way, and he had every faith a perfect opportunity would come soon enough.

ANJEE WAS ALONE IN the library, reading a book of ancient prophecies, or trying to. Reading was difficult, and the prophecies were vague and ludicrous. She didn't know what Dinah thought she might learn from them. Her own visions were clear, sharp, and brutal. It was only because they were fragments of future possibilities that they were difficult to interpret. They had no context. She gave up on the book and instead rifled through the papers piled on Dinah's long table.

She found the bronze-hinged notebook Dinah often scribbled in. She skimmed through the pages, barely able to decipher the archaic version of God's Tongue. She saw the symbols for beast and weapon, the werelings, and ran her finger down the page until she found a pictogram that resembled a wall bristling with lightning strikes. That must be the barrier.

She'd been drawn to this book, this image, and the hairs rose along her neck.

"I must see him," she said aloud as she dug out the black scrying bowl.

Her hands shook as she poured water into the repaired bowl. She'd hated the endless hours spent staring at her reflection, but the Lady had taught her to summon the visions on demand.

The water rippled. She rested the bowl on the floor and peered inside. When the surface stilled, she saw her eyes wide with fright. Something was wrong, she felt it, but she needed to see it. She stared deep into the reflection and let her mind slip out of her control, let it open up, wider and greater than herself, so that her sensations, her skin and ears and vision filled the universe, past, present, and future.

Was this like being a god, she wondered, a true god?

No. She was not all-seeing. She saw only Ralen.

The dead army. An endless battlefield under night skies. The earth itself roaring and tearing apart to form a chasm as the black sky grew blacker. Stars dying ... Ralen was older, a scar on his left cheek. She had seen this all before—all except for the scar.

Her pulse raced as the images shifted, flying away from her, leaving. Werelings. There were always fragments of other scenes dancing at the edges of her visions, but they faded away as Ralen's possible futures collapsed, leaving only one vision. It filled the bowl and swallowed her mind—his staring eyes, his body torn to shreds.

He was trapped. He would die ... was dead. It felt real to her already. She had seen it.

"No!" She slapped the bowl away, and the watery vision trailed across the wood floor.

She hurried through the longhouse to find Dinah; only the Lady could control the werelings. "Something is happening," she called, "Ralen..."

The massive double doors in the entrance hall shook. "Lady!" A Drakein's sibilant voice shouted from the other side. It sounded like an army, pounding on the bones, making them rattle.

Anjee was too shaken to let them in.

"Dinah," she called again as she reached the workshop.

Her legs suddenly went limp, and her heartbeat became sluggish, as though it pumped something thicker than blood. She collapsed in the doorway. Dinah was feeding. Several mages already lay on the floor, weak and drained.

"Lady," she croaked, staring into the Mark on her hand. The magic that bound her worked through it, and Dinah would hear her better if she focused on it.

The pull on her veins eased. Dinah stood over her. "I told you to stay out." The Lady finally noticed the pounding on the doors. With a gesture she allowed them to swing open.

A Drakein stumbled into the entry hall. "The Conquered are rebelling," he said. Dinah's expression went rigid with fury. She stepped over Anjee and glided out the door without another word. The guards followed.

Anjee couldn't summon the energy to stand, but she made it to her knees. The mages were worse off, some shivering feverishly, some unconscious and not moving at all. The daily feedings had grown more severe as Dinah's experiments demanded more power.

She looked into her Mark and called Dinah's name. She had learned to detect the tingle of nerves that indicated Dinah's magic at work through her Marks, but the Lady's attention was elsewhere. "Ralen is dying!" she screamed. There was no response. There was no one but her.

She climbed to her feet and grabbed tools from beside the blacksmith's bench. She went to Waverly and helped the old mage stand. She leaned him against the forge and said, "Lay your shackle out. I'm setting you free."

"You can't..." he began, but he obeyed.

She placed a chisel's point against the inside of the metal cuff and struck as hard as she could with the hammer. Sparks flew and power flowed: she saw the strange red light within the metal mingle with her own aura and twist, just as the metal cracked.

Waverly felt his free wrist with his other hand and shook his head. "I would have said no one but the Lady could break this enchantment—but you did. You are far stronger than you know, child."

All she knew was that Waverly and the other mages had constructed the wereling enclosure, and now they were the only ones who could free Ralen from it. "I need your help. Gather the others."

There were only a handful of mages strong enough to stand, and she quickly broke their shackles, telling them, "This is your chance at freedom, but you must aid me."

They each nodded as she set them free, but when she stepped into the entrance hall, only Waverly stood beside her. She couldn't make them help, so she left them behind and hurried toward the bone doors.

Saren appeared in the doorway, and she stopped.

"What are you doing here?" she asked.

She had surprised him too, and the twisted expression on his face made it clear he did not like being surprised. He smoothed his scrunched lips and forced a smile. Anjee had seen gobels smile more genuinely.

"I'm delivering the daily reports," he said. She noted the armor he wore and the group of Conquered that moved up behind him. Had Dinah sent them to watch her and the mages?

"Drakein deliver the reports each morning," she said. "It used to be Ralen."

"Ralen." The older boy's face contorted again. "What is it with you two? He's all you ever talk about, and when I talk about you, he attacks."

"You saw him? Did you tell him what I asked you to?" It didn't matter now. Ralen was in danger, and she needed to get to him.

"Anjee," Saren said, stepping closer, too close. He grabbed a strand of her hair like before, but this time he yanked it. Her head was forced back, neck exposed. "I want to talk about you."

"Let me go. Ralen..."

"Is dead. I saw to it myself." His armor was sharp where it pressed into her clavicle, and his freckled face looked down at her with a sneer. "And now I need you. You're coming with me."

Ralen had been right to hate him. There was something wrong with Saren. Had she been so desperate for companionship she'd overlooked the obvious? He was just another monster.

The mage had taught her to see magic, the movement from one state to another, from thought to will, to earth and air. It was like having another pair of eyes, different from seeing the future, but just as terrible. Waverly called up magic now, a strengthening of will, a thickening of the air, and it pounded into Saren like a fist from above. The message runner crashed to the floor, but he held on to Anjee's hair and dragged her down too.

The Conquered soldiers barreled through the doorway, nearly stepping on her as they surrounded Waverly. She kicked and punched at Saren, but his armor protected him, so she grabbed the base of the strand he held captive and rolled away, tearing free and feeling some of her hair pull out from the roots.

She stood just in time to see more magic stir the air. A bullet of flame shot from the workshop—the other mages were helping—and melted through armor to pierce one soldier's heart. A cloud of black smoke formed around the other soldiers' heads, and they choked and coughed, striking out blindly with spears or swords, but Waverly had moved out of their range.

She looked to Saren and saw his expression rigid with fright. He didn't even look at her before running back down the staircase.

The soldiers caught in the cloud suffocated and fell, lifeless, with a thud onto the wooden floor.

"We have to go now," Anjee said, "before Saren comes back with more Conquered." She took Waverly's arm and pulled him along behind her.

She heard Saren banging arms and shoulders against stone as he dashed down the steps ahead of them. She stepped over pieces of armor he'd cast aside. Waverly was old and slower than she liked, and soon she could no longer hear Saren. She knew the quickest way through the labyrinth, but when they reached the great cavern there was no sign of the traitorous message runner.

"Dinah," she desperately called one more time into the Mark on her hand. As much as she hated and feared the Dark Lady, she did not know if Waverly would be able to stop the wearlings alone. They needed Dinah.

Chapter Twenty-Nine ~ Too Late

Dinah thrummed with the power absorbed from her mages. She flew across the surface of the lake faster than a horse could carry her, dress and hair blown back by the wind of her passage.

The Conquered were in revolt. She would never have believed it if she had not seen it in the Drakein's minds. Her power over her subjects should be absolute. The Marked could not disobey, but the Conquered had never dared dissent before.

Ralen.

She could no longer sense his whereabouts. The Mark did not work as it should with him anymore, which is why she had left him in the Keeper's care. The abomination was charged with his protection—and his taming. Yet, how was she to have predicted the discord Ralen's mere existence would cause? He had given her freedom of thought and the will to rebel, but she had not imagined how others would be influenced by his gifts. How was she to tame that?

When she reached the city, she saw shattered lamps, pools of blood on the streets, and houses burning. Dead and wounded humans and Drakein lay against one another. This was intolerable.

She made her way to the Command Center. The room was empty except for the First Commander and a few officers. She noted Drakein and Conquered among them. Good. Not all of her soldiers had turned on one another. "What is happening here?" she said.

"Lady." Gordon bowed. The other officers fell to their knees, frightened they would be punished for the circumstances. "It began near the old temple, Drakein accusing Conquered of treason, while humans claim they are to be enslaved and fed to Drakein."

"Absurd." She paced angrily. "What did you plan to do from in here?"

"I sent guards to surround the mob, but even they have turned on their comrades. I cannot fight a war against my own soldiers. I hoped my messengers would reach you, Lady."

"You will put a stop to this, Commander. When they see my solution, they will have real reason to panic." Dinah turned and headed for the old temple. She would have answers.

Whenever she passed a band of fighters, she sent out her aura. She killed many in her anger, but she restrained herself. Most fell unconsciousness—they were not the lucky ones. When they awoke, their fears would come true and everyone responsible for this mess would suffer.

RALEN CLUNG TO THE rope, trapped beneath the barrier, and the werelings' growls were growing louder. They were still hungry.

Let go.

He was not safe where he was, and losing his grip anyway, so he listened to the mad thought and let go of the rope. A pile of putrid meat cushioned his fall.

The rope dangled just a few feet above him. It was still attached to the wagon, but there was no point climbing back up. The barrier let things in, but nothing could get out, including him.

It was dark, darker than the slave caves. His eyes had no time to adjust. He felt a hard piece of bone near his hand and grabbed it. He sprang to his feet and put his back against a wall.

Wereling jaws clacked. There were wet slaps of meat and gulps as they swallowed the last bites from the wagon. He turned from the sounds of their feeding and ran, one hand brushing along the wall to guide him. The glow from the Mark slowly revealed stone. Narrow stone walls, uneven stone floor, small stones to trip him ... stone and more stone.

The werelings took notice of his flight. Growls rumbled through the earth and into his fingertips. He heard the scratch of claws on the ground and the jangle of metal behind him. It sounded like chains, shackles.

The path ended at the waterfall Gar had described. It was nothing more than a trickle that dampened the stone around it. The hole it fell into was edged with excrement and hair and no wider than his thigh. He reached in, hoping to widen the opening, but his fingertips stung as they hit another blue barrier. Dinah had trapped the werelings well.

He wedged himself in the corner and climbed, using his legs and elbows to brace himself against the damp stone. When he reached the upper barrier, he touched the spot where the water passed through, hoping the constant flow meant the magic was weaker there—but it wasn't. A shock danced along his nerves and all the way to his spine. His muscles turned flaccid, and he fell to the ground. Blood oozed from gashed knees.

Dozens of green lights winked in and out in the darkness, growing larger, coming closer. He noticed their ovoid shape, how a pair would disappear and reappear together. Blinking. Blinking eyes.

He moved on instinct. A wereling's arm swiped the place his head had been a moment before. Sparks flew as its claws struck stone and gouged a line, limestone dust filling the air. He jabbed the sharp end of the broken bone he carried into the creature's side, but it could not penetrate the thick fur.

He was too close now. The tip of a sword-length claw stung his left cheek. In his hyperaware state, he felt his own warm blood on his skin and smelled its iron tang above rotten meat and animal musk.

He rolled beneath the massive creature, flipped onto his feet, and dodged a blow from the next wereling in line. He weaved between them, soft fur brushing his arms, hungry growls shaking the ground beneath his feet, the rush of air from swiping claws cold on his sweat-drenched skin. If they were not in chains, he would never have outmaneuvered them. They were fast and strong and could kill him with one blow—if it hit. The angels had taught him to be faster.

He ran back the way he'd come. The long trench—he had decided it was more of a trench than a pit—ended at the pile of meat. He groaned with frustration.

He kicked through the refuse until he found a long bone with tendrils of tendon still attached. He pulled out the gobel claw knife from his pocket and used the sinews to fasten it to the bone. Now his reach was as long as theirs. He turned and brandished the weapon.

The clink of chains on stone warned him of their arrival. Green eyes filled the darkness around him.

Ralen was surrounded. Nowhere to run

One set of eyes moved in front of the others, and he felt a tremor as the heavy weight of the creature crashed onto the ground before him. The wereling's claws clattered against the stone, and metal shackles glinted in the dim light. A wet growl poured from its open mouth.

Ralen raised the bone spear and said, "Kill me if you can—but I will hurt you before I die."

The wereling reared back on hind legs, standing like a human, and glanced back at the others. "My-eeee preeey." The words were a growl, but they were words. The wereling alpha had claimed him as its food.

Ralen acted without thinking. He grabbed the rope that hung from the wagon above and swung past the encircling werelings.

The alpha followed, claws tearing up stones, hungry growls shaking the air. The wagon above teetered on the edge and finally crashed over. The wereling ploughed into the fallen wagon, pushing it along with a grumble of gouged earth. Wood splintered as the beast fought to get free of the wreckage, but it was entangled in the giant spokes of a wheel.

Once more, Ralen moved on instinct and ran back toward the wereling. Claws slashed wildly and cut into his side, drawing a trickle of blood. He dove and twisted and came up behind the animal. Its head was between the spokes and the axel. Ralen braced his feet and heaved on the wheel. The wereling gurgled as its neck was slowly crushed.

He expected the other werelings to climb the wreckage and stop him, but they hung back. The alpha had one claw between the spoke and its neck now. The wood cracked in its grip. It would be free in a moment.

Glowing green eyes stared into his, yet they weren't the eyes of an animal. "I am preeey. Killll meeee." The alpha released its grip on the spoke. One claw was stuck between the wheel and its skin, and the pressure forced the wereling's claw into its own flesh.

Ralen felt the wheel press against the soft tissue of the wereling's throat, saw the claw dig in deeper. Red blood flowed.

He couldn't. He wasn't one of the monsters. He released some of the pressure. "If I let you live," he asked, "will you let me live?"

"Killl preeey... I am Dead Mother's preeey. Better to die," it said.

"Dead mother's prey? You mean Dinah?"

"I smelll herrr on you. Know this: she is not yourrr pack mate. You arrrre preeeey too."

"The Lady protects me. She cares for me in her way. She even ... she hugged me."

The creature laughed, a sound like boulders bouncing on a drum. "And she strrrroked my furrr. We arre all herrr pets. Betterr to die. Kill meee."

He couldn't.

He released the wheel completely. "Go. I leave you alone, and you leave me alone. That's the bargain."

Green eyes stared into him and their light turned cold. Black pupils narrowed, fangs protruded from wrinkled jowls. "Insult!" it barked.

The wereling jumped to its feet, broke the wheel choking it into a dozen pieces, and tossed the wagon aside as casually as a cloak, leaving kindling at the feet of the other werelings.

Ralen never had the upper hand. The beast wanted to die—it had never been truly trapped. He shouldn't have tried to bargain. He should have done the easy thing and killed it. Now, it and the other werelings attacked.

He remembered how the wereling's own claw had drawn blood, yet a broken shard of bone had been unable to penetrate its hide. Claws were the key.

He dodged the alpha's swipe and plunged the gobel claw knife into soft tissue. The wereling yowled, spattering warm saliva against his arm. Only one eye glowed now, but the creature kept coming.

Pain seared across his shoulder. The cut felt deep, and he knew he suddenly stank of fear.

He backed away from a blur of claws and teeth lit red by his Mark. Even that faint light dimmed. Was it his vision fading? He gasped for air as his muscles burned from twisting and dodging. It was the Mark fading. It was as though Dinah's connection to him was withdrawn, as though he'd been abandoned here to die. Food for monsters after all.

No.

The angels had taught him to fight without seeing, and so he fought.

ANJEE REACHED THE MASSIVE gate that closed off the wereling lair and hesitated at sight of the two Conquered guards on either side of the opening.

"Why aren't they helping Ralen? Don't they know something's wrong?" Anjee said.

"I think they work with the ones who attacked us... Is that the city?" Waverly asked, pointing to flames in the distance.

The pinpoints of light had become a wall of fire. The city was burning—yet the guards did not stir. What was wrong with them? She spotted gobel corpses floating beside the shore. They were pitted with wounds, their twisted shapes disturbing the reflections in the water.

"I'll distract them," Anjee told the mage. She ran up to the closest soldier and said, "You! Open this gate. The Lady commands it."

The guard pulled his sword, and Anjee stepped back before the blade sliced her in two. The metal was already wet with yellow blood. They had killed the gobels.

The Conquered soldier readied for another swing, but lightning rose out of the ground and danced between the spaces of his armor, between sword and helm. He convulsed and crashed to the ground, writhing.

Waverly called up more lightning and felled the other soldier, who contorted like a marionette, twisting with pain. It seemed forever before he stilled, dead.

Anjee stuck her fingers through the holes in the latticed gate. She couldn't see Ralen, only the fire-lit tunnel that led to the wereling pit. Growls shook the limestone beneath her feet. "The barrier," she reminded the mage.

Waverly closed his eyes and mumbled a few words.

Her hairs stood on end. Power. Even more than the old man had used to call lightning. It was a very different feeling from what Dinah did. This energy was pushed out from the heart of the mage, directed through the latticed gate and into the lair. It gave to the world rather than taking away.

"It's done," Waverly said. He drooped, his skin ashen. The Lady had already drained most of his reserves, and it looked as though Anjee had forced him to use the rest of it.

"Ralen!" she called. "Ralen! Can you hear me?"

There was no answer.

"Those are werelings," the old man said. He meant there was no hope.

"Ralen!" She spotted the mechanism for the portcullis and ran to it. She pulled the lever, but it wouldn't budge. The gate was too heavy. "Help me."

Waverly put a hand on her shoulder. "The barrier is down. If we open the gate, the werelings will get out. They're immune to fire and lightning. Even if I had the strength to call such power again, we can't fight them. We've done all we can for your friend."

She took his hand off her shoulder and placed it on the lever. "Pull." She braced her legs and used her whole body. The portcullis raised a fraction. A latch held the metal gear in place, so she was able to take a breath. She pulled again, red faced from the strain, but it moved faster when the old mage started helping.

Her legs and back screamed with pain. The jagged lower edge of the portcullis was high enough for her to crawl beneath, but, before she could lock the lever in place, it dropped a few inches. Waverly had let go too soon.

"Don't give up..." she chided then stopped as soon as she realized Waverly was on the ground, his blood pooling around leather boots. Saren stood over him with a dagger.

"No," Anjee cried. "You've killed him. Why would you do that?" Since she'd been trapped with Dinah, her best moments had been with Waverly, learning from him, listening to his creaky old laugh....

And now he was dead. Like her parents and brothers and everyone she had ever known before coming here with Ralen.

"Isn't it obvious? So, we can be alone." Saren smirked. "And so this will be a fairer match. I've been shadowing you since the tunnels. The Locum won't be happy if I come back empty handed."

He reached for her. She kicked, but the blow hardly fazed him. She dodged behind the portcullis mechanism before he could grab her.

"You're not being nice. I thought we were friends."

"You were wrong."

"No use delaying the inevitable. Adarmis wants you, and what the Bringer wants, he gets."

"You don't have to obey him. You serve Dinah."

"You don't understand. I want to. I want my reward." He grabbed the sleeve of her dress, and the satin tore.

She fell, but he maintained his grip, and the tear widened. The teeth of the portcullis gate were right behind her, the gap almost wide enough. She pulled herself beneath it, and the chain creaked. If it slipped, if Saren touched the lever, the gate would fall and kill her.

Her chest caught on an edge of metal and trapped her. Saren grabbed her leg. "Quit fighting me. You're a nothing slave. Accept it and do what I tell you to do."

She kicked at him with her other leg, the portcullis teeth digging into her skin. She let them bite deep and draw blood. She ignored the pain and wriggled farther beneath the gate. He kept pulling, and her leg felt like it might come off.

Waverly had taught her some "unnatural" magic, but she'd never tried anything more than setting a scrap of paper afire. She'd felt the flow of energy between Waverly and the earth, though, felt the charge build, and knew what she needed to do. She let it build now, between her skin and Saren's. She thought of pain and fire and the blue flash of lightning in a dark storm. A black ocean...

"Little bitch!"

Then Saren contorted as electricity danced between his arms. His eyes rolled into his head, and he collapsed. It was far more lightning than the old man had managed, and it didn't stop when Saren stopped moving.

The bright waves moved harmlessly across her body, played between the gaps in the latticed gate, and arced to the chain and lever. She smelled burning metal.

She moved her legs out of the way as fast as she could, but her dress was caught. The gate crashed down on it. Metal fused, sealing her in. Slowly, slowly, the electricity faded, leaving only her jangling nerves and shaking limbs.

Women are more powerful, the mage had said—powerful enough to kill without meaning to. Saren's body smoked, the skin burnt and blackened like one of Dinah's victims. She'd only wanted to get away. She didn't want....

She shook her head and stood. There were a thousand things she would undo if she could, and this was not the worst.

The satin dress fell to the ground, ripped in two. The old rag underneath was stained with blood from the cuts on her chest, but it was all she needed. She turned and looked into the wereling tunnel. The barrier was down, the portcullis sealed. The smell of Saren's burning flesh filled the air, and the monsters were quiet.

"Ralen?" she called. "Are you there?"

Chapter Thirty ~ Kill Me

Sweat stung Ralen's eyes and burned across the gashes on his face and arms. He had wounded more werelings, but he was tired, and they had grown cautious, slowly circling him. Soon, he'd be surrounded, nowhere to go, but that was okay. He wasn't sure he could run anymore.

"Ralen," Anjee called. She was close, the sound echoing through the tunnel above—the sweetest sound in the world.

He held the claw spear tight, never taking his eyes off the alpha wereling. "I hear you."

"Ralen. Get out of there. The barrier is gone. Get out!"

The werelings shifted closer.

The stone walls that held him were twenty feet high. He might be able to scale them, but not without being torn to pieces first.

"I can't." It took the last of his energy to say those words.

Dirt and pebbles rained down on his shoulders. He glanced up. Anjee hung over the ledge above, her arm outstretched. "Yes, you can. Take my hand."

She shouldn't be here.

The alpha laughed its scratchy laugh again and bared teeth, the fluid from its punctured eye oozing along the side of its muzzle and into its open mouth. "Morrre preeey."

The alpha lunged, and Ralen reacted. He was surprised by how fast he moved, surprised he had anything left inside to give. He grabbed a handful of fur and swung behind the wereling, naked toes digging into its pelt. He climbed up its massive back and jumped the remaining distance to Anjee. She slipped as his weight caught her arms, but he did not linger there. He swung his legs, caught the edge of the trench, and clambered up beside her.

Her eyes were wide. "How did you...?"

He grabbed her elbow and pulled her back from the edge of the trench. The alpha landed right beside them, and the force of its impact shook the ground.

LOCUM PAERIS TRUSTED no mortal to do the god's work as well as he could, least of all a mere message runner, no matter how well connected to Caleb and the other Conquered traitors. Thus, he had sent competent soldiers with Saren to secure their quarry. Even so, none had returned. They were likely dead. It had been a gamble sending them into the heart of Dinah's lair, but that was why he had used those more expendable than he. It would be safest to flee through the Portal now, but ... the power of the female mage was too alluring.

And he could not serve God and Bringer without courage.

He crossed the lake in a boat propelled by magic. The chained mage at his feet was weary from the day's activities, but Paeris did not care if he were drained dry. His spies had seen Dinah in the city restoring order, which meant this was his one opportunity to enter her longhouse, and there was no time to waste.

As soon as his feet touched the shore, he wrapped himself in power, an invisible shield meant to deflect weapons just in case the battle had spread this far. He took a step, but his mage did not follow. The man clung weakly to the side of the boat.

"Come," Paeris commanded.

"I can't, Master."

"Then you are no longer of use." Paeris pulled with his will and stripped the last shreds of energy from the man, storing it inside his hollow center rather than emanating it through the Portal to his god, as he would have done if he weren't so desperately in need of the magic himself. The mage splashed into the shallow water face first and lay there, stripped of life and soul.

Paeris headed for the Lady's labyrinth, prepared to kill anyone who got in his way, but the Drakein guards were gone. He made for the rose stair, expending a tiny amount of power to make the climb easier on his old legs.

He hesitated at the ancient bone doors, feeling an icy trickle of fear at invading Dinah's domain. What if she caught him here? Courage, he reminded himself. He would get what he came for and join Adarmis before the Lady knew what happened.

He put a hand on polished skull handles and pushed. The scene on the other side surprised him. The Conquered he'd sent with Saren were dead on the floor. Mages were loose, chains jangling as they pored over books or hung out open windows to judge the distance to the valley floor below.

"If not the Portal, we must try overland," one mage told another.

"There is no place she will not find us!"

"We stay," another argued. "Obey, and she might let us live."

"Like him?" The one hanging out the window pointed at a human skull embedded in the wood frame. He caught sight of Paeris. "Priest!"

The warning came too late. Paeris raised a hand and pulled their power into him. The hollow core in his chest filled as he chained them to his will.

They didn't need to be bound to be controlled, but he enjoyed the symbol. "Hand me your chains," he told them.

The mages nodded as one, all arguments over. They placed the ends of their broken chains in his hands—a dozen leashes, more than a dozen powerful men at his command. He had never controlled so many at once. It was a heady feeling.

"Where is the girl?" he asked. While the mages were a boon, she was the real prize.

"Anjee and Waverly ran off," one of his new thralls said. "We don't know where."

With a frustrated sound, Paeris yanked on the chains and dragged the men after him. He flew down the rose stair. He'd jealously watched the Lady move this way often enough, but now similar power was his.

DINAH FELLED THE BATTLING groups between her and the Last God's temple. They weakened and slumped, weapons clattering to the paving stones before their skin blackened, leaving bones in her wake. These were her soldiers, she chided herself, but her anger was unquenchable. They had betrayed her.

A Conquered woman and a Drakein were locked together in combat. She separated them, snapping the Drakein's neck. The woman was wide eyed when Dinah tore out her throat. Warm blood filled her mouth and coated her tongue. She licked every drop from her delicate fangs, relishing the taste. It had been a long time since she'd needed to feed that way, but it satisfied her as nothing else could.

Her shaking limbs stilled, and the frustration lessened enough for her to think clearly. The soldiers had not betrayed her. They were too weak-minded, with no will of their own. The god's influence was gone, and hers was silenced by Ralen's presence. In the vacuum, the priests' words and subtle magic had swayed them. There was the scent of Adarmis behind this as well.

She wished she had killed him when she first captured him. The General had been an annoyance ever since. His followers, however, were within her reach, and she would not fail to destroy them.

The copper doors to the old temple were barred from the inside. She unleashed her aura and blasted them off their hinges, spraying marble dust into the air. She stepped through the cloud of debris and glided into the sanctuary, her slipper-shod feet inches above the rubble.

White robed priests hid behind pillars and stared at her from the shadows of their hoods.

"Where is the Locum?" Her voice held power, swirling the dust, and making the priests tremble—all but one. One stood defiant, the three mages from the Command Center crouched at his feet. He thought they were enough to protect him.

"This is the Last God's house, Lady. You do not rule here."

The gall. She was immobilized by shock for a few seconds, but the frozen feeling was quickly replaced by a warming fury that started in her loins and moved through her chest and throat and out through her arms. She stretched out her hand, and a ribbon of shadow spun from her palm and encircled the priest.

He summoned a column of swirling flames, but she absorbed it into her aura. The fool screamed in agony, his white robes torn away by shadows, followed by his hair and eyes and strips of flesh. She stopped before he was dead and left his skinless body quivering on the floor.

"Now," she said, looking at the others. "Tell me where the Locum is hiding."

The priests scattered, heading for the side doors, but she caught each one in her aura and dragged them bodily through the air and across the ground until they were heaped at her feet. A few struck out with magic, sending shards of stone at her head or electricity that rose from the ground. Her aura absorbed it all: their energy along with their lives.

A dozen priests were now leathery skeletons. They had never been more useful. Priests were good at keeping enslaved mages in check and the populace of Conquered devoted to the god, but first and foremost, she needed her people devoted to her. The moment the priests turned against her, their existence lost all meaning, and their lives were forfeit. They thought they had a connection to the divine and were superior to other mortals, but they were wrong. The god did not care for anything, not even His sycophants. They would not be avenged.

Then she felt the wereling barrier go down. Paeris. That's where he was.

She sent out her thoughts, trying to feel the beasts, connected to them through the shackles, but her vision of them was hazy, as though hidden by dense cloud. She had not seen anything clearly for some time, not since Ralen arrived, and it grew worse each day.

She hurried from the temple, dead priests already forgotten, and ignored the fighting on her way to the lake. She sped across the surface, her thoughts intent on destroying Locum Paeris.

The Keeper and a swarm of gobels intercepted her mid way.

"Lady," the Keeper said. "Have you quelled the uprising? I sent Drakein, but there were too many Conquered traitors. I warned you about Gordon and the others..."

"Enough!" She frowned, noting the mass of green-skinned gobels that surrounded the Keeper. "Where is Ralen? You were not to let him out of your sight."

"Lady." His fingers fluttered. "He is never beyond my reach. Gobels escorted him to the wereling cave, and that is where he is now."

The frustration was back. "Useless. Surrounded by useless..." If Grin had any blood in his veins, she would have drained it. "The werelings are free."

The Keeper trembled. "What? I will go to him at once."

"No. You will help the First Commander achieve order. If you do not, or if Ralen is dead, then I will spend the rest of eternity devising tortures for you, Grin."

He nodded violently, but she was too weary to enjoy his fear. She flew across the lake, unsure whether she preferred to discover Ralen alive or dead.

Her realm was falling apart. She felt the disorder in her marrow, the filamentous connection to her Marked, including the Keeper. The priests' treason, the war between Conquered and Drakein.... She did not like this feeling of things slipping out of her grip, as she had slipped out of the grip of her god.

Ralen was the cause. He was her freedom, her hope for the future, but he was also destroying what little she had. Something had to be done.

RALEN STOOD HIS GROUND before the wereling leader and said, "Kill me if you can, but I will never let you touch Anjee."

A fallen torch guttered in the dirt, and its light allowed him to finally see the creature. The alpha was ten feet tall and thick with muscle. It sniffed the air between them, black nose glistening. Anger poured from its one remaining eye along with that eerie green glow. "I am not prrrey." It stepped closer.

"Run. You can't fight it," Anjee said.

"I <u>have</u> been fighting it." Ralen pushed her out of the way and swiped at the creature's forearm with the gobel claw spear. The wereling side-stepped, its movement hampered by the nickel shackles around its ankles.

"Watch out." Anjee put hands over her mouth when the monster struck in a blur of slashing, saber length claws. Ralen avoided them all. He moved just enough to evade instant death but not so far that his own weapon was out of range. His answering attack was a blur too, but one that drew blood from the creature.

"Stop." Dinah's imperious voice echoed down the tunnel behind them from the other side of the portcullis. The wereling's shackles glowed red like the Lady's Marks, and the wereling stumbled, falling to all fours.

The alpha spit, saying, "Dead Motherrr." The red faded from the shackles, and the wereling stood up again.

"I said stop," Dinah repeated. But the shackles no longer obeyed her command.

"I am not prrrey. Not yourrrs!" The monster sprang. Ralen thought it would charge after Dinah, but it twisted in mid-leap and reached for Anjee.

Ralen reacted and raised his spear. The gobel claw cut through the flesh beneath the wereling's ribcage, and the weight of the creature as it fell shoved the weapon in deeper. It died with a shudder, its one remaining eye looking into his. The acid green light slowly faded until the eye was empty as a bead of black glass.

Ralen sank onto the ground beside his latest victim. He had warned it to leave Anjee alone—and so it had known exactly what would make him kill it. "Something always dies," he said. Death had become a part of him.

Anjee touched his shoulder and then the gash across his cheek. He winced. She said, "All that matters is that you didn't."

Metal groaned and shrieked. Dinah's form was silhouetted in the tunnel opening, the portcullis twisted and broken at her feet. She stormed toward them, and her gaze fell on the wercling's corpse.

Red Marks burned across Anjee's arms and legs, and she collapsed. Ralen held her. "Anjee?"

Her lips trembled, speechless, until the Marks faded. Then she said, "The Dark Lady is angry."

Dinah's voice was as calm and cold as ever. "The Drakein and Conquered are at war. You two will seek shelter in my home. It is the only safe place. Go."

Ralen nodded and took Anjee's trembling hand, leading her toward the exit. She kept staring at Dinah with wide, frightened eyes.

ONCE THEY PASSED THE mangled portcullis—and the bodies of Saren and Waverly—Anjee ran. Through the Marks she had sensed Dinah's fury. She knew how close both she and Ralen were to death, how slim the Lady's control. They had best obey. But before they reached the labyrinth of tunnels that led to the longhouse, Ralen stopped her.

He stared across the lake. "The city is burning."

"It is not our concern."

"Gordon and his family ... I have to help," he said.

"You are not Conquered." She felt a stab of jealousy at his concern for them.

He took another step toward the lake.

"There you are."

Anjee spun. A white-robed priest wearing a gold mantel stepped out of the Lady's labyrinth. The mages from the workshop were with him, their faces slack, eyes glazed.

The priest made a gesture, and she felt a hand around her heart, squeezing. It was as though he had reached inside and was scooping out her soul. She arched back on tiptoes, mouth gaping, trying to cry out, but no sound emerged.

"What are you doing to her?" Ralen said. "Locum! Pay attention to me. I thought it was me you wanted to see burn?" Ralen tore the gobel claw dagger from the bone spear he'd used to kill the wereling and took a menacing step towards the priest.

Anjee's feet left the ground, and she felt herself flying. She landed in a heap before the Locum. She fought the paralysis and lifted her head enough to see that a dozen yards now separated her and Ralen. He ran toward her, but a hand squeezed her heart and power flowed out of her and into the priest. The Locum used what he stole from her to rend the earth. Limestone cracked and fissures formed, blocking Ralen's path. The fissures filled with phosphorescent water from the lake, and stalactites, disturbed by the tremor, tumbled from the ceiling and crashed all around them.

"Ralen," she gasped. A chunk of stone struck him, and he went down. "Ralen."

"Your power is glorious," the Locum whispered into her ear. "I am gorged with it. Imagine what I can achieve with you chained to me." The Locum ripped the depleted core from one of the mages—Yira his name was—and the man fell dead. The Locum snapped the dead man's wrist bones and pulled off his manacles. He tried to put the bloodied things on her, but her hands were too small, and they slipped right through. "Just a bit of adjustment I think..."

Talons of ice cut into her left shoulder, chilling her to her marrow. The Dark Lady was there, and her touch felt like death.

Dinah let go of her shoulder and stepped in front of her. The priest's link to her core was cut off, as though the Lady's body had physically blocked it. "Run," Dinah ordered.

Anjee was compelled by the Marks as much as by her own desire to get away from there. She was on her feet in a second and running toward Ralen, hopping the fissures at their narrowest points.

Behind her, she heard the Lady say, "Here we are at last, Locum. No more pretenses."

Anjee reached Ralen and was relieved to find him already stirring. There was a massive scrape down his right arm, but the fallen stone had missed his skull.

Anjee felt the Lady's anger wash over her like a hurricane. It was aimed at the priest this time, but it made her knees buckle. Ralen helped her up and half dragged her toward the lakeshore. She heard his ragged breathing. He must be exhausted, but somehow, he kept going.

"What happened to you?" he asked, taking a breath when they were beside the water.

"Magic," she said. "He tried to steal my magic." She'd never felt anything like it. Dinah drained her nearly every day, but that was like being weakened by blood loss. The core of her was still present, still able to make more. The priest had nearly taken it all in one gulp. She felt disjointed, like things had been moved and not yet slipped back into their rightful place.

"What magic?"

She hadn't told him, and now, with Dinah's attention elsewhere she felt free to speak. "Ralen, I have power, have always had it. It's what Dinah feeds on instead of my life, what makes me valuable to her." She still did not mention the visions. She'd already been down that path in her dreams. "You think she took me in only as a favor to you? She gains by it, by everything. She wants you, and you can't let her have you. You're too special."

He looked towards the burning city on the opposite side of the lake. "Special. That's what Dinah says, but what does that mean? I think I'm a slave, but Dinah won't let me be. I think I can be Conquered, but I can't be that either. I don't know what I can do, so why should I try to do anything? It all falls apart."

"Don't just accept." Anjee shook him, more angered by this than anything. "Don't you care what happened to our world? What's still happening in other places? How can you not want to stop it?"

"Don't think you know what I want. Not even Dinah can read my thoughts anymore."

"Then tell me."

"What I want is dangerous. I'm dangerous." He wouldn't stop staring at the city. "Blasphemers are tossed into cages and burned. They die in the millions. I saw that the Last God has a face, Anjee. I saw. That was but the first blasphemy. I don't want you to suffer for what I want."

"Dinah could kill me tomorrow," she said. "You can't protect me from everything."

"She wouldn't."

"You don't know her anymore than she knows you. You don't know her half as well as I do. It's <u>because</u> you're dangerous that she keeps you and me alive. She wants to use you."

"Then maybe I should let her."

"No. You can choose your own fate."

"I don't see any choices." He finally looked at her, and his expression was so lost she couldn't stay angry with him.

"There are endless choices. If only you knew..." She wanted to tell him everything, make him believe, but she didn't know where to start.

A dying mage screamed, and she noticed the fissures were widening all around them. Things were about to get much worse. "We have to go now," she said.

They found a boat further along the shore and dead Drakein. Ralen helped her into the boat and then grabbed a sword from a fallen soldier. He held it poised at his side and turned back to where the priest and Dinah faced one another.

"Don't," Anjee warned. "Who would you fight for, anyway? The Dark Lady or the Last God's priest? Find your own way."

Ralen clenched his muscles and made a sound of frustration before tossing the weapon in the boat and picking up the oars. Columns of flames rose from the city to the full height of the cavern, like an aurora tearing across the sky. Her first visit to the city would be as witness to its destruction.

Behind them, magic seared the air. Anjee felt the ebb and flow of it, the priest attacking, the Lady consuming. It left afterimages in her mind and began to turn the lake around them to steam.

Chapter Thirty-One ~ Power

The power in the mages cores drew Dinah like gravity, but she couldn't reach them. The priest blocked her way, his hold on them tighter than it had been on Anjee. "You think you can oppose me, Locum?"

"I have a dozen mages, Lady, more than any priest has ever wielded. Shouldn't I at least try?"

"You are mortal. You will burn from the inside and consume them along with you. I want them back."

"Would you spare me? Let me go to Adarmis' side and serve the new Bringer?"

"Of course," she lied without hesitation.

"You have shamed us all in the eyes of Our Lord, and you show no shame now. I have the opportunity to destroy you, and I will take it." He squeezed the mage's chains in both hands and pulled their souls into his.

"Fool." The cave darkened. Glow worms, torches, the fire that consumed the city, even the few remaining slaves nearby—all but her precious mages—were drained as she pulled in everything she could.

The priest's attack began as a tingling in the air, the scent of ozone. Orange streaks of fire rained down from stalagmites, molten bits of stone breaking loose and incinerating the moss and lichen not already blackened by her aura. She took the heat into herself. Everything he did fed her. She absorbed energy just as the Last God had absorbed all other beings of power.

"You can't kill me, priest. I am beyond your understanding," she said.

She took a step forward and reached out a hand to push through the thick barrier of air Paeris had erected as a shield. If she could get close enough, she could rip out his throat before he wasted any more of the mages' power on fruitless attacks.

The ground shook. A crack appeared at her feet. It filled almost instantly with superheated water from the lake, and mist blocked her view of the priest and his captives. She came inexorably on, feet floating over the gap, but when she got there, he was gone.

<u>Invisible?</u> She listened for heartbeats, felt with her aura, and located the burning cores of the mages in the center of the lake. Teleportation. Costly and wasteful. Another mage was already dead from the effort, his powerful core pulling free of his corpse to form an apparition as she watched. Paeris would consume the ghost and kill all the remaining mages just to get his miserable hide closer to the Portal and escape. She would not let that happen.

RALEN WATCHED DINAH'S battle with the Locum as he rowed. When the glow worms went out, Anjee grabbed the sides of the boat so hard he heard the wood creak beneath her fingers. The flames in the burning city vanished as well, leaving them in utter darkness.

The battle shifted to the Keeper's island. Flashes of lightning and the purple glow from some twisting gaseous cloud of magic reflected on the water. He was acutely aware there was a gobel caught in the middle of the destruction, trapped in a cage. Ralen had nothing else to steer by, so he shifted course and headed towards the center of the lake.

"What are you doing?" Anjee said. "You should stay out of this and pray the Locum kills her."

He couldn't pray for that. As a child, he'd never prayed for anything—not even when Mother told him to pray for mercy for his damned soul. He had always pretended, clasping his hands and closing his eyes, but he would never think the words. It was one thing to know God existed and another to risk catching His attention. The first time he truly prayed was when he pleaded with the Lady for the Conquered, for Gordon, and for Anjee. He would pray for others—and the only being he knew who would answer was Dinah.

"Claw needs our help," he said. "He saved your life when you would have drowned, don't you remember?"

"I remember." It sounded like she was anything but grateful.

By the time they reached the limestone isle, Dinah and the Locum had vanished again, but moss still burned and even some of the stones glowed red hot, so there was enough illumination to see by. Anjee stayed on the boat with the sword while he hopped ashore, bare feet carefully avoiding the scorched areas.

The small island was deserted, the Keeper's chest of belongings blasted into pieces and the charred contents scattered everywhere. There was no sign of the small cage.

He squeezed the hilt of his knife and called, "Claw, are you here? Are you hurt?"

"Here," a pained gobel voice whispered.

He made his way towards the sound. The gobel was caught beneath a shattered stalagmite, the bent remains of his cage entangling his legs. Ralen shifted the stone aside and tore away broken metal wires until Claw was able to drag himself out of the wreckage.

"You came for me!" Claw said excitedly. "Thank you, Master."

"I'm not your Master."

"Yes, Master." The creature bowed, head on the ground.

DINAH FLEW ACROSS THE surface of the lake so fast the water split into a deep trough and waves spread out from the line of her passing. She must not let Paeris flee again, must not let him waste more precious power.

He stood on the lakeshore, braced wearily against the golden staff of office he carried everywhere, captive mages flopping like dying fish at his feet. They had not yet regained their strength, and already he drew on them again to create a barrier of summoned stone. The force of her approach pushed her halfway through it.

She felt like a bug caught in amber, and it was a feeling she did not enjoy. A physical barrier was more difficult to absorb than the pure energy of a lightning bolt, but she concentrated and breathed in. She no longer needed to breathe, but the gesture worked to turn the stone syrupy and pull it into her, into her skin and pores, where it dried into dust and vanished like lost ages of time.

"What are you?" Paeris asked between exhausted gasps.

"The one thing you should not have crossed." She felt him reach for more power, and she sent a thread of darkness out, looping it around the mage's chains and ripping them out of his grip. It startled him, but his connection to their cores was unbroken.

A wave of water rose out of the still lake and crashed over her. The force was enough to pound her into the rock. She stood her ground, absorbing even that, turning the pressure inward to fill the void in her core, a void greater than the priest's.

The coil of darkness under her command spread out from the fallen chains and reached for the hem of the priest's robe, black fingers clutching hungrily at his legs.

"Lord, protect me," he cried.

"He no longer listens, Locum. Not here. This is my Hell." She pulled the tendrils through his body, parting his limbs as she had the water of the lake. He fell to his knees on bleeding stumps, his mouth gaping. A trickle of blood ran between grey stones and pooled beside her feet. She bent down, touched a fingertip to the glistening surface, and licked the ruby drop from her cold skin.

"Because of your treason, this rebellion you and Adarmis devised, I feel … frustrated, Locum. Fortunately, I have a favorite remedy for this mood." She bypassed the rivulet of blood and went for the source.

Paeris prayed to his god as she tore out his throat. She was connected to him in that moment as intimately as she was connected to her Marked. She knew all his hopes and ambitions, all his piety and sacrifice, but it was his hatred for her that tasted most sweet.

She rested a moment, feeling the priest's life warm inside her. Why had she ever stopped feeding this way? She reigned in her aura, and the glow worms on the cavern ceiling brightened, blanketing her in blue light.

It was a brief moment of peace. A chain encircled her throat, and the mage holding it pulled with all his strength. Another picked up the priest's staff and ran the sharp point into her heart.

Like her lungs, the organ was no longer necessary, but her anger flared out of control. She caught them up in her aura, smothering them with fury, and her two assailants collapsed. Their hearts gave out in terror, and she instinctively consumed their dying cores, but her reflex began to drain the other mages as well. Already weak from the priest's demands on their power, their souls began to gutter and die.

She needed them alive. She focused her thoughts and directed her power from accustomed paths to the unnatural course, toward life. She gave back the energy she'd stolen, hoping it wasn't too late. A needed breath, a vital heartbeat, she heard their bodies clutch at existence. Their cores steadied, a link to the source of All, and relief washed over her.

Six of them lived, but they were as rebellious as the Locum. She had hoped the Mark, combined with the primitive version of her shackles, would be enough to control them, but she was wrong. The shackles had failed to control the werelings too, at least when Ralen was near.

She could not see him, but she could sense the girl with him. They were on a boat and drawing closer.

How strong was the boy's influence? Was it unchecked because the Last God had withdrawn his Presence from her realm? Or ... did Ralen's Presence war with the god's?

She remembered their first meeting, the emotions she'd been free to feel, even with her Lord beside her, and she knew it was no war—the boy's Presence was unstoppable.

Ralen was her hope for freedom, but if he could not be controlled then it was too dangerous to let him live.

As she wrapped the weakened mages in magic restraints and used her aura to drag them across the water, toward the safety of her mountain, she avoided crossing paths with Ralen lest she act too rashly. Perhaps there were alternatives.

The Drakein remained loyal, but they were not an effective army. She needed the Conquered's adaptability and the werelings' ferocity to defeat Adarmis and the others who would stand between her and her goal. And she needed Ralen for the rest of it. There had to be a way.

She did not return the mages to the longhouse. Instead, she went into the labyrinth to where the ensorcelled cages from the wagons were stored and locked them inside. Let them sleep on iron, shivering in the dark for a night, and pay the price for disobedience.

GORDON HAD DIFFICULTY convincing the Drakein he was loyal—so many of the Conquered had turned—but he made sure he was surrounded by guards of both races as he made his way through the city and to the Portal tunnel. It was packed with fleeing families. He'd given Caleb long enough.

Conquered shrunk from Drakein as Gordon and his squad passed, but he did not stop to arrest any of them. He needed to secure the Portal before anything else, stop the tide of deserters.

When he reached the eastern valley, he saw that the encampment was overrun, tents trampled into the dirt. Only the stone buildings remained, like rocks in the ocean of people swirling around them. He had to bash a few soldiers with the blunt end of his dagger to make his way through the crowd. They glared but recognized the First Commander's insignia and a lifetime of discipline stayed them from striking back.

When he reached the marble arch, he found Caleb and his wife, Lillian, there, directing the exodus. They should have fled already. Gordon took Caleb by the arm and dragged him aside, outside the range of Drakein hearing. "I said only your family, Caleb."

"Why should we be the only ones? Everyone here is in danger of being Marked. Dinah has her Drakein and her werelings and no lands to conquer. She doesn't need us."

"You believe that nonsense? There's no truth to any of it."

"Would Dinah tell you if she planned to turn us into food?"

Gordon chewed his lip and did not answer.

The Drakein he'd brought moved to block the Portal with massive bodies and crossed halberds. Lillian and several other Conquered tried to push them aside, but they were shoved back. Hands went to sword hilts.

"Stop," Caleb said to the Drakein. "You cannot keep us from leaving."

"You are traitors," the grey-scaled creature growled down at him. "Fleeing also makes you cowards."

Caleb drew his sword.

"No," Gordon shouted, moving between them. "We will not turn on each other!"

"We already have," Caleb said, not taking his eyes off the Drakein. His friend struck out, forcing Gordon to dodge away. The Drakein blocked with his halberd.

"I order you to stop," Gordon said.

"Dinah's orders come first." The Drakein lunged at Caleb.

Gordon's friend moved aside, but the other Drakein sliced down and caught Caleb in the neck. Blood sprayed across them, his friend's blood.

"Caleb!" Lillian cried.

It had happened so quickly, so foolishly. He couldn't believe it, but in an instant Caleb was gone. His body thrashed at Gordon's feet. When Gordon reached down to hold him, he saw that the eyes were empty, the soul already gone to the god, and nothing but twitching muscles remained.

He drew his own sword and cut down Caleb's murderer. The other Drakein stepped backward through the Portal and onto the God's Plain. Lillian's lip curled into a snarl as she went after them. He couldn't let her die too.

Gordon stepped across into a hot wind and squinted at the strange blue sun. Conquered surrounded the Drakein guard, and he was torn, wondering who to help, until the halberd cut through Lillian's shoulder guard and nicked her chin. A bit lower and she would have joined her husband in death. He ran the Drakein through. "Get to safety," he told her.

She nodded her thanks and turned toward the horde of God-fed on the Plain. He stared wide eyed as people continued to push past him, tearing off red tabards and streaming toward the distant green of Adarmis's army. He had killed his own guards. This couldn't be. It mustn't be. Conquered had betrayed their lady.

The shame was his, but he could not let his children bear the consequences. With a growl of frustration, he fought against the flow of people and hurried back to the cavern city.

GORDON ORDERED EVERY soldier he saw to begin a bucket brigade to extinguish the flames, but most ran in the opposite direction. It was chaos. He wanted to bash heads and bring order, but that instinct was overridden by the fear he felt for his family. He had nearly lost them to plague, he could not forsake them now, even if it meant temporarily abandoning his duty.

Then the fires went out, along with the lamps, and his breath went cold. A strange hush filled the darkness—magic at work.

He fumbled through his pouch until he found a fire striker, tore a fragment of cloth from his undershirt and lit it. The fire struggled, a dim orange, until it finally came to life. He singed his fingers but got a lamp burning and held it aloft as he made his way between stone buildings. The clamor of battle and screams of dying, momentarily hushed, now returned.

His house was intact, the door locked. He pounded on the wood and shouted his wife's name, "Kiera!" until the maid opened it. He pushed past her, still calling to his family. They came down the stairs in full armor.

"Gordon." Kiera put her arms around him. "What is happening? Who is the enemy?"

"Everyone." He held her at arms' length and looked into her eyes. "You must take the children through the Portal."

"What?"

"Conquered are joining Adarmis' army and Drakein are slaughtering everyone. It isn't safe here."

She frowned. "Are you joining Adarmis too?"

He couldn't bear the look of betrayal in her eyes and rushed to defend his actions. "No. Drakein turned on the Conquered, or the other way around. I don't know. All I know is that Dinah will end this any way she can. I want you out of danger. Wait on the Plain. I will return to fight for Dinah, but there is no guarantee she will spare us. You may have to don green with the others."

"Did you know this was coming?" she asked.

He looked down. "I knew Caleb and the others were unhappy. They bargained with Adarmis."

"How could you let them?"

"Because it was Caleb—and now he's dead. I can't lose you too. Come."

RALEN WAS SHOCKED TO see the city in disarray. It had been a place of discipline. Now, broken windows looked like eye sockets in buildings gutted by fire, and the dead were left where they fell. Few living humans were to be seen. Drakein ruled the streets, and gobels peered between the columns of smoke that billowed from newly extinguished pyres.

He held the sword he'd found tightly in one hand and Anjee even more tightly in the other. She didn't speak, but the firm set of her features, visible in the light of the lantern she carried, meant she did not approve of coming here.

A Drakein reared out of the gloom, poleaxe leveled at Ralen's head. He pushed Anjee out of the way and turned to the side, slicing through the wooden handle with his sword in the same movement. The metal end of the poleaxe clattered and bounced on stone.

The Drakein bared his fangs angrily, but his gaze took in Ralen's sword and Anjee's Mark, and he stepped back. "You are Dinah's special ones."

"What's going on here?" Ralen asked.

"The humans have turned against us. My brothers will see your small fleshy forms and strike first. Anyone headed for the Portal is stopped. It is safer for you on the mountain."

Ralen ignored him. They were almost to Gordon's. When he reached the house, the door was open. He hurried inside and searched both floors but found no sign of anyone.

"Perhaps they went through the Portal?" Anjee said.

"Gordon is no traitor."

"The Drakein don't seem to care whether Conquered are guilty or not. What's beyond the Portal?" she asked.

"There is nothing on the Plain but armies of God-fed and the troops of other lords who despise Dinah. There is nowhere to go."

"Oh."

Had Anjee been thinking of escape? He squeezed her hand. "The Marked can't go through the Portal." Besides, he thought, there might be worse dangers outside Dinah's service, and he was not ready to face them.

"Come on," he said, hoping to catch up to the First Commander. The Portal was a key strategic point to hold, whichever side Gordon was on. He would be there, and if anyone could return order to the city it was him.

GORDON STEPPED OVER corpses as he propelled his family through the bedlam in the eastern valley. Night had come and it was as dark as the cavern, except for weaving lamps and torches where warriors fought. Conquered and Drakein who had trained together, defended one another in campaign after campaign, now stood locked in combat, jamming swords into each other's chests.

He shouted for them to stop, bellowed orders at the top of his lungs, but only a few Drakein obeyed. When they did lower their guard, Conquered speared them from behind. Someone had to stop the madness.

He pushed his wife toward the Portal. Blue daylight on the other side passed through the arch and shone on the Conquered who fought to hold the ground all around it. There was a clear path. "Go," he said.

"What about you?" She had one hand on their youngest son and a dagger in the other. Their oldest boy was similarly armed, as was the maid.

"I must stop the fighting. No more should die."

She looked at him with tearful eyes, but there was strength in her stance, the set of her jaw. She understood. I love you. Her mouth formed the words, but the only voice he heard was the wheezing rasp of the Keeper's, fuelled by magic as much as air over a larynx:

"I knew you could not be trusted," Grin said behind him.

Gordon turned to see the Keeper who was monstrous in his deformity and lounged on a palanquin held by a swarm of gobels. The Conquered defending the Portal threw spears at the new arrival, but the weapons were caught in an invisible field of magic, like flies stuck in a web. Soldiers stepped forward to swing swords, but they were caught in the Keeper's barrier as well. Gobel claws cut their throats.

"Go," Gordon told his family.

His wife was halfway through the Portal when more gobels swam out of the dirt, parting the soil like water. They grabbed her legs and arms and pulled the dagger out of her hand. His sons collapsed beneath the creatures' weight, crushed to the earth while claws and teeth tore at them.

All nearby Conquered were caught in the frothing mass of death. Not even the maid was spared, unarmored, bleeding from a hundred wounds. Gordon hacked his way into the melee. Thick yellow blood sprayed across green skin and into his eyes. He looked for his family, but there was too much blood.

Gobels swirled around him now, nipping at the borders between gauntlets and bracers, boots and greaves. He cut furiously, killing scores before they climbed his back and weighed down his sword arm. Teeth bit into his neck.

"No!"

Gordon heard the shout like an echo of his own unvoiced agony. Distantly, he was aware of the boy. Ralen had a sword. He'd foolishly come to save him, but there was nothing left to save.

RALEN SAW GORDON GO down. "No," he said again, as though he could command events. He left Anjee beside a ruined tent, outside the fray, and dove into the swarm of gobels that stood between him and the First Commander. Their claws lacked the reach of the werelings'. With a sword in his hand, instead of a broken piece of bone, it was effortless to slay them. Their skin cut like butter, and he danced between their outstretched arms, seeing them moving as slowly as the angels must have seen him move in his first stumbling attempts at combat.

Soon he stood in a sea of yellow ichors, and he made out piles of Conquered armor—the small suits of the boys, the silver engraved hauberk of Gordon's wife. Their faces were unrecognizable, bite marks where there should have been a nose, or ears, or lips. He looked away when he saw the maid's white dress, now dyed as red as Dinah's.

Gordon lay face down. Ralen turned him over. His eyes were closed, and the torn artery in his neck, which no longer bled, made it clear he was gone. At least he had been spared mutilation. The First Commander deserved dignity in death.

The surviving gobels hung back, either terrified of Ralen's sword or awaiting new orders from their master. "Boy..." Grin began, reasonably.

He faced the Keeper.

Anjee moved closer and shook her head. "Don't." It was a frightened whisper.

He remembered how terrified she had been in the Keeper's pool, the monster's putrid hands petting her, and he would never forget Gordon and his family, never erase this scene from his memory. He did not ask why. The Keeper did it because he could. That was the lesson Ralen had learned at Dinah's feet: do what you could.

He clenched his hand around the hilt of his dripping sword and leaped. For a moment there was resistance, like jumping onto a mattress of feathers, followed by a flash of light as the magical barrier around the Keeper vanished. His bare feet landed on the wooden litter with a thump. The gobels holding it dropped their burden and ran or sank into the upturned earth. The litter tilted side to side and jarred Ralen's teeth when it hit the ground, but he kept his balance.

The Keeper's mouth gaped with shock. His fingers fluttered wildly, and he stammered, "It was my duty."

Ralen had no duty, nothing but a desire to live, for Anjee to live, and he had wanted the maid and Gordon's family to live. He knew all their lives belonged to Dinah, that they were merely counting time before she chose to take it, but she was powerful. At this moment, the Keeper had no power.

He aimed the tip of his blade for the monster's eye, the first eye he had given to Grin. The Keeper muttered an incantation in an effort to defend himself, but whatever he was doing failed.

Ralen took both eyes, and then the Keeper's head.

Chapter Thirty-Two ~ Remains

Ashkal and Amseel saw the Keeper die. They watched from their perch on the rose arch.

Dinah has lost her most loyal subject, Ashkal said.

She can replace the First Commander, Amseel said.

I meant the Keeper. Ironic. She never trusted him, but he was loyal to the end.

Is it her end? Amseel asked. Has the Last God's best beloved servant been defeated by a boy?

Come, Ashkal said. Let us take a closer look.

Invisible to everyone below, they beat their wings and circled the battleground like crows, surveying the butchery. Dead Drakein and Conquered covered the ground, and the doors of the new white temple swayed on broken hinges. The interior was dark and empty of priests.

All this is his doing, Amseel said. Ralen.

Ashkal felt a thrill inside, something stirring. Yes. Can you imagine the chaos if he were at the core of the god's army?

I do not like your thoughts, my brother. I do not like my own.

Be calm. A blade in your hand is less terrifying than the same in your enemy's. Let us be the ones to direct this mad weapon, brother.

We watch—we do not lead.

Things are changing, brother. Can't you feel it?

All I feel is fear.

DINAH WENT INTO THE city to survey the damage. The
Keeper and First Commander should have restored order by now,
but new fires raged. She extinguished them with a thought. She
gathered scattered Drakein to her side as she traversed the carnage.

There were too many dead. She needed an army to reclaim her
rightful position. The few living humans she encountered were taken
into custody. She would sort out loyalists from traitors later. She
held on to the hope of finding Gordon and an intact army mustered
around him, until she reached the Portal valley. The encampment
was deserted. Conquered and Drakein corpses were scattered around
the Portal, along with butchered gobels. Ralen stood with a dripping
sword over a quivering pile of flesh.

Anjee lowered her head when she approached. The girl's
thoughts were clear: <u>Mercy</u>. <u>He only wanted to protect the First
Commander</u>.

Dinah looked about for the commander and spotted his body,
the ravaged throat, and the other Conquered obviously killed by
gobels. Her Mark glowed on every piece of flesh at Ralen's feet. The
Keeper.

"What happened here?" she asked reasonably, while her
thoughts roiled with angry questions: Where was her army? Why
were both her Keeper and her commander dead?

Ralen fell to his knees in the gore. "Lady."

Dinah saw the scene in the girl's memory, witnessed Ralen's
ability with a sword, his effortless defeat of gobels and Keeper.... And
he had stood against werelings.

Dinah had the sudden sensation of holding a writhing serpent
in her hand, knowing it could bite her if she released her grip for an
instant, yet no matter how tightly she held, it would wriggle free of
its own accord. What could she do?

"Grin is not dead," she said. She put a reassuring hand on Ralen's
shoulder, felt the pulse in his neck next to her thumb, and imagined

slicing the artery open. It would be the safest course—but also a pointless one. She had lived an eternity without a future. The boy gave her a chance at one, if she was daring enough to risk the dangers. She had always dared.

She pulled him to his feet and said, "You did well. The First Commander was valuable to me, a keen mind unmatched by many leaders before him, and a useful servant. More useful than the Keeper of late." She summoned a fire from the remains of a trampled circle of tents. It grew into a bonfire. "I am displeased by Grin's actions. Throw the remains of the Keeper in the fire. It is my will that he be executed, a permanent death."

Ralen nodded and hurried to toss the bits into the flames.

Dinah caught the Keeper's last thought. Through agonizing pain, he whispered, <u>Thank you</u>.

Dinah's fury flamed to life again, and she fought to control it. Ralen had laid her lower than her disgrace in the Last God's eyes. She had nothing left—no army, no commanders—yet she dared topple a god?

She laughed.

The boy looked at her curiously. Once more she fought the urge to kill him.

For now, she must salvage what she could. She sent a Drakein scout back to the workshop atop the mountain, while Ralen helped the other Drakein gather the bodies of fallen. When the scout returned with nickel shackles, she said, "Stand back," and looked at Ralen in particular. His Presence might interfere.

When the living were far enough away, Dinah clipped one bracelet around Gordon's left ankle and the other around his left arm. The chain was long and barely constrained the limbs.

She had designed the shackles with two purposes: to force obedience and to channel her life force. The effects were linked; the wearer was both fed by her power and enslaved to it. She had used it to control the mages and the werelings—when Ralen was not present—and she had planned to use it to transfer control of the God-fed to her. She would be the source of their power, not the Last God.

What she was about to attempt had not been part of the plan. She had never raised a corpse before. Such power belonged only to her Lord. But she believed it was possible, and she thrilled at the idea, even as fear tickled her stomach. Ralen had thought her a goddess, but this ... would doing this truly make her one?

She sent her aura into the earth, into the molten core, not unlike the mages', to draw upon its strength. She hungered for life in the air and soil nearby but concentrated on limiting her circle, so it did not envelop Ralen and the others. She could not let her aura cross the edge of the Portal either. It was tempting to draw from the god's Presence on the Plain, but He would sense what she was doing.

When she was filled with energy, she sent it through the shackle beneath her fingertips and into the dead flesh of the First Commander. She had donated life before, but never to revive. This was something else entirely.

She pushed energy into the corpse, but there was nothing to direct it, nowhere for it to go and nothing for it to do. The flesh was on the verge of exploding, so she withdrew. She did not remove her hand from the shackle, however. She was unwilling to admit defeat.

She looked up into a night crammed with stars and sent her aura into the sky, feeling for something that was distinctly absent from the corpse. Gordon. His consciousness watched the scene of his death. He felt her coming for him and rose higher, but she snatched his soul before it could depart.

She drew his energy into her, through her veins and out again through her aura and into the shackles. She did not consume it so much as tame it in the process, akin to how she tamed the souls of the Marked. She forced the essence back into its flesh then infused it with power. It took only a little to get the limbs twitching, but the heart would not beat.

She felt thoughts stirring, Gordon's agonized thoughts, memories of death and sensations of pain as he reconnected with his body, but he did not bond with it as before. Dinah could not get the flesh to heal or the brain to fire. Gordon's consciousness animated the parts out of memory, moving them with his will as Dinah had moved the Keeper across the floor of her house. Each time he tried to lift his arm it drained some of the energy she had given him. She shifted the connection between her and the shackles, so he wasn't fed through her anymore but from the core of the world. She kept a tendril of her will linked to Gordon and sent a command: <u>Stand</u>.

He stood.

Anjee gasped.

Dinah looked for Ralen's reaction, but the boy's impassive expression was unreadable.

Power flowed into the shackles and Gordon's hungry soul. He fumbled with his limbs. When he gained control of them, he turned toward the remains of his family. His bulging eyes did not blink or moisten as they should. The voice that issued from him was as dry and rattling as the Keeper's. "No."

Dinah stood, triumphant, chin held high. She had done what only a god could.

The shackles were not completely useless. At least one experiment had worked. Once the initial euphoria subsided, she ordered Ralen to oversee the Drakein as they continued to collect the bodies of the fallen. She wandered the battlefield and the city in search of more souls to trap in their bodies. If she could sort them all out, she would create more Risen, as many as she had shackles for. Then she would force the remaining mages to make more shackles.

Gordon hunched over his family, and his unearthly wails echoed through the canyon behind her.

RALEN WATCHED GORDON gather his wife and children into his dead arms. He hugged them to him, one after another slipping out of his grasp as he struggled to hold them all at once.

"Don't let her," Gordon said with a withered voice. "Don't let her have my family. Let them stay dead. Please." He looked at Ralen as though he were the Commander, as though it were his orders that mattered.

Ralen's throat was tight. He could barely swallow let alone speak. Instead of answering Gordon, he hefted the maid's tiny form. She had always seemed larger than him, but now she was like a bundle of dried wheat. Her scarred leg showed through her torn dress, and he shifted the fabric to cover it. He ached, thinking of the pain she had suffered, all the dreams stolen away ... because of him. He had never asked Dinah to heal her, never found the time or the words, and now it was too late. Had he become one of the monsters without realizing? Had he been so worried about his own life and Anjee's he'd given up on everyone else? Tears poured down his cheeks, tears for the maid and the children, and the dead all around, tears for everyone he'd failed.

Drakein gathered the other fallen. Grey men, yellow-spattered gobels, and red-smeared Conquered were piled together like autumn leaves. Ralen turned away from them and tossed the maid into the bonfire that had disposed of the Keeper. The Drakein did not question him—Dinah had left him in charge.

He pried the body of Gordon's youngest boy out of his embrace and carried the torn flesh to the fire as well. When he came back for the next one, Gordon gripped him with shriveled fingers and kissed his hand. "Thank you."

Ralen let Gordon take his wife and oldest son to the pyre. His reanimated limbs shook oddly as he lowered them into the flames.

For a moment, Gordon looked as though he would throw himself in after. He crouched, ready to jump, but froze, as if given an order he could not disobey. Ralen left him there, bowed before the fire.

He went to Anjee, worried by her haunted expression. Her features were slack as she stared at Gordon. "It's happening," she said.

"What do you mean?" he asked.

"The army of shackled souls." She focused her eyes on him and reached out her hand, hardly aware of what she was doing, like a sleepwalker, and traced the new cut along his cheek. "I don't want to be alone."

"You won't be," he said for the millionth time, putting his arms around her. She felt almost as hollow and lifeless as the maid.

Chapter Thirty-Three ~ Aftermath

For months after the Conquered rebelled, Dinah refused everyone entrance to the longhouse, saying she was conducting sensitive experiments, so Ralen and Anjee spent every moment together.

Sunset colored the tree trunks orange as bird calls were replaced by the squeak of fruit bats and buzz of cicadas. The scent of warm fig drifted from the terraces above. They lay beneath a giant apple tree, trying to spy the first star through branches thick with new leaves and white blossoms. Anjee saw it and pointed. "I wish ... I can't say, but you know what it is."

"Yes."

"Do you think Gar made it back home?" she asked, as she sometimes did.

"Yes."

"I saw his butterfly wings high above the battleground. You were busy with the bodies, and I don't think anyone else noticed him. He went through the Portal, but I didn't see where he went after that." She told the story excitedly every time, as though it were proof of happy endings.

Ralen didn't believe in endings, happy or otherwise.

He rested his head on her lap and fell into a deeper sleep than he could achieve in the most comfortable Conquered bed. Not that there was a bed left in the burned city.

Later, he woke to her singing and enjoyed the feel of her fingers as she stroked his hair. The moon was high and full, and she noticed his open eyelids. "We should go back," she said. "The soldiers will need you in the morning."

She continued to call Gordon and the others 'soldiers', even though they weren't even people anymore.

"All right." He reluctantly climbed to his feet then helped her up. He kept hold of her hand as they made their way across the moonlit valley to the cavern entrance.

The yellow-eyed Drakein guards nodded to Ralen as he passed, and he nodded back. The slaves' side of the lake was crowded. He avoided their angry looks. Every surviving Conquered—those not killed and Risen by Dinah or escaped to Adarmis—were now Marked. His fault. He knew it, and he suspected the Lady did too.

Anjee's Marks burned red. She clapped a hand over the first one, but he'd seen. His Mark no longer even glowed. "What is it?" he asked.

"She's calling me." Anjee cocked her head as though she could hear the Lady's voice. "I have to go."

No one had seen Dinah in so long, and Anjee was the first person she summoned. He worried for her and would not leave her side until they reached the base of the rose stair. He hadn't been invited, so he could go no further.

"Will you meet me in the apple orchard tomorrow?" she said.

"Of course."

"This is important. Be there at noon." Her expression shook, the muscles in her face fighting each other, her mouth half open. There was something she wanted to say but couldn't.

"Anjee?"

"I have to go," she repeated. She climbed the stairs two at time, leaving him alone and dazed.

He could not sleep in the destroyed city or among the Marked slaves without nightmares, so he curled up in his rowboat on a pile of blankets. He kept thinking about Anjee's expression, unable to shut his eyes.

Black feathers with blue highlights rose over the side of the moored boat, and a down-covered hand reached out to touch his shoulder. He rolled away and came to his feet, steel dagger in one hand, gobel claw knife in the other.

"Impressive," Ashkal said.

"I didn't hear your call," Ralen said. His weapons remained unsheathed. The angels' arrival meant either mock battles to come or a real threat. The last time they were here, Amseel had wanted to kill him. "Where's your brother?"

Ashkal twitched and flexed his wings. "Observing Dinah."

"What do you want?"

"To continue your training."

"What use is it? You didn't teach me enough to save Gordon's family."

"You did well against the Keeper's horde."

"You were watching?" Ralen pictured them, vultures, enjoying the carnage.

"That is what we do."

"You could have saved them!"

"Why? You are our sole concern."

"Am I? You didn't save me from the werelings." He tightened his grip on the gobel claw knife, the one thing that had kept him alive. After the battle, he had set the claw in a proper handle to make it more comfortable to wield.

"No one is omniscient."

"Except for the Last God."

Ashkal laughed his shrieking laugh. "No, not even the god. Else we would all be dead. He believed us when we told him Dinah ordered the Keeper's execution."

"She did."

"Only when she no longer had a choice. She is stirring on her mountain, and you have rested long enough. Let us see what you remember." He pulled his dagger and advanced.

Ralen wanted to sleep, but with a Blessed Blade slicing the air in front of his face, he had no choice. He balanced on the wooden seat as the boat wobbled and tried to survive—or learn—there was little difference in his experience.

THE NEXT MORNING, RALEN could not shake his worry. Anjee had seemed so strange when she told him to meet her in the orchard. The image of her twitching face would not leave him.

He folded his bedding, hitched the oars, and rowed to the Keeper's island in the center of the turquoise lake. He should give it another name. That monster was finally dead, as it should be. Unfortunately, Gordon was dead too.

Most of the Risen wandered through the ruins of the city, but some, like Gordon, whose minds and souls were more intact chose to dwell on the island, far from living things and the memory of their old lives.

The surviving gobels had abandoned the place. After their master's death, they scattered and now lurked in the depths of the lake or in underground rivers throughout the mountain. Claw was somewhere with them. No one saw them except when they crept into the storehouses to eat the mice and rats that infested the grain. They were never far away, though. Wherever Ralen went, he caught glimpses of silver eyes watching from the dark and heard his name whispered in a fearful chant.

He had recovered a few trinkets from Gordon's house, a necklace from a jewelry box and a notebook and pen from the study. He pressed the pen into Gordon's skeletal hand and said, "I want you to write down the stories you were telling me yesterday."

The First Commander's withered body was decayed and smelled so awful Ralen tried not to breathe through his nose. Even more unsettling was the chill. Standing next to one of the Risen was like standing next to a ghost, their souls torn loose from their bodies. It made his hairs stand on end.

"I tell you, so I don't have to remember," Gordon said. The necklace glinted in the light of Ralen's lamp and Gordon snatched up the gold chain. "My love." His swollen eyes looked feverish, an edge of madness.

Some of the Risen nearby shifted uncomfortably. This island was for forgetting. They shambled to the water, shackles scraping against stone, and sank beneath the surface.

"You remember her, don't you?" Ralen said.

"Lord help me. Kiera." He continued to stare at the necklace.

"More Drakein have hatched," Ralen said, trying another tactic, "but the captains don't know whether to sow fields for grain or clear land for livestock." Drakein were always twitchy and unsure without commands.

"What do you think?" Gordon said.

"Both. A bigger herd will need more food."

Gordon nodded, but Ralen had already given orders to the Drakein. What he needed was the First Commander back. A bit of bone and tooth was visible beneath Gordon's moustache. It was hard not to stare.

Ralen heard a scream in his memory and remembered gobels dragging the Marked slaves he'd chosen to repair the rotting Keeper. He shivered and wrapped his arms around himself. He didn't like this spot.

He tried to picture the orchard. Moments with Anjee were his one hold on sanity. The look she had given him... There were things unsaid, things he did not want to know, and he understood all too well Gordon's desire to forget.

DINAH LOOKED DOWN ON the farming valley from the window in her library and narrowed her eyes at the newly Marked who worked the fields. They were a reminder of the rebellion, of her failures, which far outweighed her achievements.

She would remedy her mistakes.

She hefted the Fae tomes, debating. She had spent the last months studying them as she restored her realm to a semblance of order. She wanted to keep them with her for reference, but they were too dangerous. Like Ralen.

Was Fae magic the answer to her problems? There were hints of ancient spells in the books, spells that might save her plans.

Like so many others, Fae stole magic from creatures with a link to its source in their cores. The ancient Fae had been so adept at it they were able to cloud the minds of their victims, making them believe they were living out their lives in freedom, when really they were imprisoned and subject to the will of their Fae masters.

The art had been lost along with their Emperor's head. He had been too dangerous for Dinah to let live, especially when she began to feel herself swept up in his illusions, but she had kept the books.

She knew it was possible to bind someone as powerful as herself—would it be enough to bind Ralen? She needed the full spells to test, not just hints, which meant she must go to the Fae homeworld to find what she was missing.

But the tomes contained other information she did not want the Fae to have access to again. Their Emperor had been very dangerous and very difficult to kill.

Decision made, she placed the books back into their ancient wooden chest and activated the seal. No one could get past her wards except for the boy, as all magic seemed null around him. The books were useless to him, still, she decided on extra precautions. She sent the chest flying through the open window and into the ground beneath the bleached olive tree on the edge of the cliff. The barren soil shifted and covered it completely, leaving no sign.

She dreaded going among the Fae, but the remnants of her army were too weak to stand against a host of the god's devoted followers, so she must once more rely on stealth to pursue her projects.

While she feared leaving Ralen behind, it would be madness to do otherwise. His Presence would disturb the lands she passed through and draw the god's attention. Let Drakein and her new Risen defend him. He could cause no further turmoil among them—the damage was done.

"Is everything packed?" she asked the girl.

Anjee bowed her head. "Yes, Lady. I've sent for Drakein to cart it all to the docks."

"Then you are free to say your goodbyes."

"Yes, Lady." Anjee did not hurry from the room but walked at a stately pace, as though carrying a weight. Dinah felt the stone on the girl's heart, but she was too angry to pity her. While her links to the rest of the Marked had weakened, her bond with Anjee had grown stronger. It alone seemed impervious to Ralen's presence, and for that she was thankful.

The seer was coming with her, a hostage. The Mark alone could no longer keep Ralen here. One day, he would realize he could cross the Portal, but he wouldn't, not when he awaited the girl's return. And Dinah would have the seer's visions to guide her, to warn her of any threat to her plans. She hoped more training would improve the child's reliability. Anjee had spotted the danger with the werelings too late. She needed to do better than that.

After a time, Dinah returned to the window. The green fields and terraces of flowering trees made her fury rise again. The children could run beneath the leaves, laugh, and taste the air, but the most she could do was experience it second hand through her connection with the girl.

Why did she tend things she could never touch? Why was Ralen—who had destroyed her realm—able to enjoy life when all she had was death?

She rose over the windowsill and hovered to the edge of the cliff. This time she did not think of throwing herself off it. Rather, she imagined the land as dead as she was, and she had the perverse desire to make the image reality. She stepped off into air.

RALEN WAITED IN THE orchard. He had been there a while, because nothing else, not even comforting Gordon, mattered to him as much as each moment spent with Anjee.

When she arrived, she tossed a stick at him before dodging behind a tree. It was one of their games. Normally he chased her down and tickled her. This time he easily blocked the hurled twig and just stood there. "I know something's wrong."

She peeked around the tree, and her smile faded. She came up to him and took his hand, tugging him to the ground. They sat cross legged across from one another.

"Dinah is going on another trip," Anjee said.

"That means we'll have more time together."

"Ralen.... We won't have more time. I'm going with her."

He shook his head. "Why?" For a moment, he thought it was Anjee's choice, but then he remembered they were slaves. Ordering the Drakein about had made him forget. It was stupid to forget.

"She commands it."

He tore a clump of grass out of the dirt and squeezed it until pulp stained his hand. The scent was stronger than the fragrance of apple blossoms. "She was gone more than a year last time." He couldn't stand to be alone for so long, with Gordon. He couldn't.

"This will be different. She has only one place to go." Her tone was reassuring, but he noted the way her gaze darted to the side.

"Everything changes," he said. It was truth, hated and inescapable.

He leaned forward, feeling the strain in his folded legs, and kissed her. This was not like the peck they had shared when they were little children, but something more. Heat and frustration coiled inside him, joy and sorrow warring. The kiss was a command, one that demanded she be his one piece of life in this place of death. It demanded she come back to him.

She returned the kiss, and the electric sensation pushed all fear away. He touched her hair, her cheek, her neck... it felt like fire tingling through him. The scent of her was sweeter than all the flowers in the fields and terraces around them, a scent that made him hungry for more. He shifted closer, unwilling to stop the kiss for even a moment, not caring about getting air or the pebbles digging into his knees.

He reached for her with his other hand, but she took it in her own, wrapping her small fingers over his knuckles. She gently removed his hand from her hair, and then pulled away from the kiss with a gasp.

"Anjee," he said, longing for her, wanting to hold her again, but she stayed frustratingly out of reach.

She slowly opened her eyes and said, "I will make you cry."

"No. You are my joy."

"I always feared you would be the one to go, but I'm the one leaving. Why didn't I see that?"

"How could you?" He touched her cheek again, and she seemed to shiver from the touch as much as he did. She closed her eyes and smiled, but then another flicker crossed her features, and she winced as though in pain.

"What aren't you telling me?" he said.

She put a finger to his lips to quiet him, and her touch seemed to burn. He wanted her to keep touching him, but she pulled back again and studied his face, as though trying to really see him—or to remember him. "Everything changes," she repeated his words, but she smiled, filling each syllable with hope.

There was a universe of things Anjee was keeping from him. He knew it. He was about to demand she tell him, but then his insides twisted with fear. Something was wrong.

He smelled death.

He looked up and saw Dinah. A dry wind blew before her, bending the branches of the trees, making his skin prickle. She glided through the orchard, bare feet inches above the ground, pale, corpse-like toes pointed at the earth, blood red dress billowing behind her. Apple blossoms, shriveled by her presence, suddenly filled the air like ash, and he remembered that day in the square on Earth, the air thick and gray with debris from the volcano, from the coming of the Last God, and fear filled him. Was it the end of the world again?

Leaves wilted and yellowed ahead of Dinah and fell brown and lifeless to the ground as she passed, like the seasons sped up, pushed past autumn and deepest winter to a dry and silent death. The ancient trees blackened and oozed amber sap, bleeding wounds. Anjee gasped at the destruction, as though she was the one hurting, but all Ralen could do was watch, frozen. The Lady never disturbed the fields, never. Now a vast swath was ruined, gone forever.

She stopped a few steps away and looked down on them, sharp teeth bared, green eyes almost as bright and acid as the wereling's. What was she thinking? She held Ralen's gaze for a moment, and he saw a wild anger in her he had never seen before, one that instantly made him want to beg forgiveness for whatever he had done, but he was too shocked to move.

She looked at Anjee. "Come girl, it's time."

"Yes, Mistress." Anjee bowed her head with a disturbing reverence. It reminded him of Gordon's irresistible obedience, as though she both loved and hated Dinah in the same moment.

The wind swirled around them, blowing dust and the decayed remains of spring into the air. Dinah put an arm around her and Anjee groaned, veins standing out on her skin, eyes wide with unvoiced pain.

"Stop it," Ralen said automatically, forgetting he addressed the Lady. "You're hurting her."

Dinah's features flickered with hatred once more, but then her usual, stern expression returned. "She will survive. I will bring her back safely. Farewell, my young Ralen."

They turned and walked away.

"Anjee," he said, reaching out, but she obediently stayed beside the Lady and did not look back. He watched until they disappeared in the distance.

Alone, he took a ragged breath, fighting the pain in his chest. Anjee was gone. He fell to his knees in tall grass.

Something niggled at the edge of perception. Grass? He looked around and saw he was in a circle of greenery. The tree he and Anjee had sat beneath was alive, while the rest of the orchard, as far as he could see in every direction, was dead. Somehow, Dinah's power had stopped at him.

"What am I?" he asked the empty air.

The voice that had begun as whispers in his mind, telling him which slaves to choose for the Keeper, making him think he was going mad, now answered loud and clear. *Something new.*

Dark Days Will Continue in Part II

Also by Lorel Clayton

Dark Days
Dark Days

Eva Thorne
A Thorne in Time
Tangle of Thornes
A Thorne for a Crown
Blood and Thorne
War of Thornes
Nest of Thornes
The Fortress

Watch for more at https://www.lorelclayton.com/.

About the Author

ABOUT THE AUTHORS

Lorel and Clayton were teen sweethearts. Clayton has severe dyslexia, but from the moment Lorel read 'Magician' aloud to him at age thirteen, they began to share magical worlds and dream of writing novels together one day. Hundreds of books later, and a wedding as well, those shared hours of reading, discussing and laughing, as they embellished their favorite stories, culminated in the completion of their first manuscript in 1996. After many more years of honing their craft, the Eva Thorne series was born. After the main four book series of Eva is complete, they are planning a new series of mysteries, as well as a science fiction series and a young adult fantasy. Stay tuned!

Connect with Lorel Clayton
Website: lorelclayton.com
Twitter: @lorelclayton
Facebook: https://www.facebook.com/AuthorLorelClayton/
Instagram: https://www.instagram.com/lorelclayton/
Read more at https://www.lorelclayton.com/.

www.ingramcontent.com/pod-product-compliance
Lightning Source LLC
Chambersburg PA
CBHW031106030726
47496CB00002BA/400

* 9 7 8 1 7 6 3 8 0 0 8 0 9 *